I Feed Her to the Beast

the Beast

AND THE BEAST IS ME

JAMISON SHEA

SQUARE
FISH

HENRY HOLT AND COMPANY

NEW YORK

TO THOSE WHO FIND FREEDOM IN BECOMING A MONSTER WHEN DENIED THE SPACE TO BE HUMAN

An imprint of Macmillan Publishing Group, LLC
120 Broadway, New York, NY 10271 • fiercereads.com

Square Fish and the Square Fish logo are trademarks of Macmillan and are
used by Henry Holt and Company under license from Macmillan.

Our books may be purchased in bulk for promotional, educational,
or business use. Please contact your local bookseller or the Macmillan
Corporate and Premium Sales Department at (800) 221-7945 ext. 5442 or
by email at MacmillanSpecialMarkets@macmillan.com.

Library of Congress Control Number: 2023938255

Originally published in the United States by Henry Holt and Company
First Square Fish edition, 2024
Book designed by Rich Deas and Meg Sayre
Square Fish logo designed by Filomena Tuosto
Printed in the United States of America

ISBN 978-1-250-34658-2
1 3 5 7 9 10 8 6 4 2

— AUTHOR'S NOTE —

Though I could probably wax poetic for pages on end about the purpose of "art" and what elements of the human condition I wanted to explore in *I Feed Her to the Beast and the Beast Is Me*, this book's primary goal is to entertain. As a result, I want to make sure readers know what they're signing up for by forewarning of some potentially disturbing content and topics that can be triggering, stressful, or just unenjoyable to read. Different strokes for different folks, you know?

Foremost, this book contains copious depictions of blood and features ritualistic self-harm (with the purpose of summoning a nonhuman entity). There are also descriptions of bones and corpses, body horror and an instance of body-shaming relating to ballet, non-graphic torture, and murder. Finally, there are references to classism and racism as well as parental neglect and abandonment that, while not graphically depicted, still permeate the work.

Now, let's have some fun.

What do you crave?

I lurched back, tumbling flat on my ass as a voice spoke from within my marrow. Muscles in my arms and legs trembled at the vibrations. The knife skittered across the floor as it repeated its question.

"P-power," I stammered, blinking rapidly. "So they can't deny me."

My skin prickled. Still, I inched closer.

And what would you give for power?

"Everything." I prayed by clenching my bleeding fist against the shiver that rolled through me. Willing more blood to flow, willing all this to be true and more. And I meant it, I had to.

I wouldn't go home with nothing.

"Take it," I dared.

I crawled until the knees of my jeans were wet, until the tang of blood filled my nostrils. Until my hands were submerged in red and it had no choice but to take me.

Something hot and sharp gripped my ankle. Then the rock floor vanished beneath me, and I was pulled under, down into the void.

PART ONE

DEVOTION

CHAPTER 1

We were desperate to be the girl who dies, always. Eager to show how dolefully we danced, how prettily we perished, in every ballet, at every audition. In every room was a chance to have our graceful suffering acknowledged.

Today was no exception.

The clock ticked toward auditions for *Giselle*, and the hallway air was thick with desperation, with hunger. Pale ballerinas swarmed the studio windows, elbowing each other to get a better look at the demonstrating soloists, the judges, the board of directors, and our instructors. People who held our futures in their frowns got acquainted with the teachers who had watched us both soar and plummet for eight years straight, six of which I spent at the top of my class. They always told us that dancing meant sharing a part of yourself with your audience— well, now we were ready to give them everything. Once we crossed that threshold, none of us would come out whole.

Take it, the palm prints on the glass pleaded. *Have all of me, I'm offering.*

Fighting the urge to gawk at my executioners, I squeezed out of the crowd. With our final year at the Ballet Academy of Paris drawing to a close, every audition was more important than the last. Today, it was for *Giselle*, our last production before graduating, and next, for the company, *the* Paris Ballet, swirling in luxurious satin and tulle on one of the greatest stages in the world. What we gave today mattered because it was all they'd remember of us tomorrow. The girl who claimed the heroine became who they craved in three months' time as an apprentice.

So my shoes had to be perfect, because now wasn't the time to over-compensate for a dead pair, and that mattered more than analyzing any judge. Madame Demaret, who taught for both the academy and the company, had said during our very first pointe class, "The shoe is an extension of your foot." And the best shoes required a delicate balance—rigid enough to prop you up but beaten into silence and the shape you needed. Firm but still broken. And always beautiful.

Just like the perfect ballerina.

"Of course they brought Joséphine Moreau to show us how it's done," Vanessa remarked loudly from the window, twisting the twinkling diamond necklace at her throat. "As if we don't get enough of her with *Cinderella* posters all over the city."

Keeping my head down, I focused on the pair of new pointe shoes in my lap. The soft pink satin was still unblemished, the scored soles and darned box not yet darkened from scuffs or worn away, fabric still neat on the sides and back where I'd stitched elastic and silk ribbon. I'd started customizing them the night before, working my nerves out in the crack and pop of the vamp and shank, rapping on the floor and shutting the tip in doors to reach that sweet spot. I didn't have diamonds or famous parents or a milky complexion to sway the world, but I had this. And by the end of the instruction period, when it was time for the judges to watch me, they'd be perfect.

And I'd be perfect too.

Girls like me didn't have any other choice if we wanted to belong.

"Last week, I heard someone in the locker room say that Joséphine kills lesser ballerinas and drinks their talent." Olivia, with her straight, dark hair in a neat bun, grinned from her place by the window.

"That's ridiculous," I muttered, turning the shoes over and giving them a shake. Stories of broken glass, thumbtacks, and pins hidden inside before auditions were too abundant for it not to be habit.

And every month, there was another rumor about the new étoile Joséphine Moreau and her rapid rise to fame, stories dark, wild, or twisted. She was an urban legend made flesh, where everyone knew someone who saw something untoward. Seducing board members, handling large wads of cash, drinking blood. The only thing we knew for certain was that every door was open to her, and she had more opportunities than she could carry. She'd even turned down Moscow last month.

But it didn't matter what any of us thought of someone like her. Almost everyone who made it into the company also had a legacy name or an inheritance big enough to make you blush, while Joséphine had neither to pave her way. It was rare for a nobody to climb high society's ladder, and for Joséphine to reach so high so fast... that was terrifying for them. Enough to inspire endless gossip. People always manufactured excuses to deny us our successes.

"Obviously she's a witch," my best friend Coralie Baumé grumbled as she shoved her way through the thicket without a glance inside. "There's no other way. Even my mom loves her."

Her nose wrinkled with disgust before she turned her attention back to the sticky toffee bun in her hand. She was the only one with an appetite, easygoing in her poreless, ivory skin as she flopped down in a graceless heap beside me. Times like these never got to her the way they did the rest of us. Wisps of golden ringlets sprang free from her sloppy French twist.

I declined her wordless offer for a bite and smoothed back my already gelled hair, resisting the urge to point out that Rose-Marie Baumé wasn't capable of loving anyone but herself. In some ways, though Coralie descended from ballet royalty, she had it worse than I did being on my own.

Vanessa threw a scowl over her shoulder. "Coralie, you just hate her *because* your mom likes her. Your mom is wasted on you."

The last part came out a dreamy sigh that made Coralie freeze mid-chew. No one saw the hesitation in her jaw, the blankness in her eyes, but me. It was there and gone in a flash.

"Anyway," Olivia drawled, "I heard she's a witch too. When she was in the academy, one of her classmates caught her stealing hair from a brush for a spell or something. She even tried to recruit Nina Brossard into her coven—"

"Was that before or after she was spotted bathing naked in the Seine under a full moon?" I quipped as I slid caps over my toes.

The hall fell silent, frosty. And when I raised my head, Vanessa, Olivia, and the others were glaring at me, making it abundantly clear that I wasn't meant to be heard. Because I wasn't like them, not in any way that mattered: rich, white, born with the moral high ground. Breaking the stark silence, Coralie threw her head back and laughed, exposing chewed, gross globs of toffee for all the world to see.

The metal door to the studio lurched open with a loud shudder just as I shoved on my shoes, and my heart skipped a beat. My classmates streamed out of the hall, chatter turning to whispers while I remained on the floor. The pointe shoes' drawstrings and ribbons fell loose at my trembling fingertips.

"If Vanessa climbs any higher up my mom's butt, she'll get stuck." Coralie sneered through a mouthful before licking the cinnamon and toffee from her fingers. "Ready to get this over with, Laure?"

I didn't move. Too loose, not loose enough, ribbon bunching instead of lying flat, I stayed put, tying and retying my shoes, ignoring her and that open door, waiting for my pulse to steady so I could walk into that room and claim my future.

Small, warm hands closed over mine. Big, green eyes like a doll's inched into view. Eyeliner clumped in her long lashes. "Hey! Don't be nervous—"

"Easier said than done, Cor," I snapped through gritted teeth. "You realize President Auger and Hugo Grandpré are in there, right?"

Coralie cocked her head to the side and smiled. So innocent and amused, like she knew some secret to the universe the rest of us didn't, and it made me want to shove her. "I know. And who's ranked number one in every subject?"

My eyes fluttered shut. A flush crawled up to my ears.

"Well?"

"I am," I mumbled, unwilling to look at her and her smug grin. It wasn't that I forgot my rank, or that I had any other choice but to out-perform when my scholarship was on the line. The problem was the same as ever: *What if rank wasn't enough?* And certainly my calves could stand to be stronger. "But—"

She wasn't done. "And *just* this morning, who did Madame Demaret call 'a joy to watch' and 'a vision to behold'?"

A knot untangled in my chest. Always did when Coralie was here, hands in mine, radiant in the afternoon rays like some angel with words of affirmation to soften my edges. It was just the two of us in the hall, sitting on the floor, just like the day we met twelve years ago. We'd waited for our parents outside an empty studio, alone, late into the evening, and though her mother's driver was the first to show, she refused to get up until my dad arrived from the construction site. And look how far we came. Together.

I sighed and pushed to my feet. Though my hands were no longer shaking, my heart still raced in my chest, but we couldn't put it off forever. "Let's go knock 'em dead?"

"And then bury them."

Coralie looped her arm through mine, and we faced the massive studio, inseparable. By the wall of mirrors, our classmates huddled with their things and took seats on the floor; and behind a row of tables, the board of directors perched stiffly in wire chairs, wearing bespoke suits, day dresses, and mostly pinched mouths. It wasn't until I was settled with my legs outstretched in front of me that I finally saw them all, the demonstrating soloists and the people who would judge me.

"Sabine looks good considering she was cheated out of *Cinderella*," one of the boys observed, sending my stomach into free fall.

There, stretching with an ankle propped on the barre, was Sabine Simon, a recently promoted première with the Paris Ballet, graduate of the academy, and my ex-girlfriend. There was no mistaking her pixie face and butter-blond hair, her small frame and sugary pink leotard with ruffled sleeves. For them, President Auger and Director Grandpré, Sabine was the blueprint for the ideal ballerina, and so they always picked her for demonstrations, but for me, she was an inescapable reminder of how love and ambition couldn't seem to coexist. Time with her was time better spent perfecting my technique, and no love could withstand how ugly she was beneath the lacquer of ballet silks and perfect pirouettes. There wasn't any love that could withstand the ballet but love of the ballet itself. Not family, not yourself, and certainly not a doll-like girlfriend.

And in avoiding that eyesore, my gaze found Sabine's junior who had surpassed her, Joséphine Moreau. The newest étoile. In fact, the youngest ever to be promoted so, having managed to ensnare the judges and seize the honor of opening the upcoming season in *Cinderella*. Just before her rise, there was even an article interviewing current and former dancers from the company, some of whom moved to other cities because the board refused to promote any new étoiles for years. Former dancers blamed their departures on favoritism and bias, stalled careers, forced retirements, damning exclusion policies the ballet would never admit to. Anyone who had walked the gilded halls of the academy knew it was more than coincidence how the roster managed to stay gold-plated. And that's what made Joséphine so noteworthy—she was the only new étoile in almost a decade, so special she couldn't be denied, so commanding she just *took* it.

She looked just like her flyers that had gone up the day before: hardly older than us, milky white skin, long neck of a swan, pink rosebud lips, the slenderest hips, legs for days, shiny chestnut hair. She was so coveted, they'd pulled her out of the academy early to begin her apprenticeship, and now she was filling seats, Grandpré reserving roles for her while she guest featured in Saint Petersburg, London, and Milan.

And with every kind of murmur attached to her name.

Joséphine stood in conversation with a tall and slender man, face fine with East Asian features and long, full hair bleached ash white. He wore an expensive-looking white suit fitted nicely to his frame, and when she said something to make him laugh, it became undeniable how handsome he was. Model-esque and hard to look away from. The two together, in intimate closeness, drew the eye: two beautiful people fully absorbed in only each other, the gravity of the room tilted toward their glow.

"Okay, he's not my type, but that is the most attractive man I have ever seen," Olivia mumbled.

I rolled my eyes and swept the room.

The man in white easily ignored Rose-Marie Baumé, seated at the table and watching. Glaring, really. Coralie's mother, with the same flax-colored hair but smooth and a heart-shaped face, decked in jewels and dripping wealth, hands clasped before her and round lips pursed in displeasure. A look I knew well, of a bad smell, that designated other-ness, that conveyed you didn't belong but it was uncouth to say so aloud.

Vanessa gasped. "That's the new board member! Remember I said I ran into Joséphine at a bistro, and she was seeing a guy who looks like a model? Totally nouveau riche."

"My mom said his name is Ciro Aurissy," offered Coralie to our cohort with marked indifference, pretending to study her nails chewed down to stubs. "Won't say what he does though. He just showed up one day, totally legit."

"How could Joséphine have everything and *not* be a witch?" Vanessa lamented to a sour chorus of agreements.

What I found more interesting was that Joséphine never denied the tales of drinking blood and spells with hair, only adding to the aura of mystery around her. Fears of curses and dark magic psyched out her competition, making her nothing short of genius.

Ballet was warfare, after all.

Rose-Marie stared at both of them now: the guy far too young to be on the ballet's board and the girl who skipped too many rungs of the ladder on her ascent.

There was an order to the ballet, a structure for who was featured and when. Étoiles then premiers, sujets then coryphées, and finally quadrilles, with apprentices in the gutter. When a role opened up, the ballet worked its way down the pyramid *except* where Joséphine was concerned. She'd sped through her apprentice and quadrille statuses in a matter of weeks instead of years, bypassing coryphée altogether as the youngest sujet ever. She made première and étoile look like a cakewalk with her competition cowering in her dust and Adonis incarnate at her side. Now together, they *really* got under Rose-Marie's skin.

Suddenly I liked them a lot.

Because who were they, Ciro and Joséphine, but nobodies capable of upsetting the order of the ballet? How did they, so easily and completely?

Joséphine waved to a dark figure sitting behind the table. He was the only other brown-skinned person in the studio aside from me, with dark hair piled on his head in some haphazard fashion, his black suit neat and working hard to obscure how young he also was for his place there. He scrawled into a notebook in his lap, brows knit in a contemplative scowl, and when he noticed her, he nodded in acknowledgment. Light fell on his broad face, exposing the beautiful sculpt of a strong, wide nose and melancholic downturn of his eyes. Striking, even, if you're into that sort of thing.

Which I wasn't.

Strangely, all the room's daylight appeared dimmer in that corner where he sat, like a photo gone fuzzy around the edges. Broken TV static and shade obscuring an image I had to squint to see.

I nudged Coralie. "Did your mother mention a second new board member?"

"Nope, why?"

"Does he seem *off* to you—?"

Turning back, I saw Ciro's nameless friend had returned to his notebook, face hidden again, pen moving fast. The eye-straining dimness adorning his frame was gone, leaving just a normal boy dressed in finery, nothing for Coralie to see. Just my imagination then, dust or something in my eye.

President Fiona Auger clapped her hands and strolled to the middle of the floor. Everyone sat quiet and still, arrested by the timbre of her soft voice. "Welcome to the evaluations for level eight's final production, *Giselle*. Let's get started, shall we?"

Watching Joséphine dance was like watching a sculptor carve, knowing they were onto something before the masterpiece even revealed itself to you. She struck invisible lines none of us saw, tapping into currents in the music none of us felt. Her sissonnes were textbook, attitudes beyond reproach, and pas de bourrée as light as a feather.

To kick off the audition, Joséphine, Sabine, and some muscled male soloist I didn't know danced variations from the finale of *Giselle*. The man, a hero in mourning; Sabine, the vicious queen forcing him to dance until his death; and Joséphine as Giselle's ghost, adamant in saving him from beyond the grave with her love. His jumps, Sabine's turns, and Joséphine's grace set the standard, showing the board what proper soloists looked like before we students dared to try.

Even Coralie in all her pretend apathy couldn't resist staring, her mouth agape, transfixed by the spell Joséphine cast. The whole room was enraptured by her sorrow. We hung on every half-turn, hoping she'd save her duke. And when the music ended and she curtsied, not even flushed or breathing hard, not a hair out of place or a falling bead of sweat, we applauded loud enough to shake the walls.

My toes twitched in my shoes to get up and have my turn. Not just dancing, I wanted to fly and glide and spin like that. I needed to channel her, subsume her essence in mine. *Become* Joséphine, the board of directors soft as putty in my hand, ready to offer me everything.

Moving like that, Joséphine was untouchable. *That* was the kind of power I didn't know I wanted. To be undeniable.

"Very well done," President Auger said, clearing her throat and rising from her seat among the judges. Her silver hair was pulled back into its usual high bun so tight it lifted her brows, her navy pantsuit pristine, and as she returned to the center floor, she scanned our class with her falcon's gaze. Searching for mice.

Nearly everyone was afraid of her and the man at her side, Hugo Grandpré, the company's creative director. They shaped and shattered careers, though the sight of Auger's severe expression warmed me just as much as it made me want to run. She'd presided over auditions for the academy all those years ago, grey eyes shining when she realized that I came alone, by bus no less. Eight years old but wholly devoted, shoving my way through a lobby full of dance moms with my chin high. Auger gave a single, almost imperceptible nod that said we shared the same drive, wore the same fierceness. That said she saw *me*.

When she told me I belonged at the academy, I marched back through the shark-infested waters of desperate parents bitter over their children's misfortunes, grinning victorious. Indestructible.

I wouldn't let her down now.

"While they have their break, students, please take your lines for individual evaluations."

Coralie was the first to leap to her feet, impatient while the rest of us tensed our shoulders. My paltry breakfast went sour in my belly as I shuffled up toward a place at the barre.

Before auditions, they liked to line us up to be evaluated, and we complied wordlessly, standing in first position, heels turned out and together, in our academy-issued uniforms of black leotards, soft pink tights, and matching buns.

All cuts of meat in a display case while they prepared a dinner party. The board of directors waited hungrily at their tables.

As they examined us, President Auger whispered to Grandpré, a muscular man with a shaved head and too-tight clothing, known for both his temper and creative genius. Our future choreographer if we were lucky. He scowled, disappointed with what he was served. He always seemed in a foul mood, whether I passed him in the halls or he was taking bows onstage. During the warm days of spring when all the studio and theatre doors were propped open to combat the stifling air, his screams of rage filled the opera house.

"From the top of the roster with Vanessa Abbadie," Auger mumbled, prompting Grandpré to look at his clipboard and then at the first girl in the row.

In evaluations, we braced ourselves as they cataloged our parts for muscle-to-fat ratio, pitting the curve of my arms against Olivia's ruthless precision, loud enough for everyone to hear. Six months ago, it was Vanessa's emoting we had to strive for, worthy of every night on the main stage, but lately, the rubric was Joséphine Moreau. They wanted necks longer, teeth whiter, arms slenderer, hips narrower, and thighs shapelier. And we had only months to fix what he labeled as flaws before company auditions came along.

"Joséphine is the girl they should all kill to be," Grandpré grumbled loudly, his eyes shifting to the newly minted étoile on the floor, dabbing at her neck with a towel. "Raise their standards to be more like her." Only the air-conditioning whirring overhead gave him a reply.

And so we all studied Joséphine, lithe and pale and pretending not to hear. Not even two years ago, she was one of us, getting told to be like Sabine or some other older model that she studied and later moved on to replace. Maybe two years from now, one of us would be cannibalizing her. We hated her as much as we loved her, because she had our dream caught between her perfect, pearly white teeth, dangled in front of our faces.

The director lingered in front of Vanessa, and Auger offered like a merchant eager to sell her wares, "She has Joséphine's proportions."

And Grandpré stared at Vanessa for a long while, taking in every detail from her full, brown hair and dimpled chin to her long, muscled calves. The silenced dragged on, not even the professionals on the floor daring to make a sound. In the mirror, the only trace of life in Vanessa's face was in the upward twitch of her lips. The board sat up in their seats, squinting to estimate the width of her hips.

"Yes, but she's too tall," Grandpré muttered, waving a dismissive hand. Auger scratched notes on her roster. "Taller than the rest, so putting her in the corps may be difficult. She'll stand out."

Auger nodded. "What about pas de deux? Imagine her dancing Princess Florine with Alain—"

He shook his head. "Joséphine can do everything. We want versatile dancers who will shine in any role."

And like that, Vanessa's turn was over, her lips trembling toward a frown, and they moved on to the next.

"She reminds you of her mother, no?" Auger asked before Coralie.

Rose-Marie Baumé was one of the ballet's greatest étoiles, who went on to become a model, cosmetics mogul, and chair on the ballet's board, and my best friend was her spitting image down to the permanently flushed cheeks and perfect posture. The kind of disgusting beauty everyone craved, though everything about Coralie from her hair to her manners was wild, almost out of spite.

No one cared to notice the annoyance in Coralie's set jaw as she stared straight ahead, daring them to say more. Auger couldn't have chosen a worse attribute.

Grandpré hardly glimpsed her. "Yeah, we all know Rose-Marie's daughter. Too many freckles, but she'll be fine if you keep her out of the sun." He said this directly to Rose-Marie, whose painted smile hardened. She narrowed her eyes at her daughter when he stepped aside.

Then came a nobody at the middle of the pack, a pretty face but too weak a turnout, and though Olivia Robineau's turnout was near perfect, her waist wasn't small enough. Leading the boys was Rémy Lajoie, too muscular, and Geoffrey Quý, bafflingly not muscular enough, but his broad shoulders were certainly appreciable. The girl before me cried when Grandpré said her hair was too short. But bodies mattered to them as much as our skill and devotion, and many talented dancers were chased away over the years because of things they couldn't change. Or shouldn't have been asked to.

We didn't have the power to say otherwise. Still, I stiffened when my turn came.

"Laurence Mesny," Auger announced, using a small, cold finger to lift my chin, raise my eyes to Grandpré's. I was a puppet, waiting for strings to be pulled. Over her shoulder, the board watched on with muted interest. Ciro Aurissy's brow furrowed as he contemplated me. His friend didn't bother glancing up from his notebook at all.

"Final marks are in, and she finished at the top of her class in all areas. Astute, dedicated, with innate artistry."

I resisted the urge to smile in case I appeared confident. They didn't like too much confidence in a soloist.

Grandpré scanned me from head to toe, closing in on the remnants of kinky hair burned and gelled into submission, my complexion darker than the rest, shoulders wider, pulse racing in my throat. Over the years, I'd received every type of criticism veiled as critique, sometimes kind and occasionally cruel. Some found me charming, others boring. Depending on the day, I was too thin or not thin enough, simultaneously vibrant and dead behind the eyes, hair too big and expressions too cocky. I swallowed it all with a blank face.

I held my breath, both eager and reluctant to know what he saw. What if they wanted something I couldn't give? Some*one* else?

Finally Grandpré shrugged. "I guess."

Freed from the spell, I blinked rapidly and released the tension in my shoulders, though I didn't remember flinching.

"Her shoulders are a little too wide," he said before moving on, having had his fill and leaving me hollowed. After two steps, he glanced back and added, "And she could stand to be softer too. Not so uptight."

I tasted blood from biting my tongue.

Uptight.

No one looked at me now. Sabine turned back to her snack, Joséphine worked her calves with a muscle carver, and the board devoured the next poor girl down the bar. Even the dark-haired boy kept scribbling in his notebook, probably taking notes on our humiliation.

I mulled over that word in my head again and again while the rest of the critiques went by in a blur. Unseeing, unfeeling, my only sensations the tang of blood and ringing in my ears. Not sore from morning class, nor hungry from the breakfast I hardly stomached through the nerves. My knuckles popped in fists balled at my sides, because of everything I'd heard, this was a new one to fixate on.

Now I was too *uptight.*

And then, it was time to dance.

CHAPTER 2

In the center of the studio, Coralie danced a variation from *Giselle*, and she was doing it badly.

"Looks like she finally learned how to balance," Olivia muttered snidely behind me.

I tucked my cheeks between my teeth, willing myself not to turn around and say something vicious. Each of us prepared a solo for this audition so the judges could assign featured roles, and like many others', Coralie's strategy was to make her desire plain. She didn't want Myrtha the queen or Bathilde the noblewoman; she wanted to be the star, which was always a risk if the judges thought her more suitable in some other position.

She clasped her hands at her chest and turned out, the ends of her long gauzy skirt swirling. I recognized the variation from the first act, when the shy and lovesick peasant girl twirls to entertain a party of aristocrats, full of turns en pointe that sink into gracious, sweeping bows.

And it was spit in all our faces how beautifully, effortlessly she still fit, despite her flaws.

She beamed brighter than the setting sun's rays as she moved through the steps. Doe-eyed and demure, round cheeks caked in blush she didn't even need.

My eye twitched at the sight.

"Do you think her mom gives her private coaching?" Vanessa whispered.

"I would, if my daughter got held back a year."

I inhaled sharply through my nose, but still didn't turn. Before us, Coralie stepped into the temps levés en pointe. On the toes of one foot, she hopped again and again, small and steady, while the other foot did petits battements to the rhythm. It was a feat both gentle and athletic, to be perfectly in time and make it look easy—the supporting leg bent slightly, body perfectly upright. All the while, the facial expression remained serene, skirts fanned with both hands. It was hell on the knees, yet Coralie's full, pink lips were quirked in a soft smile as she gazed out past the board. As if she could hop for days and weighed nothing at all.

Beneath the gold plating, however, her work was only passable. Her movements were listless, sloppy. Her hops half a beat off-rhythm and stilted. If I danced like that, they'd laugh me out of the academy.

It took all my strength to stop cringing, as I admonished myself for how easily I too dissected her mistakes. And I was worse than the evaluations, not even saying it to her face. Me, her best friend, no better than the rest.

"Imagine the embarrassment," Rémy said, voice dropping low. "Anyone else would've quit or run off to another ballet already. She only got to repeat the year because her mom's on the board—"

I whipped around and gave my most scathing glare. Three of our classmates, Olivia, Vanessa, and Rémy, who only smiled in Coralie's face to sidle up to her mother, fell silent immediately.

"Is someone paying you to be this bitter," I hissed, "or are you doing it for free?"

Coralie was my best friend—my *only* friend—and I loved her. I wouldn't let them talk about her like that, as though they didn't see me sitting right here. Even if they weren't wrong, exactly.

Vanessa pursed her lips but didn't respond. I stared her down a moment longer before turning my attention back to Coralie's wobbly attempt at piqué manège.

In a tornado of blush pink, she spun through a series of small turns, wisps of golden curls coming free. From here, we all saw there wasn't enough speed. Even Joséphine stopped flirting long enough to wince because Coralie didn't have enough momentum to carry her across the arc.

Sure enough, on the next step she lost her footing, stumbling roughly out of the turn. A chorus of sharp inhales echoed through the room. Rose-Marie's frown deepened. But Coralie righted herself, finding her place in the music once more, only now she was trying to make up lost time, pushing faster. And that was a mistake. I chewed my lip to stop myself from shouting directions at her. She needed to turn *with* her rib cage, not restrict its movement. She looked inexperienced, and that was the last thing they wanted their Giselle to be.

Not that it mattered. The judges' warm, indulgent smiles barely slipped—*maybe* there was a dash of pity on Ciro's face, but that was all. The boy in the corner even glanced up from his notebook.

When Coralie's music finished, she sank into a deep bow, dipping her head with convincing modesty. Her shoulders rose and fell, her neck and chest flushed as the room broke into a small round of applause. It wasn't the thunderous roar of a full house by any means, not the sky-shattering applause that Joséphine's Giselle had received. Still, it was louder than the other solos had gotten.

Coralie was a demigod competing against mortals. She *belonged*, born of the ballet with stardust in her blood. And it took everything in me to fight back the bitter taste in my mouth at the thought.

She smiled and scurried to her seat.

"Mademoiselle Baumé," President Auger said from her seat among the panel, wire glasses low on her nose. "Very charming, as always, but please take extra consideration to anticipate the pace of the music."

Coralie, fanning herself as she crossed the floor, paid her no attention. Everything was a game to her when her mother was in charge.

"Still delightful." Auger motioned to the next dancer. "Olivia? Ready for my Candide fairy?"

Coralie flopped onto the floor beside me with a happy sigh, smelling of fresh sweat and muscle cream. "Well? Did I do her justice?"

I dragged my gaze away from Olivia, who pranced to center in a tutu with her arms waving like willow branches. She looked confident. Candide from *Sleeping Beauty* was a good choice. "Huh?"

"You were watching me like a hawk." Coralie wriggled her brows, but within her grin, her lip quivered. Her eyes watered.

So I flicked her nose and offered her a smile. "You were disgustingly angelic. It was some of your best work."

And I technically wasn't lying.

My turn came after Olivia, so I leaned forward in a quick stretch, eyes drifting closed for a second with pleasure as my hip popped, relieving pressure. When I opened them, I found the boy in the black suit glancing at me from his corner. There and then gone, eyes turned back to his notebook, pen moving.

What is he writing?

"Last up, Laurence," Auger called out. "Ready for Kitri?"

No.

But my feet were already carrying me to position. A heavy silence blanketed the studio, eyes boring into my skin as I crossed the floor. The air felt thin. My heart drummed in my ears.

Still, my body struck the starting pose, even as the shrieking chorus of questions began to loop in my head: *What if I fall?*

What if they've already seen what I can do, the polish chipped and peeling, and they finally find all the ugly things underneath? Too desperate, too sharp, too uptight?

What if I'm not enough?

The questions didn't stop, but the opening strings of music stirred through the studio announcing Kitri's fiery variation from *Don Quixote*. I'd listened to the music so many times, it played in my dreams. Ready or not, my body sprang into action, and before I decided to move, I was already galloping across the stage.

One leg folded under me, the other extended, I leapt high and fast.

The solo was meant to be upbeat, dazzling. A bold young woman in the market square, declaring her love with the sweeping arms of a toreador and the kicks and jumps of an angry bull.

I rose on the tips of my toes in a quick développé, then kicked my leg straight up. The movement was crisp, precise, but my cheeks were already aching from the strain of my smile. Kitri was meant to be impetuous, vivacious, but all the muscles in my face felt rigid. I twirled into the double pirouette, blessed heat rushing my joints. In motion, the studio faded until it was nothing but a blur of white, and I was transported to a higher plane. I couldn't make out anything or anyone except the flurry of violins encouraging me to move faster, jump higher, kick sharper, *be more than.*

I flitted back to my starting spot, toes numbed in my shoes. Skin sticky with sweat. But I only had time for a single, hurried breath before taking off at a gallop again. More spins, more flirty little flutters. My pulse took flight along with the ends of my skirt.

But the grands jetés were still to come. They were the type of move that every ballet used in its promotional shots: a ballerina contorted in midair, split a perfect 180 with her head back, arms up, ephemeral, intense.

A great Kitri had to be fearless. It demanded everything she had, everything she *was.*

My legs moved me through the développé and grand battement by memory. Then came my time to soar.

Into fourth position, and up I sprang.

The thought rang out in my mind, loud and clear, cutting over the music: *What if I'm not enough?* But it was too late.

I split my body as far as it allowed, against gravity and sinew and time, stretching the moment—the pose—for as long as possible. The tip of my pointe shoe nudged the crown of my head. My eyes drifted shut.

Then the floor reclaimed me again, too soon. There was no time to fumble in the music. My body couldn't pause, couldn't rest, already moving into the next step, arms sweeping wide. Because the ballet didn't wait for you to catch your breath.

I leapt into another grand jeté, crisper, less languid, and snapped back to the ground on bouncing heels. Too early, but acceptable. Lingering en pointe, I gave the crowd sweet, little battements while the knuckles of my toes stung. Sweat ran down my arms.

Gazing over at the tables, I made out the stony faces of the judges, the squint of Rose-Marie Baumé, the purse of President Auger's lips. Was she disappointed? Even against pirouettes, I caught the stares of Ciro, his friend, Joséphine, and Sabine. Olivia was practically salivating in her seat, waiting for me to fall.

So I channeled Kitri, chin held high, and blew them a kiss. Proof that I could be cheeky and sweet. Fearless. The very opposite of uptight.

The music didn't stop, and in three heartbeats, I sailed into my third jeté. And this one was perfect. My body became extreme and exalted. Even as makeup ran in my eyes.

I landed weightless before flying into the ending. Twenty pirouettes down the length of the studio, back-to-back, push spin push spin while the room disappeared. I became a bird of prey in motion. There was no

Coralie, no Auger, no judges or classmates—only me and the lights, the wood and the mirrors. I belonged to the music, and we only had each other. My breath was shallow, lungs burning as I swept myself away.

Unbound from my body, from myself. From time and mortality, even.

Until I stretched into the final arabesque, contorted in a pose, and the stillness claimed me. Face flushed, eyes unseeing, chest wheezing, skin buzzing.

Applause scattered slowly around the room, but compared to Joséphine, it only felt hollow. My pulse throbbed in my neck as I dropped my trembling leg and straightened. Limp and wrung out, I slunk back to my seat with my eyes locked ahead, too afraid to glance back. I knew what I'd find on the other side of the tables: the panel's distaste. Who else could follow Princess Coralie and Joséphine? They'd already seen what they were after.

My eyes stung. Someone's whisper prickled at the back of my neck, not that I heard anything.

"Well done, Mademoiselle Mesny." The president's voice floated my way, faint over the blood pounding in my ears, the same comment she'd given everyone who just did "okay."

But I wasn't allowed to be "okay." Without Giselle, I'd fade into the background in the corps. The board would forget about me, and when company auditions came around, I'd be dispensable. Insignificant. Cast out of the house and back onto the street with nothing. And certainly separated at last from Coralie, from the only person who cared about me.

Coralie rubbed my shoulders, but I hardly felt it. Geoffrey Quý danced Hilarion's death next, and we all knew he'd capture the part.

When it was over, President Auger gestured to the door. "Once again, well done, students. Assignments will go out later this evening, thank you."

Everyone stood. Bags were stuffed and slung over shoulders, and the studio filled with the clamor of dancers chattering, murmuring their bests and worsts of the day. On the other side of the room, Ciro Aurissy and Rose-Marie Baumé butted heads. They engaged in a battle of hissed whispers too low to make out, Ciro scowling, still seated and arms crossed while Rose-Marie leaned over the table, sneering and red-faced. The other board members' gazes flicked between them nervously.

Clearly, he didn't appreciate Coralie's number.

Meanwhile my classmates filtered out through the clanging metal door, back into the hall.

"Laurence, a moment?"

President Auger stood by the table, head bowed and close with Grandpré. The creative director nodded to her and moved aside as Rose-Marie Baumé stormed out, expensive coat thrown over her shoulder. No one seemed surprised.

I licked my lips, cycling through what Grandpré might have told her. Was I still too uptight? Or maybe my scholarship didn't renew, and there was a huge bill waiting for me in the office. Both options were equally terrifying.

My heart skipped a beat as I neared, as the older woman placed a hand on my shoulder and leaned in.

Is my father dead?

"We're still figuring out the cast list, but I wanted to tell you before you left."

Bile rose in the back of my throat. I was going to be sick, and my life was over.

"Grandpré has assigned you the role of Giselle. You've done a marvelous job this year. Your devotion has paid off, congratulations," President Auger whispered, with Grandpré's grunt of approval behind her. Her lips curled in the closest I had ever seen to a smile.

But I only stared, ears ringing, completely numb. Breath caught with incredulity, my feet carrying me away and into the hall. Coralie waved a hand in front of my eyes, took my shoulders, and shook me.

"What?"

"What. Did. She. Say?" She was nearly growling, our faces so close our noses touched. Her eyes were wide and wild, anticipating.

Finally my face cracked into a smile. A shaky breath.

"I'm gonna be Giselle."

Coralie screamed, so loud a board member stuck her head into the hall to shush her. But she didn't care. She crushed me to her chest and spun us around, tilting us off-axis until we both crashed hard on the floor.

I was spared to dance another day. *As Giselle.*

"Olivia suggested going to Pont Notre-Dame to chill. And now you *have* to come celebrate!" She turned her head to our classmates, all huddled together conspiratorially up the hall.

They eyed me. I eyed them.

Gnawing at my lip again, I willed one of them, any of them, to smile. To offer me a bead of warmth or congratulations. Anything.

It didn't work. They remained silent.

I pushed up into a seated position and fixed my bun, averting my gaze. But sweet, oblivious Coralie didn't wait for an answer. "Laure's coming!"

As we climbed to our feet, Coralie took my hand, fingers threaded through mine, and squeezed. Our classmates continued to look me up and down, unconvinced.

"I *said* she's coming. Now, what's the plan?"

And just like that, there were no objections. There would be no hugs welcoming me into the fold, but Coralie's charisma was impossible to deny. She wanted me around, so it was simply made fact like everything else she wanted in her life. It scared me a little, that unearned influence, and in these moments, she truly resembled her star-powered mother.

Not that I'd ever say it aloud. She'd never talk to me again.

After a hesitant pause, Olivia explained that her cousin was fetching booze, and the group resumed their discussion where they'd left off.

For now, I'd take it. I smiled at the idea of being ordinary for one night. In this, at least, I wasn't so different from my classmates—they were playing a game of pretend too. Drinking wine by the water like we were normal kids about to graduate from a normal school and celebrating our last exam the normal way. We'd stare at the stars, and for a little while the crushing pressure of our looming careers might lessen. For a moment, they'd pretend to not care about *Giselle* casting or the company's audition, ignore that not all of us would make the cut. And I'd pretend that I wasn't Laurence Mesny—a girl who could never allow herself to falter, for there were monsters nipping at her heels, starving for their chance.

For one night, maybe I could just be Laure, a normal girl who belonged and had the leading role to prove it.

When Coralie noticed me smiling, I stopped.

The Seine's dark waters sparkled under lights from the lampposts as we marched down the old, yellow stone steps off the bridge, welcomed by the warm damp air of early summer. They passed around a bottle of expensive rum from La Réunion that I didn't drink, and Geoffrey Quý, with his wide smile and an offer from La Scala already waiting, howled at the moon, his volume rising as the alcohol went down. When the rum ran dry, someone cracked open a bitter merlot. I passed on that too.

"It's too cloudy," Olivia groaned, her eyes already bloodshot and nose pink. "You can't see anything!"

"Just keep drinking until you can," Rémy Lajoie, tied for first of the boys with Geoffrey, quipped.

Not that funny, but I laughed because it felt like somebody should, though it sounded strange and false, even to me. Olivia narrowed her eyes at me and brushed past, her gaze so cold I rubbed my arms without thinking. Then we all followed, clambering down to sit at the landing. We were a cohort of ballet dancers who finally stopped spinning long enough to enjoy the night.

Coralie nudged me with her elbow, offering yet another bottle until I finally relented. It burned all the way down. I'd glued myself to her side, cowering like some stray because I couldn't bear being completely on my own. Not with them. Her cheeks and neck were flushed red, and she squinted at me suspiciously.

"What?" I asked, twisting my gold ring on my finger. It was the only real gold I had, not that it was actually mine. It had been my mother's once, though now I didn't know who it technically belonged to. Still, I wore it always, fidgeting with it as a harsh reminder that I had to keep climbing, never pausing to catch my breath.

My best friend grinned wide, leaning in. "If you want them to like you, you really have to stop trying so hard."

"I'm not trying anything," I sniped back.

She held the bottle between us. "Admit it—you're only drinking because that's the only way you can stomach these people, and we both know Rémy's never funny."

I scowled, but my face already stung from the alcohol and the cold and smiling so much in evaluations that I struggled to rearrange my features any other way. Still, she leaned her head on my shoulder, and I ground my teeth at how right she was. The second our cast list went out, I'd really have to watch my back. "What else can I do, then? Go home?"

"You can't make them like you. Just be yourself. It works for me."

"Yeah, well, *you're* rich and pretty, and your mother's face is all over

TV," I snapped, and though the words felt jagged, she simply laughed. Sometimes I wondered if there was anything about my sharp edges that could push her away. *She* didn't mind me being uptight.

"They're all vultures in people-suits," I continued acidly, wanting to test her. See how far I could go. "In cotton candy tutus, ready to devour me if I give them the chance."

She laughed again, a high little trill that warmed my chest. Or perhaps that was the rum. "You're a vulture too Laure." A smile curled on her cherry-red lips, like it was a good thing that I was. Like she was envious of my claws.

"Guys, we're graduating in three months," said Vanessa, gazing out at the lapping water with a stunned expression. "From the fucking Ballet Academy of Paris!"

Olivia threw her head back and shrieked.

"This is our last time to unwind," Rémy added. He ran a hand across his face, and I supposed in the low light, he could be handsome enough to play the hero Duke Albrecht. "It's all serious after this. We run *Giselle* and then it's straight to the company."

Vanessa fished around in her bag for a lighter, cigarette propped in her mouth. "God, don't remind me. If I screw this up, it's back to the middle of nowhere for me."

Olivia snorted. "My dad has been planning my Parliament career since before I was born. If I fail, he has a ten-year dossier ready to go. What about you guys?"

"I'd go to school, study physics," Rémy supplied. We all glanced at him, incredulous, but he just shrugged. "I have beauty *and* brains."

For a moment, the group fell silent, watching the plumes of Vanessa's smoke drift over the water. It was more peaceful than any moment at the academy, bellies warm and shields down, not having to watch for teeth lunging at each other's throats.

So then, lulled into a false sense of security, I offered up my truth. "Without ballet, I'd be dead."

Because I meant it. I didn't see a world for me without my art in it, where I didn't live this beauty and torment every single day.

But they all stiffened around me, and I squeezed my eyes shut. *Too* honest. So stupid to let myself forget that, for all this pretending, I wasn't actually one of them. We might all be vultures, but they weren't the same kind of hungry that I was. Or if they were, they had the luxury of never letting it show. Tomorrow they'd be back to picking at the still-warm bodies of each other's careers. *My* career, now that they smelled my desperation.

The silence stretched on.

And then, a little too delayed but having my back like always, Coralie cackled, and the rest of them followed.

PART TWO

SCHISM

CHAPTER 3

THREE MONTHS LATER

The handsome Duke Albrecht took his sweet time crying over my grave. I paced the wings, my "afterlife," fighting the urge to gnaw my nails off while he rolled around in his lament—face contorted in anguish, sculpted body stretched taut like a rendering of some ancient Greek hero.

Blood pounded in my ears, so loud I kept losing my place in the music. And the longer he drew it out, the more my muscles grew cold and stiff, the louder my panic sang.

What if they forget me?

Rémy Lajoie plunged his face into the bouquet of plastic lilies laid at my tombstone, milking his finale for all its worth. An impatient scream tried to force its way out of my chest. We were in the great amphitheatre of *the* Palais Garnier, our farewell performance to the Ballet Academy of Paris, and in some of those gilded seats were the company's directors and board members. This was my time to become someone who mattered.

I flexed and extended my feet to keep moving, ready to take my bows, to soak in the audience's attention once again. Nearby, a pair of Wilis—dancers who made up the chorus of ghost girls—glanced at me and whispered, giggling behind their hands as they leaned into each other. I was a tiger pacing the length of my cage, voracious and biding my time in the dark. My classmates kept their distance, like

I might pounce and drag them into the shadows with me. Like I was something to fear.

The taller chorus member drew a silver flask from the bodice of her gown and slipped it under the ghostly white veil obscuring her face. She threw it back, her pale neck arching, and held it out for her companion. They didn't offer me any, and I didn't ask.

Applause made my heart stutter, and my attention snapped back to the stage, where the audience cheered Rémy and his melodramatic suffering. My nails dug half-moons into my palms. I didn't remember them applauding like that for *me* after I danced myself into a grave.

Then heavy velvet curtains began to finally, slowly drift shut, prompting Duke Albrecht to rise to his feet and make his way to the scuffed white tape that marked center stage, to bid our audience adieu. Meanwhile, a flurry of anxious energy exploded backstage as the rest of the cast rushed in for final bows. Veils were straightened, stinking bodices smoothed down, dandruff brushed from shoulders, makeup smears wiped away. The two drinking Wilis giggled and scurried to their places in line. They hugged and squeezed each other, sneaking sips and whispering words of celebration: They'd reached the finish line.

And I stayed in the dark.

Alone.

It's supposed to be this way. After all, I was an equation that didn't add up, the unwelcome guest who'd stolen the crown, the soloist while they were merely the corps. So I wore the loneliness like fine silk on a bespoke gown.

Bright and golden at the center of the huddle, Coralie's gaze found me, and she flashed me a grin. To her mother's dismay, she was an ordinary Wilis, laughing as she attempted to tuck a loose ringlet back in her bun. It slipped free again, and a flurry of white hands reached out to help—delicately lifting her veil out of the way, sparing a bobby pin, basking in her effervescence. But then the curtains closed with a thud, and Rémy swaggered offstage, and I lost sight of my friend in the storm of white.

Onstage, two perfect rows of ballerinas struck the same pose, stiff and waiting for the curtain to reopen.

The applause swelled to a hum.

And then the curtains parted, revealing the Wilis with their hands crossed at the wrists, heads tilted the same angle. Identical. With a romantic sigh, the girls took their bows in unison, fluffy white skirts pooling the floor like fog.

I wiped my sweaty palms on my bodice, wincing at the sting. They were scraped raw from drying and redrying on the rough tulle and beads of my funeral gown, my hands twitching under the urge to crack my knuckles, *do something.* My time was almost here.

But—what if I bow and nobody claps and it's just endless, oppressive silence that clings to me, following me out of the weekend and into auditions on Monday?

I smoothed the intrusion away by smoothing out my already gelled hair, aggressively pinned into an angelic bun. Never a curl or unruly coil in sight. Especially tonight.

"Laure!"

My head shot up to find Rémy standing in the wings, extending a hand. I dipped the bottom of my shoes in the box of rosin powder for extra grip and felt my feet carry me to my place at his side.

The other soloists darted out one by one; Vanessa Abbadie, who never ceased to remind us that her sister just married an actual Italian prince, and then Geoffrey Quý as the valiant hero Hilarion, all cheekbones and shiny black hair. Against the rules, he grinned as he bowed, and the audience howled with approval anyway.

My fingertips stung when Olivia Robineau entered as the ghost queen Myrtha. I was sure she'd hidden a razor blade in my shoe last week—removing it left scars on the pads of my fingers that ached whenever I saw her. The stony, puckered stare she gave the audience as she curtsied low wasn't a performance but her usual expression.

When she backed away, Rémy tucked a firm hand around my waist. The stage had cleared. It was waiting for us.

For me, really.

From the wings, I glimpsed beyond the stage, the golden sculptures and filigreed columns visible even with the house lights off. Angels with trumpets and lyres stared down from the ceiling in judgment. The grand chandelier glowed like the painted heavens were watching. Just looking at it, you wouldn't know it fell once in the early days of the Palais, crushing the audience below under several tons of gold and burning light. A woman even died.

I'd always found the story poetic in a grim sort of way. Wasn't that what art was meant to be, transformation through sacrifice? It was why we endured the endless blisters and bruises and broken toes and hidden razor blades—all so we could touch god. When I'd told Coralie, she'd just laughed.

Rémy took my hand. "Are you breathing?"

"Of course I am," I snapped.

But I wasn't. He could feel how uptight I was, seeing it all: me falling, crashing to the floor, sliding into the orchestra pit. I imagined my shin bone snapping, bloodied and poking through for the audience to devour. Eight years at the ballet academy undone because I couldn't take bows properly. Proof at last that people like me would never belong to places like this.

The boning of my bodice dug into my ribs—*how had I ever breathed in this dress?*

The applause rose to a rhythmic rumble, which did nothing to ease my panic. Silly maybe, but now I couldn't shake the idea of their hands growing tired before we arrived, for the first time in Palais Garnier's history.

"Ready?" asked Rémy, only we were running before I answered. For all my panic, I still remembered the way.

The star-crossed lovers as Giselle and her Duke Albrecht, Rémy and I sauntered to center stage. To stay upright, I clutched his hand so hard the knuckles popped, but ever the performer, his smile didn't budge an inch. Under the blinding spotlights, only the rough shapes of the audience's bodies were visible, packed into lush velvet seats beneath gilded cherubs. Cameras flashed. Tuxedoed blobs surged to their feet.

My heart climbed into my throat like bile, like a scream.

I raised my hand.

A roar climbed in response, louder than Rémy's, than all the others' combined. The crowd, *my* audience, was applauding for me, and I was their star.

Standing amid the clamor of their devotion, I was transformed into a great étoile. Not just Laure, but something better, something more than. Something reminiscent of Joséphine Moreau—she'd claimed her godliness on this stage, after all.

I held my spine straight, reinforced by the ghosts of other greats who had come before me. My eyes stung under those unrelenting lights, and I blinked back tears that probably looked like joy or gratitude from afar, to anyone who didn't know me. My starving sneer would soften to a smile.

There came pressure on the hand that Rémy clutched, and together we bowed. My foot pointed behind me, and I sank down ever so slowly on one knee, unhurried and decadent as if I were sinking into a hot bath rich in rose petals and lavender oils. I took my time—head low, no wobbling, no slipping shoes, no falling into the pit. My arm swept the floor with an elegance I had never possessed offstage.

In this moment, I let myself be carried away by this glittering altar covered in sweat and calloused feet while my heart raced, not with humility or gratitude, but with hunger. I was going to carve my name into the bones of this ballet. They'd enshrine this gown in their museum—Laure's first, the skirt sullied by sweaty palms.

Soon I'd be a name no one would forget. A raging fire they couldn't escape.

For two hours, I'd glided across this stage with vicious perfection. Never missing a beat, it was the best I'd ever done, and now I deserved the glory that followed. Like we rehearsed, I stood and allowed my costar to plant a dry kiss on my hand. Rémy gestured for me to bow again, and I obliged in the halo of that brutal, burning chandelier. The applause became thunder. I was their god.

Finally Rémy and I shuffled back to join the rest of the soloists, Olivia jostling me slightly as we took our places, but I didn't waver. We bowed together. Then again with the full cast, and again with our director. I smiled and smiled, so rigid and wide my cheeks hurt, but the pain was welcome. It made all of this real.

The audience, my disciples, never tired in their devotion. The cheers carried on, so loud they drowned out my breaths. I needed to savor every second of it, of being a darling before high society in the hopes they might remember me and one day make me immortal.

But too soon, the curtain drew to a close. It happened so suddenly I flinched; the velvet cut me off before I had my fill, and then the roaring applause died down to a murmur. My arm was still raised and trembling.

Too soon, the world moved on without me. Stage lights flipped on in a blare, flooding all the dark corners of backstage with harsh, clean light. The backdrops and set pieces were corralled to their places, cables rolled up and tucked away. My fellow castmates streamed into the wings until it was just me standing there. Alone again and gasping.

At last, I dropped my hand. Pins and needles vibrated through my skin; high from the dancing and applause, I couldn't feel my face, arms, or legs. On this stage I had transported to some divine place, and it scraped my insides raw to have to drag myself away. How did Joséphine manage this every night? The ringing in my ears and spots in my vision refused to fade.

I stood there until the last of the crew trickled out and the lights dimmed. Until the stage door shuddered on its hinges and plunged me into the dark. One girl drunk on euphoria left behind and forgotten. Limbs heavy and weak from exertion, I staggered offstage, as though the thousands of watching eyes had drained me. Every step wrung me out more than the last, and then in the midst of the rising ache, I felt it.

The air went cold and still.

A chill brought the hairs at my nape on end, as though my body sensed the presence of someone—or some*thing*—lingering in the shadows. Though I hadn't seen him since I left the studio that day, the feeling reminded me of the dark-haired boy with fuzzy edges, of Ciro Aurissy's friend in black silk, scrawling in his notebook, bending light in his corner.

It was the same flavor of uncanny. Of weird.

"Hello?" I found myself asking, like there was anyone left but me.

After all, this was Opéra Garnier, inspiration for *The Phantom of the Opera*. It was often that the air stopped completely in certain corridors, and we all heard the ghostly footsteps that accompanied walking the halls alone. There were strange doors in the dressing rooms that didn't open and tunnels beneath the stage, and no one knew where they went. We didn't know what lay in the pools below, and just earlier that day, I'd sworn shadows flickered in the corner of my vision. We seldom talked about it aloud—if you asked an older dancer, you'd only be met with the same advice: Ignore it.

But instead I asked again. "Hello?"

There came the faintest whisper of . . . something. My name, maybe. Too low, too soft, or maybe nothing at all. Maybe I was just delirious from months of nonstop rehearsals. My ears strained to hear, but the sound—if it existed at all—was swallowed by the thousands of retreating voices on the other side of the curtain.

With a shiver, I gave up and hurried out to the hall. The Palais was an ornate tomb, and though I didn't consider myself superstitious, I cared little to find out what might be lurking in its shadows.

Up ahead, the rest of the cast traveled as a pack. Rémy carried Olivia on his back, and together they weaved excitedly down the hall. A train of lesser Wilis held hands and ran after them, squealing. And I trailed at the end, no longer divine under these glaring fluorescent lights, the reality making me sick.

"Where are we going for the after-party?" someone shouted.

"My dad brought half l'Assemblée nationale to see."

The hallway eventually split, and the entire cast turned left toward the creamy marble stairs to the atrium, where a loving mob waited. There would be extended families alongside neighbors and preschool friends, not to mention politicians, oil barons, and assorted glitterati all eager to heap flowers and praise and pride on my classmates for their average features and form. Congratulations for years of blood, tears, and the occasional lost toenail if you were devout.

Every one of them veered left without thinking—never questioning if someone waited up above.

Everyone but me.

I turned right. Kept my eyes locked straight ahead, not allowing them to stray, to so much as glance in the foyer's direction and the waiting crowd. No one was here for me—no one I knew had come to a perfor-mance in years, since long before the academy.

The first time it happened, I was seven and a snowflake in *The Nutcracker*. I'd searched and turned up empty, climbing platforms and standing on chairs to peer over a crowd of strangers. The pang sat with me the whole carpool home. Then again, a year later, a whimsical solo as the Lilac Fairy from *Sleeping Beauty*. Maybe they'd show up with a bigger role. Maybe they'd do it to surprise me. But the humiliation of searching—of hoping, of my classmates and their rich, supportive par-ents watching me fracture again and again when I walked away alone—that hurt worse than the absence itself.

There was a litany of excuses, even for smaller missed recitals and late pickups: an extra shift, a flat tire, exhaustion, no money for a ticket, forgetfulness. My mother's radio silence was complemented by my father feeling out of place; ballet was supposed to be *her* thing. So I didn't look after that. And I'd never looked since. Somewhere along the way, I stopped having a family altogether.

At first, the loss was an aching bruise. Then a callus. Now, a hunger.

I didn't need pats on the head or velvet boxes of bracelets with balle-rina charms. Not when I tasted applause. Head high, features schooled like I was still onstage, I strolled down the hall to the dressing room. The noise of families and friends and well-wishers faded as the door closed behind me.

The room was blissfully empty. Once safely out of sight, my steps warped into a haggard hobble, the balls of my feet aching as I dragged myself over to my table. I was eager to change out of this costume and these damned tights and remove all fifty-seven pins digging into my skull, but for a moment, I posed for the reflection in the mirrors. Angled chest, long neck, soft brows. One day everyone I knew and some I didn't would be in that foyer waiting for me, when I became an étoile and danced Cinderella or Odette for a sold-out theatre of adoring fans. I would be a star like Joséphine Moreau, and they'd bask in *my* glow too. For one moment, I allowed myself to pretend, because there was no one around to catch me.

I surveyed the hawkish girl in the mirror, face painted heavily in stage makeup, all coarse hair and burnished brown skin and dark, sharp eyes.

Not so uptight.

"You were *glorious*," I told her, because no one else would, tone fierce so she wouldn't argue back.

And before any voices came floating down the hall, before tired, flushed faces trickled into the room, I wiped my face clean, packed my bag, the program with my name next to "Giselle" tucked neatly inside and ready to be framed, and hung my gown on the rack. I cleared the lead's station with mirrors twice the size of everyone else's, erasing any evidence I'd ever been here—for now. Then, on my way out the door, I tossed the complimentary pack of free foundation and blush several shades too light in the trash and bade the ballet good night.

CHAPTER 4

The atrium of Opéra Garnier hummed with voices. Beneath the glow of the glass dome, people ambled in formal evening wear, crisp black tuxedos and sparkling gowns, posed beside gilded statues holding lanterns. The air was stifling, thick with heat and too much cologne, and tonight's patrons batted silk folding fans and programs as they crooned over the dancers. My classmates all stood out in their costumes and dirty slippers, grinning proudly and gripping bouquets.

And on the other side of this ocean of wealth lay my exit.

I clutched the stone railing tight and braced myself. My practiced ballerina smile clicked into place—gentle in the eyes, soft around the mouth, chin raised, shoulders down, neck long. Glances of recognition followed my descent—how could they not after a procession of moon-pale faces? Still, my smile did not waver. It was my armor.

At the bottom of the stairs, I hit a wall of muscle and jasmine perfume. "Excuse me," I called out in my highest and most agreeable voice. No one heard me. The dangling platinum around one woman's neck caught in the light as I squeezed through the narrow gap formed by her and an older woman in a lace gown. It was the tiniest crevice, hardly more than a few inches, but I made myself small enough to fit. "Pardon!"

Guests looked down on me with saccharine smiles as I continued on my struggle through the crowd. Someone's grandfather touched my arm like a devotee stroking an effigy in prayer, and at his example, a woman in purple chiffon patted my shoulder, more goat at a petting zoo than deity. I escaped through another space only for two suited men to step back, crushing me between them. While I wormed free one limb at a time, the men drifted apart of their own accord like jellyfish in the sea. Neither apologized or even noticed me.

I couldn't breathe. I was drowning here, and when I looked to the exit, it only seemed farther away.

A spiked heel dug into the toe of my shoe. My gasp turned to gagging on a mouthful of cloying cologne, while the shoe's owner laughed. And then a familiar, rich alto called out, "Oh! There she is!"

Chills ran down my spine. Acting on pure instinct, I pivoted to run back the way I came.

"Laurence!"

From the throng, a small, icy hand closed around the crook of my elbow. Hair raised at the nape of my neck. But before I could scream, I was yanked around to face my captors—Rose-Marie and Émeric Baumé, Coralie's parents. Coralie grimaced at their side.

They conversed with a man I didn't recognize, the adults all gazing at me in appraisal. The measured way they took in my features, my hair, and the proportions of my face, the collarbones visible from the neck of my dress, my height and shape, made my stomach uneasy. I should have been used to it with all the ballet evaluations, Rose-Marie's hawkish interrogation of my body in comparison to her daughter's, but here it felt predatory. Like I wasn't a real person but an assortment of parts.

My hands tightened around the strap of my bag, and I brandished my ballerina smile like a weapon.

"Here is our little star," Rose-Marie cooed in my ear, though her smile was stiff and polished and didn't reach her eyes. It *never* reached her eyes. "The stage loved you, my dear."

Her talon nails sank into my shoulders, pinning me in place while she kissed both my cheeks. Émeric, bronzed with full, shiny hair and a permanently bland smile, kissed with three.

"Have you met Émeric's business partner?"

Rose-Marie gestured to the tall, old man with a barrel chest wearing a velvet tuxedo. I didn't hear his name over the scarceness of my breath and the hum of the crowd, but I shook his hand anyway, my eyes darting toward the exit. Somehow, the doors looked even farther than before. Soon they might vanish and leave me stranded.

"I was just telling him how proud we are," Coralie's mother went on, "how far you've come, our little American plucked by way of Clichy-sous-Bois."

I stiffened.

The old man's bushy, silver brows shot up, the imagination running wild in his watery eyes. It was as though this additional detail painted the perfect portrait of who I was and how I got here. I saw him just picturing what it must have been like—the poor little girl out of place, her tragic childhood growing up in a housing project, the terrible things she must've seen. He nodded like everything about me suddenly made sense now.

Only it didn't. Because first, I wasn't really from anywhere—we'd packed and moved all over the north side, living in all kinds of houses. And second, I didn't see or experience anything terrible or gruesome either, which Rose-Marie knew, not that it mattered. These people viewed everything touched by the lower class as dark, depraved, and violent. To them, surely I was either exactly the same or exceptional not to be. If only they knew what cruel traits their precious ballet gave me.

"Clichy-sous-Bois? Your parents must be so proud!" the old man said, shaking my hand even harder.

I opened my mouth to respond—ready to breathe fire and make

him cower in his rightful place—but nothing came out. Just dead air jammed in my lungs. Rose-Marie took the opportunity to throw a thin arm around me.

"Oh no, Laurence is an orphan. She's all alone."

My eyes watered from the sting as I clamped down on the inside of my cheek, to ground myself back in my body.

"Alone?" Again, he nodded deeply, as if that one word conveyed everything. Beside him, Coralie's father was equally grim. They looked like we were at a funeral, and I was the surviving, pitiful orphan.

And Coralie just stared at the marble floors, flush rising beneath her collar. She didn't say anything though. At times like these, it took so much not to resent her too.

No matter how hard I strained, willing my jaw to loosen, lips to part, vocal cords to stir, I couldn't find the words. That I wasn't an orphan, and I wasn't a receptacle for their charity either—it all lodged in my throat, and instead, I was the one left burning with shame.

"And now you've come so far to dance Giselle! What a feat!"

I bit down harder until I tasted blood.

"So fortunate to have been given the opportunity, yes," Rose-Marie said with paper-thin enthusiasm. And considering her own daughter was relegated to the corps, her coldness was unsurprising. Though it was easy to outperform Coralie when she didn't need to try, I couldn't say as much. No matter how I wanted to, the Baumés owned our apartment.

Mustering as much grace and poise as I could, I wrenched myself from Rose-Marie's grip. "Yes, well, I also *earned* the rank of first in my class six years straight—"

"And she speaks French like a native, Rose-Marie!" the businessman remarked, as if I were a rare specimen in her collection of glass figurines. A trained animal.

Now I only smiled and shook his hand again. "Someone's waving for my attention over there," I lied. "Please excuse me."

His skin was dry and warm, and as I clasped his hand firmly with both of mine, I flicked the gold watch from his wrist. It slid away easily, into my pocket with one hand while I gestured to the door with the other. A seamless movement I learned pilfering wallets from tourists when I started dancing en pointe because specialty shoes didn't come cheap.

"Laure—" Coralie started, too little, too late.

Before anyone else tried to stop me, I turned on my heel and melted back into the mass of guests. My hand still in my pocket, I fingered the warm, rigid dials of the man's watch. It gave my coat a pleasant weight, and the bland, plastic smile I'd performed for the old masses finally transformed into something real.

Prick.

Someone's mother ambled sluggishly out of my way, opening the path just enough to see beyond the front doors, black wrought iron lamps illuminating the opera's small courtyard. Only steps away from freedom, I made out the rumble of cars over the din of the crowd.

"...No, you're right, André," a man said from the alcove by the door. I recognized him from the board of directors: a film producer with a blond, pointed mustache. "There is some...*roughness* that she brings to the stage."

My feet refused to take me farther.

There were a few of them gathered in the alcove: President Auger and her finely dressed colleagues. Though I hadn't made a sound, one of them noticed me and then they all turned.

Auger charged forward nervously. "Brava, Laurence! We were just discussing—"

"You are a fine dancer," another older man started. He clapped a hand on my shoulder and squeezed tightly, pinching a nerve. "But I was saying, there is a perception when one comes to see the Paris Ballet, you know? Opéra Garnier signifies luxury, exclusivity, delicate performers. It's not typically what our audience expects, to be forced to think of inequality and social issues…"

I tightened my grip on the handle of my bag until the cold metal bit into skin. But shot from dancing, my tendons wouldn't budge an inch.

"Ghislain, perhaps not now—" Auger tried interrupting. Her eyes darted to me warily.

"Well, let's talk practically," he continued, though nobody had asked. The stench of hard alcohol on his breath made my head swim. "What about the swans? Can Grandpré put you in a ballet blanc? *Swan Lake?*" And for a moment, he paused as if he really expected me to answer. To agree with him, even though it's been done plenty of times before, if he bothered to check. When I didn't budge, he nodded as confirmation. "It would ruin the illusion! I'm sure you're nice, but you'll stand out. Maybe in *La bayadère*, something exotic. Or modern. Classical ballet wasn't made for your kind."

Bile rose in my throat. *La bayadère* was a yearly staple starring caricatures of Indian dancers, the photos full of white girls in fake bindis and synthetic black wigs. "Exotic" indeed.

"I'm—" I stammered, my voice trembling and quiet, jaw working at the words for my defense. My gaze switched between the man and his colleagues, as I waited for someone to intervene and came up blank. For all their silence, they might as well have agreed. "But I'm at the top of my class. I have glowing praise from all my instructors—"

"We must consider how dancers assimilate into the culture of the stage, not just their grades. Ballet is an art that requires finesse, and Paris Ballet Company has a reputation as one of the best in the world. Others like you do quite well in America, I'm told—"

The metal buckle of my bag split my palm open, thin skin peeling back, pain jolting my muscles awake. Sucking in a breath, I backed away without another word. Then I was turning. Running out into the night.

Giselle was supposed to be my chance to show them that I was ready. For months and all this evening, I'd fantasized and paced, wondering about their impressions of me, but I never imagined this. That my technique wasn't the problem.

It was *me*.

CHAPTER 5

"Last time," I promised the tired, disheveled girl in the mirror as I cued the music. Never mind that *last* time was also "the last time." But this time I was close, I could feel it.

I hit RECORD on my phone and walked back to my starting mark, feet screaming in protest with every burning, shredding step. Still, I'd run Giselle's variation from the second act, going until my toenails cracked and bled if I had to.

Until I was undeniable, every time.

Pose struck, chest raised in yearning toward the camera, I waited for the music to start. The brittle smile and weary eyes full of doubt in my reflection stared back at me while the violins stirred awake.

I'd been at it for hours already, cloistered away in this small rehearsal space in the basement of Palais Garnier, the music running on loop. Every attempt was recorded, and in each video I discovered some new way my variation was lacking. Jumps too tight, then too loose; turns too fast, then too slow. It also felt hollow, joyless, and typically performed with a partner while all I had was myself. As usual.

But now the music swelled, and it was time to move. My body swept up onto my toes, a heel flicking behind me like clockwork. My legs were heavy and overworked, but still they flitted under me before I sank into plié. Thighs burning but I didn't flinch, smile steady even as I rose up on searing toes. It was all practiced precision, ankles perfectly straight, shoulders down and slicked with a sticky sheen of sweat. Flawless, though my knees trembled and threatened to buckle, because this was the easy part. There was still a dreaded grand jeté in the repertoire.

Just thinking of what those men from the board said made my heart rate spike again. *Classical ballet wasn't made for your kind.* But it was all I had. A ballerina was all I had ever known myself to be. So I'd jump and twirl again and again because it was the only thing I knew to do. The only thing I could control. If I pushed at it a little longer, became more focused and refined, *softer*, less uptight, less *me*, maybe the judges would see it too. This was the only power I had before company auditions tomorrow.

My aching heels slid into fifth position and sprang up. Once, twice, thrice. And this time, I approached the great leap like an attack. My body hinged at the middle, back leg swinging with all my power to meet my arms raised above my head. The shoe's satin brushed my fingertips, and my mouth began to part in a grin.

Only, instead of sinking out of it gracefully and into a demi-plié, I fell.

Hard.

My ankle rolled, and the landing foot slid out from under me. A harsh cry slipped past my lips as I dropped to the ground, the air torn from my lungs. Pain bloomed bright and loud through my knee and hip. The back of my skull thudded against the floor, sending stars dancing—*gloating*—in my vision.

And the music ambled along, indifferent. Horns blared where I should have been jumping, spinning, dancing with my duke. The Laure who'd earned that role was nowhere to be found.

Meanwhile, what was left of me lay broken on the floor, staring at swirls in the ceiling. Blinking away tears. Breathing hard through clenched teeth to stop the sob quivering in my chest. Every part of me throbbed.

It took a long time for the pain to subside enough to push myself upright, and even then, I stayed seated, head in my hands. There was no strength in me to keep fighting, to get back on my feet and go again. The runs were only getting more strained. And the harder I tried, the further out of reach total perfection moved. No way I could just give up, but if pushed any more, I'd dance my way right into physical therapy and a season-long injury. If I even had a season left.

A shudder forced its way down my spine. Where would I go?

"You okay?" called a voice from the door.

My head snapped up, and a fresh wave of pain flared through me. The walls spun a little as my vision settled on Joséphine Moreau. She leaned against the frame of the studio entrance, her arms crossed coolly in a leather jacket. There was a grimace on her crimson-painted mouth.

"I was on my way out and spotted you through the window."

Did she see me fall? I hadn't heard her approach, so she couldn't have been standing there long. Still, I imagined her wincing as I dropped, as the floor shook, maybe shaking her head in pity.

Unmoving, I gripped my knee, nails biting into bruising flesh until the pain screamed loud enough to keep me from unraveling. The last thing I needed was for her to remember me like this, my mask cracked and body grotesque.

I nodded woodenly. "Yes, I'm fine."

Joséphine arched a brow at the unsteadiness in my voice, as if she saw my bullshit from across the room. More insistently, she asked, "You sure?"

Against the stinging in my eyes, beneath the blur of tears, my knee had already started to swell. And I was too tired to deny: I was falling apart. I *hated* it—the weakness, the frustration, the wet rolling down my cheeks. Girls like me weren't supposed to get tired or fall apart. I was supposed to be exceptional, every time.

"It's just," I started, but that ache in the pit of my stomach reared its head again. A single, choked sob filled the air between us before I could stopper it, and then the rest poured out. "It's just—I did everything I was supposed to, gave everything they asked of me. I did everything right. I was perfect! And it's...it's not *fair*."

My head collapsed back in my hands, nails raking through my scalp as embarrassment burned in me. I sounded pitiful. Nothing a future prima ballerina should be.

"No, it isn't," Joséphine admitted softly. Her gaze pinned me in place, and a long silence stretched out as she studied me and the sad, desperate things I said, finding all my chips and cracks, the layered paint that covered up the fact that I wasn't wanted here as I was. All the while I squirmed where I sat, unable to escape.

Besides, what was the point?

"It doesn't get any easier either," Joséphine said, pushing off the doorframe to saunter closer. The click of her heels echoed around the studio. "We're puppets for the board, and the stage and the music own our bodies. It never changes. It doesn't hurt any less."

Then she glanced around the room, eyes seeking little details I couldn't see. Her sigh had a melancholic tint to it.

"I used to come down here every night when I was an apprentice. Everyone thinks it's all smoke and mirrors and a decent push-up bra for me, but it's really just practice. And a lot of tears."

After another long beat of silence, Joséphine's head tilted, as if she heard something I couldn't, and she finally dragged her attention back to me with a rueful half smile. Her hand floated out, offering to pull me up, her nails manicured and painted deep red like blood.

I stared at it. There was no way Joséphine Moreau busted her kneecap in an empty studio at night, desperate to be someone—*anyone*—else. She was one of those people who changed the air of every room she entered, who made you turn and stare. She walked as if the world would rearrange itself at her feet, and it did. She danced without a shred of doubt in her steps, a titan always in motion, poised to conquer the world.

Here I was on the floor, no money, no status, no *future*—nothing to offer, yet she stood waiting for me. A hand outstretched like we might be equals.

And because the mortification couldn't settle any deeper, I took her help. She tucked an arm around my sweaty back and pulled, hoisting me to my feet like it was nothing.

"Thanks," I mumbled as I turned to shut off the speaker and grab my stuff. Every step was like walking on molten glass, but I refused to cry again. Taking my time to gather my things gave her an opening to walk away, her random act of kindness complete.

But when I rounded, Joséphine was still there. She was watching me in that inscrutable way again—mouth open, eyes glazed over in thought. Then she slid her hands into her pockets and chirped, "Come have a drink with me."

"What?"

Startled, I dropped my phone. It clattered on the floor, Joséphine laughing as I stooped to pick it up, as if people fumbled around her all the time and it thrilled her to catch us unprepared.

"It's nice to have a drink after hard practices," she explained casually. "It helps you unwind."

What I almost said was, "I can't."

Because I was seventeen, and no one would serve me more than a club soda with lemon.

Because maybe if I ran the variation again, this time I would be perfect, and the judges would see differently.

Because I couldn't remember the last time someone looked at me by *choice*, and the warmth of it fizzed brightly under my skin. What would I do when she changed her mind?

But instead, I nodded and said, "Okay."

Because Joséphine Moreau was extending an invitation to *me*, as if she and I were alike.

Because maybe some of her grace might rub off and give me a fighting chance.

Because she of all people could teach me how to conquer the universe too.

Joséphine waited outside the locker room while I got ready. I moved in a stinging, aching flurry, afraid it was all a dream and she'd vanish by the time I was done. I ripped away ribbons and pointe shoes, grimacing at the spots of blood that mottled the insides. Red seeped through the tape, all over the satin and toe box at the end—it was a massacre. The blisters and loose skin of my veiny feet were grotesque even beneath the tights run through with holes. A pinkie nail had split and bled and now hung free. My feet blazed in the water of the shower and took forever to wrap, and my left knee, distended and purple, twinged with the effort.

"How about that drink?" I breathed as I flung the door open.

Joséphine glanced up from her phone. She didn't seem to notice my heat-damaged coils dripping ice water down my coat, the bunching of my shirt underneath, my shallow breaths. She only smiled, and we were off.

The dark sky was clear, speckled with stars as we left the metro near Jardin du Luxembourg. Following Joséphine to some Italian restaurant in the 6th, which she assured me was the best in the city, I prompted, "How did you find this place?"

"I discovered Il crepuscolo when I was still at the academy, but now I just come here after rehearsals to relax," she confided, her eyes glittering as she led me toward a crimson awning. The place looked tiny, wedged between a kebab shop and a phone repair front on a narrow, cobble-stoned alley that reeked of piss. String lights decorated the standing menu, and just two small wicker tables sat out front, but the noise from within filled the otherwise quiet street on a Tuesday night.

"It has the best atmosphere," she continued, "music, fresh pasta, grappa. Have you had it before?" Up close, she was animated, taking short, hurried steps and waving her hands when she talked. I caught a flash of red ink on the inside of her wrist, a tattoo peeking out from beneath her sleeve. Only she could get away with being tattooed in the ballet.

I answered honestly. "No, but I'd like to try." I didn't want to deny her, and Joséphine didn't bat an eye—only continued babbling, effusive and warm. Her sentences were rushed, as if her thoughts were always on the verge of getting lost, and still she carried me away. Where I wasn't enough on my own, she overflowed in every way.

Before we'd even taken our seats or removed our coats, small, round glasses were brought out. As Joséphine sank into her wicker chair, oblivious, staff and guests alike lit up behind her. It reminded me of the rare occasions when Coralie's mother took us to dinner—all the world soaked up Joséphine's splendor, and I was just the lucky person in her periphery.

I talked myself out of texting Coralie. She'd never believe this was happening.

"Shall we toast?" asked Joséphine, raising her glass to mine and meeting my eyes.

In a reflex, my shoulders tensed with the feeling that she was trying to see more than I wanted to share. But I forced myself to relax and sniffed the translucent yellow liquor, pretending to be a connoisseur versed in fancy Italian alcohol. It was harsh, strong enough to singe my nostrils even though it looked no different from white wine. *Am I really doing this?*

"To smoke and mirrors," she said.

I was.

"À la tienne," I replied.

The moment the grappa hit my taste buds, I shuddered, rushed by heat and fumes and a bitter aftertaste. It rippled through me like an earthquake; meanwhile Joséphine swallowed hers unflinching and picked up the menu. A waiter materialized at once, and she ordered an assortment of antipasti and desserts that rolled off the tongue of someone well-practiced in Italian.

"Impressive for a former street rat, huh?" Joséphine asked without looking up, hands rummaging through her leather purse, the gold YSL label catching in the light. "You can't even tell I grew up on ham sandwiches and instant ramen. It was shocking all the things I didn't know when they 'plucked' me from obscurity."

The way she said "plucked" made me think she was less than grateful.

I found myself mirroring her conspiratorial grin.

"Wealth and power are foreign languages you have to learn to speak fluently if you want even a chance of surviving that place. But I wear the mask well." She offered a hand-rolled cigarette from a gold case with a grin.

Prima ballerinas didn't smoke; we couldn't afford stained gums and blackened lungs. But Joséphine could. I hesitated and shook my head, but without missing a beat, Joséphine turned and batted her lashes at our server. The young man with a ruddy complexion rushed over, a light at the ready, his gaze burning with longing and intoxicated at the sight of her leaning into the flame. She looked like the starlette of some art house film, her straight, mousy hair shiny and loose, wearing understated but still expensive black pearl earrings and matching necklace, pale shoulders bare in the moonlight. Even I found myself leaning forward in my seat, entranced.

When her cigarette caught, she angled her regal face toward him, lips pursed, eyes heavy-lidded, and whispered warmly, "Thanks, Antoine."

I cleared my throat and sat back, trying to look comfortable and at ease though my heel wouldn't stop bouncing under the table. Any moment now she'd notice how the rest of the world saw me—or rather *didn't* see me. How no one's gaze lingered on me unless they were waiting for someone to escort me off the property. I was still at a loss for why she'd even invited me here because surely, she wasn't desperate for my company. Not that I was foolish enough to question it. She'd realize her mistake.

Joséphine took a drag on her cigarette. "If they see you fall apart, that'll only confirm the bias against you. I think they make this process as hard as possible to thin the herd. See who breaks so they have fewer people to evaluate later. Are you ready?"

"I'm doing everything I can, I guess," I said with a shrug. It was too stiff to come off indifferent like I'd hoped. "It's hard to stand out when there are thirty of us and only six spots. And you know who I'm up against."

I didn't dare utter my friend's name because the thought was a betrayal—she would never think of *me* that way. So instead I twisted the grappa glass between my fingers and let those five syllables remain unsaid.

"Well, it'd be embarrassing if another ballet gets you. I've seen you dance." She tilted her head back and exhaled clove-scented smoke, each motion inhumanely beautiful. Light bent where she sat. "You're fantastic."

Heat rushed to my cheeks. I didn't know why she was being so kind, what she wanted from me when I had nothing to offer, but still, it was nice to hear. Especially after *Giselle.*

Between us descended more grappa and plates of food, colorful arrangements of bruschetta and burrata. My empty stomach growled at the sight, having been fed for years on frozen dinners, deli salads, whatever my stipend afforded. The *ballet* made this possible for her, elevating her from value meals to fine dining.

I downed the next dose of grappa to kill my nerves, keenly aware of sweat pooling under my shirt. The burn in my throat made me hiss, and Joséphine laughed, sharp and mirthful, clapping her hands. "I thought you might like it."

Absolutely not, but I beamed anyway.

Another server placed a hand on her shoulder as he introduced every plate, speaking to her and her alone. She listened with rapt attention, and I watched her, bewitched. I wanted that. To be her and be bewitched by her. So badly it hurt.

When the waiter retreated, she turned her focus on me. "Thanks for joining me, Laure. It's not so fun to eat alone."

It took a moment for the fog to recede, a moment to release my grip on the napkin in my lap. She knew my name, had spoken it aloud and made me real. It melted the pain in my knee and feet. I hardly remembered why I'd been crying in the studio just an hour ago.

She speared an olive. "Let's share?"

So I ate perfect halves of everything and studied Joséphine up close. She groaned at the taste of mozzarella di bufala, fermented olives, and fresh bread. Squealed at the chef's dish of squid ink pasta and forced a forkful into my mouth before ordering glasses of Aperol to wash it down. She insisted we share the house-made gelato, and I memorized every bat of her lashes, flip of her hair, and wave of her wrist. She knew the chefs and servers by name, thanking everyone because she waitressed her way out of dance fees the same way I picked pockets.

Joséphine lounged back in her seat with a happy sigh. Every bite we shared was rich and decadent as it sat heavy in my belly, but my head felt light enough to float away. Her radiance was infectious. I pictured doing this every day after hours of rehearsal: gracefully smoking, drinking, eating, laughing. My every action a work of art for people to admire.

"For the ladies," offered the attractive server as he sat two small espresso cups on the table. Behind him, the last pair of customers trickled out with their coats on their arms and their eyes on Joséphine. They waved, and she waved back.

I shook my head, astounded. *How?*

The server winked at me, and while it was obvious that his target was Joséphine, I lowered my lids and smiled anyway. Just to see how it felt. It was thrilling.

"Is every night like this?" I had to ask. The room tilted when I pitched forward, and my skin buzzed. Was I intoxicated from the alcohol or her?

Joséphine blinked large, hazel eyes at me, surprised and confused, as if all of this was normal. As if people dissolving at her feet was simply the natural order of things. "What do you mean?"

I want it.

I retrieved the slip of paper from the handle of her cup, the server's name and number written neatly inside. "The food, drinks, people, *Cinderella*! This is just … your life? Every day? How do you do it?"

She waited until our little cups of espresso were replaced by little complimentary shots of a dark liquor from a bottle labeled Fernet Branca. We clinked our glasses in meaningful silence, and I took a slow sip, the digestivo deliciously herbal and spiced after our meal. In a flash, she gulped hers down and sat up in her seat, evaluating me with narrow eyes again. As if I'd passed some test, she nodded resolutely to herself.

"Do you trust me?"

Perhaps it was the hot food, or the flush from so many drinks that swirled my thoughts like spun sugar, or the pink of her cheeks, but I didn't hesitate. "Of course."

How pathetic that I meant it, even knowing she hadn't answered my question.

She took my hands in hers, her skin feverish, and held my gaze. "No, Laure, I mean it. Do you trust me? Because . . ." She pursed her lips—bright red lipstick somehow still perfect—and threw a glance to the server, who was pretending to dry an already dry glass. *Subtle.* "You can have it all: the ballet, the money, the food and drinks. I can help you, but only if you trust me."

Under the full wattage of her attention, the heat where our hands clasped, there was no running. It burned down to the very center of me until there was nowhere left to hide, until she saw it all. I was all rough edges and hunger, and here was *the* Joséphine Moreau, refusing to look away or let go.

So I nodded, unblinking, flushed and reeling, undying loyalty beating hard against my ribs as I whispered, "I trust you."

And then she grinned, patted my hand, and took out her designer wallet. "Good. Then let's go."

CHAPTER 6

"You aren't taking me to prayer, are you?" I asked jokingly, wiping my sweaty palms down the front of my jeans and scanning the empty courtyard for flickering candles or a congregation lying in wait. After the restaurant, I'd followed Joséphine to a quiet but imposing cathedral nestled somewhere south, waiting for an explanation. "My mom already tried the whole baptism thing one summer in Georgia. It only made me meaner."

She snorted. "Definitely not, we're just cutting through. What I want to show you is underground—it's sort of hard to explain. Easier to just see for yourself."

I eyed the stone archway. The courtyard wall was old enough to have survived a few wars and maybe even a revolution, judging by the jagged scarring and mismatched concrete. It threw the cloistered space into heavy shadow.

My phone buzzed in my pocket the instant I crossed the threshold. The name JULIEN danced on the screen when I fished it out, a faceless blob bobbing up and down, beckoning me to answer. But I ground my teeth and powered it off instead, sure that Joséphine could hear my heart pounding and might see it as hesitation. The last thing I needed was for my father to stand in the way of my destiny. Again.

In the dark, Joséphine led me to a short iron gate built into the recess of a stone wall. Even in this moldering place, she carried herself with the same ease as in the studio, wrenching the gate open with a smile and—without another word, or any explanation at all—ducking inside.

She held it open, waiting for me.

Automatically, I took a couple cautious steps, drawn to her still, though my feet paused at the threshold. Beyond the gate, the alcove was damp, and there was the unmistakable shape of stairs descending into darkness.

A slick sensation blossomed in the pit of my stomach as I remembered Olivia's offhand comment. What if Joséphine *did* kill ballerinas?

As if sensing my thoughts, she took my hand in hers. I tensed at her touch, but she maintained a gentle smile, her hand pleasant and soft, melting my panic. My racing heart slowed, and in the quiet a voice sang her promise back to me far louder than my fear.

You can have it all.

So I closed the gate behind me and let the dark swallow me whole.

"I'm not sure who found it first, but I think some parts lead all the way to the ossuary. Not that I've tried," Joséphine called out over the volley of our footsteps. Her voice remained chipper, its pitch bouncing off the walls and making me dizzy. "But no bones where we're going, I promise."

It certainly smelled like the Catacombs. Years ago, Coralie and I ventured into the underground ossuary on Halloween night; the air down here smelled just like the rest of the musty tunnels that wound beneath the city, like mold and stone and death. It felt wrong too, reminding me of the opera, like something *more* lingered nearby. Waiting for me. I shuddered at the memory of the dark calling my name and had to grip the crumbling wall to avoid tipping forward down the steep, mile-long flight of stairs.

"I've been studying it," Joséphine was saying when we reached the bottom, "ever since Ciro brought me. Researching every interaction, every deal, reading up on the history of the city, philosophy, theology, even *alchemy*. It's maddening how much we still don't know. I think it's older than written word even."

She wasn't talking about the Catacombs anymore.

The lighting down below was terrible, sconces so weak in places that my hands faded into shadows in front of me. We crouched at junctions with low ceilings that dripped in my hair. My blistered, bloody feet, once numbed by the pleasant buzz of grappa, burned again as we walked on and on. When the sound of our footsteps traveled less, we rounded a corner and the tunnel opened into a grotto where the air tasted heavy and sweet and pressed against my lungs.

"Don't be afraid," said Joséphine as she gestured around. "Now I'll explain everything."

Stalactites the color of blood speared from the ceiling, and a pool lay in the center of the room, filling the cave with a soft, red glow. Silence was thick as I took wary steps inside.

I turned back to Joséphine. "If this is a joke, I don't get it."

She knelt beside the water and waved me over. "Take a look and then tell me I'm joking."

"What is it?" I approached.

"This," she answered, "is my gift to you. This is how you ascend."

The pool was a red-tinted mirror that served my reflection back when I gazed down. It was opaque, its depths unfathomable. And maybe it was the drinking or maybe not, but a foggy heat rose from its shimmering surface and plumed in my face, making my head spin. It smelled like blood. I glimpsed an old-looking dagger lying at the pool's edge.

Then, faintly, came the music.

"Hear something?"

"I feel silly," I said, even though I sank to my knees too.

"Don't. Just take a breath, close your eyes, and listen."

My thoughts were so hazy I had to press my palms into the cold, damp ground to keep upright. But because Joséphine asked, I closed my eyes and listened.

It was definitely music, like the kind from a music box. In fact, it was the same melody as the one my mother got me after we saw *The Nutcracker* for the first time, a brown ballerina spinning inside. Tchaikovsky's "Waltz of the Flowers." I played it for hours the night she left, when we realized she wasn't coming back, and had hated the song ever since. But this version was corrupted, the pitch off, the speed too slow. Warped and . . . alive.

Even with my eyes closed, I felt Joséphine's focus on me, making me self-conscious.

She rested a hand on my shoulder, and her voice came out high and fast. "I know it's hard to believe, but this can do things. *Make* things happen. You've seen what it's done for me. You know what it's like—the ballet is so political. All they care about is money and tradition, and they only let you get so far. No one cared about me, who I was before. You and me, we're cut from the same cloth, but this—this changes things!"

I opened my eyes and blinked in the low light, saw the feverish excitement on her face as she pressed the cold handle of the rusted dagger into my hand.

"What—?"

"Money, fame, success, luck, love—anything you want. If you're serious, if you're worthy, it doesn't matter what the ballet won't offer because you can take it. Like I did. I'll help you. Like Ciro helped me."

"And at what *cost?*" I snapped, raising the blade between us.

From what must have been the nervousness on my face, she rushed on, "Nothing you aren't willing to give. A little blood to start the process, a wager to prove you're serious, and bargain for whatever you want." And then she rolled up her sleeve, exposing the tattoo on her wrist, a stencil of a river etched in red ink. *"Trust me."*

I swallowed, my mouth dry. While we talked, the water's surface rippled, and the music grew in volume until it was like they were both shouting at me to decide. And for all my fears, of dying down here, of how long it'd take Coralie to find my body, of never *being* somebody, I did trust her.

There was no hiding my grimace as I asked, "Why does it want… *blood*?"

"I don't know," whispered Joséphine, staring at the pool of red. "Does it matter?"

The dagger was heavy in my grip. For the ballet, I was serious enough to try anything. It was all I had and all I was, but then something else Joséphine said stopped me. *If you're worthy.* And the words of the board filled my thoughts, shrouding everything back in doubt.

"But what if I'm not enough?"

What if it doesn't want people like me?

Her smile faltered for a moment, eyes still downcast at her own beautiful reflection. "Then you try again. You come back when you're more deserving. Acheron will always be here waiting."

So will tetanus. I chewed my tongue and tightened my hold on the handle. *Am I this desperate?*

But how could I forget evaluations for *Giselle*, getting picked apart before a line of judges, hoping they'd find me acceptable? Only to be perfect and *still* told I didn't belong? All the defects they manufactured for me to fix, too uptight and too tragic? Not like them on some fundamental level? They wanted Joséphine though—everyone did.

So now I'd become her. Or at the very least, walk out of here with a new scar and a story to tell. With the company audition tomorrow, I was out of options.

The skin of my palm smarted under the knife. It ran red like the stalactites in the ceiling and the water below, and Joséphine leaned forward in my periphery, trying to read the ensuing ripples like tea leaves or charred bones. I felt foolish and broken, far deeper than the knife's edge could reach.

Then, it spoke.

What do you crave?

I lurched back, tumbling flat on my ass as a voice spoke from within my marrow. Muscles in my arms and legs trembled at the vibrations. The knife skittered across the floor as it repeated its question.

What did I crave? A nap, an apprenticeship, a future, *a goddamn break*, I wanted to respond. But something pulled inside me, invisible string wrapped around my heart tugging, pressure against my sternum building until another answer slipped out from between my ribs.

"P-power," I stammered, blinking rapidly. "So they can't deny me."

It was a whisper between me and the red water and its gravity. I couldn't see or hear Joséphine in the room, not anymore, not when liquid life ebbed from the ripples. My skin prickled. Still, I inched closer.

And what would you give for power?

"Everything." I prayed by clenching my bleeding fist against the shiver that rolled through me. Willing more blood to flow, willing all this to be true and more. And I meant it, I had to.

"Laure," Joséphine warned, a disembodied voice too distant and too weak to reach me.

I wouldn't go home with nothing.

"Laure, you're too close—"

"Take it," I dared. "Have all of me, I'm offering."

I crawled until the knees of my jeans were wet, until the tang of blood filled my nostrils. Until my hands were submerged in red and it had no choice but to take me.

"Don't—" she cried out.

Something hot and sharp gripped my ankle. Then the rock floor vanished beneath me, and I was pulled under, down into the void.

It was warm in the dark, wherever I was, the dizzying kind of heat like the hottest days of summer, when the humidity chafed against your will to live. I was frozen, a constant and heavy pressure bearing down from all sides, trapping my limbs in place, both suspended and sinking.

What have I done?

Lightning struck, revealing all the world above and below and within me red. Violent, gory red like warning signs, like poisonous mushrooms, like poppy flowers and destruction. Rising from the shadowy corners was that tinny music, that awful waltz, scattering my thoughts like a flock of birds. It was here.

Do you want to be a god? prompted the darkness, buzzing in my bones. The voice was ancient and primal like thunder, and its question had a seductive quality that tempted me to say yes. If I could move, I might have crawled into its lap.

"I want to be a star."

Are they not the same?

My neck strained to look around, to find the source, a face to talk to. It terrified me, which was all the more reason to try, though the entity stayed hidden. Overhead was the muffled sound of a racing torrent, and I was far below it, in the smothering dark where I struggled to ball a fist or grit my teeth to rail against it.

Your life must mean very little that you bargain it so freely.

"If I can't dance, it's no use to me anyway—"

Then three days of the power you seek, but the thread that binds it is your will to dance. Let's see how voracious your appetite is, mortal girl.

Though it didn't reveal itself to me, I still heard the smile in its voice, and a pang lanced my heart. Gambling my life to save my future was one thing, but a life *without* dance—it was everything. I was nobody without it. But there was nowhere for me to run, nowhere to go if they refused me. It was Paris or nothing.

Remove my mark, sever the bargain early, and you dance no more.

My jaw set. "Deal—"

It seized me before I finished, filaments of lightning latching on to the gash in my palm. Blazing tendrils parted skin, inching up my wrist through muscle, burrowing deep into bone. A laugh ricocheted through my veins. I gasped.

And hot, thick, and acrid, my mouth filled with blood.

Like the collapse of a dam, the current resumed motion, throwing me around as I too lurched out of suspension. Down was up and up was down, the rapids churning debris and gore in every direction as I writhed against the fire working its way into my chest, to my heart.

Kicking. Drowning.

I tried to shout, only taking in more fluid.

Then something fisted my shirt and jerked me up. Out, dangling and limp. From the dark into the light of dawn, free from the oppressive wet heat onto cool dirt. I dropped down, sputtering breath and blood on my side, trembling and raw. A sob lodged in the back of my throat.

"You're alive," someone observed through heavy breaths. More question than fact. The voice was soft and low, emanating from the blur of a shadow standing over me that then sank into the dirt with a boyish sigh. "I thought we were the only ones here..."

I used the heels of my hands to wipe the wetness from my eyes. It hardly worked—I was drenched in blood. It seeped through my clothes and skin, coated my mouth and lungs, stuck to my hair in a sopping, stringy mess. Everything around me was dipped in rich shades of crimson too: the coursing river that spat me out, the coppery dirt, the waxy leaves on hanging vines. Even the sky above was bloodred. And the cave, Paris, and Joséphine were long gone.

My pulse lurched. I snapped up to a seated position and turned to the voice. My bag and phone were still in the cave. "Where exactly—?"

The scream that came out surprised even me. My feet were propelling me back, away from the river and my savior, back toward the tall grass.

Because it wasn't a person beside me so much as a creature in the shape of one. A twisted imitation that forgot its frame of reference. It wore fitted, human clothes draped over its human-shaped body, but instead of skin, the exposed arms and angular face appeared viscous—wet and moving, like they were formed from blood. It was wide and tall, with imposing stag-like antlers that ended in sharp points. Blood dripped from long black hair, its maw full of jagged teeth pulled in a grimace. And two pairs of inky black eyes stared at me. It was a mimicry at best.

And absolutely monstrous.

Yet the creature stared at *me*. It cocked its head and mumbled in a very human, baritone voice, "I know you—"

"Laure!"

Leaves rustled in the distance, snagging our attention. My racing breaths stuttered—Joséphine.

"Laurence!" she called again, frantic.

When I risked a glance back at the creature, it was gone, and in its place sat...him. The boy from evaluations, nestled in the corner and absorbed in his notebook, Ciro's friend. And up close, he was *beautiful*. Skin rich like warm clay. *Two* normal eyes, dark as a moonless night sky, narrowed suspiciously. His long, dark lashes were clumped with blood, and his bow-shaped mouth hung open. Breathtaking and human, at least, wearing the same bloodied clothes as the monster.

Maybe I imagined it. Maybe the river was playing a trick.

The boy climbed to his bare, bloodstained feet to tower over me, the tired set of his wide shoulders dipped in gore. Even now, he was striking, maybe more so because he'd dived into a river of blood to save me.

But I took a step back just in case.

"Who brought you here?" he whispered in the same voice as the monster, a furrow settling in his thick, dark brow.

Joséphine broke through the trees then, her eyes wide with panic. At the sight of me, she picked up speed, ducking under branches, trailed by a deathly pale figure at her heels. *Ciro.* And he didn't look happy. Did the ballet know about this place, what they were doing?

"You're okay," Joséphine assured me, brushing sticky hair from my face and cradling me to her chest like I was a child. It wasn't even convincing, with me bloody and quivering and very much not okay, gaping at the blood-drenched boy who gaped back. Vexed. "You're fine."

Her hands and expensive silvery satin sleeves were soiled now, but my shaking slowed a little under her touch.

Over her shoulder, the bloody boy thrust a hand angrily in my direction and rounded on Ciro. "What have you *done?*"

I winced.

"Why did I just fish her out of Acheron?"

Ciro, still handsome in his annoyance and dressed all in white, raked a hand through his long, ashen hair. "It wanted another. Joséphine said she got too close, and it pulled her under..." He cast a glance at me and shook his head. "Let me see her home and then I'll fill you in—"

"You do its bidding now?" My savior sneered, fist clenched.

But Joséphine was already leading me away by the shoulders, into the high grass and among the trees before I could hear the reply. Before I could ask, *What* wanted another? Another of *what?* All those thoughts got tangled. I might have been in shock.

"Let's get you home," she cooed in my ear. "We'll explain everything tomorrow, okay? You need some rest."

Home, bed, rest all sounded great. I let her pull me along, through a door, into the dark, moldy catacombs with my bag in tow, out into daybreak, and into a waiting black car that carried us across the Seine to my apartment. It didn't even occur to me how she knew where I lived.

But in the morning, I'd force Joséphine to explain everything: the red-stained grotto and the red-stained river, the red-stained boy who was born out of the red-stained monster. Ciro at the center, who knew it all. I repeated it over and over again, that Joséphine would explain the dark that talked and the things it gave and the things it took. The blood. Then she'd tell me what I'd become, what staggered over the threshold of the place I shared with Coralie.

Let's see how voracious your appetite is, mortal girl.

Because the entire ride over, I couldn't look away from my palm. My *smooth* palm. The gash was gone.

CHAPTER 7

The loud, brassy, squawking melody of an Édith Piaf song filled the room, jolting me awake with gasping breaths. Body tense, I lurched up in bed and spun.

I can help you, but only if you trust me.

This was my iron-frame bed, my flannel sheets, my annoying alarm still set to my ex Sabine's favorite song—the one I loathed so much it never failed to get me up. This was my apartment in the 19th under skies that were blue or grey but never red, my symphony of honking horns and police sirens in morning traffic.

. . . It doesn't matter what the ballet won't offer because you can take it.

My head throbbed in the stillness, a hangover beating at the backs of my eyes. I clenched them shut against the light streaming through the small window. I was home, and it was all a booze-fueled dream.

Do you want to be a god?

There wasn't any blood. None on the nightshirt I wore, on my arms and legs, in my matted, frizzy hair. The river and the catacombs were far away in my subconscious, slipping further still as I pushed out of bed, across the fuzzy rug to my desk. Coralie's snores were soft on the other side of the wall.

Madame Piaf croaked when I slammed my fingers down on the button, cutting out to the bliss of morning silence. Today was just another day to dance my best, and that was all that mattered. My night and my dream of Joséphine Moreau were far behind me.

And it was only a dream, right?

My bedroom was spotless, just as I always left it, though I frowned as I circled it, trying to find something as *off* as I felt. Stacks of folded leotards and skirts were still neat, rolls of tights still arranged like a bouquet of roses for easy picking. All the magazines and books on ballets and Palais Garnier filled the bookcase in alphabetical order.

In the middle of the floor, I examined my palm, truly unblemished, free of scar tissue and split skin. But running my thumb over my life-line, I found something that made my heart skip a beat.

There was blood under my fingernails.

Real blood. Real as my fall in the studio and Joséphine Moreau's coquettish smile beneath the crimson awning and the burn of the grappa in my throat and the cold, winding Catacombs. All ten fingers, in fact, were stained around the nail beds as if from scrubbing, but I didn't remember doing it.

When did I—?

Seeing the fresh tattoo on the inside of my wrist knocked the air right out of me. I cursed Joséphine and rushed into the shower.

It was the same mark as hers, the stencil of a river inked bloodred, impossible to scrub away and stinging like fire. I pressed my thumb into the center of it, hard enough to bruise, and the searing pain made my head spin. Made it hard to breathe. It made me think of lightning in the dark and a broken, dissonant music box.

And in response to my kneading the skin, something awoke, crawling in my veins and writhing up my spine.

A shudder rolled through me. I pushed off the shower wall, then lathered and shampooed myself three times for good measure. In the water, I discovered other oddities—the swelling of my knee had vanished completely. There wasn't a single black or purple bruise dotting my knees or shins, no blisters or loose, broken skin to pick clean on my feet. All my toenails were whole and attached and healthy. Disgustingly, unrealistically perfect. Those badges that marked me as a dancer, the calluses I'd earned over the months and years, erased.

Just like the gash in my palm.

Just like the blood. Most of it, anyway.

"Where *were* you last night?" Coralie mumbled when I stepped out of the bathroom. She leaned against her doorframe, rubbing her eyes.

"Practicing."

And thankfully she was too tired to notice how high and false my voice sounded. I never had to lie to her before.

While Coralie showered, I got ready. There wasn't enough time to smooth my hair into a neat bun with gel, not after all the scalding water and shampoo, but I went through the motions anyway, dressing for the audition, packing a full bottle of aspirin for the headache splitting my skull in two and cursing Joséphine again. And then again after I discovered a bloody footprint near the door and my stiff, blood-soaked clothes sitting at the top of the trash.

I didn't remember any of this.

But today was too important to be distracted by anything, much less whatever game Joséphine was playing. The gash was gone, the tunnels below, the blood washed away, and I would keep it that way. I couldn't reconcile what happened, what to make of the night—one minute, it sat hazy in my mind like a fever dream, and the next, every touch and smell was crystalline again. The monster and the river, that *boy*—it couldn't have happened. It was impossible, yet the blood was real. I remembered the taste.

"Everything okay?" Coralie asked as we clambered down the metro stairs.

No. Joséphine could afford to be hungover but not me. I could feel the board already shaking their heads, imploring me to stop trying while I was ahead. Showing up like this, I'd only prove them right: unrefined, not belonging. It'd be better to give up now and book a one-way ticket to London before the disappointment shattered whatever was left of me.

Only this was my home, and I didn't give up so easily.

"I'm fine," I chirped with my most stage-ready ballerina smile, wide, white, shoulders back, chin up. My reflection in the dark subway window confirmed as much.

I would get what I wanted one way or another, even if I had to take it by force. Even if I had to turn away from the window to avoid the little monster staring back at me.

Coralie arched her fine brow through all this, though she practically bounced at my side. "Great, so now you can tell me all about your night. Even *you* don't stay in the studio that late. Something's up."

In the middle of our crammed car, everyone looked at us. Not that she cared. People like her never cared how they affected the world. Meanwhile, Joséphine and I were just grains of sand in the ocean, thinking we could shape the coast and influence the tide. Rather, Joséphine *was*, if what happened the night before was real.

Which it couldn't be.

"Was it a date? Are you seeing someone?"

"Because I want to lose my focus during *the most important audition of my life*?" I squeezed my eyes shut, willing the train to move faster. Any slower and we'd be late for morning class, and the board was probably already tossing my file in the trash. "Just some extra practice. Let it go."

Another station rolled into view, a swarm of travelers spilling out and more cramming back in. I felt Coralie's eyes narrowed on me, as if something I said didn't add up. As if she knew better, which she didn't. Finally she sighed. "I already told you, you'll be fine."

And we rode the rest of the way to Opéra Garnier in silence.

While my classmates filed into the amphitheatre for our audition, Joséphine and I stood off to the side. We ignored the passing glances and whispers, her small hands kneading my shoulders like a coach and their boxer before the ring. The entire way over, all through morning class, I'd convinced myself it was all a dream, and now she was here.

Seeing me off.

She looked like she belonged on a poster today, so radiant with her big eyes and long lashes, but now, live and up close, the fidgeting was more apparent: the way she shifted weight from one foot to the other, the tension housed in her brow. I felt how on edge she was, her nails pinching bare skin around my leotard straps.

"Is everything … okay?" I asked softly.

When she grinned, her smile didn't reach her eyes. "Of course! How are you feeling? Are you ready?"

I didn't believe her, but I swallowed and nodded anyway, nerves high, sweating, and eager to stake my claim. Buried beneath layers of foundation and concealer, my tattoo throbbed as if in anticipation, as if it could sense greatness within reach just beyond those doors. It was a living thing under my skin somehow, and now it only needed her to tell me how it worked, what I had to do to seize it.

Real or not, this time, they wouldn't deny me. They couldn't. Whatever was going on with Joséphine could wait.

"Yes, I'm ready. As soon as you explain."

"Right, sorry, the bargain," Joséphine sighed, raking a hand through her luxurious hair. It ruined her French twist and brought strands into her face that framed her alabaster neck. "Don't worry, it'll work. Think of it like a little boost—do exactly as you would normally, and when your blood starts calling, just give in."

"When my blood starts—" I repeated stiffly, but she cut me off.

"—and after you find out you're in the company, how about you come over to my place and we'll talk through all I found on our mutual friend Acheron?"

From the bag on her shoulder, she flashed her phone in a gold confetti case that caught in the light. Full of secrets about that pool whispering in the dark. Her smile turned sheepish. I felt the smooth skin and soft grooves of my lifeline again. Even beneath the opera's skylight, there was no sign of a wound, no trace of the lightning or the previous night at all except for the concealed tattoo on my arm, the headache, the memories. And Joséphine right here.

We were really doing this.

Pushing the thought away, I turned the gold ring on my finger, focusing on twisting and twisting until the metal warmed. Until she noticed and took my hands to stop me. I pasted on a smile. "Okay. Yes, I'll come over."

Joséphine pulled me into an embrace, squeezing me in her constantly feverish, bony arms. Against my ear, she whispered the ballet expression for good fortune onstage, "Merde."

So I rushed inside, afraid to look back. For what was coming, I needed to cling to her belief in me a little longer. Coralie eyed me suspiciously as I sank into the seat beside her.

"Since when do *you* know Joséphine Moreau?"

Rather than answer, I just shrugged and turned my attention to the stage. Immediately bile rose in the back of my mouth.

Sabine Simon conversed onstage with Director Hugo Grandpré. The stage lights illuminated her lily-white face and butter-blond bun, and she beamed under his attention, a living doll known for the popularity of her Sugar Plum Fairy. This year was supposed to be her time to dance more variety, and just seeing her evoked memories of how badly she wanted it, how she'd cried herself hoarse at the thought of her career stagnating. And when finally Grandpré promised more, along came Joséphine. It must have hurt.

Not my problem, I had to remind myself, gritting my teeth.

"Today's audition is broken into two parts: the tutorial and then the group numbers..."

In the neighboring section, cozy in their seats, sat the judging panel, all frowns and stiff suits that only seemed to tighten on them as President Auger introduced them in a flurry of names. Rose-Marie Baumé gave that smile with her eyes that models do, provoking whispers of how effortlessly cool she looked that also made Coralie dig her nails into the armrest cushions. I straightened in my own seat at the sight of Ciro Aurissy down the row, elegant and stone-faced with Joséphine at his side to observe, both showing no indication of what happened the night before. The sharpness of Ciro's commands by the river was replaced by his eagle eye as he prepared to judge us. He must have promised the river something big to be here, and there was no reason to think it stopped at just me, him, and Joséphine. There were probably more of us harboring shadowy bargains, in the orchestra or costume design. Did he lure her into this like she lured me?

Thankfully, his dark-haired friend, the one who took the place of a monster, was nowhere to be found this time. I didn't need to see *that* particular reminder right before I danced for my life.

Dread settled deeper in my stomach.

I spotted the group of three men from the night of *Giselle*, practically interchangeable with silver hair, weathered faces from their vacation homes in Corse, and their air of disapproval. When I proved them wrong and took the whole ballet for myself, would they stammer out apologies and beg for mercy?

My thumb pressed into the inside of my wrist as the tattoo burned with anger. Was this normal? Was this what Joséphine meant by my blood calling? There was no time to run over and ask her, not as Grandpré beckoned us to begin. Now there was only time to show them all exactly who ballet was made for.

We spread out across the stage, marking through Grandpré's rapid-fire instructions. His choreography was Nureyev-inspired, and for once, I was grateful for our morning classes, already prepared for the word soup thrown my way. Sabine demonstrated every command, but the routine was easy to remember. Enough that my eyes kept drifting to Ciro, his blank face observing, occasionally marking down notes. And every time, his gaze flicked up to me, like he could sense it, and our shared secret sent heat to my face.

Would he stop me? Or maybe this was all going according to *his* plan.

"Think about your motions before you move," Grandpré lectured from nearby.

While we ran through the piece again and again, the director roamed among us and offered corrections, his noxious cologne closing in and gagging me. I brushed up onto the muscles of my toes with the music, my eyes trained on an empty box seat, expression placid. Even as the stench sent me fumbling out of pointe and off-balance. It burned the way grappa burned, and every muscle in my body reacted to the sensation by seizing up.

"Mind your posture," he commanded in my ear, placing a dry palm where my neck met my shoulders, pushing down. His other rested on my ribs and stayed a little too long for comfort while he hovered close.

For a second, I imagined how good it'd feel to break every bone in his hand and shove it down his throat. The fear in his eyes. The sound of him choking. The urge crawled up from the depths of me along with the music of plucked steel teeth, darkness tunneling in my vision, ready for me to reach out and make it so—

Horror flashed through me.

Ballerina gaze, développé, turn out slowly, I reminded myself, grounded back in my body. In the moment.

Grandpré moved on, and I hissed out a long breath until the tingling in my fingertips ceased. The viciousness drained away, that music receding back into the core of me, having come out of nowhere, and my heart slowed apace.

Soon Grandpré ushered us back into the wings, where panic set in. The variation wasn't too complicated, more a test of technique than of memory. It wasn't enough to just lift the leg—they cared which muscles the lift came from, how the other leg stood rooted, the positions formed, the lines smooth and in time. And amid thoughts of extending into my fingertips and toes, in the breath of my movements, now I also had to ensnare the judges and pay attention to whatever called from my blood and hope it worked.

"Vanessa's totally gonna get chosen. Look at her turns."

We watched on from the sides as the first group was called, in alphabetical order, featuring Vanessa and Coralie. The others crooned in awe and envy at the length of Coralie's legs, how Vanessa glided across the floor.

My heartbeat hammered against my ribs.

I could do this, because I didn't have any other choice. It had to be Paris, no matter the cost. The darkness had promised me power, and I'd be a fool not to use it when it mattered most. If it even existed.

Still, my nails dug into the soft wood of the barre as the memory of tinny music and that voice resurfaced: *Do you want to be a god?*

"Vanessa is my friend and all, but is it bad I hope she messes up?" Olivia muttered.

Backstage, Sabine floated around, handing water to a dancer who crouched in a corner with her head between her knees, tucking the tag back into Geoffrey's crisp white shirt. Her gaze skipped pointedly over me. Auger called the second group. And then the third, the fourth, and the fifth with me and Olivia.

My moment.

In ballet, there was always someone better than you. That was the universal truth—no matter how perfect your form, how high your jumps, how hard you worked, or how many toenails you lost over the years. It was something our teachers drilled into us when we lost a casting and on the front steps of the academy as we said our goodbyes.

But it was consolation for losers.

I didn't have to be *better* than the world's sujets, premières, and étoiles. I didn't have to surpass the elite either; I just had to be better than my competition, and my competition, Vanessa, Olivia, and all the rest, didn't have Joséphine on their side. They didn't have *my* hunger.

When Auger announced, "Laurence Mesny," I walked out with my head up and shoulders back, rising to the tip of my toes and then sinking in a bow as instructed. Ciro's unblinking stare followed me to my position center-left. His mouth gave nothing away, no sign one way or the other that he even remembered crossing paths.

Grandpré shouted from the seats, "Cue the music."

The intro bars of a symphony filled the great hall, and immediately the tattoo on my arm burned, blazing awake. It was ready. Now was the time to make it count. Now I just had to . . . give in. So I did.

Watch me, I thought clearly, desperately, turning heavy focus to the panel as we took our poses. The words felt heavier, headier, different from anything I'd done before. They felt real.

And one by one, all seven judges turned my way, a domino effect so sudden it made me flinch. The dark, the power—*what I willed*—moved fast and unrelenting.

In the first steps, I felt something unwind in me. Every muscle loosened when I sprang into motion, energy in abundance with every step, beckoning me to let go, and I did that too. The turns were faster and tighter, expanding into jumps that soared higher. Every fear and worry melted away. The angles my body struck were perfect like never before—through adrenaline or something darker, I didn't know. And in time with the music, it didn't matter. Lines from my toes in pointe shoes to my fingertips went unbroken, alternating between soft and lilting and strong and defined.

The blood river had promised me three days of power right before it slipped under my skin and stitched itself inside, I knew that much. And the way the judges stared now, they locked on me as if I was their sun. Their *god*.

Don't look away, I ushered. **Don't let me fail. Don't deny me.**

The chains that bound my movements as merely mortal broke and fell away then. It was like I left my body and watched from the outside. Even my face transformed to hyper-expressive, serene, full of yearning down to tempered joy when sweat should have been burning my eyes. I was untethered, liberated from confines I hadn't known I wore.

I danced as if I'd been performing the variation all my life, drawing surety from stage lights, channeling energy from ballets past, building gravity from the ensnared gazes of the board in the dark. All of it sang loud and bright and hot in my blood, until I was the only star, thrusting an arching arm high in the air to the final beat.

And between panting breaths, it was over.

"Thank you," Grandpré said, curt and a little distant.

My shoulders heaved as I slunk into the wings. The judges blinked groggily and marked their notes, all except Ciro, who alternated gazes between them and the place where I'd stood. As if he'd felt the shift in the room, the weight of my presence growing. As if he recognized exactly what transpired. What *I* did.

A fog of fatigue subsumed me the farther I retreated into the seats, light-headed and dazed. Rémy rubbed his tired eyes and gawked at the stage, though he couldn't possibly understand. Vanessa squeezed past, pinching her nose, blood running down her front while Auger called the last group.

All the adrenaline coursing through me ran dry as I slumped, spent, just shy of dropping dead. In place of that dark confidence flowed only guilt now, burning in my belly. And regret.

Because if the power was real—and I felt it coursing through me, somehow—then so was its cost and what would happen if I changed my mind. So was the monster, the boy, my ability to dance as collateral. And if I had to cheat, it occurred to me that maybe I really wasn't good enough to be here. Maybe this power had many other gaps to fill, ones not even I knew, just to level the playing field. After the bargain expired, I'd be back where I started—begging to be seen as a contender.

"Look who's gonna be an apprentice." Coralie beamed, tugging my arm a little harshly.

I gave her a weak smile. With her flushed round cheeks, golden hair, and royal pedigree—she'd never need a deal like this. This was her world, where power spun the wheels, kept you fed and warm and loved. She once confessed that she never felt guilty when teachers ignored all her absences and late arrivals, when she'd smiled her way into features at the academy. She never had to wonder if she was enough.

But I spent too long fighting for scraps. Now that I had a chance for more, why should I be guilty? What did I do that others hadn't in one way or another? My guilt would fade, I decided. Power and influence were the costs of belonging to this world, and wasn't this what Joséphine intended?

I deserved the world to bend to *me* for once.

"Well done!" Director Grandpré shouted from the edge of the stage.

In his gruff way, he gave us a parting speech, probably praising us for how hard we worked and teasing that contracts would find the very fortunate few in the coming days. It all went in one ear and out the other, however, because I made the mistake of glancing over at the judges' panel, where something far more interesting was unfolding.

President Auger stood in a row of seats, huddled close to Ciro and Joséphine and speaking rapidly. The old woman's head shook with the emphasis of her words, and the rage rolling from Joséphine as she sat with her arms crossed, her round features warped in a sharp glare, was enough to burn the whole theatre down. They were too far away to make sense of the harsh, hurried whispers, but it attracted the other judges' attention too. And there was no missing Auger's flushed cheeks, or the venom in Ciro's pursed mouth.

With a rattle, Joséphine shot to her feet. "If you think I'll just roll over and play dead, you're in for a surprise!" she snapped, loud enough to make everyone flinch. Grandpré's speech trailed off as she shoved past the president and charged up the aisle.

Ciro rose too buttoning the front of his white coat, eyes narrowed severely at President Auger for whatever she'd said, like she caused this. His silence was somehow even worse. He marched up the aisle after his girlfriend, and when he reached for the crook of her elbow, Joséphine whirled around like a snake and shoved him. Coralie gasped beside me. Everyone in the theatre was quiet, leaning in to hear.

The tenderness we'd seen between them the day of evaluations was gone. His light smile, her twinkling eyes, both extinguished, even as the gravity of their world still pulled at us.

Their angry voices were reduced to little more than hissing, the sneer he gave her as he leaned in indistinguishable. But Joséphine didn't shy away from him or his message. She didn't move at all, her spine turned rigid as Ciro whispered something that left her fuming. Far worse than

Auger, than anything I'd ever seen. I strained in my velvet seat, dying to hear what made her shoulders heave in her leotard, anger building fast. I didn't breathe and found my thumb idly stroking my tattoo.

Joséphine cast her glower at the judges for one long second before she turned on her heel and let the opera doors slam behind her.

"Trouble in paradise?" Olivia whispered, summoning a round of giggles.

CHAPTER 8

For the first time since we started dancing there, the main studio of Palais Garnier was silent when the final workshop dismissed for the day. Not only were we frenetic from anticipating audition results that might arrive at any moment, but the shock wave of Joséphine's outburst in the theatre the day before worsened with her complete absence today.

There was a saying—miss class once, you feel it. Twice, the directors see it. Three days without dance, and the audience knew it. Girls left their deathbeds to dance on the barre, waiting only until the music stopped to faint or puke. Sabine once danced Sugar Plum Fairy on a sprained ankle just to keep her alternate from gaining favor. So it was reckless for Joséphine to tank her own reputation so soon after her spat with Auger. No one said her name, but I saw how their eyes flitted to Joséphine's usual space at the barre, then back to the door.

I sprawled on the floor, legs extended while I got to work on my third pair of pointe shoes of the day—anything to keep my hands busy. It took a concerted effort to keep from also acknowledging what hung over us like a blade soon to drop, from swiping at my phone, refreshing my email in search of what I knew I deserved. The others filtered around me with the same agitation, an undercurrent of fear tremoring through our group.

Coralie was the first to break the silence. "*Does this mean we're free* forever from Demaret and her *Joséphine* obsession?" She didn't notice the glances her way as she added, "I would kill to hear about anybody else."

Olivia snorted and leaned into a deep stretch. "I don't know how they expect us to not want to push her in front of a bus."

I held my tongue and kept my eyes on sewing elastic to a shoe with dental floss, because it held better and frayed less than thread.

Coralie still didn't know about my deal, the blood river, Joséphine's part in it. She didn't know that I had Joséphine's address and was supposed to visit tomorrow night. Hopefully with an acceptance letter in tow. It was still too early to share anything in case it didn't work. Or Coralie disagreed. It was as though everything had changed while nothing had, and only Joséphine knew how different I'd become inside.

"Did you hear Nina Brossard lost her spot on the cover of *Pointe*?" Olivia chirped, and the tension in everyone's shoulders began to loosen. Only a little. "Apparently the editor-in-chief changed her mind and wanted a younger star. You can all guess who."

Some wicked part of me wanted to interrupt by divulging what I'd done, brag about what Joséphine Moreau was really like. Not the diva in the theatre, snatching photo shoots like a thief, but the girl who shared food and drink, the way she charmed an entire restaurant with *me* by her side. I wanted to illustrate just who I was worthy of brushing shoulders with.

But instead I mashed my thumbnail deep into the fading ink of my tattoo, until black spots danced in my vision. Until the pain brought me center.

Patience. They'd see soon enough.

An electronic bell dinged.

"Whose phone was that?" Vanessa shouted, rigid where she sat, but Rémy was already rustling through his bag. Then she lunged for hers.

Another phone chimed.

The announcement was here.

Everyone groped for their phones, Coralie tossing her shoes carelessly aside to find hers, but I didn't move. Part of me was too afraid to know, in case I failed and this power was all in my head. I wouldn't survive the embarrassment.

My fingers were stuck on the needle, stitching over the same strip of fabric again and again. When I read that email, it'd change me for better or worse. We'd bring out the teeth and claws again, and I'd transform to either predator or prey. Would Coralie forget me if the latter?

She looked down at her glowing screen and chewed absently on her necklace, the one with her name carved in gold, gifted by her mother when she got into the academy. The one she swore she hated but never took off.

"Results are live," Rémy announced to the room. Vanessa climbed into his lap to get a look. His hands trembled so much he almost dropped his phone.

Yet I remained still, stitching, looping, my heart crashing violently against my ribs.

"I got the email, I got it!" Olivia stuttered. "Vanessa Abbadie!"

Vanessa's hazel eyes became saucers. Disbelief for her, but not for us. She *was* good. Then Rémy released a sigh of relief, his shoulders dropping and eyes fluttering shut. He was safe too of course. The dashing Duke Albrecht lived to dance another day.

My eyes squeezed shut, both dreading and dying to see for myself. It had to work—I'd felt the force of my hunger, the gravity of my dance pulling at the judges from the stage. It had to be *enough* either to make them realize or to force their hand.

"Geoff, we did it!" Olivia shrieked.

Geoffrey shot to his feet like a rocket, his fist thrust in the air. He laughed, high and proud, and pulled her into a hug. The others cheered and celebrated, standing tall over the rest of us and clinking half-empty aluminum water bottles.

And finally I broke down, the shoe and floss dropping in my lap as I fumbled around for my bag's zipper, the pocket, the fucking *power button*. Was I one of them or on my way out? Would any of them tell me either way? I swiped through notifications, a voice mail from my father, a text from Joséphine about tomorrow, because all of it had to wait until I knew—

An email from the Paris Ballet Company arrived. And in the body, welcoming its new apprentices, the names appeared in stark black lettering.

Vanessa ABBADIE.

Rémy LAJOIE.

Laurence MESNY.

Geoffrey QUÝ.

Olivia ROBINEAU.

A strong shudder rolled through me as my fingers went frantic, refreshing again and again to prove it was really true. It worked. The deal, the begging, the blood, all those years and playing god, and it finally paid off.

I read the list again, and again. There was a chasm between the academy and the company, and somehow, I'd leapt and made it. I had their attention now, became so great they couldn't possibly deny me, and now all that was left was to keep running. This was proof that I was worthy, that I belonged, that I was *someone*.

"Cor—" I started.

Beside me, my best friend held her phone in a tight grip, but a deep frown had carved its way onto her face. She stared ahead, stiff, seeing but not really, her right hand fidgeting with the necklace and so brittle I expected it to break off. And looking to the email again, I realized that the list only had five names. The company took *at most* twenty percent of academy students, which meant they could always take less.

The revelry of the four others was punctuated by the harsh quiet and soft weeping from the rest of our class.

"Maybe they made a mistake—" I said, resting a hand on Coralie's shoulder, but she shrugged out of my touch.

"I guess they'll just take anyone," she muttered to herself but loud enough for all of us to hear. We watched her climb to her feet and sling her bag over her shoulder. And with my stunned silence in her wake, she weaved through the tangle of classmates and out of the studio.

It didn't matter who she was referring to, or if she even really meant it. Everyone was lesser compared to Coralie.

A hollow sensation carved out my chest. The truth sinking in was a double-edged sword: Coralie had failed another exam, and I didn't know whether it was through merit or machination that I'd passed mine.

On the cusp of disbelief and giddy, the rest of us packed our things and streamed out into the hall. The victors had family to notify, everyone else had bruised egos and crushed dreams to console. But me—all I had was Coralie, who was getting away.

What if I stole her place?

The question bubbled up as I scurried after her, knocking into the frames of once-vibrant girls who now looked like empty husks, the warmth in their eyes snuffed out. The apprenticeship didn't *belong* to anyone, technically; Coralie didn't deserve something just because her mother once held it. And really, nobody else with power stopped to question whether they earned their places. It belonged to the most powerful.

A nervous giggle escaped my lips, earning me sideways glares.

Most powerful.

I clamped my teeth down on my knuckles to stop another, though it was futile. Against the laughter, I bit hard enough to draw blood, to taste that this was all real. Tears welled in my eyes. A sob lodged in my throat. My feet stopped, and I doubled over, weeping and laughing and gasping in the very heart of the opera house regardless of who saw.

Because I, Laure Mesny, a nobody with nothing, beat Coralie Baumé, the daughter of titans. *My* power exceeded hers for once—her name, her face, her legacy. Those judges saw a replica of Rose-Marie and still chose *me*.

It was such an ugly thought, but I wanted to scream it into the gilded chandeliers. She was always the shoo-in, the guarantee. I never had to worry if she'd be accepted because she always was, so what could I possibly say to make her feel better now that I'd tasted power?

Sucks to suck.

"Bon rétablissement, Sophie!" someone shouted in the gallery that opened before me.

There was a gathering of company members surrounding a woman on silver crutches beneath a sign that read GET WELL SOON. Gold balloons framed a table full of untouched éclairs. Despite the open doors, the air was stale, and there wasn't a smile in sight. President Auger's expression, in fact, was grave.

"Sophie Poullain," whispered Vanessa as she slowed. "Guess she can't put off surgery anymore."

"How sad," Olivia mumbled flatly, not even looking up from her phone, where she texted excitedly. She was practically beaming. "What's wrong with her again?"

"Broken hip. It was all over school."

Partial hip replacement, actually. The friction over the years to the bones in Sophie's hip grew so severe that it finally displaced her for an entire season, triggering Joséphine Moreau's promotion to étoile. And though it wasn't the end of the world, this was the end of *our* world—Sophie would be fine to walk and run and play with puppies post-recovery, but this injury was a death sentence for her career. I'd looked it up: *years* of physical therapy just to reach corps standard, but then she'd be too old. And the ballet waited for no one. Only being named an étoile made you immortal, and Sophie didn't make it.

I spotted the première as we walked by; her round face had been on giant posters for *Sleeping Beauty* last year. Now her eyes were red and puffy, the corners of her mouth turned in a fraught smile. Under rays of light from the gold leaf chandeliers, she looked pale; and the boundless mirrors served back her dismal reflection in ridicule.

There were already students at the academy waiting to devour us the same way we hungered for demises like hers. Itching to rise up in the place she left, like Joséphine did. Every broken girl was an opportunity.

"She'll be lucky to teach kids," Rémy muttered with cold indifference, though he looked away and picked up his pace. In an added flair of the dramatic, Vanessa crossed herself and followed, though I was sure she'd never even set foot in a church—she once said ballet was our religion.

We understood this omen before us loud and clear: *This could happen to any of you.* Poignant, sure, but I wouldn't let that be me. *I* was going to take it all—the apprenticeship, the corps, the glory of being crowned an étoile, and the worship that followed.

I wouldn't accept anything less.

So I grabbed an éclair from the table and kept walking.

"The ballet definitely isn't what it once was with that woman in charge," said Coralie's mother from behind a frown, tossing glossy hair over her shoulder.

Rose-Marie's favorite restaurant was particularly crowded tonight, and often a camera flashed in the direction of our booth, someone eager to capture their proximity to greatness. Her every movement was so perfectly posed and picturesque—so very *polished*—that I was dying to know how she looked when no one was around. Especially when she was forced to swallow the bitter news about the apprenticeships.

After all, she was a classical ballerina first, formed from clay to perform for an audience.

"Handing out yet another honor like hard candy to that ungrateful little harlot who can't tell her bust from her pointe shoes. If I see her polluting all I've worked for, I will wring her pretty little neck."

"I know, chérie," Coralie's father, Émeric, crooned, remarkably monotonous, without looking up.

She put a hand on his arm. "The board too with that *boy*. A boy, nothing more, and just as arrogant despite how welcoming we've been."

It was Rose-Marie's idea to take us out, to celebrate the audition results as we crossed the threshold to professionals at a world-class ballet. Only she made the reservation before she knew how it all played out. Invitations from the matriarch always slicked my stomach with oily dread, as the outings involved dressing in finery that I clearly got from a thrift store—I'd rather cut off both my legs than *borrow* from Coralie—and trekking over to the 16th, where Jardins du Trocadéro so wealthily gazed upon the Eiffel Tower. The venue was sandwiched between an upscale hotel-apartment frequented by filmmakers and Michelin-starred bistros with year-long waiting lists. There was always a long line of black cars idling for their owners out front.

And tonight, she was exceptionally agitated.

"And then there's *you*," said Rose-Marie, her eyes narrowed squarely on Coralie. I felt my friend grow rigid beside me. "When I was your age, I was already promoted to soloist, you know."

We know, I wanted to snap. Instead, I buried myself in the egregiously priced wine Émeric ordered for the table to avoid drawing her ire.

She reminded Coralie every chance she had, especially after Coralie failed her final exams at the academy last year. Having her progeny repeat a year while the little friend on scholarship caught up was the worst tragedy to befall their family, somehow. At least until today.

Under the table, Coralie folded and refolded the napkin in her lap. "They have more requirements for apprenticeships now. And the classes are twice the size. There are eighteen other girls with the same qualifications and only—"

"Excuses," Rose-Marie interrupted without a dent in her thin smile.

Coralie deflated in her seat, shoulders slumping forward. Once, I'd asked if she wanted me to throw a plate or cause a scene, something to distract from her mother's constant criticisms, and she looked horrified. But this was worse, so weak of her to just sit here and say nothing. It was surprising after my earliest meal with the Baumés and then maddening the next that the dynamic hadn't calloused her yet. She should have been hardened by her mother's harsh behavior by now. She shouldn't still be so *soft*. What did she have to fear when she was rich and pretty, the daughter of a celebrity? Both of my parents *abandoned* me, and I was doing just fine.

Mercifully, before anyone said more, a server approached the table carrying meager plates of steaming food. My stomach growled at the smell of roasted garlic, hungering for more than olive oil–dipped baguette and wine. With Joséphine, I'd eaten more liberally, sharing plates of hearty platters that tasted like life itself. Here, the appetizer consisted of a lone shot glass of tomato pulp and lemon foam.

Minimalism was en vogue.

"I talked to Demaret," my friend said in such a small voice I had to strain to hear over my chewing. She cleared her throat and idly stirred her pale soup. "She's confident that next year I'll—"

Rose-Marie raised the wine glass to her lips and snorted. "'Next year.' You're being outperformed at every turn by your inexperienced junior. I don't find her *confidence*"—

I clenched my jaw, wishing she'd back off. A blaze sparked in my blood with the desire to make her eat her words.

—"to mean..."

At her sudden pause, I glanced up from my plate.

"...much..."

She knit her brows and lowered her glass.

Interesting.

Coralie hung her head, eyes clouded with tears, but her mother did not seem to notice. Rose-Marie's expression was vacant, as if some thought— something like *me*—had swept her away so suddenly that she was too wrapped up in herself to care. And Émeric certainly didn't. He hadn't looked his daughter's way since we arrived, didn't know that Coralie was one insult shy from vanishing in her seat. Instead, he ate with his eyes glued to his phone. His world of venture capital was so far from ours.

Rose-Marie's blank face resembled a doll for me to play with, ensnared by a hidden command. *My* command. And I just gaped, shocked and delighted, because the power wasn't confined to the audition or dancing.

If it weren't for the red ink etched in my skin, I would have forgotten the power altogether. Since the audition, there'd been no more impatient writhing in my veins, no more wicked whispers, no burning impulses. With its job done, the river went dormant, and it seemed like it was over, my dalliance with power only temporary. Until now.

Now I did it again: lassoed a person into bending to my want. In moments like these, I used to wish someone would stop her, and now *I* could. That whispered prayer and the river's response replayed in my mind, and this was just as easy as wrangling the judging panel.

I smiled into my plate and tried one more command. And instantly,

Rose-Marie turned toward me, robotic and stiff, the table thudding with the motion.

Mouth slack and face empty, she said, "I...apologize, Coralie. Laurence." Each word was clipped, pulled from her gums like teeth, but she'd *apologized*.

Stunned, Coralie passed me a sideways glance, but she was too defeated to do anything but keep eating and fiddling absently with the dainty gold chain around her neck. Sometimes I wondered if she hated ballet like she swore she hated the necklace, if she was too much of a coward to quit while I'd surrendered everything just to be given a chance.

Now that I had it, I wouldn't look back.

Something beneath the tattoo shifted in my muscle, turning, waking up. I could feel it wanting me to try again, to embrace the dark urges, encouraging its use. And since tonight was my last before the deal ran out, I figured I might as well throw Coralie a bone.

Eyes on my plate, I let fly another hope. An *order*. For the first time since we sat down, Émeric raised his head. Mechanically, like a puppet beneath strings, he extended the phone in his hand, dropped it into his glass of water with a *plunk*, and smiled at his only daughter.

Rose-Marie gasped. Coralie gaped. I kept eating to hide my grin. And for once, I knew deep down in the dark of my marrow that things were going to turn out just fine. I had a way to see to it myself.

After dinner, the Baumés delivered us to our apartment in silence. Coralie's mother hissed something in her ear as we climbed out, and I was so tired from a day of classes and the news that I hardly registered the figure standing in front of our building until it was too late.

"Laure?"

I ground to a halt. That voice was one I recognized anywhere, one I'd never forget, one I'd known since childhood, since birth. The rasp carried the inflection that only a parent had when they called their child.

Julien.

I might have hissed my father's name aloud, pulse erratic in my neck. The tall man leapt in surprise at the sudden movement and took a cautious step back. The light shone on his close-shaved head. Coralie narrowed her eyes possessively.

Julien Mesny stood at our door still dressed in his neon construction vest and dusty boots, a wary smile on his face the color of steeped black tea. It was a far cry from the last time I'd seen him, the expression of resignation I came to understand as his default state. There was new animation to his eyes, wide and bright, nothing at all like my own, though six years had only made him look even more tired. And the only things we had in common were surface level: the dimpled chin and widow's peak. My only inheritance, while Coralie had millions.

Not until I nodded for Coralie to go inside, until she was far out of sight, did I breathe again.

"Papa?" I rasped. I hadn't used that name in years, but it spilled out of me. A reflex. My voice belonged to someone I didn't recognize. "What are you doing here?"

There was a box tucked under his arm, peppered with black prints from oil-stained fingers. It jostled in my hands when he offered it to me, light, half full. My jaw clenched so hard at the sight of him *here*, after all this time, I could have cracked a tooth.

He scratched the back of his head nervously. "I was doing some cleaning and found some stuff of yours—leotards, skirts, the like. And your graduation certificate got sent to me. I guess the school still has the old address on file."

Then his gaze flicked to the gold ring on my finger with its fat emerald, the one he'd picked out for *her*, the one she left behind. He never looked for it after I'd swiped it from the table. Or her.

I shoved my hand into my pocket and stared at the box.

If it was just a couple leotards, chiffon skirts, and a piece of card stock, he could have mailed it. He didn't have the right to just show up here unannounced, acting like he'd ever shown up to anything in my life. I was already used to his absence, comfortable with the space he'd vacated. With my mother across the ocean and me all grown up, there was no need to pretend we were a family anymore. Anything more than strangers, really.

"Thanks," was all I managed to say. There was nothing else *to* say.

So when he took a step toward me, I lurched back. "What?"

It was sharper than I intended, but I was too tired for this. Whatever he thought he was doing, it was too many years too late. Though I ran away six years ago, my father was gone long before that. And I wasn't a helpless little girl anymore. *He* created this distance; I was merely maintaining it.

Julien cleared his throat and held up his phone. "How was your audition? You haven't been answering my calls. I was worried—"

"I don't need you to worry about me," I countered, stepping back farther into the recess of my door. "I can take care of myself."

Today was proof of exactly that.

CHAPTER 9

The cathedral was easy to find, even in the dark of dusk: The fracture in the wall stood out starkly, the iron gate an inviting well of shadows. I marched down those stone steps with my head high, armed with my phone flashlight to figure my way to the grotto. It turned out to be a mostly straight path until the air turned warm and metallic, the red glow more saturated, my footsteps heavy, the pull undeniable. As if *it* was guiding me back, more than I was guiding myself.

But oh, how the wicked dark had earned my faith.

I hadn't slept the night before, refreshing that email again and again, pinching at the rapidly fading tattoo on my wrist to assure myself it was real. Me, an apprentice at the Paris Ballet Company while Coralie had nothing, all because I was daring enough to bleed for it.

The mark had vanished completely by the time I woke this morning, leaving behind only smooth, brown skin, and in the dark magic's absence was a persistent chill I couldn't shake and fatigue deep in my bones. My skull had throbbed over breakfast trying to force Coralie to do something—pick her nose, release a primal scream, *anything*—but she kept eating, oblivious. And curiously, even my ability to dance remained intact; I'd danced a tired variation in my room as proof. It was just as the dark god had promised: I let it ride around in my veins for the full term, and it granted me all that I asked. Bargain fulfilled.

So here I detoured, on my way to Joséphine's, to do it all again.

"I'm back," I announced, my voice bouncing around the jagged red stalactites.

There was no one around to answer, of course. Only that same tinny version of "Waltz of the Flowers" that plucked around inside my skull as soon as I sat down, still out of tune, out of time. The wicked dark's way of greeting me. I was careful not to wet my knees this time as I leaned forward to bargain. And I was ready to heed Joséphine's instructions exactly, to drink it in instead of letting it swallow me whole.

With the same rusted blade, I cut the back of my hand, moving fast to fight the shaking. Thinner skin, more blood vessels, more time, I reasoned. I tossed the blade aside, and its sharp clatter echoed against the walls. Having tasted power and success, knowing it could do what it promised, there was no chance I could will my hands to be steady or patient.

It was as if my body craved more.

Thick red ran down my knuckles in rivulets, and I forced myself to wait longer. I wanted the river to hunger for me the way I longed for it. But when the surface rippled from the falling drops, in the silence, doubt hit—I was worthy once, but would I be gifted again? Would it say no?

Well, I wouldn't give it a choice. There was no way I could walk out with nothing, not after tasting possibility. Just because Coralie had lost didn't mean I had to stop climbing. In fact, Coralie *needed* this as much as I did, because if the ballet promoted me quickly, if I ascended as fast as Joséphine, it would make room for Coralie among the apprentices. She'd do the same for me if my future dangled by a thread.

I could help her with this just like I'd helped her with her parents the previous night. We were in this together, forever.

Hissing, I sliced the back of the other hand, just to be sure. Skin broken right below the wrist bones, jagged and sloppy, smarting with need, and instantly lightning flashed beneath the surface in answer.

Do you want to be a god now? asked the voice that rumbled in my spine.

"Yes," I breathed, my hands trembling as I cupped the liquid. The heat stung my icy fingertips. "With more blood and my will to dance again to prove I'm still serious."

My pulse pounded in my ears as I waited for its reply. The silence seemed to drag on, to thicken and wrap around my throat like a noose. I could feel it smiling from deep amid the pit of blood, savoring how I shifted on my knees and winced from two desperate gashes. I didn't know how much more I was able to give.

Three months, the dark god decreed, jolting me from my trance, **as you worship at my altar**.

I sagged with relief. Or exhaustion. Or blood loss.

Better than three days, better than nothing at all. I couldn't be more eager to accept, steeling myself against the bitter, acrid warmth as I drank deeply. The taste, where the blood came from—none of it mattered where I was going. To the ancient thing that commanded it, I would only be grateful. I would take anything it offered me. I needed the power to buy myself time, to let it finish guiding me along, to turn the ballet to my side—

My breath caught.

Electricity surged through my veins, climbing up from the incisions in my hands. My arms burned, and my lungs seized. My jaw clamped shut, while my blood roiled until everything went dark. I threw my head back and tensed, every muscle on fire and *alive*. The wicked god had taken more and hurt more this time, infiltrating every inch of my body, but I wasn't afraid. As it poisoned my blood, it dissolved my fear too. My anxiety, all my doubts incinerated to nothing. Until I was sanctified.

Even as the pain delivered me to the ground, writhing, back bowed, gritting back a scream, it held my steadfast loyalty because I knew I wasn't alone.

For once, I had help.

Joséphine's neighborhood straddled the 5th and 6th arrondissements, some of the wealthiest places in the city. There were no publicized break-ins or murders, no beggars policed out of sight in the hub of revolution-aries and intellectuals, where monuments to de Beauvoir and Sartre and institutions like le Panthéon and la Sorbonne rested around every cor-ner. The few people on the street when night rolled around wore tweed, trench coats, and corduroy, the finest in academic chic. But I learned early that respectable society kept their viciousness hidden *inside*.

Despite the heavy exhaustion in my limbs, I bounced on my heels as I walked, eager to dive into planning with Joséphine. Gaining an apprenticeship was the first of many milestones, but as I watched Rose-Marie begrudgingly apologize, as Émeric tossed his phone into the glass, as Sophie Poullain tried not to cry, a plan had begun to take shape. I wasn't meant to stop after an apprenticeship—I was meant to go all the way, scaling the mountain until I was a star in the sky. Until I was untouchable forever. Joséphine was going to help me.

The entrance to her apartment was situated next to a corner bis-tro touted to be Hemingway's favorite in all the city. I rang the buzzer outside the big apartment gate next door, watching staff in crisp, white shirts and red aprons stack wicker chairs and drag tables inside, closing for the night while I waited.

Trickling rain and the sweet scents of petrichor and bread softened all the harsh angles and severe façades of the neighborhood, making everything shiny and new and romantic. The soft glow from a red traffic light reflected on the steel toe caps of the new leather boots I got to celebrate: sturdy, pointed, *luxe*. They clicked against the cobblestones like I belonged here, a steady beat pulsing through the veins of the quartier. Like the whole city could be mine if I reached out and asked for it.

The return of primordial shadow making its home in my veins confirmed just as much.

No one answered the door.

I checked my phone for messages and rang the buzzer again, my pulse climbing at the unease. It'd only been a couple days since we last talked, but with her busy schedule, she could have already forgotten. Or rehearsal ran late like they often did, especially so close to opening night. Maybe a family emergency or she stopped for something, and when she arrived, I'd look clingy for worrying.

But what if something *was* wrong?

A woman in a long tan coat pushed open the gate and strolled out. She didn't bother to look back as I caught the door with my boot and slipped stealthily inside. For once it was helpful that, in neighborhoods like this where people lived in a bubble of goodwill, no one paid attention to well-dressed people on the street. It was enough to curl my lip at.

Joséphine's building sat in the far back of the inner courtyard, and instead of rickety wooden stairs like mine, there were flights of marble and lush red rugs in an elegant spiral. It felt unused and too quiet, no one stirring anywhere inside, the rug eating up even the sound of my footsteps. At the top floor sat apartment H with the letter embossed in copper, but when I moved to knock, the door budged under my fist and swept open. The hair on the back of my neck stood tall.

"Joséphine? Are you here?"

Silence.

The wood floor creaked as I waded in and latched the door behind me. The living room was spacious, with large windows and tall, folding mirrors propped in a corner on top of a Marley mat, next to a barre for home practice. Rows and rows of shelving were filled with framed photos of Joséphine and people who looked like her parents. Siblings. Friends. Patrons and fans.

I shouldn't be here.

Standing in her apartment, it felt like I was prying. Like she'd come home any minute and catch me intruding. But something could be wrong. She could be hurt, or bedridden with a bad flu, waiting for anyone to notice or care, and I wouldn't let her feel discarded; I knew firsthand what it was like when no one showed up for you.

So I stopped twisting that ring on my finger and straightened, determined. Blood pounded in my ears as I stepped into the kitchen. The air smelled fetid and moist. Humid with decay. Flies swarmed around something dark and fuzzy at the bottom of the trash.

"Joséphine?" my voice rang out.

Still no answer.

Finally I moved into the bedroom. It was messy, her wardrobe exploded, piles of clothes on the floor, in a chair, on the vanity littered with perfumes. More clothes than I owned. Two jewelry boxes on a marble-top dresser overflowed with strings of black pearls from the night at the restaurant. And on the floor, on the other side of a blue velvet bed, lay a shadowy mass.

One step closer and I gagged.

Joséphine.

The mass was in the shape of a person, as if Joséphine had collapsed on the spot. Pale skin sunken and sallow, chestnut hair fanned around her and dull in the light. Her mouth hung open, brown eyes wide in their sockets and capillaries burst in a flood of red, hands splayed at her sides. Her neck bent at an unnatural angle. The river's tattoo on the inside of her wrist was gone; the flesh there and around the crook of her throat had been burned away. Charred, as if she'd been garroted by flames.

Joséphine Moreau was dead.

I spun away. Gasped for air.

"*Does this mean we're free forever from Demaret and her Joséphine obsession?*" Coralie had joked the day before while we all brushed off the principal's absence. I couldn't tell from the smell how long Joséphine had been lying here, but the question of her rotting all day and night, during all the workshops, made me gag again.

Doubled over, head between my knees, I felt my stomach flip. If I didn't breathe, I was going to be sick.

My fingers were already fishing the phone from my pocket, trembling and dialing 112 when the apartment's front door clicked.

"*Emergency response—*"

A creak in the wood slats by the entrance lanced my heart. Someone was here, and it wasn't Joséphine.

The lump in my throat dissolved as I hung up and clambered away, leaping over the body. Over Joséphine, once a living, human person, and into the dark, narrow closet with the door drawn. I didn't exhale.

Soft footsteps moved through the apartment, ambling closer at a leisurely pace, and every thought bled out of me. Glass shattered in the living room. Objects from the shelves clattered to the floor. The intruder was looking for something. Then through the crack in the door, I saw it: Joséphine's cell phone. Right there in its gold confetti case, resting on the bedside table and plugged into a charger.

It was all I came for, really.

If this was what they wanted, they couldn't have it—it had my answers about the river, what it gave me. My future. Maybe even Joséphine's killer. Swallowing, with a glance into the hall, I darted out and ripped the phone from the wall. Its charger tangled around my legs as I retreated, panicked.

I'd only just slipped back into the safety of the closet, pressed behind what was no doubt a real mink coat, when the bedroom door whined on its hinge. Light footsteps waded inside, calm, unhurried, *unbothered* by the body that lay there. I clamped a hand over my mouth, stifling my breath. Sweat pooled under my coat.

The intruder whistled a familiar song as they moved, riffling through a drawer, pulling it off its slider and letting it crash loudly to the floor. Then another. Jewelry boxes rattled on the dresser. Tears rolled down my cheeks as I silently begged them not to raid the closet for whatever they were looking for. I didn't dare take a peek—between my stuttering heartbeat and my wish to distance myself from whatever got Joséphine killed, I was meant to be a prima ballerina, not another corpse.

Down the street, a lone siren wailed. For me.

Rapidly, the whistling cut out, and the footsteps rushed away, growing farther and farther until the wood in the entrance creaked, the front door clicked shut, and finally they were gone.

The breath that came out of me was closer to a sob. I barely managed to push my way out of the closet before my body sank to the floor of its own accord, fingers trembling while I turned on Joséphine's phone. It was too late to turn back now.

Tears wouldn't stop spilling over, blurring my vision, but I could still read the prompt: *Fingerprint ID.*

I cursed, squeezed my eyes shut, and took a deep breath. If I didn't do this, it'd all be for nothing. Then—

"I'm sorry," I whispered to the skin and bones of the once-great Joséphine Moreau as I crawled over and pressed her cold, rigid thumb to the screen. Her rancid stench made me shudder. She used to smell like clove smoke. "I'm so sorry."

And as the sirens grew closer, as I disabled the lock in settings, turned off cell data and wifi, and stashed the phone in my pocket, I realized I recognized the intruder's melody: "Danse macabre." It continued playing in my head as I leaned over and puked on a discarded silk blouse.

By the time I finished with the police and came home, Coralie was asleep on the couch. The new tattoo on the inside of my wrist seared and throbbed beneath my coat sleeve, and death clung to me like a gummy residue. This morning, we'd passed each other like ghosts around the apartment, drifting from room to room with vague acknowledgment. She still hadn't bothered to acknowledge my place at the ballet, and I didn't have the nerve to ask what she was doing now without it. So the sight of her unconscious, knowing I was spared another awkward encounter, relieved me. Especially when all I wanted after romping around a filthy, bloody cave and then uncovering a dead ballerina was a shower.

I listened to the drone of the showerhead while I scrubbed Joséphine Moreau away and let her rinse down the drain, reliving that first trip to the river. How in the morning, when I discovered the tattoo, I'd wanted to kill her.

And now she's dead.

When I finally smelled of orange blossoms instead of a corpse, I sank my feet into my routine ice bath. The shock of it soothed my aching muscles, gifting me the kind of pain I savored, that I looked forward to every night. A shred of normalcy while I went through the dead première's phone. Though I'd shared with police exactly how I found her body, I didn't tell them about the device. Sure, there was a *chance* that something on it could help them find her killer, but it was only a chance, and what about what I needed? Was that less important to even a dead girl? What if whatever got her killed came after me next? I deserved to know. So they'd have it when I got what I wanted. I'd even help avenge her when I was safe.

The phone was remarkably slow, bloated with hundreds of thousands of files: photos and videos, so many unread texts, unopened emails, and missed calls that it stopped bothering to count. Anything could be a clue to better understanding the red god or who killed her. The entire device could be a cautionary tale of things—or people—to avoid on my climb.

I tapped through the latest from Ciro, from this morning, that simply read: *I warned you.* Earlier in the thread, there were only meeting places and dates, but nothing of whatever he'd warned her about. Nothing to prove he hurt her, or that he knew whoever did, not that I expected a written confession. It could have been anyone for any reason.

It could have been the blood river itself.

Flicking through the photo gallery wasn't any more fruitful: mirror selfies during rehearsals and out shopping, posing on a balcony with a cigarette on her lips and a smile, so many plates of food and colorful cocktails.

"Come on, Joséphine," I mumbled, swiping back to home, "show me *something.*"

Her wallpaper was of her and Ciro at night, the Eiffel Tower twinkling in the background. His arm was tight around her waist, her hand on his chest, matching red ink on their wrists exposed. She beamed. And staring at her face, I almost missed a folder icon, the only item without a label and so unlike the colorful apps that surrounded it. A secret hidden in plain sight.

My jaw dropped when I tapped inside.

It was a drive full of files—bookmarked web pages about astral planes, Sumerian myths, the big bang theory, entire texts of Aristotle's *Metaphysics* and Dante's *The Divine Comedy.* Joséphine had organized subfolders even, for more photos, videos, voice memos, and notes.

There was so much my head ached and my thumbs twitched, unsure where to go first. I shut my bedroom door behind me, curled up against the headboard, and started at the beginning.

The first of the videos was a landscape, and my hands shook at that flood of red. Red sky and red silt, a river of blood ebbing calmly behind Ciro's brown-skinned friend, who stood on its banks. Even on camera, he was unusually breathtaking, dark eyes piercing through the screen, a sardonic brow arched at Joséphine, who handled the phone.

"*Okay, Andor, ready?*" she shouted, and he cocked his head in answer, eliciting a giggle. "*Go!*"

At her cue, the video glitched like an old television. Like a file, corrupted. Static flashed where the boy stood, distorting reality around his body like it did the day I first saw him. The edges of the recording darkened, the air blurred and burned around him. It lasted only the span of a second, but what followed, the thing that stood in the boy's place, made me flinch.

The monster. No longer a human boy but blood made sentient, huge, with great antlers primed for goring and claws just as lethal. It was a thing of nightmares, of demonology and myths, the thing that pulled me out of the river.

Behind the camera, Joséphine laughed. Intoxicating laughter, like she'd witnessed a party trick. Then followed applause and Ciro's voice, "*Bravo*," while that monstrous boy just scratched the back of his neck shyly. His skin rippled iridescently. It looked like magic, like special effects and editing, and I would have thrown the phone away if I hadn't seen that thing with my own eyes. If I hadn't just made a pact with something like it only hours ago and let it nestle inside.

I backed out of the file called "Andor," knowing exactly where I had to go, what I had to do next. Then I swiped to the next video and hit PLAY.

CHAPTER 10

anessa Abbadie twirled herself dizzy around the room, showing off her new, expensive leotard from Rose-Marie Baumé's line, and all I could think was how much I wanted her to fall. Face-first, teeth loose and trickling out like candy, eyes watering from the pain. I envisioned it all—the blood, agony warping her features, her embarrassment, even as I told myself I didn't want it. Most of me didn't want to see her hurt, but part of me craved it.

My fingertips ached to reach deep into her flesh, through blood and muscle, and send her crashing down, so I drummed on the floor to keep them busy. I didn't know if I *could* do such a thing, but I didn't want to find out. And ever since I'd renewed the deal and found Joséphine the previous night, the darkness remained alert and ready to feed.

"Isn't it so cute?" Vanessa prompted, basking in the attention, twisting this way and that for Olivia and the others to get a better look. "My brother-in-law, the *prince*, called in a favor to get this prerelease."

It *was* a beautiful leotard, of course, soft lavender with petal sleeves, and she even donned a purple lipstick to match. A commendable choice for our first rehearsal, one hell of a way to stand out when no one knew our names and the professionals were already assessing how much of a threat we posed. Principal Nina Brossard sized up Vanessa as she stretched on the barre, ready to hoard her privileges like a fire-breathing dragon hoarded wealth in case Vanessa turned out to be another Joséphine.

Only she wasn't. I was.

No one even knew that Joséphine was dead.

Suddenly my drumming fingers weren't enough, and I was up, carrying myself across the room, chasing a deep breath I couldn't draw. I felt eyes follow me into the hall, judging as the door shut behind me.

The police didn't share how long it would take before the ballet was notified, but all I kept thinking was that everyone could see it on me, smell the decay lingering in my hair. All through morning class, I could hardly focus or remain still, clenching and unclenching my fists, tuning in and out of instruction. It was enough to earn me a chiding from Madame Demaret, but nothing quelled the unrest.

"Not up to your usual standard today, Mademoiselle Mesny?" she'd commented, tutting her teeth in condescension while a secret was adamantly trying to wrest itself from my ribs.

From the bottom of the nearest stairwell, the voice carried up, partially muddled by the clapping of pointe shoes on concrete. "Still no Joséphine?"

My head snapped up, and I inched closer.

"My friend said he saw her dealing outside a club last week, and then police showed up. She's probably in jail," another suggested. "They had to pull Sabine from rehearsal yesterday and ask her to fill in for *Cinderella*."

My nostrils flared from such horseshit. Joséphine was gone, and rumors filled her place. And it could have been any one of them lashing out in a fit of envy, wanting to do worse than thumbtacks in a shoe. We all joked about killing each other, but how many of us meant it?

She didn't deserve her fate. Nobody did.

Then, alone in the empty hall, in the middle of pacing across the opera house's lower levels to temper the flames in my blood, I felt it— the wicked darkness shifting under my skin, disquieted, followed by a flare of light. It was a basement without any windows, yet the hall grew so bright for a moment that I could have been standing on the top floor in summer. So bright it hurt.

Though I threw up a hand to shield my stinging, blinking eyes, it was too late. Like staring into the sun with none of its warmth, I couldn't see.

A chill ran down my spine.

"Hello?"

Silence.

The air turned stale as a mortuary, deadened to any outside noise and unmoving. Not even the whirr of heating vents could be heard down here, and though I squinted for a source of my unease, there was nothing to see. There was only me and the tinny music in my blood, telling me to *run*.

I took a step back, then another, and another, footsteps picking up speed until I was engulfed by the din and heat of tourists crowding the atrium.

Though it once seemed glamorous, it was burdensome now to have my workplace so full of voices and cameras, people salivating over ceiling carvings and leaving fingerprints on all the mirrors. They clogged stairwells, regularly choking off passageways I needed to get to class. I cut through the center in search of the locker room, breath racing through gritted teeth. Oblivious heads inclined to stare at the shining glass dome, taking pictures of yet another chandelier.

Fuck pretty crown moldings while a star was missing from the sky. What did it take to make them remember us?

My hands freed a wallet from a tourist's coat pocket as I wedged by. His camera was pressed to his face, attuned to the cherub etched at the top of a pillar. The wad of warm, brown leather was already being shoved up my sleeve as I drifted away.

His penance for forgetting. For the audacity of not seeing me.

"Laurence!"

At my name in *that* voice, I pursed my lips. It sounded just like it did the night by the blood river.

Ciro Aurissy blocked my path in a cloud of star anise and tobacco, a mischievous grin on his beautifully sculpted face. He nodded toward a quiet hall housing an old Raymonda costume, and I begrudgingly followed.

"What are you doing?" he asked in a low voice, eyes on my now bulky sleeve. Not a speck of dirt to be seen on his perfect white suit.

Does he know his girlfriend is dead?

Instead of asking, I only sneered and pushed the wallet farther out of reach. "Just be happy it's not yours."

That only made him laugh instead of bothering him like I'd hoped. As a board member, he had to know how expensive this all was, the pointe shoes and massages and muscle creams, how little it all paid. If he was going to turn me in to security, he would have done so already. But since I had him here…

"Have you talked to Joséphine lately?" I prodded, doing my best at a casual tone.

His grin sharpened considerably. "No, why?"

There was no way *I'd* be the one to tell him. Not if he did something to her. So I pivoted, mumbling with a shrug, "I just saw you arguing at auditions. It looked serious."

A long moment passed with Ciro eyeing me, probably considering how much I weighed so he could plan where to stash my body. But then he rubbed his jaw. "President Auger made a last-minute change and reassigned some of Joséphine's shows this season. I guess whatever dirt Joséphine had on her wasn't working anymore."

"She was *blackmailing*—?!" My voice pitched high through the empty corridor. Glancing around, assured we were alone, I stepped in closer and whispered, "Why would Joséphine *blackmail* President Auger?"

"I told her to be patient," he continued without answering. "Said I'd take care of it, but she was angry. She didn't want to wait."

I blinked, stunned. He was lying, of course. He had to be.

But Ciro stood calmly, chest open, preternaturally still—none of the telltale signs of a liar, unless he was a good one. Capable of murdering his girlfriend and returning to work with a smile on his face.

"That doesn't make any sense. Why would Auger cut her shows? She's perfect—"

He only laughed again. "Haven't you realized? The ballet's a chess game, and you're all pawns."

Up ahead, President Auger entered the corridor and waved in his direction, her expression serious as she was flanked by two uniformed officers. The news was here.

"I must get going," said Ciro as he clasped my hand in both of his, leaving behind a folded scrap of paper in my palm. He was already turning on his heel as I unfolded it and read:

Through the tunnels, past the red cave, iron door on the left.
Elysium.

"Wait—"

But he sauntered away, calling out over his shoulder, "Come see us when you're tired of being sacrificed for the king."

Though President Auger stood at the front of the studio like she always did for her end-of-day announcements, her demeanor was off. She rubbed her wrists constantly, losing her train of thought even while she droned on about the rehearsal plan for *La bayadère* and not leaving our tutus all over the halls. And having seen what I saw, her expression with Ciro, and the police, I knew why.

"... to the costume closet in the basement for preliminary fittings."

Fidgeting in my own seat on the floor, I pressed my thumb into the mark, deep enough to bruise and disturb the concealer I'd carefully applied over it. If I remained careful, hiding all traces of my deal as I climbed through the ballet ranks, there'd be no reason for whoever killed Joséphine to come after me. No one would ever have to know what I did, what I sacrificed to get it, and Coralie's own reemergence as an apprentice in my wake wouldn't dare be questioned either. There didn't have to be any connection between me and the fallen étoile.

"Lastly, you may have noticed Joséphine Moreau's absence."

My attention snapped up to Rose-Marie Baumé, who sometimes joined our announcements to deliver news on behalf of the board. Now she glanced around the room, and beside her, Auger's expression was impassive, cut from stone. At the pause, Demaret hung her head. Ciro was nowhere to be found.

"We were notified by police that Joséphine is no longer with us. She was found in her apartment yesterday."

Murdered, I wanted to pipe up. She was found murdered, and no one bothered to look for her. If she hadn't invited me over, how long would it have taken for someone to find her rotting corpse?

My fists balled in my lap. If anyone dared cry, the wicked dark in me would rise to stop them. No one here deserved to mourn her; not with how they whispered, sneering behind her back while they cooed in her face.

Instead, Nina Brossard yawned. Olivia whispered something into Vanessa's ear, and they both snickered. Sabine studied her manicure.

As her gaze swept through the group, Auger dismissed us for the day with advice: "You can honor her memory by giving the ballet your utmost devotion."

And everyone around me, the professionals and apprentices, all nodded, resolute like little soldiers. Everybody but me. Because we weren't soldiers—we were ballerinas with careers like mayflies, gliding onstage in gossamer wings. The only enemies we knew were time and each other.

CHAPTER 11

For my first appearance with the Paris Ballet Company, I transformed myself into a god. The gala d'ouverture took place every year to mark the opening of the ballet's winter season, hosted with powerhouses like Chanel and Balmain, and while apprentices weren't *true* members—not full-time until we were promoted to quadrille—we were still expected to attend. Dead prima ballerina be damned. A dress hung on my door, power flowed through my veins, and all I had left to do was finish painting my face and not think about Joséphine.

No one else did.

More pressing was the crowd I meant to sway tonight, seeds to plant for my promotion and Coralie's salvation. With or without Joséphine, I needed to bend the world to my will, to prove them all wrong. And if I was to play god, I needed to look the part.

"Your mom's *making* you go?" I repeated Coralie's news, letting the words fall dead from my lips as I peeled tape from my temples. My eyeliner wings were as sharp as blades. "Are you...okay with that?"

My throat thickened whenever I imagined how much she must be hurting, how I'd hurt if the roles were reversed. Being promised something all my life only to have it taken away. Living with the reminder of what I lost. After today's orientation, there was now a locker in Palais Garnier with my name on it and a paying contract in place, which was more than she could say. Her mood was wretched still, had been ever since the announcement went out and she stormed off, and now, sharing the bathroom mirror as we got ready, she appeared determined to scowl her way through the party.

Still, it shouldn't have surprised me when Coralie came home with an evening gown and her father's invitation in hand. *Of course* Rose-Marie had a plan to strong-arm her daughter into the company.

Gaze focused on her curling iron, Coralie explained, "I'm supposed to talk to President Auger and convince her to make room for one more."

She sighed, as if riding on her mother's coattails dressed in couture was a chore. My nails pressed half-moons into my palms as my pity dried up and I fought the urge to slap her.

"It's so unfair," continued Coralie, over the smell of burning hair. "I worked really hard for this, and she *swore* this time would be enough. If anybody deserves to be there, it's me."

I concentrated on applying a deep crimson shade of lipstick so I wouldn't make a face. But the liquid reminded me of the whispering river, the boy named Andor who transformed into a monster, being covered in blood, and I squeezed my eyes shut to chase it all away.

When I opened, green eyes in the mirror settled on me, beseeching. "Not saying you don't deserve it!" Coralie added hastily, throwing me a half-hearted smile before dousing herself in a cloud of hairspray. "You're good too, obviously. It's just . . . You know, it's easy for you. You wouldn't get it."

She was right about one thing—I didn't. And I didn't know why it bothered me, but I kept my breath steady to hide the pang in my chest. We both went quiet.

"Hey, what's that?"

Cold fingers gripped my arm like a vise and tugged.

"Watch it—!"

Coralie pushed up the stack of gold-plated bangles on my wrist, exposing my river's marking to the light. Her gaze widened on the stark red ink. For days, I'd been covering it with long sleeves or in powder and foundation when leotards left my arms exposed, but tonight, I thought the bracelets would be enough. I was wrong.

I wrenched from her hold and shook the bangles back down. Maybe too quickly, for the way she stared. "It's nothing," I piped up, squeezing past her to get my dress. "Just a tattoo I got on a whim a while ago."

She arched her brow. "Since when do *you* do things on a whim? Staying out late, getting tattoos—"

"Maybe you don't know me as well as you think you do."

It came out a barb, far harsher than I intended, and she actually flinched. For a long time, we just stared at each other, but I didn't apologize as I slipped into my room and shut the door, and neither did she.

Outside the opera house, a cool breeze rippled under my black cape, covering my arms in goose bumps. My dress was beyond protection from the aggressive departure of fall—full skirts of tulle and organza to scream wealth, bodice beaded and covered in gold-embroidered constellations. I'd even burned my hair into submission and weaved it half up with little gold stars. So when a photographer aimed their camera to appreciate my hard work, I raised my chin and beamed.

I'd arrived at Opéra Garnier with a thirst for blood and no clear reason why.

Revelers, a mix of models and millionaires, climbed out of shiny cars all around us, adorned in bespoke luxury and posing for cameras on the red carpet. The building's façade was aglow ahead, and still hanging above, sandwiched between two gilded angels, was a poster of Joséphine Moreau, midpirouette, her lips parted in a breath, eyes dancing with allure. This was supposed to be her opening, and even in death she drew an audience. Attendees pointed up at her as they strolled inside. She and the Palais's splendor both sold season tickets, filled seats, and charmed rich donors out of six or seven zeros. And after champagne and walking the costume displays, those who weren't performing would sit for *Cinderella*.

With Sabine Simon as the replacement.

Pride and unease prickled my skin as I cleared the doors. Though we'd spent nearly a year dancing in the opera house, we stuck to side entrances, rarely venturing through the great foyer filled with guests who marveled at carvings of cherubim faces on marble columns. Suddenly, I was one of them. And then security gave my invitation a second, more scrupulous glance.

My smile hardened as I waited, twisting that ring on my finger, body flashed hot with embarrassment.

The exalted sculpture of Handel, a composer who also got rich off the slave trade, pinned me in place, unrelenting, and a voice that sounded curiously like Rose-Marie reminded me that, invitation or no, I didn't belong here. I was meant for a lifetime in the margins, in obscurity. I stole my invitation from a more deserving girl. It grew louder, even when they finally nodded me along and I had to scurry to catch up to Coralie.

"Hurry, before they run out of champagne!" she grumbled, oblivious and dragging me through the atrium with her hand entwined with mine. The glitter of her plum-colored bustier shimmered in the light.

We crossed beneath golden filigreed chandeliers, in front of large, gilded mirrors and walls inlaid with veined, creamy marble, all the way to the grand hall where waitstaff offered glasses of champagne at the doors. The gallery beyond, wrapped from floor to high ceiling in gold and light, stung my eyes. Chamber musicians played a Baroque waltz beneath an old painting of dancing nymphs.

The opulence made my head spin.

"Your gown is amazing," gushed a squeaky voice I recognized.

Behind us, Vanessa beamed, lifting a flute from a nearby tray held by an expressionless, dark-skinned server who wouldn't meet my eyes when I walked in. I didn't know for whose sake. She faced me, while I braced for her punch line sure to follow. Her niceties always felt fake.

Coralie snorted, taking a second flute for herself. "Yeah, I wonder how many conned tourists at Notre Dame it cost."

My cheeks burned. I'd stopped targeting tourists years ago—too much risk for so little reward. More lucrative were parties and recitals like this, with wealthy parents losing pocketbooks and watches and too apathetic to notice. And even then, it was mostly out of spite, like the man with the watch. It was hard to temper my rage at the stink of entitlement.

"Do you want me to compliment *your* dress, Cor?" I whirled around, a jab prepared about her mother's hand-me-downs.

But the moment was gone; Coralie was downing her drink with her eyes closed, and Vanessa, if she'd even heard, had already moved on to detailing how her brother-in-law—the *prince*, she sang sweetly— managed to get some designer on the phone for a last-minute request.

Deflating, I surveyed the room. The drinks, the lights, the overture of *A Midsummer Night's Dream* that began playing. Reflections of the city from beyond the open balcony doors twinkled in the mirrors. Everyone mingled, reconnecting over summer homes on the Mediterranean and necklaces insured for more than I'd ever earn and poor, poor Joséphine.

Beneath these golden lights, before all these people, everything that made me different was laid bare. No amount of tulle, gold thread, and heat straightening would make me soft and shiny and expensive; instead of talking, laughing, or networking with people who smelled like money,

I stood around, chewing the inside of my cheek. Rose-Marie Baumé, posed by the fireplace and swarmed by adulating sycophants desperate just to breathe her air, glanced around the room, and her gaze jumped over me like a scar to avoid.

What am I doing here?

A thought stirred in me to walk over there and make Rose-Marie bow, assert my dominance and *make* her look at me, but I forced myself to turn away. The skin of my wrist stung with power and need.

My mark.

I refused to shrink. If assimilation into the powerful was what they wanted, then I came armed. They'd see how influential I'd become, taste what I was capable of.

Show some respect, I commanded, shoulders back, head up, as loud and clear as my thoughts would go. After all, they needed someone like me, someone hungry. The savior of their dusty ballet was coming through.

I walked the length of the room, skirts fluttering the floor around me, skin humming as gazes followed with the same vacantness I'd elicited from Rose-Marie at the restaurant. A touch fearful, even, as if I'd ripped the worship from their reluctant hearts. While Coralie was tucked in a corner trying to smooth-talk President Auger, people were parting around me, a sea of fine silks and charmeuses punctuated by real gold and diamonds, and like a shark, I passed through.

Good.

And then, poised with primordial power bolstering my spine and surrounded by unknowing prey, a temptation to take it further rose in me. A question with only one answer. Like the sight of freshly fallen snow, or poured concrete set to dry, or a newly painted building begging to be tagged. I wanted to do more than assimilate. I wanted to cause a mess and leave a mark.

Before the command was even fully formed, there were already gasps on the other side of the gallery. The first man in my line of sight, in a deep cobalt suit, stirred and stared down, his cheeks flushed a brilliant red. A wet stain blossomed at the front of his pants and grew, traveling down, down. He blinked, dazed, and someone rushed to take his arm.

My mouth twitched in a smile.

"You gonna drink that?"

I jumped. Coralie arrived beside me, nodding to my full glass with a frown and totally uninterested in the scene unfolding before us. The chandelier washed out her usual honeyed glow and exaggerated the purple circles beneath her eyes.

"When was the last time you slept?"

She snatched my drink and rolled her eyes. But I wasn't done—I wanted to force her into fighting back.

Cheer up, I insisted silently, the order harsh enough to leave the tang of blood on my tongue. It was still too soon to share my plan of joining the company early and opening a spot for her. Telling her meant exposing everything, and she'd make her failure my fault. I'd lose her. **Be happy for me.**

Coralie's expression didn't change, however. No smoother brow or softness in her pout. She was still cold, unaffected by my commands. Prickly. My gaze narrowed on her, the hollows of her cheek and dullness of her hair, as if it would reveal how she'd resisted. After a beat I shrugged, realizing that I liked her this way, couldn't imagine her more agreeable. This was how we were, full of sharp digs and interlaced hands.

Turning my attention back to the crowd, an old woman shrouded in sapphires did a pirouette. A man in a black tuxedo asked Olivia for a tour of the costume displays, and she rushed away giggling. And from my corner, I just smirked, knowing all of it was me. *Watch me* and *Show some respect* were simple commands, but *Adore me* and *Worship me* yielded no results. Perhaps manipulating flesh, *blood*, was simple, but the mind, not so much. I could compel the world to bow, but I couldn't make them believe. Which meant the rest relied on me, and my dancing at the audition was all mine. It had to be.

There were still so many files on her phone to sift through, but I pictured Joséphine practicing just like this, *making* Grandpré give her a solo. Now I was the new puppeteer making high society dance, and blood rushed to my ears from the euphoria of it.

"Laure?"

I blinked out of my daze and spotted a familiar part-boy, part-monster slipping out of the gallery. His rich, tawny skin was hard to miss when there were only two of us among the crowd, and swathed in emerald jacquard print and black silk trim, he looked more sumptuous than the Palais itself. He looked distinctly otherworldly.

"Laure, you're bleeding." Vanessa's eyes were wide as saucers.

My fingers flew up to my nose and came away wet, red. Like dominoes, the others turned to gawk, but I was already plowing through the crowd, out of the gallery and after Andor. My savior from the river, Ciro and Joséphine's friend. My heels echoed on marble in my wake as I went to have a word, my tattoo itching for a fight.

Only the moment I rounded the corner, he was gone. The long hall was empty, just endless mirrors and columns reflecting on each other and me, swiping at my bleeding nose to stop from sullying my dress or the fancy floors.

"Damn—"

"Nice to see you all cleaned up," said Andor from behind me, in the same soft, smoky baritone. I jumped and spun around to find him lying in wait, a glass of champagne in hand. Up close, I recognized the lines of his face and fullness of his mouth even without all the blood or static, and his black gaze, decorated with heavy eyeliner, still narrowed on my face curiously. Like I was a puzzle to be deciphered. As if the monster inside him was not far beneath, and it saw something it recognized. Then he added with a smirk, "Mostly."

I swallowed, suddenly, inexplicably parched.

"And congratulations, by the way. Few can say they apprenticed with the Paris Ballet," he continued, pulling a white silk handkerchief from his pocket and gesturing to my nose.

"Thanks," I mumbled, and the fight drained out of me. Was I really going to just come out and accuse him and his friend of murder? With no proof, alone, and knowing what he turned into?

Andor's smile was immovable and disarming as I accepted the fabric finer than anything I ever owned, his warm hand covered in gold rings brushing mine. With little choice, I dabbed blood from my face, and it felt like an act of desecration. One I liked a little too much.

"Listen, I wanted to make sure Ciro talked to you," Andor started, guiding me down the corridor and away from the party. My legs fell in step beside him, and though he made no effort to walk close, I made sure to stay out of reach. Lest I turn up dead too. "Or offered our help. We watched you in there. You're pushing yourself a little hard, don't you think?"

I tightened my grip on the cloth. The skin where we'd touched felt tingly and numb. "What do you mean?"

"Exercising power has a cost. It takes from you as much as it gives..." He glanced pointedly at the blood-soiled cloth.

I stopped walking. If he meant to say that the mark was doing this to me, I didn't care. A nosebleed and a little headache were a small price to pay for power, especially when I'd suffered worse as a ballerina, especially when I had my future on the line.

"What's the point of having all this power and not using it? I've spent my whole life under the boot of others who had no qualms about using *theirs*."

No, it was my turn to be formidable.

Fire flared in my veins in agreement, just as, out of the corner of my eye, I saw a blur of white dart past. Ciro stepped out from wherever he'd been lurking and clapped his hands, eyes bright and verging on feline. He looked expensive the way simple things often were, dressed in a skinny-fitted white tuxedo and posed like a luxury ad. His milky complexion was clear, his smile shiny, as if his girlfriend hadn't been found dead two days ago.

"Glad you two finally met—I've been meaning to introduce you. Laure the ballerina, meet Andor the painter. Andor, Laurence."

I glowered. "Don't you have a girlfriend to mourn?"

Andor winced beside me, and Ciro's eyes narrowed to slits. He stepped in close, so that I could smell his expensive cologne and see the rage in his brown eyes. In a low voice, he bristled, "We don't *have* to help you, you know. And you don't know anything about me *or* Joséphine. Who do you think taught her everything?"

For a second, I faltered. I knew that Ciro was her recruiter, and probably Andor's too. He'd said that night, *It wanted another*, right after I fell in, and here was Andor trying to clean up his mess. But to what end, I didn't know.

I folded, impatient. "S-so then why did Joséphine take me to the river that night?"

"It wants more of us."

"For what?"

"How should I know? Acheron has its own plans for the world." He said it so smugly, it was impossible to know what anyone saw in him.

"And now that she's gone?"

Ciro shrugged carelessly and turned on his heel. "Go ask it yourself—"

"**Don't walk away from me**," I growled, the words unfurling from my tongue like darkness, heavy and raw. His haughtiness, this place and these people, Joséphine—all of it was gasoline to the wildfire in my blood.

And Ciro went rigid. Still as a statue.

My hand floated up to my scratchy throat in disbelief. It was hard to get used to but exhilarating, this new, brash imposition of mine, having some power that demanded to be heard, that he couldn't just walk away from. It was so far from where I'd been, and so beautiful where I was going.

I turned to Andor, ready to threaten him too but stopped. As he watched Ciro, he raised his brows, neither horrified nor angry but *endorsement* curving on his lips. This close, the scent radiating off his wide shoulders and tall stature was earthy, sweet, and a little sour, like dying roses and wet leaves. Not wine or brandy or sweat or expensive cologne like his friend, but real, fresh wilderness. The heat from his form sang invitingly.

But thinking of the tingling skin and the monster underneath, I inched away.

Ciro shivered, his face flushing and his body spasming. As if he was fighting through whatever had bound him. His expression turned wild when the chains broke, as he rounded on me, snarling. "Try that again—"

He managed two charged steps my way before the lights flickered, calling us to our seats. The halls flooded with people heading to the theatre. Rose-Marie Baumé scowled at the sight of him as she passed, Coralie on her trail, and I grinned, his threat lost.

"We're not finished," I warned him, watching him seethe as, with my head high and a lift in my step, I strutted away. My mother wasn't an étoile, my parents didn't gift millions in endowments, but I had something better. I wouldn't be underestimated again.

And in my orchestra seat, I couldn't stop smiling, even as I sat through two hours of Sabine Simon's dreams coming true. Because of Joséphine's death, she was finally a star.

CHAPTER 12

The scent of wet rock engulfed me as I followed Ciro's directions to the iron door. I'd passed through it once before, when Joséphine led me home. Now like a hook through skin, there was a pull from behind my navel growing stronger as I neared. The air thickened, turning heavy and warm as I passed the archway to the altar, curls of steam rising above the red pool. As if the river god was calling my bones home.

I'd spent my nights on Joséphine's phone and all my waking hours thinking about it, replaying that video of Andor, watching Joséphine roll die and flip coins again and again. *Luck and charm*, her deal was for. It wasn't a lack of talent, flexibility, or height in her jumps holding her back—she just needed a chance to show what she already had. And in that video, she couldn't fail.

So where was her luck when she was getting murdered?

I loosed a breath when my hands found the door beyond, tucked in a dead end and built into a stone recess. The metal was cold, and I froze in hesitation. It could all be a trap, and I was next: Ciro's argument with Joséphine in the theatre, his sudden rage at the gala, the burns on her body, the lack of cell reception underground, the monster for a friend.

I could be next.

And maybe I couldn't take them, but Elysium, the blood river, the bargain—if any of this played a part in Joséphine's death, I had to know in order to save myself. If it happened to her, the rising star with thousands of eyes on her, then certainly it could take me too unless I knew what and how to stop it.

So I set my jaw and shoved the door open.

In the matter of a step, I was back *there*, under the violent red sky, crossing through a rock-pile arch in the middle of a meadow, surrounded by tall white flowers. The smells of struck matches and the bite of blood carried on the breeze. Down the hill, a vein cleaved the countryside in two, and another, its twin in silvery white, lay beyond that, days' or weeks' hike away.

"*How do I even describe Elysium?*" Joséphine had said in one of her videos. She'd laughed and panned across the black trees that stretched for miles. "*It's everything: a place, a time, a living being all in one. Andor's theory is it's the resting place for the proto-god Chaos. An immortal plane to counter our mortal one. Acheron*"—she focused on the red river—"*is its blood, and Lethe*"—then on the white—"*came from its bones. Life and oblivion. Chaos and order, all in one. The paradise to our earth.*"

"*Or hell,*" Andor had muttered off camera.

This place had dominated my dreams, vibrant every time I closed my eyes long before I found her phone. The quiet of the woods, the flow of Acheron, the heat of the blood, Andor's monstrous face. It was a fever dream I sometimes didn't want to shake.

I took another step, lured by the sudden urge to run, dive into the red, and submerge myself. Again, that sudden craving for more that made me question if maybe I wasn't in control when I'd decided for another deal. Maybe it *wanted* me to come back now.

"So this is it, huh?" I whistled to myself, plucking a white flower. The petals were marked down the center with crimson drops like bloodstains, but they held no scent.

Sobering my resolve, I dug my thumbnail into the mark on my wrist to stop from running away, pressing and pressing until it broke skin and stung. Then I started toward the river. In all of Joséphine's videos, there was a stark white cottage nearby, the only sign of people around, and I took it as the best place to start. As I broke through the tree line, the only sound came from leaves on the forest floor rustling at my ankles. Warm air tickled the back of my neck.

"Ciro?"

If it wasn't him that killed Joséphine, he had to know who did, why my nose bled at the gala, why she really brought me to the river. No more running—I'd make him look me in the eye and explain the files.

I marched quickly across the uneven forest floor, stumbling over the fallen logs and tangles of vines. Twigs lashed at my bare thighs. And all the while, I was conscious of the red river flowing fast on the other side of the trees, whispering to my blood. My mark throbbed.

Finally I found a well-trodden dirt path leading down to the river in one direction and the old cottage in the other. An old, worn-down pergola stood surrounded by a yard piled high with firewood and over-grown gardens, and someone lounged in its shadows before a firepit reduced to cinders.

And at the sight of the creature that took shape as I neared, my feet stuttered to a stop.

Four black eyes glanced up at the sound, staring back beneath great antlers, and its—*his*—bloodred arms held a large sketchpad and charcoal in his lap. It was incongruous, the size of them compared to his hands, the very *notion* that such a thing might be capable of art, and then, his entire façade, the extra eyes and sharp teeth, his moving, inky red all flashed like static until he took a shape more human.

My thumbnail broke skin over my mark again, forcing air into my lungs.

Andor climbed to his bare feet and moved deftly around the firepit. With his bushy, curly hair decorated with flowers and his white shirt billowing, the mask of refinement that he donned for the gala had evaporated. Standing before me was someone wilder, as feral as his human face was beautiful.

"I-is Ciro around?"

"No, but he should be back soon." As he approached, head tilted, his brow furrowed. His eyes, dark irises inseparable from the pupils, were gentle. "Listen, Ciro's not always like that, you know. Last night, he was... We thought she was just ignoring us. She'd do that sometimes when she was really into her experiments or busy with the ballet."

He cleared his throat, and I looked away, out into the forest as if saying the boy's name might conjure his specter in white.

"We didn't even know it was possible—she was divinely lucky. As long as she had her favor, it would take... I don't understand. You found her?"

"I did," I replied blankly. Ballerinas were known for our composure, our grace—we were never things to be pitied. Even when we fractured, we never fell apart; we kept dancing with a smile. I didn't feel like smiling though.

Though I came to ask who did it and how, if it could happen to me, instead I said, "Is it possible to *lose* Acheron's... favor? Like, could it be taken away?"

Andor studied me as if he could see through my words, and there was so much movement—flickering shadow—in his eyes, it made me nervous. He was far different from Joséphine and me, and I couldn't help but squirm, fisting the cuff of my coat until he finally relented. And frowned. "Well, we never tried it, but I suppose it's possible. Acheron's power is bound to our bodies through the mark; I can't say you'd still have yours if you lost your arm."

Which meant that burning it off left her vulnerable to anything.

I nodded thickly and turned away, trying to fit the pieces together. "Okay, thanks."

Beyond Ciro, there were a dozen people with countless reasons to kill Joséphine. Olivia, Vanessa, Rose-Marie. There was the spat with Auger, her blackmail, if Ciro could be believed. She'd eclipsed Sabine Simon and Nina Brossard on more than one occasion. Maybe she also stole her friend's spot at our prestigious ballet company and lied about it—

No, Coralie wouldn't do *that* to me. Especially because soon I'd make her an apprentice too when I put this behind me to focus.

But how many people knew to do something like burning off her mark?

"Before you go, will you stop by the river with me?" asked Andor as he fell in step beside me. He didn't notice how I leapt. "Just for a moment? I'm sorry, it's just—I've been thinking about you ever since the gala. What you did to Ciro."

My face flushed hot. Last week had been a momentary lapse of my perfect shell, a flash of anger that seeped through the crack and onto the nearest target. It was all instinct, no thought, and unbecoming for a prima ballerina. I raked a hand through my hair. "I should apologize, I wasn't thinking—"

He rushed closer. "No! Don't apologize. Ciro was being a dick. He deserved it."

And I eyed him warily as we descended, his eager smile, his dark lashes feathering his cheeks. But maybe in exchange for his curiosity, I'd get some answers of my own. "Okay. What do you want to know?"

At the end of our path, the river shimmered seductively. Like it was beckoning for me to wade in and let it consume me. My chest thrummed loudly in anticipation, its current running through me.

Andor clasped his hands behind his back, reinstating the arm's length between us. "Well, everyone's *gift* from Acheron is different, which is why I want to learn more. I . . . well, for me, it's complicated, but its favor doesn't always manifest in the way you'd expect. That *or* its consequences."

An understatement—I asked for the power to make others see me and now I controlled people's bodies and risked a nosebleed. And *he* transformed into a walking nightmare.

The river churned, frothing viscous red on dark sands and blood-stained rocks. It was a body sliced open for us to venerate. And I stood exactly where it all happened, what plagued my dreams when I closed my eyes at night: kneeling in the pool, begging and being dragged under, the lightning and the voice speaking from my bones, dizziness as Andor hauled me to safety with gore saturating his hair. He was still imposing then as he was now—the blood on his skin, the clot clinging to his antlers, as if he was a fearsome hunter who haunted these woods. The hairs on my arms stood on end. That pull of thread from my spine tightened.

"Will you try it on me?"

It took all my strength to pull my gaze from the hypnotic rapids. "What?"

Andor gestured to himself, stretching the fabric of his shirt that opened at the chest just a little. "Direct it at me. Here, now, I want you to compel me."

"To do what?" I laughed with disbelief. Who *wanted* to lose control of themselves?

"I don't know," he said, shrugging, with a smile that mirrored mine. "Name every species of tree in the world, go for a swim, dance the Swan Queen—"

I scoffed. "You can't dance Odette. Do you know how long it takes to—"

"It's just a test."

Slowly I nodded and tried to focus on seizing control. Of every suspicious glare, every doubt thrown my way while I had to be perfect. Perfect and never recognized for it. Hiding in a closet afraid, forgetting I had power now. I was more than just Laure—I took divinity into my veins, and that divinity demanded respect. Not to be underestimated and laughed at. The command was already bubbling up.

Bow to me, your new god.

Andor went still.

I wasn't sure if it was really me or the river then, screaming on the banks and encouraging me to give in and do my worst. And it was always so tempting to be worse.

His jaw clenched, the muscles from his throat to his exposed collarbone straining, fists tight at his sides. He was rigid, not even breathing, because he was fighting it. Fighting me. Even as his shoulders inched forward and his foot slid back, he resisted more than anyone had. Blood rolled from both nostrils across his lips.

Then the tension snapped, and Andor doubled over with a shuddering breath, sinking his knees into the sand. Head hanging low, he bowed to me, by giving in and letting me win. My eyes widened.

"That…" Breathing heavy, he swayed back on his heels and wiped the blood from his chin, smearing it along the back of his hand. "…was amazing."

I uncurled my toes and stared down at him.

"Laure, I felt you in my veins. You felt…inevitable. I bet it's because you went in before. You took more than usual." Instead of scared or angry, he sounded impressed. And when he glanced up, finally meeting my gaze, my stomach flipped. His face had changed under duress— though the antlers and blood-toned skin were still hidden, all four eyes locked onto me, the whites of them gone, and the teeth in his grin grew long and wolfish. Here he was, terrifying, yet so enthralled by what *I'd* done.

Just like Joséphine laughing, applauding when he transformed: acceptance in spite of the horror. Or because of. I wanted to both run away and have him tell me more.

"What does it feel like, controlling people?" asked Andor, and he looked so eager to know that for a moment I would have given him everything just so I could share it with *someone*.

My mouth opened and closed, working back to my lapse with Ciro. The gala. Dinner with the Baumés. Auditions. Even a class with Demaret. There was always a cocktail of emotions stirring in me, but mostly...I was angry. Even now. All the time. At the way people looked at me, what they said, how easily they dismissed me. Reduced me to nothing. I had enough rage to go around.

But rather than risk that honesty making me appear petty or vengeful, I gnawed the inside of my cheek and countered, "How come your nose bled this time instead of mine?" Then I reached to help him to his feet, only to recall the pins and needles when his skin brushed mine at the gala and stop.

"Maybe you don't know your own strength." Andor drew himself up to his full height without taking notice of my aborted effort and shrugged. "You'll get better at wielding it with time, I'm sure. And I'd love to help too, if you need it."

As if I had several weeks, months, years to spare. It had already been days—a week—since I found Joséphine, and her killer was no closer to being caught.

"And how come you and Ciro get to fight it? No one else does."

He maintained his devilish grin, even as his fangs shrank and dulled and the extra eyes melted away to leave only smooth skin. There was sinister beauty to the gleam in his gaze and the curve of his mouth, crafted to appear warm and inviting where Ciro was cold and unforgiving. A predator in both his forms. "Because we're like you—with Acheron's favor, we aren't just merely mortal anymore."

At his start, we turned from the river, climbing back up the slope toward the cottage and the forest beyond, where reality waited behind the door. And torn between eagerness to leave and fear of what more I'd find on the surface, I let my pace linger and studied him. With his sleeves down, it was impossible to glimpse his mark, and as he moved, tree branches and wildflowers along the path leaned toward Andor. As if all the forest was caught in rapt attention. He held his chin up and walked with his broad shoulders back, oblivious to his sway over the world, but in a softer way than Coralie. Like he'd earned their deference through gentleness alone.

"So what, you can just turn into a monster? That's your thing?" For all that transpired, I couldn't hide my smile. His easygoing manner, his bright disposition even after I'd made him kneel, the wildness of him—it all disarmed me.

"If you're wondering what my favor is, I'd asked for beauty," he offered in a way that said there was much more to it.

I knew it. Under the red sky's glow, he was attractive, the highlights and shadows easing all the angles of his face, and the affability made it easy to forget he was something *made.* Not natural. He asked for beauty, but then it also made him a monster.

"It was a mistake—I wanted someone's attention years ago, Ciro had already made his deal for money by then, and well, things aren't always what you expect them to be."

"What about the other river? Lethe? What are those people like?" I forced myself to keep straight ahead instead of craning back for a glimpse of Acheron's pale twin.

"There are none," Andor explained, his voice low and warm,

soothing. Surely he understood the effect he had on others. "Or rather, we've never heard of them. I don't even know if there's a source outside of Elysium to be found. Not like Acheron, who found a tear in this world and crawled through."

I nodded though I didn't understand, the exhaustion in my body calling while his words swirled aimlessly in my thoughts. All of it was dizzying, too much to make sense of and know what to do with. "So the river just gives us whatever we ask? Why?"

"To sow chaos? Must everything that exists have a reason?" He shrugged, like it didn't matter to him at all what our mysterious benefactor wanted. Like the primordial thing lurking inside him was negligible.

"You're strange," I murmured, not intending to say it aloud, and unsure if it was a good thing or not.

Andor threw his head back and laughed anyway. It was light and airy, like music, provoking a trilling sensation in my chest that I tried desperately to suppress. "Need help getting back?"

"No, I—"

A figure in white darted out from the trees and into the high grass, like a fox after prey. We turned and watched, the smile on Andor's face fading until his mouth was a grim line.

Ciro hurried toward the cottage, a hand pressed to the back of a tall woman to urge her along. Her light-colored afro stood stark from her smooth sable skin and grungy black clothing. She glanced around, the confusion on her face made plain.

"Not again," breathed Andor before leaving me there to bound after them.

I stood rooted in place, forced to remember when no one else would that beyond this river, this place, Joséphine was dead. Rather than grieving, Ciro was *here* with another woman, and if the blood down her front and on her hands meant anything, he'd just finished recruiting another one of us to replace her.

"Nice of you to finally join us, Laurence," Ciro quipped as I scurried through the gate, though his voice was tight. He led the woman into the cottage, which looked far older than any of us, the wood battered and worn with weather and time. Inside, the furnishings were a mismatch of secondhand collections and antiques crowding the shelves and tables.

Andor vanished into the back.

"Who is this?" I asked, heart racing in my ears, following Ciro and the woman into the living room. I was afraid of the answer, of the blood, but I needed to know what it meant. To hear him say it.

"Meet Keturah Whiting, a friend," he pronounced, giving her a stiff smile that didn't reach his eyes. When Andor returned with a bowl of water and a cloth, Ciro offered it to her, and either my eyes deceived me, or his hands were shaking. "The latest of Acheron's children. Excuse me."

I inhaled sharply, while Andor dragged Ciro out of the room by his collar.

The woman smiled while she washed her bloodstained hands. Her afro was not just light but dyed a very toxic shade of yellow, arranged in a neat mohawk and shaved on both sides. She wore some faded shirt of an '80s rock band and baggy overalls, and rings looped through either side of her bottom lip, spikes jutting out of the bridge of her nose. Her arms were covered in tattoos: tribal and traditional, hearts lanced with safety pins and lightning bolts, skulls with spider legs. I couldn't see her river's mark, but I didn't doubt that it made itself at home.

"Did Ciro help you too?" she said in a high British accent, brown eyes feverishly bright. "I don't know what I would've done without him—"

I pressed a hand to my mouth and turned on my heel. I was going to be sick.

In the hall, Ciro's voice was low and insistent. "Please understand that I had to, okay? It kept saying it wanted her, and Keturah needed help—" He fell silent when he saw me standing there, staring.

"It's getting late," I mumbled, reaching for the door. "I should go."

Andor's brow wrinkled. "But—"

"I'll be in touch."

A lie.

Whatever they were into, it was much bigger, much worse than ballet hierarchy. The recruiting, the dazed girls covered in blood, this place called Elysium—whatever it was—got Joséphine killed, and I'd have no part in it.

All that mattered to me was dancing, and as I fled into the woods, back through the iron door and into the tunnels, I vowed to mind my own business.

CHAPTER 13

On Monday, I dressed my best for the first day of rehearsal. The leotard and soft ribbed wrap, the tights and leg warmers—all in the color of dusted rose that turned my hickory complexion as warm as a kiss. When I walked through the doors, the thicket of dancers, *my colleagues*, fixed me with a gaze that said I was an étoile in the making, glorious in my own right. And I hadn't even compelled them. Yet.

"This is such a good look for you, Laure," admitted Olivia begrudgingly.

Across the way, even Sabine watched me slack-jawed, and my head swelled with vindication as I denied her a glance.

"I just felt like dressing up today," I lied, adjusting my perfect bun, carefully curled into a uniform, sleek pattern. Little did anyone know how much I'd tossed and turned last night, tormented by dreams of a blood river, a white fox, and the dead woman's phone ringing in the dark. Between covering the tattoo on my arm and the dark circles from restless nights, I was blowing through concealer.

In truth, today we were vying for parts as yet another troupe of dead girls in *La bayadère*, and I was going to do everything to stand out. Just seeing the schedule reminded me of that man from the board and put me on edge, but I'd still stayed up late the previous night learning the choreography. Thanks to the worship of Marius Petipa, a deity in the ballet pantheon, it rarely changed from production to production.

I gave the room my modest ballerina smile, crossed my ankles, and dipped into the perfect curtsy. Feigning humility was one illusion we excelled at, as easy for us as breathing—taking gracious, delicate bows as if everything I was didn't require eight-hour days for years on end, unbridled obsession, an endless supply of tapes and creams, a dash of masochism, and praying to a dark god with an oath of blood. And my only ally dead.

My throat bobbed at the memory of Joséphine's body, and I pushed it away. I was good at pretending, better than most.

It had occurred to me that I could simply compel President Auger into a promotion. But just like with Joséphine's successes, I knew it wouldn't make my colleagues understand my superiority. I couldn't even get Coralie, my best friend, to congratulate me. Instead of well-wishes, the others would only meet my ascent behind closed doors with suspicion, so instead, I had to prove that I was better in a slow conquest. I planned to wear them down starting now, leaving Elysium and that mess behind me.

As Joséphine had said, it wasn't divine intervention or smoke and mirrors that made me better—it was practice. Grit woven into the tapestry of my person.

A short, thin Russian woman with acid-blond hair and blunt bangs marched into the studio.

"'Kingdom of the Shades,' right?" Yelena Ivanova barked as she dropped her bags at the front of the room. She was Grandpré's star assistant, with the same deep scowl honed to perfection, and her voice carried well. "Welcome to the Himalayas. The scene calls for thirty-two girls, and if you count, there are thirty-four of you here. Everyone learns the choreography, and apprentices float from number to number to fill in gaps as needed. Understood?"

Olivia and Vanessa turned their focus on me. This began our standoff, assessing who would be chosen as the final shade, marking their official debut with the company. It wasn't a solo—just one of many in a very long act, mostly spent at the back, but it was the biggest professional production of the season, and a number where you had to match the others perfectly. More so, we technically weren't in competition anymore. The game was no longer to best each other but best ourselves, and if we weren't cast in this, there remained the lesser shows—*Roméo & Juliette*, *Petrushka*, and a series of contemporary pieces in this season alone.

So I bared my sharpest, most monstrous grin, which was enough to make Vanessa wince. Olivia turned away. This one was mine to take, to snag a visible role out the gate and show President Auger that I belonged. That the ballet needed me. Perhaps even remind Vanessa and Olivia that I was an apprentice too, one of them and worthy of a little kindness. That maybe I wanted some warmth by proximity.

I can compel them.

I gritted my teeth at the temptation. It'd be easy to make them beg for my friendship, my affection, have everyone tripping over themselves, clambering to my side, hands clasped in supplication.

But no, I wasn't that desperate. I was just lonely, used to having Coralie at my side. For the first time in years, we were really, truly apart. I was at lessons and exhausted when I came home, and she was out doing … whatever it was aimless rich girls did. And despite all she said before the gala, her absence still ached.

Yelena dived quickly into instruction, and I propelled myself from the barre and toward the front for a better view even though I already knew the steps. It was a simple but haunting number, starting with one lone ghost leaning forward in a slow and elegant arabesque and then sweeping back adage. All thirty-four of us moved like seaweed on the ocean floor, swaying forward on one bent leg while the other swept up straight behind us, and then spines arching back. Small steps to shift the line, and repeat.

"Think about your extensions, please!" she called before scanning over our group. "Now for progression—Nina, you'll take the lead.

Four groups of eight, and I guess the last group of alternates. Who else downstage?"

She began with the principals, since those closest to Nina would not only be the most visible but also have the most stage time as they entered soonest. And what better way to show I belonged than by dancing downstage near Nina Brossard, fresh from her tour with London?

Choose me, I commanded without hesitation. Without even thinking it, really. A shadow flickered across my vision as I narrowed on her, willed my intensity onto her, like a storm cloud invading the sky. **Invite me into the front row.**

The junior director's frown softened, the lines around her mouth and brow smoothing out as my order took hold. She pointed to me at number four, right behind Flora Silvestre, a sujet newly promoted following Joséphine's truancy who also danced her first Kitri to a full house's round of applause last year. Flora adjusted her strawberry-blond ponytail and looked me up and down like she might eat me. Her black pearl earrings caught in the light, familiar.

"Don't make me regret it," Yelena said sleepily before turning back to the others.

I fluttered into the line with my best ballet scurry, feet turned out and light on the balls, chest angled toward the makeshift audience. The placement wasn't official until they fitted me for an ivory tutu and I stepped onstage, of course, but it would get the director used to seeing me here. And since apprentices were never featured, always relegated to the back, no one could overlook my skill positioned front and center.

Olivia glowered in the mirror. Her lip curled in anger, as if where I stood was a personal slight against her. At her side, Vanessa rolled her eyes, and together they shuffled to the end of the line the way good apprentices should. I'd hoped they'd look at me with awe, endear themselves to me, but instead now I had to get even better at hiding my slippers. I wanted them envious, enraptured even. Not resentful.

My frown was cut short by Yelena's yelling again. "All right, ready!"

In front, Nina took her two steps and, for the entire room, showed what it meant to fill out the music. She extended every muscle along to the lilting melody. The song was slow, but she was in constant motion—when she arched back, she dragged her arms until it was only her fingertips left to reach, unfurling knuckle by knuckle. And then came her unhurried steps into a lean forward again. Aiko Watanabe, famously recruited from Nagoya based on her recording in the International Ballet Competition, followed, then Flora Silvestre, then me.

Like them both, I lifted my arms ahead of my run, and then I was stretching forward, copying Nina's pace. Luckily, I spent all my life imitating prima ballerinas. Careful to savor every note, every second, the length of every breath, the point of every toe. Each sequence of hers was perfect, no sign of fatigue or boredom, and so I approached every one of mine with precision too. Yelena walked the length of the studio, shouting her critiques and studying us all. Her eyes fell to Flora, and she mimed angling her shoulders. Then she looked at me . . . and moved on without a word. As good as an endorsement.

I smiled.

The procession continued until all the dead had taken over the studio, rocking on the current. We moved and breathed in unison, our arms and legs reaching the same height and sinking in the same sweep. An ocean of beauty. Not one, but part of a whole.

Finally Yelena thanked and dismissed us.

Back in the room's corner with my bag, I dabbed the sweat from my neck and chest with a towel. Ache burned in my thighs, back, sides, and arms from the repetition. At trying to be perfect every single time. It was easy to understand why "Kingdom of the Shades" was one of the most difficult corps pieces around—deceptively hard in its simplicity. Still, warmth effused through my skin at the sight of Nina's nod in my direction when she left. Flora threw a glance my way too.

I did it.

We trickled out slowly, me at the tail end and high on exhaustion. Like my head was full of air and this was all a dream.

This was what I was *meant* to be doing, not stumbling upon crime scenes, walking beside a blood river, or cloistered in some little room learning about Ciro's new acolyte. I was meant to dance until the pads of my feet burned and I felt so faint it could only mean I was alive—*this* was what I'd given everything for.

My promotion was so close I almost tasted it. Soon Coralie would be back by my side as an apprentice, the color returned to her cheeks, helping me figure out how to keep this momentum when I didn't need a bargain anymore. Because it wasn't Acheron's mark making me dance this way—I was god material long before it started. The others would come around soon enough.

I was floating down the ghostly halls when a voice rang through to me.

"Laure isn't a witch—she doesn't have the personality for it," someone complained just around the corner.

My steps slowed.

The voice was Vanessa's, infused with a jagged and bitter tone I rarely heard from her.

"You heard what Grandpré said—she's too uptight. Either she's cheating or everyone feels sorry for her because she's an orphan. But how long can she milk that tragedy?"

"I don't think she's actually an orphan. Coralie said her dad lives just outside the city," Olivia theorized, unaware that I was right here out of view, holding my eyes shut. She cut clear through the blood rushing in my ears. "He just doesn't like her, that's why he never comes to see her. It *is* a ploy so the ballet doesn't seem elitist after that article though."

Of course, the one accusing favoritism as to why the ballet was hemorrhaging talent. I leaned against the cold marble pillar and fiddled with my gold ring, squeezing my fist so tight the stone bit into my palm. The pain was grounding.

Vanessa snorted. "Something's *always* been off with her. There's no way she's that good."

But I was. Proven time and again. We all went through the same process, finished at the same academy. They just didn't like that I beat them.

"Don't know how Coralie slums it with her—"

I stepped out of the dark, fists clutching the straps of my bag, unsure if I'd hit Olivia or invite her to repeat it to my face. I bathed in their shock—the four other apprentices gathered around the balcony, wide-eyed, Geoffrey glancing warily between us.

This was what it meant to be a star: Vipers hid around every corner. But Joséphine never stumbled at rumors, so neither would I. In fact, she did one better by dancing her heart out every night to prove them wrong.

I breathed in and held steady despite the flush of warmth to my neck, despite tasting blood on the inside of my cheek, the fire in my veins. Buried beneath a ton of makeup, my mark screamed to be used, to show them just who I was. I wanted to have my rage felt.

Acheron has its own plans.

No, I wasn't its monster. It didn't control me. And I was better than them in all the ways that mattered.

Shoulders down, neck long, ballerina smile impenetrable, I brushed past, back into the light of the atrium. If I had to, I could make do without their acceptance—I'd be performing *La bayadère* within my first month. That was enough. I was enough, and they'd see.

Then Olivia snickered. The group rounded the balcony to descend the steps, laughing like it was a game and I wasn't a person at all. Just their entertainment. A *toy*.

So I snapped.

It was a rogue thought, fast and dark with too much feeling behind it, and suddenly my will was reaching for her blood. With a single hunger and gritted teeth, I made her hurt too.

A shout tore through the atrium as something—*someone*—clattered down the stairs.

Gasps followed, faces, including mine, darting out over the balconies on all sides to glimpse what happened. Olivia lay on her back, whimpering on a landing, clutching her arm to her chest. Her cries drifted up like a song, tasting sweet and soothing my aches. The tension in my muscles faded a little. My fingertips prickled and my eyes stung with euphoria. And though I knew I shouldn't have, I even breathed easier.

In the wall's mirror, I still smiled. Soft, elegant, and so very refined, like an étoile should be. Like Joséphine was and I was soon to become. I was looking at the dream in real time, everything I wanted to be within reach.

And then the dream split.

A long spiderweb of a crack spiraled from my face's reflection, stretching the full height of the mirror and making me flinch. So it took a moment to look past the fractures and notice my irises had changed— bloodred spots grew and grew, until all the brown was encircled. Until my eyes were ringed in crimson. It took a moment to register the pain too. That my fists were smarting from my nails, which had sharpened, elongating to claws until they pierced the skin of my palms. Blood gathered in both hands and dripped onto the clean marble floor.

I wasn't becoming like Joséphine at all, I was becoming like Andor. A monster.

CHAPTER 14

Another restless night and fitful morning class left me on edge. Olivia's fractured collarbone and the reflection waiting for me afterward had managed to worm their way under my skin, into my thoughts, near impossible to shake. I left Madame Demaret's studio needing to do something, move *toward* something.

Break something.

The bell over the door to the office rang when I entered, and my racing heart slowed a little to see we were alone.

The ruddy-cheeked woman with frizzy, gold hair who always manned the front desk was humming to herself. She was obscured by a wide computer screen and a small army of nutcrackers, but at the sound of the bell, she leaned to the right and smiled.

"Laurence, what can I do for you today?"

At the front of her desk sat a golden nameplate that read Isabel Gorces, and today, she'd planted a smiley sticker on the small *o*. I was still in my leotard, tights, and sweatpants, my stench probably warring with the frankincense pumping out of her humidifier.

My anxious fingers with freshly trimmed nails picked at the loose thread on the end of my wrap sleeve. Olivia's fall had awakened some eager hunger in me, and now my nerves were all live wires that wouldn't calm. This, at least, was a harmless idea, monstrous in a small way that could sate it. Sate me. A heavy pressure built against the base of my spine, threatening to send me careening over. It was like a joint that needed to pop. It wanted more.

I wanted more.

"**Madame Gorces**," I started, using the most syrupy voice I could manage.

The woman hesitated. Her half-formed smile went rigid, while a shadow ascended from the depths of me. It crackled in the air like ozone. The woman's eyes, a sea-tinted green, widened a little. Her hands, once clenched on her desk, loosened.

"Yes?" Gorces whispered like a prayer.

The lightning rippling through my veins rose to a crescendo as I threw a glance behind me nervously, sure that there was no one else to see. I stepped closer, feeling my smile harden, the mark on my arm itching. This was it.

"Do you have the clearance to change an employee's pay? **I think Laurence Mesny deserves a raise for her hard work.**" My words were as strong as iron and as rich as chocolate when they bound her to me. No room for escape.

The woman nodded slowly and turned to her screen. Clicking and typing slowly. "How much of a raise?"

I glanced at the window, where outside, cold rain pelted the sidewalk and sent tourists running for cover. The city became so grey and hostile in the later months, and that was when I felt most at home. "Another five hundred—no. Let's double it. **Effective immediately.**"

Gorces keyed in the value and went back to clicking. I shifted weight from one foot to the other, waiting. Then my beaming turned to a grimace.

A bead of blood ran from her ear. One long, dark line starting from the canal and catching on her dangling silver earring. It looked like a fresh piercing. Like the blood from Andor's nose and mine. Like the classmate who rushed out after my audition, pinching her face.

You'll get better at wielding it with time, I'm sure.

My shoulders stiffened despite Andor's voice in my head, his misplaced confidence in me. It soured the taste of victory. How could he be so sure when he didn't know anything about me? What if I was out of control and this was yet another thing to worry about?

I cleared my throat, pulled a tissue from a nearby box, and offered it to her. "You have a little something there…"

Without a word, she swiped at both ears and balled the bloody tissue in a trembling fist. The unscrupulous nature of her motions was unsettling. Inhuman. When she looked at me, her green eyes flickered unsteadily, the pupils blown wide. Unfocused.

I shivered.

The receptionist smiled blithely. "All done. Can I help you with anything else?"

It took several tries to find my voice, to back away and push the door open, to say with the same heavy tone, "**Forget I was here**."

And then I hurried into the hall, quick steps carrying me toward the cacophony of the tourist areas. Rounding a corner, I collided with a warm wall of clean linen perfume.

With President Auger.

The old woman yelped, and I stumbled back, stretching my sleeve over my wrist just in case she sensed how it hummed now that it was plump and well-fed. She only studied me in surprise. I was sure my pulse was audible.

"Hello, President Auger."

She inclined her head in greeting. "Laurence. How are you adjusting so far?"

"It's great," I chirped, voice a little too high and loud, rubbing the back of my neck so hard the skin stung. "I'm learning so much already."

"Yes, I just had a chat with Yelena over *La bayadère*—she's very impressed with you. You've come a long way from the young ruffian with a little chip on her shoulder that I met years ago."

Now not so young and with an even bigger chip. And considering what I just did, still a ruffian, I supposed.

Nonetheless, I blushed, face burning at the nicest thing the president had ever said to me. She rarely deigned to give encouragement, compliments, making this tantamount to a kiss on the brow.

"Thanks. I want to show everyone what an asset I can be, how dedicated I am. Maybe even get promoted early."

Auger released a thoughtful sigh. "Maybe even free up a spot for a friend?"

I blinked rapidly.

"It's possible, but a word of advice? Be mindful of the lengths you go for the sake of ambition and loyalty. Others come and go, but you cannot escape yourself. You wouldn't want to end up like Joséphine."

And then she was on her way, and I was on mine, wondering what the hell that meant. It sounded like a threat. Or a confession.

I found Coralie where she always lurked when she was in a mood, sitting on the marble stairs near the opera's library. It was housed on the west side of the opera with narrow two-tiered corridors full of yellowed scores, worn libretti, and a rich collection of dusty, musty-smelling cloth-bound books. I fought my way around huddles of people squinting through glass displays of faded personal letters, and there, down in the belly of the exhibition, Coralie sat alone. She rested her forehead on her knees, tapping a languid foot to a song playing from the speakers. My tattoo hummed from what I could only assume was a high from my new raise.

"Never imagined you were a fan of"—I squinted at the mounted screen as I dropped beside her—"Saint-Saëns."

She stopped moving and raised her head to glance at me. Broken blood vessels had turned the bags under her eyes deeper purple, and even in the muted light, she was a little gaunt. She lowered her head again listlessly.

"Did you know, in his early years, he had a reputation for celebrating his contemporaries?" she mumbled. "Back then, they considered it uncouth to enjoy modern music, but he loved Schumann, Liszt, Wagner. He promoted them constantly."

"I did not."

She sniffled. "It changed as he got older. Newer composers and their cheap tricks started getting popular. He looked washed-up, and the shiny new boys replaced him—Debussy, Stravinsky, and even Fauré, his own student. Gone. Forgotten."

I cleared my throat and looked around. "Cor, you're sitting in the middle of his *exhibition*. His framed portrait is staring at us right now."

And that brought out a smile, still aglow even at her lowest point. A little longer, and I'd lift her out of it for good.

"I have a lot of free time now to learn about composers," she added, wrapping her arms around her torso, "since you're always unavailable. What do you want?"

I miss my best friend, I wanted to say. But that sounded needy. Weak. Nothing like the Laure she knew and loved, the vulture.

"I've come to entice you with some shopping."

I thought of Olivia flouncing her jeweled hairpins in class, the way everyone flocked to Vanessa's new leotards, how they finally looked my way. If everyone respected shiny new clothes and jewelry, and *I* had shiny new money, why not take advantage and bring my pitiful friend with me?

Coralie's green eyes glimmered. "Is that so?"

Weaving my arm through hers, I pulled her to her feet and through the gallery. She came willingly.

"I want some new leotards, we never spend time together any-more, and you could use a pick-me-up," I explained, dancing around any mention of Joséphine, Elysium, Auger, Olivia, and *La bayadère*. If it was pretty fabric that gained acceptance, I could do that. With my *real* friend by my side. "Also, are you okay? You look really ill. Do you have the flu?"

Her forehead was cold when I pressed my palm to it, and she shook me off. When we hit the fresh air of Rue Scribe, she pulled her coat tight. "Just haven't been sleeping well. So, where did you have in mind?"

I nodded up the street to where the lights of shops were already flashing, the sidewalks overflowing with people, cars congesting the intersection. "Les Galeries Lafayette since they're closest. I figure we can shop, have dinner, hang out."

Her feet slowed. "Here? Come on, you can find better stuff at Place Vendôme, *and* it's less crowded."

"Yeah, 'cause no one can afford it. You need handwritten invitations just to set foot in some of those places." I held her arm tight in case she tried to escape.

"But, but," she stammered, her lip puckering like a child's. "Next time I go with my mom, you can tag along—"

I walked faster, effectively dragging her with me. Only once had I ever gone shopping with her and Rose-Marie, and she didn't know it, but I found her mother and their wealth nauseating. Far worse than the feeling of being the only one to walk out of a store with full eyes and empty hands. "Let's go, Princess Coralie. I promise you won't catch anything from us peasants."

"Fine. For you and you alone, I would do anything," she groaned, relenting, trying and failing to hide her smile.

I didn't bother hiding mine.

We stopped first in a store full of lotions, and she drifted through the aisles smelling each one. Even while brooding. She screwed the cap off a tester and cringed. "So, what's the scoop?"

Most of me wanted to tell her about the compulsion. I wanted to spill every detail of the bargain and what it entailed, the videos, getting featured in "Kingdom of the Shades," my raise. But that meant talking about Joséphine. The secret was a weight around my neck, because if she knew, she'd march right into Auger's office, ruin everything, and never talk to me again, even when I had a plan to save her.

I could recruit her, whispered some dark part of me, *like Joséphine recruited me, like Ciro recruited all of us.*

But my stomach clenched that voice into silence.

"Is Vanessa still talking about *her brother-in-law, the prince*?" She imitated Vanessa's extreme vocal fry and rolled her eyes.

I snorted. "Wearing Rose-Marie's latest, of course."

"Of *course*," Coralie parroted back to me, looping her arm through mine as we left the store. "And what about you? The apartment's so empty lately. Where have you been sneaking off to?" She gasped and tightened her grip on me. "Are you seeing someone?"

The laugh that came out of me was loud and sharp. *If only.* "Keep dreaming."

After the creams, we made our way up to the second and third floors of the neighboring department store, glancing at all the coats and gowns and perfumes arranged like boxes of chocolates. For everything I pointed out, like the A-line gown of twinkling gold and delicate diamond wristwatches, Coralie wrinkled her nose in disappointment and went back to reporting on our classmates stuck auditioning in some smaller city or another.

I focused on the jewelry. Necklaces and earrings and dainty little bracelets weren't as showy as Vanessa's two-hundred-euro leotard, but they still drew the eye, brought the attention to perfect posture and gentle hands and prominent collarbones. Jewelry was an unspoken part of the ballerina's uniform—the right necklace could make even the roughest dancer look polished. Maybe haunt a creative director with how elegant I looked, how much I deserved that stage.

My hand froze over a string of black pearls.

Coralie arched her brow. "Everything all right?"

"Fine!" I settled on a rose-gold choker studded with small crystals instead.

It took all my effort to keep my tone cheery, smile light, even as the shop attendant showed me the choker's price tag. I bit the inside of my lip hard enough to draw blood, but it was so beautiful, and I had a raise coming. The saddest, most desperate part of me couldn't back down, knew how it would look if I refused.

I nodded to Coralie. "Want anything? My treat."

Her eyes darkened and lips warped into a sneer. "You know I don't wear *costume* jewelry."

And she spat the words loud enough for everyone to hear.

We watched each other for a long moment, the air tense with something unsaid, like there was more she was angry at than just midrange jewelry. Like, say, our roles being reversed, me treating *her* to something for once. Now I was the girl with everything, and she didn't like it.

The tattoo on my wrist throbbed. It would be effortless to make her keep her mouth shut and smile. It didn't matter if she *liked* these places, these things, so long as we played pretend. But then she chomped her teeth on that necklace from her mother—she was still fragile and hurting and lashing out. And what if I drew blood again?

So I backed down.

Things will be back to normal soon, I wanted to assure her, wishing she'd understand. But as I pulled out my card to pay, I thought of the slow, gentle music of "the Shades," the way it felt to breathe in time with the corps, how Andor gazed up at me with all four eyes gleaming when I made him bow by the river.

Maybe normal wasn't what I wanted after all.

I came home from shopping and a ramen dinner to find a bloodstained shirt on my desk.

My bloodstained shirt, the one I wore during the night out with Joséphine. The blood of the river had faded to brown and crusted. Nothing else in the room had been disturbed, however, no sign that anyone had come in at all. Just the shirt that sat there, mocking me.

On the other side of the wall, I heard Coralie flop onto the couch with a sigh and flick on the TV. Completely unaware that someone had broken into our house, and I was being threatened.

"Fuck," I whispered, surging forward.

I'd tossed that shirt in the trash along with the pants and coat and ruined shoes, and then flung that trash in the garbage chute to never be seen again. All the traces of my bargain—the bloodied clothes and Joséphine—were supposed to be gone. All except the mark. And now this.

Someone was taunting me. They *knew*.

My thoughts went quiet as I balled the shirt up and shoved it in a drawer with trembling hands. Trying not to panic. Joséphine and her monsters—I'd left them all in Elysium. My promotion was close, Coralie's revival imminent. We were too close—I couldn't fumble now.

I poked my head out into the living room to see Coralie's eyelids drooping, dozing already.

Perhaps it was nothing. Perhaps I missed it in the frenzy, and Coralie found and folded it for me. Perhaps she thought it was tie-dye or ink, some cool, funky thing. She would have said something if she thought it was blood.

Unless it wasn't her at all.

Reminded of the cold light in the basement, the intruder in Joséphine's apartment, I shuddered. The phone—

Eyes wide, I lunged. Dropped to my knees and wrenched my mattress up. Joséphine's phone still rested there on the slats where I'd left it. *Safe.* I sighed and sank to the floor, holding the phone to my chest like a buoy, waiting for my pulse to slow enough to place a call. *For now.*

CHAPTER 15

Coralie found me after class, once I'd changed into my street clothes and was heading out. I was on edge from the bloody shirt, growing claws, everyone's apparent indifference to losing an étoile, and that stinging, burning, itching mark on my wrist. After bleeding a receptionist and sending Olivia down the stairs, I wasn't sure anymore who was in control: me or the sliver of Acheron nesting in my blood. Which of us sent Olivia tumbling? It grew less clear every day where I ended and the wicked darkness inside of me began.

And so I refused its constant temptations until I met with Andor to be sure. No clearing a path through the endless crowds, no silencing cat-callers perched in building shadows, not even compelling Madame Demaret to notice me in morning class. In my refusing anything, the mark—or my own wickedness—craved everything: free pains au chocolat at the bakery, forcing Coralie to put her dirty socks away, demanding Grandpré change his putrid cologne. Everything and everyone became a problem to be fixed, and I rolled my neck, cracked my knuckles, and twisted my ring to keep it at bay.

I was so preoccupied that I didn't notice her calling until Coralie's cool, clammy hand caught my arm.

"Didn't you hear me?" she asked with a smile, zipping her jacket around her bony shoulders.

Stifling a yawn, I shook my head. "Sorry, I was distracted. What's up?"

Coralie blinked expectantly. "It's Friday."

Together we stood in the middle of the atrium, staring at each other and listening to the murmurs of tourists trickling through, their shuttering cameras and tapping shoes. Until finally it dawned on me.

I closed my eyes and swore.

On Fridays, Coralie and I got kebabs from a shop on Rue d'Alésia. It was a tradition we'd held since our earliest academy days, even when we didn't rehearse together, even when we were sick, no matter what.

"I…"

I looked at my best friend. Her curls were frizzy and almost desiccated, in the same ponytail I'd glimpsed in passing all week, and along with the dark circles under her eyes and the pronounced collarbones jutting out of her jacket, she looked sickly. Pitiful. Even the chandeliers' glow didn't help her pallor.

While I was in class and rehearsals, she spent her days sulking around the opera, apparently memorizing details in the Saint-Saëns exhibition or watching set design in the amphitheatre. And then she probably sulked at home, I assumed, during my evening rehearsals or when I ran around uncovering dead ballerinas and sneaking into Elysium. Our time together was growing less and less. And now I was blowing her off.

After her outburst in the jewelry store and how hard it was to stop myself from compelling her, I wasn't looking forward to being face-to-face alone so soon, but I didn't intend *this*.

Her expression collapsed in my silence.

"You have plans," she surmised flatly, gaze dropping to my wrist. My tattoo. "With someone else."

I adjusted my sleeve subconsciously. "I completely forgot…"

"Who is it?"

My mouth clamped shut. Because of her jab about me mugging

tourists at the gala and telling Olivia about my father's visit, Coralie could no longer be trusted with secrets—not that Andor was a secret. There just wasn't any way to explain him without explaining Joséphine and Acheron too.

Coralie glowered. "It's fine. It's not like I'm your best friend or anything!" And when she realized that I wouldn't give in, she rolled her eyes. "I never get to see you. You never have time for me. It's not like I wouldn't drop everything for you if *your* whole world fell apart! It's all so easy for you—"

I didn't have time for this.

For *her*.

"Cor," I sighed, my exasperation stunning her to quiet, "I can't. I'm meeting my dad, and I'm late."

And with the shock of that lie on my tongue, I turned on my heel and hurried down the steps and out the door.

Since I was first to arrive at the bistro, I settled under a heat lamp at an outdoor table and delved back into Joséphine's files. I had struggled to find any mention of red eyes and claws the past few nights, no sign that Joséphine ever encountered the problem of turning into a monster at all, but there were still so many folders I hadn't covered. And this was better than thinking of Coralie's face, the hurt and anger in her eyes, how much I was lying because I was too much of a coward to tell her the truth.

There were only so many times I could tell myself that I was also doing this for her before I questioned if it was really true.

I tapped into a document titled THINGS I "STOLE," and the list inside made me straighten in my seat.

La Esmeralda *(?), debut in Ivanova's* Cosmic, *that modern piece choreographed to* The Planets *by Holst (Aiko Watanabe?),* Cinderella *(Sabine Simon),* Pointe *magazine cover and spread (Nina Brossard), étoile nomination (Sophie Poullain), athletic-wear sponsorship (Alain Cornillon), interview in* Télérama *(Ciro Aurissy), original Cézanne nature morte (Andor Delestrade), coin toss (Ciro Aurissy), coin toss (Ciro Aurissy), coin toss (Ciro Aurissy)*

Joséphine kept a list of everyone her bargain had screwed over. It was here on the drive among Thomas d'Aquin writings, every lucky thing to fall into her lap and who she suspected Acheron had taken it from. On the next page were more question marks, things she couldn't attribute to a name: the last vintage wine, concert tickets, promotional bookings at resorts, limited edition gowns.

Because that was, she theorized at the end, how her deal worked: others went without so that Joséphine was fed. Acheron's reach was nebulous, and it all stretched back more than a year. She'd harbored this secret for a *year* while I barely skimmed the surface with my few weeks.

Any name on this list would have a reason to kill her, with or without knowledge of Acheron. The burned-away tattoo might've just been an accident, and I was in the clear.

It went on:

Everything comes from something. Everything exists in balance—Ciro's money doesn't just appear from thin air (otherwise the value would drop, no?). 4 June, lawsuits force company A to go under; 5 June, one of Ciro's investments pays out early. But who did company A steal from first? Why is their theft any more palatable than Acheron's rearrangement? In my case, I don't think anyone is entitled to nice bags, magazine shoots, and solo roles—they are simply things the world never intended people like us would have.

Even Chaos has rules. To receive, we must be willing to take. To win, you must be willing to fight. To drink in life itself, you must be willing to bleed. And there will be blood.

I pressed the heels of my palms into my eyes.

If everything Joséphine had, she took from others, what did I take? How was my turning into a monster balancing anything?

A brusque wind whipped down the street. Then they caught my eye—Andor and Keturah, parting ways across the street. They looked formidable as a pairing, both tall and breathtaking, made in earthy hues of brown and black. Keturah's denim coat was studded and covered in patches that earned her glares as she nodded to Andor and headed down the boulevard. And Andor stepped into the crosswalk, smiling.

Perfectly on time.

Jealousy spiked in me, curious to know where they'd been, what they'd done. I swallowed the foreign bitterness down with espresso and waved in greeting.

"Thanks for meeting me."

Andor slid the vintage coat from his broad frame and sank, full of poise, into the seat opposite. The movement blanketed our table in the scent of autumn leaves after a downpour. "I'm happy you called. I don't make it aboveground much anymore."

Right. The monstrous boy lived in the woods of Elysium.

As he perused the menu, I asked in spite of myself, "Was that... Keturah I saw?"

Cool Keturah who calmly accepted her fate with Acheron, nonchalantly cleaning blood from her hands and face after what I'd thought was a traumatic, disorienting ordeal. I didn't know anything about her, not enough to actually dislike or even distrust her, but some wicked part of me wanted to try. Even as I wanted her to notice me, find me cool and well-adjusted too.

If it showed in my voice, he didn't notice.

He only tucked a curling lock of black hair behind his ear and nodded. "Yes, I ran into her on the metro. She's a bartender around here."

And of course she was a bartender and not something less interesting.

"So what did you want to talk about?" Finally he turned his full gaze to me, the gold rings in both his ears glinting just like the mortal remains of his sharp teeth.

I cleared my throat and looked away, steeling myself against the flutter of nerves in my stomach. "Any news on Joséphine, who did it?"

"No, nothing still." Andor frowned. "Ciro's looking on his own, but her phone is missing and—"

"When I found her, I saw something strange," I blurted out. "Her tattoo—Acheron's mark—had been destroyed. I think someone burned it from her arm. I didn't think it was important at first, but there's been . . ." I shuddered, reminded of that skin-crawling light in the ballet basement, the shirt on my desk, the secrets I held. "I need to know if there are enemies of Acheron, or people like us, anything that can lead back to me."

I realized how selfish I sounded the moment the words left my mouth—not concerned with Joséphine's killer being brought to justice but rather confirming they had no interest in *me* personally. But if I failed, then what was all of this for?

That shadow behind Andor's eyes shifted. "Did something happen?"

I shook my head quickly. "No, I'm just on edge and wondering."

His suspicion didn't recede, and my voice was so high that even I was surprised by the falseness in it. After a while, he answered, "Well, no.

Ciro and I haven't come across anything like that. We don't know who'd want to hurt Joséphine."

You don't know or Ciro *doesn't know?*

But if Joséphine wasn't killed for her ties to Elysium, then she was killed over something personal, and there was a list of suspects burning in my pocket. Too bad I couldn't surrender the phone yet. Not until I'd scoured everything, until I became who I was meant to be.

"Okay," I sighed, clasping my hands on the table. "The main thing I wanted to ask was about the ... side effects. Is there a way to avoid them?"

I could tell by the darkness glinting in his gaze again that this captured Andor's interest. His eyes were a black cat's tail, flicking to reveal his moods, and I was beginning to pick up on it. He leaned close, his wild scent filling my nostrils. "Side effects? You mean the nosebleeds?"

For a moment, the receptionist's bleeding ears turned vivid in my head. The blood on my fingers at the gala. Andor by the river. Such small sacrifices compared to what followed, like Olivia, losing my sense of control. Ballerinas were supposed to be the masters of such.

Inhaling, I revealed my palms and the pink, freshly healed half-moons within. One subtle benefit of Acheron in my blood was how quickly my blisters, cuts, and scrapes healed. That vanishing gash the night of my first deal was the start. Now my arms and legs were no longer mottled with daily bruises like a dancer's should be. Before every mirror, I caught myself staring, so unused to being so blemish-free.

"These are from claws that grew when I got angry. I don't think I'm in control, and I can't dance if I'm like this."

If I'm like you.

Remarkably, Andor's expression remained open, unassuming. *Gentle.* Somehow he was now the only one to know some of my secrets. And as much as having this conversation frustrated me, made my heart race and my palms sweat, my blood also reveled in the focus of his attention. The lack of judgment on his monstrous, handsome face.

"Acheron can slowly change you if you let it," Andor admitted softly.

So I was the opposite of Joséphine: I seized the power to strike Olivia down and ceded some of myself as payment. My humanity was the cost.

"Is that what happened to you?"

The corner of his mouth twitched in answer. A deep purple flower blossom appeared between his fingertips, and he twisted its stem. Thin petals brushed against his skin. "There are counterweights to your favor, something to balance the universe, but there are also counterweights to your reliance on Acheron, and those are not always the same thing."

My brows knit partially at what he said, and also at the flower—where did it come from? It was so beautiful and delicate, twisting round in hypnotic circles. Distracting me from the fact that he hadn't answered my question *again*, was saying something without ever *saying* it.

"The more you offer to Acheron," continued Andor, "the more like it you become. I offered a lot."

Do you regret it?

A question I had no right to ask because there were times—like the lying, the bleeding, the impulses—where my own regret was impossible to even consider.

Still, soaking in his presence as we sat in silence, remembering how he'd knelt before me, grinning as he wiped the blood away, his laugh by the river, I blushed. Whether it was his charm or the slice of Acheron in his blood, I didn't know which had drawn me to him. Made me *trust* him—though had he really earned it? That was more dangerous than any creature he became.

The blossom at his fingertips, the gentle way he held it and spoke and moved through the world—those weren't the actions of a monster. I knew inhumanity better than anyone, and it didn't look like him.

So because I was running on fumes, and I couldn't do this alone, I chewed my lip and asked, "Will you help me? Learn to control it?"

The flower at Andor's fingertips stopped twirling. And face blank, eyes widened, he stared at me, my bloody lip, the flush in my cheeks down to the rose-gold choker at my neck and the nervous bob in my throat. He read *everything*, weighing my offer against...something. His own reluctance, my attitude.

"That is, if you're open to it!" I followed up, the words running together. "I don't want to be a burden—"

But then he grinned, wide and bright, flashing inhuman cuspids I was glad no one else noticed but me, shadow flickering in the blacks of his eyes like a flame. He looked more primordial than mortal even now, wearing his human face, even though he didn't *act* like it.

"I'd love to," he answered, and my silly, shallow heart leapt. "And tomorrow, we're all meeting in Elysium. To say goodbye to Joséphine. You should come."

Reflexively, I almost said no, because the last thing I wanted was to wade deeper into Joséphine's mess.

Because the Laure I knew, the Laure I *was*, didn't care about anything or anyone other than the ballet and getting ahead.

Because I didn't know if I belonged anywhere else, among anyone else.

Instead, the strange new boldness in my body met his eyes, his smile, and nodded gingerly. "Sure, what time?"

CHAPTER 16

There was a black garbage bin propped in front of Joséphine's open locker when I entered the dressing room. The slip of paper with her name on it, decorated with glitter and hearts, lay on the floor by the door, and I had to step over it to reach my things.

They were scrubbing the ballet clean of her.

The room was empty. Whoever was responsible for erasing her had stepped out for another job or a smoke break or whatever, so it was just me, her things, and the disparity. She was an étoile, she was supposed to be immortal. That's what they promised us: If we surpassed premiers, we would never die.

Yet every trace of her was headed for the trash.

Still inside her locker were spare leotards on hooks, but all the fabric was slashed to ribbons and sullied with footprints. Lipstick smeared the walls. When I reached for a lightly worn pointe shoe on the shelf, broken glass trickled out.

I turned to my own locker and got changed.

None of it made sense: Joséphine should have been everything they wanted. She was thin, white, beautiful, diligent. She did whatever the directors asked of her. So why wasn't it enough?

My thoughts went around and around like this as I rode the metro across the Seine and descended into the tunnels, conjuring ways that Joséphine had failed and how I was better suited to succeed. Maybe she got too comfortable and forgot that she could fall. Maybe she didn't appease the right people. But thanks to the costume fitting for *La bayadère* and being in my head, I was late for the vigil, so I almost missed the cursing up ahead.

"Hello?" a voice asked in the dark, feminine and gentle and in British English.

I halted so suddenly my feet slid on loose rock. "Keturah?"

The young woman sighed. I waved my phone's flashlight as her footsteps grew nearer, waiting until fluorescent-yellow hair in cornrows made an appearance. She grinned and squeezed my arm like we were familiar. My skin flushed at the contact.

"I'm lucky you came when you did," Keturah said with a laugh, "or I'd be in here all night. There should be markings, yeah?"

I only shrugged and started down the corridor. I didn't have easy words to explain how I didn't need markings, not in English, and certainly not with the pull that Elysium gave whenever I entered the Catacombs. And if she couldn't feel it, that hum in her own marrow, that only made my connection with Acheron more worrisome.

"Laurence, right?"

"Laure," I mumbled, racking my brain for something to say. The Catacombs stretched for miles underground, and the walk to Elysium's door would take several minutes at least. With my American mother so far out of reach, I didn't use the language often either. "So, how do you know Ciro?"

Keturah snorted. "I met him through Joséphine, actually. She used to come to my work, and we became mates. You?"

"Ballet." And I tried not to analyze how it came out a whisper, how quickly I wanted to change the subject. "I hear you're a bartender?"

"I *was* a bartender," she said, filing her fingernails along the rough rock walls. "Before that I was a tattooer, and before that, a drum tech for the Bleeding Harpies—ever heard of them?"

I shook my head. Noise wasn't really my thing.

"Well, anyway, I quit today. I made a mess of things, so Andor's letting me crash in the spare bedroom while I figure out what's next." She shrugged.

Her tone was so clear and easygoing, unaffected as she recounted something that, if it were me, I'd struggle with. *Quitting* ballet? Changing careers thrice when she wasn't much older than me? I'd be devastated, not knowing where to go, what to do.

"What . . . what did you make a mess of?" I couldn't help but ask, my curiosity piqued.

She only sighed again. "Ex-girlfriend—she cheated on me, so I made a whole scene. My rotten love life was actually the last straw, why I came down here. To Acheron. To bargain."

I looked at her through the dark, the way my phone light illuminated her blue-black skin and soft features, her blank expression, her nails scraping rock.

It wanted her, Ciro told Andor. And how convenient it had something she needed.

"To feel no more pain, that's what I asked it," Keturah supplied without me asking, without trembling or stammering or cowering.

I couldn't share mine—it was a secret I held too close, too afraid of how ugly I'd seem. No one but a ballerina would understand. But here she was, unashamed of what she turned herself into. Of what she did for herself. And if we weren't in pitch-black tunnels, I might have stared at her in awe. I wanted to take her courage and bathe in it. Maybe in another life, I would have devoured her every move and then remodeled myself in her image.

My brows raised. "And? Did it work?"

"I hardly feel a thing, it's bizarre. Not heat, or cold, or fear—certainly not pain. It's like, I can remember emotion, but it's quite wonderful to have a break."

Keturah's laughter filled the tunnels as we reached the door, infectious, as I found myself smiling, thinking about the counterweights Andor had mentioned. She'd asked to have her pain removed, and Acheron took everything. Because it wanted her for something just like it wanted me. She didn't sound hollow or regretful either. No, she was only open, accepting in a way I wished I was.

Ciro and Andor were already gathered around the firepit when we stumbled through the trees. They watched us climb to the pergola, Ciro's dark brows raised at Keturah and me with pleasant surprise. Andor simply inclined his head in greeting, and I tried not to let my gaze linger on his comfortable recline, the way it made his shirt hang open, the fire's reflection dancing on the angles of his face.

"I'm sorry," I muttered into the silence as I tossed my things aside. Heat from the fire seeped under my collar. "There was a last-minute costume fitting, and I forgot about the schedule changes on account of the metro strikes—"

"It's all right," replied Andor as he refilled Ciro's little glass with yellow liquor. Grappa. "We're just glad you came."

I didn't return his smile as I sat down.

There were no other vigils, funerals, or ceremonies in Joséphine's honor, and no one mentioned anything about family at the ballet. Though I once thought she had the entire world at her beck and call, now in the wake of her death, I wasn't so sure.

With his vulpine poise, Ciro proffered a tray of fresh chaussons aux pommes, flaky turnovers fragrant with apple and cinnamon. He explained softly, "They were her favorite."

I didn't know if it was grief or guilt, but it made less and less sense that he killed Joséphine. Over what, coin tosses and an interview? Recruiting me like he recruited Keturah and Andor? *I warned you*, was the last message he'd sent her, but he could have warned her about anything: me, Acheron, President Auger, her killer.

I rushed to take a pastry. "So, how did you meet?"

Ciro sipped his grappa and winced. "At the ballet, *Le corsaire*. She was in the corps. I was bringing flowers to the lead—Sophie Poullain was her name—but Joséphine thought they were for her. *Insisted* they were for her." The corner of his mouth raised in a phantom smile.

Beside him, Andor poured his grappa drop by drop into the flames. Without looking up, as if he felt me watching, he said, "Ciro and I've known each other our whole lives. Our mothers were best friends who spent all their time together, so naturally his parents took me in when mine died. When he came to Paris looking for adventure, I did too."

They complemented each other well, striking a perfect balance between dark and light, warm and cold, wilderness and city. Like Coralie and me, I imagined. This could be us when the time was right.

Keturah flicked through a stack of Polaroids and flashed one of a rainy street corner, Joséphine in a short, tight dress with a wide grin, holding up a peace sign.

"Oh god, do you remember that night at La Tempête? We were at a nightclub, and some guy grabbed me on the floor. Joséphine smashed a hundred-euro bottle of champagne to his head. Beautiful form." Her voice was filled with admiration as she took another chausson. "No inhibition at all, but she was loyal."

This drew out Ciro's chortle, defrosting his exterior a little.

Beside the pastries, they'd decorated a table with Joséphine's things:

her large painted portrait, eyes focused, mouth grinning. There were old ballet programs, a green silk scarf, and more photos—her arms around Ciro and posed on a red carpet, craning up at Andor in admiration, smoking on an ivy-decorated balcony with Keturah. All of them warm memories crystallized by people with nothing to gain from her attention, who liked her as she was without a high cost of admission.

"Remember when I broke my arm?" Andor started, now swirling the drink he never brought to his mouth. "I still hear her voice reminding me she danced Aurora on two broken toes like it was a competition."

And they laughed, like the worst parts of Joséphine were just as worthy of acknowledgment, just as much a part of her as her greatest ballet feats and glossy hair. Being a ballerina meant hiding our sharp teeth and claws under pink ribbon and gentle movements, to only show the world perfection. But they were opening her up to the possibility of just being... a person. It should have been offensive, but it wasn't.

"Then again, she also brought me a corpse lily for my birthday," Andor added, eliciting a groan from Ciro.

"It was foul."

The evening carried on like this, with stories of Joséphine throwing fully clothed people into hotel pools and charming even the largest, sternest security guards for access and extra guests. They weaved tales of her wit and obnoxiousness in equal measure and spoke of her with a reverence that extended beyond the stage. Like she was one of them.

I didn't know what it was like to have friends outside of ballet, people who didn't care what position you held and how good you were. People who weren't your competition. What was there to talk about, to gather round for, if not battle? What was friendship and love without fighting?

Still, it seemed... nice, how my spine softened knowing there were no knives being sharpened for my back.

Somewhere after my second chausson aux pomme, everyone turned their attention to me conspiratorially. My hands froze, rooting through my curly, knotted hair to massage the crinkles from my bun, and I stared back.

"Will you dance for us?" Keturah asked, eyes hopeful, brows raised. "Ballet was such an important part of Joséphine, and you know it better than we do. It'd be a nice way to end the night."

I swallowed.

She gestured to the recesses of the pergola, where handheld drums and pan flutes and stringed instruments sat, most of them collecting dust and probably out of tune. "Ciro can play! Just one thing, please!"

Ciro raised his brows, the edge in his eyes softened to something close to tender. And the others, Keturah and her wily grin, Andor rising to a seated position, were urging. It was a celebration of everything that made Joséphine who she was, but only I danced ballet. In fact, it was because of her that I still danced.

So I stood. Sweat made my coat stick to my arms as I pulled it off, running through the list of choreography I knew. I hadn't stretched or prepared anything, wasn't wearing the right clothes or shoes, and "Kingdom of the Shades" would be in poor taste. Behind Andor I spotted a tambourine, and a plan formed in my mind immediately. He followed my lopsided grin and offered it to me.

"The first time I saw Joséphine dance was in *La Esmeralda*," I began. They watched as I kicked off my shoes and socks and descended the pergola into the high grass, the tambourine jingling with every step. Without the costume, backdrop, and onlooking cast, they needed me to set the scene. "After I saw her, I immediately learned this variation, going until my toes blistered and I had to crawl back to my dorm."

To my surprise, they laughed and smiled, transfixed. Even Andor. Even Ciro. And it took me a moment to find my place again. I sank into a side split that made my knee and hip pop to gather myself.

"Normally, I'd wear this beautiful red tutu, but you'll have to use your imagination. It's the grand celebration for the Fleur de Lys, marking her engagement, and the heroine Esmeralda is the entertainer. The star of the show within a show."

Eyes closed, I took a deep breath, and, with the raise of my shoulders, struck my pose. There could be no better send-off, no bigger thank-you and goodbye than if Joséphine herself had planted the tambourine here as a suggestion. I almost heard the two long, drawn-out notes carried through the breeze from the riverbed. As if even Acheron wanted me to dance. And that dulled my nerves and drowned out my racing heart to begin.

I rapped my hand against the tambourine and jutted it out before me. It rang through the air each time I leapt to my toes for a pose, crossed my ankles, and floated up again.

My body shed its chains as I moved.

The variation was a seduction in sound, a sensual piece far removed from the demure of Giselle and the precision of Kitri. This was the dance of an étoile with all the time in the world, and I returned to those late nights in the studio pretending I was her, heavy-lidded gaze to the mirror, filling out the music with a tambourine high over my head.

Watch me. The command was an instinct.

When I swung a leg up to kick it with my toes, the tambourine rattled, accompanying my arch into another pose.

Listen to my song.

Keturah gasped.

Forward, cross, up, cross, kick, cross, pose... The sequence repeated again and again. With my hair loose, the pirouettes were imprecise, volume from the humidity swarming my line of sight where I'd mark my place, but it didn't matter. Joséphine didn't need perfection. And they didn't either—tonight, they were my sycophants, soaking up whatever I gave.

Adore me.

I glided fast toward the pergola and posed long enough for them to applaud. Arms spread, a performer's smile, ready and assured for more. They beamed under the influence of alcohol, Acheron's enchantment, me. All one and the same.

The grass was soft against my legs as I swept around into an arabesque. Back leg high, on the toes, my spine arched as far as it'd go to fill the void in the music. It was a series of expansions and contractions, fluttering pas de bourrée with my toes digging in the dirt.

I kicked the tambourine, tapped my elbow, and kicked again.

We were so close to Acheron that I felt the excited thrum of their beating hearts. Pushed out of my head were Auger's words, the smug premières sneering behind Joséphine's back, whoever killed Joséphine, my bloody shirt, Coralie's despair. All my troubles, shed. I thought of nothing at all but the way Joséphine smiled like everything was a decadent secret. She flirted with food and drink and people, so I kissed the tambourine the way she would have if she were the center of attention at my vigil.

When the tempo raced, I raced with it. The ringing, once teased, became constant, and each kick grew higher and higher until the tambourine was back over my head and my foot flying with it.

Only me and the ringing in perfect communion.

The others clapped along to the invisible accelerando, and I spun around the yard, the air jingling behind me as I broke into a run. My eyes and gums and fingertips prickled, stretching and burning and changing into that beast again.

A grand jeté brought me to the foot of the pergola, and I sank to my knees, chest heaving, face wet from sweat or tears, swallowed by high grass and their applause.

Beneath the praise, the incredulous laughs, and wondrous gazes, I dropped to the ground, sprawling flat on my back. I was spent from the day, from the *month*, from dancing and holding all the tension in my muscles. Tonight, like a dam breaking, the darkness that was pulled taut in me from deep in my ribs had finally been released.

I'd given myself over to Acheron completely, let myself lose control.

The buzzing in my skin, the *life* pulsing through me, demanded to be savored, held on to for as long as I could before I was forced to return to the surface, to who I was expected to be. But for now, for once, I had been set free.

PART THREE

ABSOLUTION

CHAPTER 17

The blood river was calm today. I strolled along the rocky banks of Acheron, watching the river's slow and silent ebb. There were some days when it roared, blood leaping as it sped around the bend, but other days it rested, just an open vein smelling of rust, the humid heat of gore filling the air. In the weeks that followed Joséphine's vigil, I learned to recognize its moods too. I grew better at feeling them as if they were my own.

I returned to Elysium nearly every evening, usually meeting with Andor to practice channeling that primeval call of power in my blood. The deal with Acheron was Joséphine's parting gift to me, my weapon to conquer the world, and so I would use it well. It was bigger than Olivia's fall, more than some savage impulses I could learn to control. And there was only so much I'd glean from the rest of Joséphine's files; her favor was luck, a passive magic that moved the world *for* her. Her temper didn't break clavicles or turn her into a monster, so I needed to be here until I was a permanent member of the ballet and Coralie an apprentice. I would learn to use the beast, its teeth and claws, instead of letting them use me, until every moment felt like I did when I danced that night of the vigil: barefoot and free, blood-scented breeze through my hair, my audience enraptured. Untouchable.

"Hello, old friend," I whispered to the river pulsing beside me.

A breeze raked my scalp, my eyes fluttering shut at the sensation. Elysium's lush forests had slowly transformed into a stillness I didn't know I craved—it was far removed from the loud and crowded world above, and with the opening of *La bayadère* fast approaching, I found myself slipping away more and more just to have a moment to myself. Like this evening, I breathed easier the instant I crossed the threshold.

Carved into this part of the dense trees, a long way from the cottage, a walled garden climbed high against the maroon sky, casting an imposing shadow. I'd been roaming for the better part of an hour when the sweet perfume of flowers pulled me out of my head. A current ran through the ground, buzzing in my soles.

And rather than go back to the surface, to reality and that tense apartment I shared with Coralie where we were both effectively avoiding each other now, I decided I'd rather venture inside. Static intensified within the labyrinth's wall. The pathway was overgrown with moss and crops of poppies, hedges choked by bushes of thorny red roses. Long since lost to its wilder nature, though the skeleton of planning was here in the uneven cobblestones, the arrangement of flowers—

I whirled around.

There was rustling in the bushes ahead, and I braced myself. If it was more than just a rabbit or fox, the river was close enough that I could put up a fight: throw a command, run, and probably survive.

Unless it was Joséphine's killer. There were no more deaths at the ballet or break-ins at home, so I could almost, *almost* forget she'd been murdered. If I tried hard enough, I rarely saw her sunken face anymore. And no one was any closer to finding the culprit, like it didn't even matter. Like she never existed at all.

The shuffling stilled too sharply, too quietly, as if what dwelled beyond had sensed me too. Then something thorny shot from the earth at my feet and snaked tight around my ankle.

"Who's there?" a voice called.

"Andor?" My head snapped up, surprised. I only barely threw my hands forward in time to spare my face as the thick, prickly vines jerked me off my feet. The hard crash onto my elbows chased the breath from my lungs.

And finally a familiar form came clambering around the corner. "Laure?"

He looked wild, hair pinned back messily but still falling in his face, white shirt soil-stained, feet bare. He carried a garden trowel and a fistful of flowers, and a bead of sweat ran past his thick, knit brows as he tried to smooth the confusion from them. Clearly I'd caught him as off guard as he caught me. Still, the sound that escaped me at the mere sight of him, part sigh of relief, part scoff, was mortifying.

"What are you doing here?" Andor rushed to set aside his trowel and flowers and brush the soil from his hands. Unsuccessfully. The vines biting into my skin were already loosening and retreating back into the hedges, slithering like serpents, when he froze midway, reaching down to help me. He curled his outstretched hand to a fist and straightened, like he remembered himself and thought better of it. "Were we supposed to meet today?"

Heart still racing, I leapt to my feet and backed away from the ominous growths. Toward him and the protection of his tall frame.

"No, you're not the only reason I come here, you know," I snapped, swiping frantically at the dirt on my palms and knees. "What is this place?"

The static in the ground was slow and steady, tugging at my tattoo. Beneath the bitter aromas of herbs and flowers lay the rust of blood, the tang coating my tongue. So familiar and strong I might have been standing alongside Acheron itself again. Poisonous flowers grew all around the labyrinth: hanging peach-colored angel's trumpets, bell-shaped foxgloves, and brilliant blue larkspurs. Hemlock with its spotted purple stems threaded through the maze. The rotting stench from a corpse flower permeated a corner. Plum-colored dragon lilies lined the paths in place of garden lights.

And all the plants were outstretched in devotion toward Andor.

"Did you make this? Is it yours?" I asked, turning in a circle.

There was an amused smirk on his mouth in place of an answer. And my gaze drifted to his wrist, his shirtsleeve bunched around the elbow to expose a smooth brown forearm covered in bloodred ink. The ink of *many* deals, it appeared, all looping over and around each other in an intricate patchwork of waves.

I gaped.

Andor caressed the petal of a violet blossom—aconite, I'd researched after the evening at the bistro—and in response, another bud bloomed from the same stalk. When he plucked it, brought it to his nose, and inhaled, more erupted in a wave, like a sigh from nature itself. Ignoring my expression and tucking the flower behind his ear, he said, "You can look around if you want. I think you'll be okay as long as you don't eat anything."

And with that, he started up the path, leaving me behind.

I rolled a bit of dirt between my fingers. It pulsated. Like this maze of poisonous flowers was alive and singing. Probably fed on blood, I guessed. Then I scurried after him. "How long did this take you?"

"Hard to say, a few years maybe." He reached around me and plucked another blossom, and then another, and continued on his walk with me by his side. With every step, the foliage bent toward him as if he were the sun, and he never lifted his eyes from his hands, weaving flowers and bluegrass together with idle concentration.

Andor had been carving himself a labyrinth in Elysium for *years* now, long before he and Ciro had even introduced it to Joséphine. He was a boy hiding away in a pocket of unreality, binding himself again and again to the eldritch god we hardly understood. Yet he was so . . . nobly human. Far more human than the girls I danced with. Than even me.

What kind of person becomes a monster only to embrace their curse and build a sanctuary with it?

I closed my fist around the spindly stem of a rose to corral my senses. Squeezing until the thorns bit in, until pain reminded me that this was what Acheron's creations did: We hurt. That sometimes the things we least expected, the things we thought beautiful, were the most dangerous. Beads of blood welled bright and fresh through my palm. "First you made a deal for beauty and then for whatever this is . . . I got that right?"

When he said he'd offered a lot at the café, I didn't realize anyone had so much to give. Which time did it turn him into a monster, then? An errant thought crossed my mind that maybe Andor hurt Joséphine. Or he was covering for someone who did. Part of me insisted that he didn't seem like the type, but I didn't know him at all, really.

"I have four," answered Andor, finally raising those dark lashes to look at me. The contact continued to burn long after he turned away and kept walking. "After a while, it stops being a big deal and makes it easy to want more—they're addicting that way. You should be careful."

How was more power a bad thing? I couldn't help but scowl at his back. He made it sound like he didn't trust Acheron, but then why go back for more? Why would he stay here, wasting his time making something that no one else would see? And why would Acheron let him?

"Don't you care what it's after? What it wants? Where it comes from?"

He only shrugged and turned us left, never pausing from weaving his flower crown. "It gives only what you ask for. Maybe even gods get lonely. Now, enough questions—we're almost at the center." His shoulder brushed mine as he picked up his pace. He smelled as wild as he looked, of dirt, fresh sweat, decaying wood, and . . . flowers. If I had any sense, I wouldn't have liked the combination, but I did.

We rounded the next few corners in silence, Andor leading the way by memory and me resisting the urge not to sniff and touch every new flower we crossed. There were countless varieties in full bloom, each more beautiful and delicate-looking and probably deadlier than the last. The heart of the labyrinth featured benches made of wicker and vines encircling a grove of oleander, the trees swollen with pink blossoms. A stack of blank canvases sat beside an empty easel.

"Right, you're also a painter."

"It's what I go to school for, yes," Andor mumbled distractedly with a pout. He raised the finished flower crown to my head, brilliant purple blossoms framed between baby's breath. It sat low on my brow, dark, waxy leaves rimming my vision, and looking up at them made me look at him. The shine in his eyes, the dirt streaking his cheek, the flush of red at the tips of his ears before he turned away again. "So, your show is opening tomorrow, right? Is your family excited?"

The bitter scoff that escaped me made him look up from the fresh Christmas rose he was twirling between his fingers. No matter how much I tried to reel it in, to press a thumbnail to my mark, I couldn't stop the poison ready to spill out. "*Hardly.* They never come to watch me. Everyone thinks my parents are dead, but they're not. They just didn't want me. I think they were even relieved to get rid of me."

The ring, proof of how easy I was to discard, seared on my finger as if in confirmation.

I knew he was staring, even without looking up, because I felt the heat of it on my cheeks. His silence was heavy with something I didn't want to acknowledge—pity, probably, as he pieced together all the sharp edges that comprised me and tried not to recoil. Because now all my desperation suddenly made sense to him. His pacing slowed.

"It's okay though. When I'm a proper ballerina, famous and adored by millions, they'll come running back. Or regret it. Either works for me." I flopped down on the nearest bench and gave my most effortless shrug. Even as my breathing hitched. These weren't fresh wounds but the twinge of scar tissue, evidence I'd survived.

He stood frozen, the flower in his hand darkening. Rotting. The petals shriveled and fell away one by one, all while I squirmed under his watch. His expression was unreadable, and I wasn't even sure he was breathing until his antlers flashed and vanished, and he whispered, "I think, if they could see you now, they'd regret it."

My brows bunched, mouth opening and closing in search of a response but coming up empty. And really, what *could* I say to that? To his stare, the darkness scintillating underneath, his own monster trying to slip out? We were locked in some pas de deux where I didn't know the steps. It was thrilling as much as it was my nightmare, wondrous, heady, and horrifying in equal measure. For a moment, I questioned if the poisonous crown was taking effect. It was reckless of me to wander into a garden full of toxins and expect not to be poisoned, but still I couldn't raise my fingers to remove it. To mistrust Andor, or the Acheron within him.

Not that I knew the difference. Not that it mattered.

I shifted in my seat, scanning for a distraction until my eyes settled on something useful. A large black notebook perched on the other end of my bench, and I reached for it with the brightest of ballerina smiles sharpened on years of disappointment and dancing through the pain. "Is this your sketchbook?"

That unlocked something in Andor because he stirred then.

"Can I see—?"

"No!"

Vines whipped out from the bench, the surrounding foliage, the ground, all reaching fast. Aiming for the notebook. They overshot their mark though, and I wasn't quick enough to pull away. Pain lanced through my side, fast and bright, taking everything in me to swallow a grunt. The notebook tumbled from my reach. And through my shirt, across my ribs, was a thin, stinging line of red.

Andor took a hurried step, hand outstretched, mouth rounded with worry. "I'm so—"

"**Don't**," said the growl that came out of me as I seized him.

The muscles in his arm clenched against the instruction, but it wasn't enough. The beast in me thirsted for more, blood for blood, gripping his very life in the curl of my fist. Clutching until the concern was wiped from his face and replaced with a wince.

Until the throb of his heart radiated through my palm, slow, then erratic and stuttering.

This is new.

I grinned. Because we were both monsters of Elysium. We were *both* capable of hurting each other. He didn't truly know poison until he crossed my path.

Andor threw out a hand to steady himself on the bench, not that I'd relent. Even as he huffed. His life was as fragile as lace in my grasp.

Bending over, the curve of his back spasmed beneath his shirt. Blood dripped steadily from his face to the ferns at our feet, spotting the desiccated Christmas rose petals beneath him. He was dying.

I'd never thought myself capable of killing—some part of me deep down maybe even *liked* his company—but still I didn't let go. He'd said before that I wouldn't kill him, but I could make him hurt like he hurt me. Make him feel weak like he did to me. He even suffered beautifully, his gaze twinkling with awe as he stared up at me, beneath my boot poised to crush him. Beholding me, Laure, the ballerina who bested *him*, fearsome in my own right.

His outline flashed, mortal, then primeval. The likeness was still there, in his broad nose and strong jaw and dark hair like silk. However, his skin melted from golden brown to the shiny, deep red of garnet, swirling with agitation, and towering antlers climbed from his skull.

Roots with long, jagged spines shot from the ground and closed around my wrist, wrenching me back and breaking my concentration. Instantly, Andor wheezed, something between a cough and laughter, and as I tore my wrist free and glared at him, I caught the four black eyes of a predator locked onto me.

Andor was no longer Andor. This wicked monster was bigger, wider, shirt stretching on his heaving form. He had the audacity to grin, and his pointed teeth shone like broken glass. Acheron's creation. Being trapped in its sight forced a shiver down my spine.

"You cut me," I grumbled to distract myself, examining the hole in my shirt, trying very hard not to forgive him. And failing. The gash was thin and would heal quickly. The sting had already faded.

Breathing hard, he drew up to full height, his antlers casting a shadow over my face before he stepped in close. "I'm sorry, but you did well. You stopped me—you tried to stop my heart from beating, actually."

The wonder in his voice, the curve of his lips...he was actually *proud*. And my skin flashed hot again.

"That doesn't sound like a good thing."

"It is." All his ferocity leeched away as he took my bleeding wrist in his hands. A gentle hold in calloused skin, dirt from the garden under the beds of his claws, and so very warm.

Along with the silence of the garden, it tugged at the very center of me, lulling me to give in, stay like this forever. Like all the flowers here, I too angled toward Andor and breathed him in. The primordial being looming over me wasn't so terrifying now, but the power he wielded—to look unflinching at my scars and weave me a crown, to celebrate a mark that only wanted to break things—scared me. I was revealing too much.

Seeing the tension in his mouth, how he was working up to say something, I swallowed and snatched my wrist back. The skin was buzzing from his touch. Pins and needles traveled the length of my arm, though much worse was the realization that I didn't mind at all.

"I have class in the morning."

"Yes, right, of course." He nodded, and, like in the first of Joséphine's videos, scratched the back of his neck in such an affable, *human* way. "By the way, the red suits you. Your eyes."

I stiffened. After rehearsal, I'd removed the color contacts that hide the steadily growing rim of red in my eyes. It began with Olivia, the whimper of her broken collarbone nourishing my insides, but it was another tally of my misdeeds just like the claws I trimmed down. The red was the monster slipping through the cracks, and playing around in Elysium right now, I'd forgotten about it as quickly as I forgot about the ballet. About saving me and Coralie.

"Do you need help finding your way out?" Though he kept his eyes on the ground, his tone was seeded with hope.

It was dangerous, drawing him close. Andor was a distraction, a thorny, maybe even poisonous one, one that wouldn't get me into the corps, and if I were a good and cautious girl, I'd keep my distance and find my own way. I'd take his hesitation and the numbness in my skin as signs to stay away for good.

But unfortunately something in me already softened against my will, and I never cared for what was good or right.

Fighting down a smile, I inclined my head and answered in an even tone, "I wouldn't mind the company." And on my way out, I snatched a bloodred rose as a keepsake, inviting the thorns to eviscerate what was left of my palm.

⬦

When I rounded the corner near my apartment, still sniffing my rose, I was greeted by a gust of cold air. It slipped up my spine and settled in my bones, and then a skin-crawling shudder followed. I whirled around in search of a source, but the street was dark and vacant.

Am I being followed?

There were only shadows and bony trees, no sign of a person lying in wait. Drawing my keys and pulling my coat tight around me, I quickened my steps—

A familiar black car idled in front of my building, and with the building door's opening, a figure in an elegant, silvery suit emerged. Hair like spun gold, Coralie's mother strolled to her waiting ride, heels clicking every step. Even from afar, there was no mistaking her pinched mouth, the flash of anger in her brow.

Rose-Marie didn't notice me as she flung open the car door and slipped inside. And I stood rooted in place as the car retreated, taking the ghostly air with it.

The sliver of Acheron in my mark squirmed.

In our living room, Coralie nestled in the secondhand bergère, her knees folded into her chest. Despondent. And I didn't have to guess why, with Rose-Marie having just left and *La bayadère* tomorrow. My first performance with the Paris Ballet, and the first time in years Coralie and I wouldn't be dancing together. The first time Coralie wouldn't be dancing at all. Even as students, we'd had our own programs. To not perform at all was the worst kind of hell: impotence. Without Acheron, that might've been me.

"Your mom's not taking it well, huh?" I spotted the lone ticket for tomorrow's show on the coffee table and pushed it aside.

She exhaled shakily, lifting her head to wipe away tears. Her button nose blushed pink.

If I were a softer, gentler girl, someone *other* than the Laure she knew, I might've held her. Instead, my urge was to recruit her. Lead her deep into the tunnels like Joséphine led me. But my Coralie wasn't a monster like the rest of us—she didn't need to be.

"She's reaching out to Stuttgart."

I went rigid. "Do *you* want to try somewhere else?"

Coralie unfolded her legs and shrugged. "Does it matter?"

My head dropped. I didn't know what to tell someone when they lost everything that was always promised to them. No one had ever cared enough to promise me anything before my deal.

"Don't give up, Cor. I'm so close to getting promoted, and then an apprenticeship spot will open for you! You won't have to leave."

Our foreheads pressed together.

"I'll take care of *you* this time." I squeezed her hands.

It was all I could say without ruining us, and it pained me like an exposed nerve. Coralie and I experienced every success, failure, hurt, and joy together for years. Even at her most rotten, she was all I had, my best friend, the girl who used to share her lunches while we waited for parents to pick us up from class. I didn't want to be alone again.

In a quiet voice, she said, "Or you can come with me."

I didn't move.

"Think about it," Coralie reasoned with unnerving calm. "If you quit and come with me, things'll go back to the way they were. And *I'll* take care of *you*. Like it's always been."

She observed my silence, my cringing, and cocked her head. Her gaze flicked to the rosebud at my side. "There isn't someone else, right?"

"No!" I objected, perhaps too quickly. And I meant it, no matter the moments I wished otherwise, how ill-advised it would be. The rose crushed easily in my fist.

"Good, so what's stopping you?"

Like a splash of cold water, all of me was awake. Present. Hearing and arching back. Her face warped from forlorn to cunning, the softness of her features rearranging into vicious and serpentine.

"You can stop sneaking around late at night to practice—you're obviously overwhelmed and need more time. It'll be fun! We'll find a nice place and get all new stuff with my parents' accounts. And we'll try again at Stuttgart, *together*."

As if she weren't asking me to upend my career before it ever really began.

I gaped. She couldn't possibly think I would. That I'd even *want* to go back to obscurity, being forgotten, ignored, powerless.

"N-no—"

"Why not? It's not like you have parents to disappoint. They don't care what happens to you. Mine do."

When she reached for me, I lurched away. Off the table and back toward my room. I tasted bile.

But Coralie's cold gaze still followed me. "It's what a real friend would do."

The hair on my arms stood on end as I retreated without another word. And at my back, she sneered. "It's not like you ever really fit in with them, anyway! I'm all you've got."

CHAPTER 18

When I dreamed of my debut performance with Paris Ballet Company, it never involved an upset stomach. The meager meal I'd forced down now threatened to come up as I stood in front of the dressing room mirrors. Coralie's doing.

I kept searching my surroundings for a pale hand reaching from the mass of dancers to cast me out. Right as I was finding my footing with the ballet and Acheron's imprint, when I might have found my place, now doubt marred my debut.

The bile in the back of my throat wouldn't go down.

"You belong here," I practiced saying to my reflection. Under such harsh lights, the rings of crimson around my irises were stark, even beneath my contacts. I confirmed the makeup blended on my wrist and checked my costume one last time. "You earned this."

Despite playing another dead girl on the same stage, I wore a slightly different ivory costume: strapless bodice this time, satin, and instead of a long skirt, I had a tutu. I attached the veil to my bun, elbows, and wrists without help—I'd been styling my own hair since I was six. Everything I knew, I'd taught myself—just another way girls like me started off at a deficit.

And I still stepped into the hall without a hair out of place, looking just as beautiful and haunted as any ghost.

"Did you hear it'll be a full house? Like two thousand people?"

Vanessa stared up at me from the floor, stitching elastic to her shoes in case we needed an alternate. Which we didn't. Beside her, Olivia, still sporting her sling, read one of Geoffrey's romance books. The stage live stream hummed on the wall's mounted TV.

Olivia shouted behind me, "Do us a favor and break a leg!"

All of me froze for just a breath, my eyes drifting shut to soothe the boiling blood in my veins, to temper myself out of reacting. Again. They both snickered when I disappeared into the stairwell leading up to the wings. And at the stage door, I collided with a solid wall of pungent cologne.

Large, rough hands closed around my shoulders to stop me from slipping.

"Lucille, hein?" Hugo Grandpré, the chief creative director, said as he kept me upright. He wore a suit for once instead of his signature turtleneck and sweatpants. So odd, it took a moment to realize he still couldn't remember my name.

He propped the door open and gestured for me to enter. "Go on."

It was crowded backstage, with stagehands hanging up quick-changes and organizing them with labels, the long line of shades already assembled even though our act hadn't started yet. Alain Cornillon, our warrior hero Solor, adjusted the costume turban he looked out of place wearing. His costar, none other than Sabine Simon, unhooked her arm from his waist when she spotted me.

"Laure!"

I bit my tongue to keep from shouting the choice words bubbling up inside. Of all days, my debut was here; I had no time for her preaching and goodwill.

She tapped my shoulder, and when I didn't turn, swerved into my sight. The braided end of her long black wig dangled over her shoulder. "Hey, are you all right?"

The stage was plunged in darkness ahead of the next act, and she had an appearance coming, to star in Alain's opium-fueled dream. Yet here she was, in a corner, bugging me. Her righteous concern was cloying—where was this for Joséphine? And her voice was high like birdcall, her gaze perpetually doe-eyed. It was hard to believe once I'd found her cute, had pledged my naïve devotion to her, when now she was only irritating. And a touch smug.

Over her shoulder, Flora Silvestre watched with a knowing smile. Because besides being a witch and a charity case, I was also the girl Sabine dumped for being cold.

I glowered. "What do you want?"

"I want to know if everything is all right. With you."

The way she leaned into the word *all right* made me stiffen. My fingers floated to my wrist. Surely there was no way she knew about my connection to Joséphine.

"It's just…" Sabine hesitated, leaning in so that the others wouldn't hear. Her eyes flicked back to the door. "This can be a stressful first performance, so Grandpré doesn't typically cast apprentices."

"Yet here I am." My toes went numb in my pointe shoes, waiting for her to just come out and say it.

"Here you are. But, the thing is, the ballet isn't liberal with opportunity. You know, I didn't dance *La bayadère* until halfway through my first year as a quadrille—"

"What are you asking me?" I demanded, my mouth dry. Tinny music crawled up from the marrow of my bones, my fingers twitching by my sides for something to break.

She chewed her lip, working it for courage, and when she came away, her teeth were stained soft pink. "Is something going on with… Grandpré?"

I stilled.

"You had a thing for powerful people, and I saw you two just now—"

A laugh scraped its way out of my chest, cutting her off.

"Really? 'Powerful people,' Sabine? Was that what you were?"

When I took a step, she shrank back, and I'd relish that alone for days on end. We lasted three chaotic months, wrapped in each other because I was lonely and she wanted to feel revered. I thought she was the last word in ballet, hoped some of her skill might rub off. Now all I had to show were jokes whispered behind my back, remembering that the only reason she was even here dancing *La bayadère* was because of Joséphine's murder. Grandpré, she was not.

"You were always so *detached*. Like you only cared—"

"**Stop talking**," I snapped, feeling that well of anger threatening to spill over. My words echoed in her big eyes. "Don't insult me. Not when you were insecure and vain, and you only liked me because I had no other options."

And still I wasn't enough for her. The only difference between her and my parents was that I was forced to see her every day, to remember how easily discarded I'd always been. How little I had to offer in terms of power. But things changed.

Beyond the red curtains, low brass from the orchestra marked the beginning of our act, but Sabine stood petrified before me. Stiff, raised shoulders, mouth ajar.

Like I was a monster.

Like I had finally become someone to fear, and I was damn good at it.

"Sabine?" Alain hissed in our direction.

With all the venom I'd ever swallowed, kept buried in the depths of me far longer than I'd even known Sabine, I leaned close to her ear and snarled, "**After tonight, I want you out of this ballet and out of this city**."

Just because I wanted to, just because I could've done a lot worse.

She trembled in my wake as I brushed past and sought my place in line. And for the first time on my wretched debut day, I smiled. My mark hummed with excitement, the slick feeling in my stomach gone. All that remained was reassurance.

From the wings, we watched Sabine take tepid steps onto the platform upstage, her silhouette flooded blue while Alain ran toward her, overcome with grief. The lights faded.

This was our time.

This was *my* debut, and I was going to be glorious.

The harp trilled, and just three spots ahead, Nina raised her arms to perfect arches. She tapped a pointed foot and lifted her chin.

I brushed my sweaty hands against my tights.

Nina at the helm in a count of six, then Aiko in perfect form for another count, then up went Flora's arms, and she was running.

A shaky breath, and my body kicked into motion. Two quick steps carried me past the black curtain, and then I was leaning forward, all my weight on one leg while the other floated up long behind me. Indulgent arms spread wide as wings. Hardly feeling the white gauzy veil that itched against my skin.

In perfect sync, the four of us swept our arms back.

My thoughts shifted from mechanical—heart to the audience, face neutral, tendu, then reach high to the violins—to memory.

The *clip-clop* of pointe shoes every few beats as we all shuffled forward. The soft blue light in the dark. The flash of a camera. The bead of sweat down Aiko's back. The flick of the conductor's baton over the edge of the stage. The twinge in my rib from Andor's vines. The jewels on the bodice chafing my arm with every sweep.

There was profound peace in dancing that made it easy to forget the allergic reactions to makeup and clogged pores and sweaty polyester clinging to skin. When the stage claimed my bones, I became an act of creation, soft steps to the tempo of breaths. We were a sea of the dead, the push and pull of the tide, the curling smoke in an opium den, and the rolling clouds over the Himalayas. I ceased being Laure, dancing behind Nina and in front of Eugénie. One of many, seen but not real, even as we folded over in puddles of white and made room for the dead lovers' reunion by fluttering back. Beating like hummingbird wings.

With the monster sated, I was the lightest I'd ever been on my feet, every jump and turn boundless. Every heartbeat threatened to burst.

I was holy.

No matter how repetitive the motions, the blood rushing to and from my feet as they swept front and back, pain spurring in my toes, I never tired. Ballet was my life. I wouldn't risk wavering or distractions because I needed them all to be on my side. To choose me again and again, even if they'd forsaken Joséphine.

Fueled by fire in my blood, some combination of my mark and my burning hunger, I would do it all day if President Auger asked. Work my toes to shards if the ballet needed it.

"Kingdom of the Shades" ran for thirty minutes, and I was onstage for almost all of it. When the soloists danced, we echoed their motions by waving the veils on our arms, numbed to the exhaustion sure to rise tomorrow. Sweat prickled my eyes. I could have wept.

"I can't feel my face," Flora muttered as we flitted backstage for our bows. Aiko mushed her own cheeks between her palms and snickered. I followed, weightless and euphoric.

On the other side of the lush red curtain, the audience roared. It was deafening, louder than anything at *Giselle*, enough for all of Paris to hear. My ears rang. The noise filled me, slipped under my skin, and quieted all the worries. Sabine was as good as gone. Coralie couldn't touch me. No dead Joséphine with wide eyes turned toward the stars to haunt me.

I was bathed in applause that rendered me invincible, the fat trimmed away until all that remained was me in motion.

The curtains parted, and we floated forward as a single, ghostly body, sweeping one arm and then the other into a bow, and then again to stage left. I'd never seen so many people. We kept our pretty smiles for the soloists, for Sabine and Alain, who shook the walls with their acclaim. The veneration seeped into the floors, up through the soles of my shoes. Veneration that also should have been Joséphine's, that someone stole from her.

And might one day try to steal from me if I wasn't careful.

Nina's shoulders sagged the instant the curtains closed. She hunched forward and melted into the trickle of departing dancers. The floor stopped humming, and the silence sent me reeling. Stage lights replaced spotlights, leaving me groggy. Like waking up from a dream.

Too numb to feel the soreness in my feet, the sweat slicking my chest. Too full on *this* to feel my empty stomach.

"I get to do this every day," I whispered to myself, prying my feet from the stage. If there were any lingering doubts I deserved to be here, this proved them wrong.

I left the stage vindicated, hoping every naysayer felt me like a blade through the ribs.

It carried me into the hall, right for the dressing rooms. Chin raised, my shoulders back. This was only the beginning. Little by little, I'd scale the ballet until I was a soloist, not just glorious but *coveted*. A dedicated following in the atrium soon after. I'd waited twelve years for a face in the audience, and soon I'd get my reward.

Coralie couldn't expect me to leave after tonight. *La bayadère* was slotted for two more weeks, and the thought of missing even one show lanced through me. If she was in the crowd, then she'd understand. If the roles were reversed, I'd know the same.

I changed quickly, hanging the pristine white costume on the rack with my veil in tow, and was in the throes of scrubbing the ton of makeup from my face when my phone rang. Ciro's name bounced across the screen, light flashing.

"Hello?"

"Laurence?" His voice was drowned out by a rumble of people in the background. "Will you not come greet your adoring fans?"

I hung up and scrubbed faster.

The explosion of energy and sound filling Opéra Garnier overwhelmed me the instant I walked out of the dressing room. Since the show had such a large cast, dancers, garments, and shoes spilled into the halls. Shouts filled the corridors as the crew ran, transporting battery packs and cables. The orchestra with dark-wood instruments weaved fast through loitering bodies. And that was nothing compared to the foyer. Huddles of people in finery lined stairs and landings, clutching wrapped flowers and gift bags.

Geoffrey Quý in a blue crushed-velvet tuxedo put a hand on my shoulder, stopping me. "You were great, Laure," he said with a smile. No punch line. No jokes. Like he actually meant it.

Then he hurried after an older couple who looked like his parents.

Gaping, confused, I turned away. And there, at the bottom of the stairs, beneath the guarding glare of a statue dipped in gold, a lithe figure in white and his dark companion waited.

I stopped breathing for a long moment.

Ciro and Andor leaned against the wall and whispered to each other while Keturah looked around, dressed in a golden gown, her electric yellow mohawk primped to perfection. They garnered glances from people around them, this misfit group of Joséphine's—or, I paused, *mine*—but none of them noticed. They were too busy looking for me.

Though I blinked, waiting for them to disappear, they didn't. My legs drew me closer. "What are you—?"

Keturah hugged me and planted a gold-lipsticked kiss on my cheek. "You're a real ballerina! You were amazing!"

My mouth ran dry, rough as I tried to swallow. Andor held out a bouquet next, and it took everything in me to not shatter when his fingers grazed mine and left them tingling.

"You—wow . . ." I stared at the flowers.

Where other bouquets held roses and bright yellow lilies, mine was eclectic: thick with what looked like violet aconites, the tender blossoms of pink laurels, small white clusters of hemlock—

"Some of them are poisonous," Andor cautioned softly, the tips of his ears flushing red. Under the golden light, he looked divine in his crimson suit, his full hair swept up neatly. Worthy of the Palais and more. "Careful."

His smile heated the room and snatched the air from my lungs.

"Oh yes, our local florist did the bouquet," Keturah added, unaware, before draping a casual arm across my shoulder. Like we were friends. She was doing what Coralie should: being here, hugging me, celebrating. And I was still getting to know her.

My mind reeled at all of them: Keturah's arm, the program clutched in Ciro's hand, and surely I imagined the glint in Andor's eyes. Beside him, Ciro knit his brows, alternating glances between Andor and me as if he read something written in the air. I dropped my gaze back to the bouquet, embarrassed.

No one had ever thought me worthy of flowers before.

"How long did you say you've danced for?" Keturah went on.

"Twelve years, but it's just a corps position, really—"

"No, it was magnificent. What did you say earlier, Ciro? About the sign of a fine dancer?"

Ciro shook his head unconvincingly and mumbled, "Wasn't me."

A snide comeback was on my lips when a cold front rolled through the room, forcing a shiver through my coat. Hairs on my arms stood tall. My mark writhed, skin crawling with unease.

I turned, scanning the hall. Keturah straightened. Our jovial air evaporated as Andor looked around, scowling. Inching closer, glad I wasn't alone, I asked, "Did you feel it too?"

Ciro gave a faint nod, frowning as he set a protective hand on my shoulder. And as quickly as it arrived, so it passed.

CHAPTER 19

The cast party at the end of *La bayadère's* two-week run was at La Tempête, a high-end nightclub mentioned in every trendy celebrity article and magazine. Entry came with a dress code and an etiquette guide to maintain the "atmosphere," and instead of a disco ball and the grinding, bass-heavy music I expected, the electronic beats were kept lo-fi so attendees could drink cognac and discuss Cubist art on the walls. Still, I was shy of eighteen, and the bouncer barely let me in.

I pulled at the sleeves of my simple black dress and followed the others to our booths.

When Flora had invited me before the final show—and I didn't even have to compel her—I leapt at the opportunity. It was better than another evening replaying shared glances, imagining secret messages in a bouquet, and Sabine's exile. And being invited meant that I was one of the professionals, like Nina Brossard and Alain Cornillon. I belonged among elite dancers, not poisonous monsters or blood rivers. Normal people in normal places. It didn't matter that I was expressly forbidden from drinking, or that the others ditched me to head to the bar as soon as I sat down. It only mattered that I was here.

"We'll be right back!" Nina shouted without a backward glance.

The rest of the cast crowded the chrome-dipped bar, shouting their fancy drink requests without hesitation. Would they drink themselves silly on kir royal and armagnac and forget all about me?

My smile stiffened, my finger chafing as I twisted the gold ring.

Across the floor climbed stairs to a balcony lounge, and a familiar figure breaking free from the throng of people immediately caught my eye. Lean and pretty, always dressed in white, I'd recognize him anywhere.

Of course Ciro knew about the party.

I smiled at Alain's approach.

"Some water for you," he said, carrying two sweating glasses with too much ice.

I studied Alain, the only other Black dancer in the company. In the dim light, his ochre skin didn't look so washed out, and he held his chest permanently puffed out, shoulders down as if a string overhead kept his spine long and tall. His dark curls, usually buzzed short, had been grown out for his lead in the show.

"Was the hair your idea or theirs?" I asked. Because, to them, anyone brown enough would do. How long until they asked something of me?

He ran a hand through his mane self-consciously. "Mine."

"And not drinking?" I jutted my chin to the bar, where Flora and Aiko brought their glasses together. They sipped from straws, exchanged, sipped again, and traded in perfect sync. I tried not to burn with envy, at missing my best friend.

He shook his head. "No, I don't drink alcohol."

"Then why come to something like this?"

Alain leveled his gaze as if it was obvious. "Because it's where everyone is."

Interrupting our quiet came Nina, Flora, and Aiko, squeezing around us and bringing their drinks together in cheers. We raised our waters.

Cast parties at the academy were less elegant than La Tempête: held in someone's parents' living room in Neuilly-sur-Seine—still finer and larger than anywhere I'd ever lived—or sometimes a ballroom, tables lined with soft drinks and gourmet snacks, the night accented by sweaty, groping hands in dark corners and re-creating variations to relive the glory. They were a long time ago, back when Coralie had braces and my hips seemed so much wider than everyone else's. I was an oddity then too, whose parents never hosted anything or showed their faces, and the middle-aged women in their pearls and pantsuits watched me in pity. It clung to me like a foul odor.

This was better.

"So, did you hear Sabine's at ABT?" started première Aiko Watanabe with a sigh, as if the gossip was exhausting. She almost hid her smile well behind a sip of her cocktail.

A knot twisted in my stomach at the name. Sabine was here one day and gone the next, from our gilded stage to snapping photos with friends in New York. It was stupid not to see this coming, a première dropping out after one show—of course others would talk. We worked long hours; there was little else to discuss.

I didn't feel guilty exactly—Sabine accused me of sleeping with Grandpré for a position in the *corps*. No, powerful people did way worse to people less deserving. I just didn't want to be reminded of it.

Flora twisted around and gripped my arm, her nails biting into my skin. Her pilfered black pearl earrings caught in the light. "Did she say anything to you?"

I shook my head mechanically, trying to school my expression into something other than nausea. "No—"

"You guys dated, right?" Alain asked, leaning forward. There was no camaraderie in his arched brow, the casual way he drank his water. It was akin to an interrogation.

"Only for a few months—"

"I heard her and Grandpré arguing after the show," said Nina blithely, drawing the cherry from her glass with a toothpick. "She was the understudy for Joséphine. He probably asked her not to come back."

I cleared my throat. "Do you think she had something to do with Joséphine?"

Nina shrugged. "Whoever it was, they deserve a medal."

"What if Grandpré did something to Joséphine?" Aiko's eyes widened. I looked up.

"And Sabine found out," Alain added, "and blackmailed him to dance Nikiya."

"Oh my god!" Flora shrieked with a barely suppressed giggle.

"Guys, that's silly. Why would Grandpré promote Joséphine just to kill her?" I argued, picturing Joséphine's mutilated body: her broken neck, the destroyed tattoo. If Grandpré knew, he wouldn't have voted her an étoile.

Unless he uncovered her deal afterward and felt lied to.

My mouth went dry. I drank down the water with no relief. I might have been dancing for Joséphine's murderer.

"You're just an apprentice, what do you know about how the company works?" Nina snapped, her voice sweet and venomous. It stung. She slid cash across the table at me after. "Be useful and fetch me another whiskey sour?"

"Ooh, good idea!" Aiko retrieved her own bills and sat them on top with a little pat. "Hurricane for me."

"Armagnac, pleaaase!" Flora shouted in singsong, tossing more money.

Alain pretended not to see but chose to say nothing.

I clenched my jaw so hard I expected my teeth to crack, my neck flushing under their expectant stares. I was a dog, guarding their purses while they celebrated and fetching their drinks when I wasn't even allowed one of my own. Never to be heard. The mark burned through my skin for a long, tense moment while I stared at the colorful notes. Soothing the monster.

"Fine," I ground out, closing my fist around the cash and my coat and then sliding out of the booth.

Forget your drinks, I threw over my shoulder, hoping the command took hold. It was my money now. Compensation for their disrespect.

I shouldered through a thicket of people in suits, catching the tail end of a dull conversation about sailing. Through another nauseating cluster griping about the length of someone's dress, the height of her heels, the tint of her eye shadow. It wasn't a private party; some of these people weren't even associated with the ballet, but I hated them all the same.

I hated their entitlement and their jokes, the way Joséphine's career amounted to nothing more than chum, how they looked down on me. These people perched above the gutter and didn't look where their spit landed, and I was starting to think it didn't matter if I danced ten shows or two hundred, wore the latest jewels, clung to Sabine's side or cast her away.

"Watch out—!"

Stewing, with my eyes focused on the exit, I didn't notice him until it was too late.

A body crashed into me, spilling cool liquid down my dress, my leg, onto my shoes. My boot sole sloshed as I stumbled away, gaping at the puddle on the floor, the stench of someone's craft IPA seeping into me.

"You…" I started, groping for the words.

There was a snicker nearby.

"Whoops," the man said with a wry smile, eyes glassy and bloodshot, as he turned back to his friends. No apology, no offer to cover the dry cleaning, no acknowledgment at all.

I might as well have been a ghost. Again.

I stared down at my feet, at my favorite shoes. Even with the pay raise, it wasn't like I had disposable income raining from the sky to just replace them all the time. I had bills to pay, my own pointe shoes to find because *god forbid* the company provide actual nude tones for anyone darker than porcelain, and commuting through this city wasn't cheap. I needed a security deposit and rent for a new apartment in case my roommate left the country. And he was *laughing* like I was nothing more than a table he'd bumped into.

Like I was no one.

"**Apologize**," I growled, the word scratching in my throat.

Almost instantly he turned, limbs rigid, and fixed his glassy stare on me. He was pasty under the mood lighting, the cuff links of his jacket sleeves expensive, and the soulless way his voice mumbled, "Pardon," only stoked my bloodlust.

"**Give me your wallet to pay for this.**"

He did.

And this time, when I seized those strings that tethered him to my primal imprint, I knew what I was doing. I understood very well what would happen when I squeezed just like this—he twitched—and closed my fist around that blistering heartbeat. Just like I had Andor. Tight enough for my knuckles to crack, for my nails to begin sharpening and breaking skin.

The man stumbled back, clutching the front of his shirt. Blood dripped from my palm into the puddle of beer, but I didn't want to let go, whatever the cost. Unlike Andor, he wasn't strong enough to fight back.

A warm arm wrapped around my shoulder and pulled me away before I killed him.

"Outside," a smooth tenor whispered in my ear. "Now."

I didn't glance back at the man, but his heart stuttered back to normalcy while I was rushed out into the crisp night air. The lump in my throat wouldn't go down.

"*Breathe*," Ciro coached as he led me away from the door. His white sleeves were rolled up to his forearms, exposing a fine tattoo identical to mine. "Deep breaths, Laurence—"

"I was going to kill him."

"I know. It's okay—"

"I should go back and finish the job, teach them a lesson—"

"Breathe," he snapped, taking my shoulders in his hands. Eyes the color of chestnuts bore into me. Taking the fight right out of me. "It's okay."

Once I'd blamed him for Joséphine, and yet I might have killed someone had he not intervened.

I raked my hands through my hair. The street was busy with cars and passersby, loud enough to drown out again and again that maybe I was already a monster and that was why Acheron chose me. It saw a familiar savagery that it could groom. And every chance I had, I let it, happily.

Tonight, I couldn't blame ignorance, not knowing my own strength. Maybe I never had an excuse; maybe deep down, I'd *meant* to send Olivia sprawling. I wanted to break her like I nearly broke this man, like I thought about breaking everyone around me all the time. I wanted the marble columns of Palais Garnier to snap under the weight of my anger, the whole ballet to crumble because of *me*.

I couldn't help but laugh. I was unraveling fast. "This night is a disaster."

"No fun with your friends?" Ciro murmured, offering a cigarette from his case. He tucked it between his lips when I declined.

"They're not my friends. They don't even like me." I frowned at the shiny, sticky spots of beer drying on my boot. "And I don't really like them."

He leaned against the parking sign, one long arm holding his cigarette aloft. Under the full moon, he really was mesmerizing. "Then why are you here—?"

"Because I need them to *accept* me," I seethed, turning on him.

Ciro raised his hands, as if to dissuade me from crushing his heart too. I swallowed and shoved my arms through the damp and smelly coat. It would be hell to clean.

In a lower voice, I mumbled, "There's no point if they don't."

It was why Alain came to a bar though he didn't drink—because it was where our colleagues gathered. Why he and Geoffrey followed the current instead of fighting: It meant survival. However, that begged the question why someone like Alain, once on the cover of *Dance* magazine and the son of *two* award-winning filmmakers, needed to go to these lengths to feel like one of them. Hadn't he already made it? If he hadn't, what hope was there for me?

"You sound like Joséphine," said Ciro gently before craning his head to the sky and puffing out rings of acrid smoke. Perhaps I detected pain in his voice. "And me. None of us seem to know what acceptance looks like."

He might've been right, but I wouldn't admit it. If he was, then that meant there was nothing I could do, nothing Joséphine could have done, no way to make it better. And I'd had enough of being powerless. There was always a way, a loophole, a crack to slip through, a riddle to outsmart. I wouldn't just accept that, after all of this, I was still nothing.

"Since when did you get all wise?" I quipped, feeling a smile creep up on my face. Calming the storm brewing in my veins. It dissipated as fast as it had amassed, leaving me to feel the chill of the air and shiver.

Ciro returned it before the two of us gazed up at the moon in comfortable silence. Exactly like a friend would.

"Laure?"

Coralie strode down the street, glancing between me and Ciro, her thin legs wobbling in tall heels. At her flank were the other apprentices: Olivia, Vanessa, Rémy, and Geoffrey. All hanging out together. Without me. *With* Coralie. They looked like the perfect group of friends, what they'd hoped for with apprenticeships until I got in the way.

Music box tinkling filled my ears.

Coralie jerked me away and sneered at Ciro. "What? Joséphine wasn't enough?"

I rounded on her.

"I don't know, let's ask your mother!" Ciro snarled, grinding out the butt of his cigarette with his fine, white shoes. "She's the one who had it out for her!"

She shoved him hard, and he fumed, shoulders heaving, nostrils flared. It was the angriest I'd ever seen Coralie, squaring off before a growing crowd. The only other times I'd seen him angry were at *Giselle* auditions, daring to argue with Rose-Marie, and the spat with Auger.

I looped my arm through Coralie's. "Come on. I was just about to go home." And then I lured my best friend toward the metro, mouthing an apology to Ciro behind her back.

CHAPTER 20

A crisp white envelope with my name and address printed carefully on the front and two American flag stamps in the corner was waiting for me when I got home.

I'd arrived at an empty apartment, having forgone Aiko's invitation to celebrate the opening of *Études*, weary down to my bones just days after *La bayadère* ended. I was living the ballerina dream now: Back-to-back shows ensured that the work never ceased. Though usually performing left me sleepless and filled to the brim with energy, lately, for some reason, all I thought about was rest. The apartment greeted me with the familiar mess of Coralie, a tornado of clothes and magazines and an empty pizza box, but the envelope on the counter was new. I froze where I stood.

Then it effectively welded itself to my hand from the moment I picked it up. It followed me in retreat to my bedroom, to the desk where I sat, frowning at me while I frowned back. Daring me to open it and reply.

The handwriting I recognized and dreaded, for I already knew what was inside. A greeting card watercolor of a brown-skinned ballerina with a coily bun on the front, *Happy birthday* scrawled in looping hand. The same two words always, nothing more, nothing less. It was always either too early or too late, and this year, it was early, and she'd even included a return address. *Bravo, Maman.* I'd only know if she was dead when they stopped coming.

Every year, I tossed it away without a response, but this time I was taking out stationery.

Maybe this year I'd finally write to tell her all the ways I'd changed, how I'd grown taller and wiser and vicious in the ways that girls without mothers often do. Learned to slick my own buns, sew my own shoes, lick my own wounds. I'd talk about *La bayadère* and *Études*, trumping Coralie Baumé for an apprenticeship. Maybe mention the monsters, the punk, the boy with his poisonous garden, his best friend in all white, the dead girl who brought us all together. There was also, of course, the bloodied shirt still wadded up in my desk drawer and the man I almost killed.

"Want to know how wicked I've been?" I asked the unopened envelope, fiddling with my gold ring. Her gold ring, actually.

But did it still belong to her if she left it behind? Was *I* still hers when she left *me* behind?

I'd been on edge ever since La Tempête, locking myself in my room for the night, trying to understand where the rage had come from, where it went. It felt like I was on the verge of collapse, but I couldn't stop spinning.

This was what it meant to be a professional ballerina—always in motion, never getting dizzy. When we first learned to pirouette, we used focal points on the wall to mark our places, but at some point, somehow, I'd lost my spot.

I swept the card into the trash bin and went for a walk.

To take my mind off the card, I dived back into the largest folder in the Elysium files: Joséphine's experiments. She'd documented pinching herself until she bruised, time lapses of cuts and scrapes stitching closed, roaming the woods by the cottage, collecting samples from Acheron's shores. By the looks of it, she'd even hiked her way to Lethe, the white river, photographing its bone-colored sands and opaque smoke rolling off its surface.

Sitting on a rock in Elysium's woods, I watched her arrange three containers on the coffee table in her living room. Two jars contained a violent shade of red, one of which was labeled ACHERON with tape. It was strange being a voyeur to the dead girl so often, seeing how much she'd existed outside of the ballet.

"*It makes my skin crawl,*" she lamented, raising the third vial to the camera.

Sinister white fog plumed inside. *Lethe.*

As she unscrewed the lid for the unlabeled red liquid, she said conversationally, "*I don't know if there's a better way to get there. It took me two days' hike, and I'm* fast. *Probably why there aren't any people with Lethe's favor.*"

Hand trembling, she added Lethe's liquid smoke to the vial of red.

"*My blood.*"

The forest was silent around me, as if the trees wanted to see what followed. I shifted in my seat as the camera jostled, as Joséphine removed it from its mount and focused the shot on what she'd done.

"*Whoa ...*" She murmured off-screen.

Inside, the blood was frozen. Tufts of frost gathered on its hardened edges, and the crimson beneath had darkened considerably. Joséphine chipped at it with a spoon, gasping as crystalline flecks fell away. She worked it harder, and her blood crunched like shaved ice.

"*Look at that,*" said Joséphine as the camera shook again, placed back on its mount. "*I wonder what'll happen if I add it to my sample taken directly from Acheron.*"

Her excited trembling intensified as she unscrewed the lid for the labeled jar, as she dangled a vial of white smoke over it. Her grin widened as it fell.

Then light erupted in the video.

I flinched at what followed: Joséphine's shout, breaking glass, the explosion. It was impossible to see anything until the flare receded. In its wake, the video revealed Joséphine pressed against the wall, away from the table, her eyes wide and terrified. Shattered glass and blackened tar spanned the table and floor.

And the place where Acheron's sample sat was charred and smoking.

Joséphine laughed shakily and looked to the camera. To *me*, as if she was telling me something. She pushed onto her knees and brushed the shards from her front. "*Guess they don't like each other—*"

A bird took flight overhead, making me jump. The hair at the nape of my neck stood on end, and though I wanted for the video's unsettling effect on me to fade, it didn't. And suddenly I didn't want to be alone.

The trees susurrated as I marched back through the woods. The vise on my rib cage had loosened. Something about the place was a balm for every ache and fatigue, working my bones until I could dance another show, run a marathon, climb a mountain. And now it did the same with the video.

Stirring in the cottage yard ahead caught my eye. I would have thought it a party they didn't invite me to were it not for the lack of laughter that usually filled the canopies. This quiet ran a chill through me. This quiet was wrong.

Keturah was pacing, hands on her hips, head hanging low. She slowed when she saw me and called my name, only for a moment before nodding to herself and resuming her stride. Andor flanked her carrying a warm coat unfit for muggy Elysium on his arm, the same grimace etched on both their faces.

I hesitated before slowly walking through the flimsy gate. "What's going on?"

Keturah rubbed her arms despite the heat.

"Ciro isn't answering my calls," said Andor, his voice hollow. Not looking at either of us. Though he attempted a blank face, it was devoid of the lightness I was accustomed to. That I deeply preferred.

I stilled. "You think something happened to him?"

Keturah slowed in the corner of my eye, but I kept my attention on Andor, willing him to say otherwise. Ciro was strange, smug but kind in his own way. Hardly a person you'd want to kill. Unless it was the same one who hurt—

"Something like Joséphine?"

Andor froze.

Maybe Ciro figured out who did it.

"No, no," Keturah said, waving her hands to dispel the idea. "It's just not like him, that's all. Maybe his phone is broken…"

I wasn't convinced. And neither was Andor, who clenched his jaw but nodded absently.

"Where does he live? I'm free, I can go check on him."

Someone had to go, especially with how everyone forgot Joséphine, how the ballet erased her from memory before I even found her body. If Ciro was fine, then I wanted him to explain what he'd said about Rose-Marie. And if something happened to him, related to Joséphine across space and time, then I had to know. Because we were…friends?

I added a touch too defensively, "I want to help."

"Let's go together this time," Andor suggested, setting out for the door. Keturah and I followed.

We stuck to the Catacombs, phone lights guiding us through a mile of dark tunnels heading south until we reached a newer segment more thoroughly lit. It coincided with an increase in the number of bones, dust and moss blanketing everything. Soon all along the floor were pale shards coated in fuzzy green beneath the lanterns, the stiff, cold, ossuary air growing stronger.

"Has Ciro ever done this before? Disappeared?" I prompted to fill the silence, failing to hide my shuddering. Every nerve in my body was on high alert. It felt like someone was watching us.

Keturah shook her head, her thick, yellow coils glowing beneath the lantern. "No. And I've been meeting him for lunch every day since Joséphine…"

"It's unlike him to miss an appointment," added Andor helpfully.

In the shadows, we huddled among the piles and piles of bones. Femurs and tibiae stacked high as my shoulders, ribs cascading from the mound. They were stained yellow with age, scratched or blackened or cracked in places. All unnerving.

Keturah pressed a finger to her lips.

Around the corner, there was the shuffle of footsteps over loose gravel. A slow-moving figure blocked the light and glided past the iron gate, some tourist with a large camera snapping flash photos of inscriptions and gaping skulls.

Ghostly fingers prickled the back of my neck. Icy condensation fell in my hair and down my face in heavy, biting drops.

Through the gate, we slipped into a brightly lit antechamber full of more bones. Skulls arranged into crosses and hearts, decorated by pitted femurs that lined the walls. Some were snapped and jagged, others smashed. At the center of the heart arrangement was a skull with an unmistakable bullet hole.

I shuddered, thinking of how many lives were lost to time, now yellowed and nameless and proffered to curious travelers.

"I'm sorry," I whispered to the dead, like I'd whispered to Joséphine when I used her corpse to break into her phone.

The city was a god of transformation, a phoenix demanding blood and bones, from the guilty but mostly the innocent, in exchange for being made anew. For better or worse. She was loved despite all the bodies she swallowed, those who gave their lives willingly and the millions who had them forcefully taken, the ones here and the others unaccounted for, never found and never buried, whole and in rotted pieces.

Paris was beautiful in the ugliest way, and I only dreamed of being loved so unconditionally.

Keturah led the way now, weaving between a pair of tourists taking selfies and a column covered in the backs of skulls and leg bones, all the way through the empire of the dead, breathing in decay until we hit the spiral staircase that marked the end of the tour. It carried us up to the exit and out into the quiet streets of the 14th.

Ciro's apartment was less intimidating than Joséphine's. Andor knew the passcode to bring us past the doors, and we climbed uneven wooden stairs all the way up. They creaked with use, the apartments humming with laughter and the clink of dishes and heartbeats. It felt as lived-in as the mismatched cottage in the woods.

When Andor knocked on the apartment's dark wood door, there was only silence.

We waited, the landing so small that I stood on the winding stairs, and Keturah bellowed, "Ciro!" in a booming voice before knocking herself. My heart beat so loudly I was sure they heard, even as Andor pressed his ear to the door, gave us both a sharp look, and took out his spare key.

"Stay close behind," he whispered as he went inside.

I gulped, remembering Joséphine and her quiet, upscale apartment with marble steps and the stench of death.

"Ciro?" Keturah called cautiously as she stepped over the shattered remains of a vase. Dirt and a vibrant snake plant streaked across the floor.

The apartment was beautiful in a neat, minimalist kind of way, the walls covered in black-and-white portraits. Some faces were familiar,

Joséphine, some actors and musicians and writers, and others not. If I closed my eyes, I imagined Ciro appearing from the back halls, dressed in all white as always, grin smug and holding back secrets. But then we found the broken end table, the fractured picture frames, the overturned flat-screen TV.

Andor cursed, stepping into the living room, squeezing his eyes shut, and running a hand through his hair. His figure twitched, four eyes and then two again, antlers crackling like thunder.

"Did you find something?" I whispered, pulse racing as I neared.

Slumped against the wall was Ciro, hair still neat, clothes mostly spotless. His pallor, though, was the pale grey of death, the skin of his cheek dried and cracked like a porcelain doll. There was a ring of burns at his throat, bones jutting out at a sharp angle, and like Joséphine, the red tattoo on his arm, the one I'd seen just last night, was charred. Scorch marks lined the floor.

Keturah lowered her gaze.

I pressed a hand to my mouth.

While I'd wasted time suspecting Ciro of hurting Joséphine, the real killer readied to try again. I was wrong. And by the overturned end table, the spilled stink of brandy from a glass on the white rug, he'd fought back. And been overpowered.

And burned…

My thoughts kept circling back to my bloody shirt, what Ciro said the previous night, them arguing at auditions. She'd even admitted to hating them both and wanting them dead.

Guilt transformed to anger, because suddenly, it made sense.

Rose-Marie knew about the river. About us.

CHAPTER 21

My alarm woke me up what felt like only moments after I'd fallen asleep. Old-time trumpets wailed all the way from my bedroom, and I stirred on the couch, cotton-mouthed and groggy, head aching and eyes dry and heart heavy. Remembering the night before.

Ciro, dead, strangled and burned. Andor, silent and rigid as stone and crumbling fast and glitching.

It was daybreak when Keturah insisted I go home and get some sleep, after the police let us leave and we tucked a catatonic Andor into bed. Only I couldn't sleep. Immediately I'd curled up on my couch with Joséphine's phone and gone searching for clues. Answers. Anything I might have missed.

If she kept lists of everyone her deal screwed over, photos and videos of her scavenging Elysium's woods, copies of esoteric and metaphysical texts, then she *must* have researched others who knew. Somewhere on this stupid glittery brick there was a list with Rose-Marie Baumé on it, proof that she knew and had killed Joséphine and Ciro would be next.

Only I didn't find anything, and I was so tired that eventually all the words stopped making sense. I hoped closing my eyes for a second would help, but it didn't. Because Joséphine and Ciro were already dead.

I groped in the cushions for the phone, a note about the origin of Acheron's altar still open.

. . . Must keep looking in the Catacombs for Lethe's altar. It is the empire of the dead after all.

All of it felt like Joséphine was on the brink of discovering something when her murder interrupted. Or maybe she was murdered *because* she discovered something, and when Ciro realized the truth, he was next. Yet I was too selfish and distracted to pick up the pieces.

All the while the blare of the horns from my alarm continued to fill the apartment.

"Turn it off!" Coralie shouted sleepily from behind her door. Something soft like a thrown pillow landed on the floor.

With a bone-weary sigh, I set the phone down on the table, skulked into my room to kill the noise, and hauled myself into the shower. The ballet was everything I'd ever worked for, all Coralie and I had, and I couldn't afford to throw it away now. It waited for no one.

My antics at La Tempête were all anyone wanted to talk about—it was the right flavor of erratic. They smelled a downfall coming like blood in the water.

"I heard she threatened to stab him," Olivia whispered loudly. She threw me a pointed glance, leaving no ambiguity as to whom "she" referred to. They no longer made any effort to conceal the rumors about me. Every day they were a swarm of gnats that moved from hall to hall, studio to studio, thick enough to choke me. And it didn't hurt any less over time.

When I met her eyes, I clamped my jaw shut in a bite, and she flinched. It was too early, and I was all out of decorum. As I saw it, she was lucky I didn't *actually* bite her.

"She's obviously got anger issues," muttered Vanessa.

I jabbed the side of my pointe shoe with a needle, willing Grandpré to begin rehearsal already. Stitching elastic was the perfect distraction from them, from my growing mountain of problems, a trance that kept my hands and mind away from the urge to crush hearts. No matter what, I wouldn't let anyone see me flustered. I was a ballerina; we never faltered.

"Don't you pay attention?" Rémy objected. "She's a klepto—obviously, she was trying to steal his wallet, he caught her, so she hit him."

There was only one person who could have fed them something so believable. Coralie. She knew all about the wallets I'd snatched growing up, desperate to buy myself tights, leotards, slippers, and costumes. This was her way of getting back at me for blowing her off one too many times. And still I was expected to perform and work my body until it cracked and bled, with no one to bear witness to how worn thin I was. So much for best friends.

The trick to keeping the ribbon steady was to breathe. Both fabrics were slippery and fickle, but steady breaths meant steady hands meant steady lines.

"Flora told me that she and Nina caught her trying to take Alain home," added Olivia with a snicker. "Once they chased her off, she went after Ciro Aurissy."

Jab, pull through, realign. Jab, pull through . . .

Rémy's laugh was dry. "Didn't his girlfriend just die?"

Olivia shrugged. "Guess Grandpré was taken—"

I yelped.

My hand slipped. Sharp and sudden, the needle and threaded floss fell away, red beading on my fingertip. The other apprentices turned, watching me lick the blood away as if I deserved it. Like they were waiting for me to screw up, and no matter if I was perfect or not, they'd find an excuse anyway.

"Good morning," Grandpré shouted as he strolled into the room. Magnanimity flowed from his shoulders, a swagger that carried him over to the pianist as if he were a celebrity and we were his adoring fans. "I hope you're ready for a run-through."

I went back to my stitching, imagining feeding Olivia to Acheron. Standing on a boulder that jutted out, her ankle in my grip, the jaws of rushing water eager for a taste. Would it devour her or spit her out? She was pretty bitter...

I blinked, unsure if it was my idea or the river's. These days, there didn't seem to be any separation between us.

"The only reason Olivia talks so much shit about you and not me is because I kicked her in the shin when we were six," said Coralie with a wry smile, settling down beside me. At my raised brows, she waved the clipboard in her hand. "Volunteering as a production intern."

Instead of the best friend offering gossip, the girl who cheered me up after a bad perm when I was thirteen, I only saw the girl who asked me to throw away my career for her. Because she knew she was all I had. If I asked her about the rumor, she wouldn't admit to it. Even if she knew what her mother was doing, the lengths Rose-Marie would go to for her, she wouldn't acknowledge it. My own mother wouldn't even pick up the phone after she left, much less murder my way into a company.

I started to despise Coralie, whose grin took on an edge, the dark hollows around her eyes deeper, the bones of her cheeks sharper. Like a dog, starved and feral, poised to devour with abandon.

Maybe she realized it too.

On the other side of the studio, Grandpré clapped his hands. "Everyone, up, let's go. We don't have time to waste."

With *Études* shows now underway, the next production on my schedule was *Petrushka*, an easier ballet to assign all the apprentices: The story of the puppet took place in a crowded market, so we danced less and stood around more, smiling, pretending to be impressed by the same variations we'd watched a dozen times.

"First tableau, please," Grandpré shouted impatiently as he took his seat. Coralie reclined beside him.

As I waited at the side for the music, something sharp hit me in the ribs.

Putting her freshly healed clavicle to good use, Olivia elbowed me, the blow snatching the air from my lungs, and smirked at her handiwork. The piano's starting notes rang through the room. She leapt out onto the floor pretending to skip with a basket, and others followed in an explosion of movement.

I glared after her. This was more than rivalry. This wasn't about dancing better than me or Vanessa or any of the others—she just wanted me gone.

At center stage, Geoffrey and three other male dancers did an impressive Russian squat to the opening "Song of the Volochobniki." They spun and dipped with precision, ankles and knees popping to the beat, thighs probably burning with the effort. The air warmed, our group clapped, the smell of sweat and harsh perfumes filling the studio.

My feet itched to dance, to do more than lean forward and back, side to side, beside myself with amazement. I wanted to prove my place here wasn't a fluke. Or charity. That they wouldn't get rid of me.

Vanessa brought her heel down on my toes. And under the guise of the jostling crowd, Rémy nearly knocked me over.

"Oops," he mumbled, though his grin never faded.

I gritted my teeth.

Our crowd backed away, making room for the two dueling variations by Aiko and Flora. It started with the former on the left, galloping with her legs flicked out beneath her. She was sweet and fast, light on her heels and with a bright smile as if this really were a fair on Mardi Gras, and we were giving rubles instead of air.

She threw money at me and told me to *fetch*.

The Acheron in my blood blazed to life. I had to show them that I was meant to be here, that I could dance circles around them all, blindfolded and bound, now just like I had for six years at the academy. That I was still the best.

Compared to them I was godly.

Flora started on the right, pretending to stretch. As she folded over, all I heard was Olivia's haughty voice about what Flora said. *Seducing Alain?* The wicked darkness yelled over the music, over the whispers of the crowd, the eruption of applause when Flora turned around in a circle on one foot, holding her other ankle over her head.

Still wearing Joséphine's stolen earrings.

The air changed. I fixed on Flora's swirling form, watching her spin along the edge of the crowd. She may have been older, a soloist, but soon she'd realize I didn't need Alain or anybody to cover for me. And though I knew I could be better than even her, it took years to land a solo, so she wouldn't know. *Years* of them doubting me, when I could just prove it here and now.

In a flash of fury, I seized the wicked dark and struck her down.

One moment, Flora was caught up in fouettés, whipping her leg rapidly, her heart pounding against my fingertips. The next, my blood called to hers, all me, all fury, so strong I didn't even have to command her, and she tilted like a spin-top. Her foot slipped. She cried out and crashed to the floor with a wet *snap*.

Aiko flinched.

I loosed a steady breath.

The crowd surged forward and then grounded to a halt. Through slippers and pointe shoes, blood pooled on the floor. Vanessa clapped a hand to her mouth and turned away, looking green, retreating. Meanwhile I admired the view: Flora curled up and clutching her leg, jagged, white bone jutting out from flesh and tights, painting her shin and the floor red.

"She just fell!" Olivia uttered with a grimace.

Panic sparked through me before quickly being shoved back down and replaced by something dark, twisted. Wrong as it was, my toes curled with delight. Want came alive in the pit of my stomach at seeing exposed marrow and her face carved in a painful wail. Even if no one understood that it was me, it still felt as life-sustaining as any applause.

My fingertips throbbed as my nails elongated.

I did that.

I gave in to the dark, and I felt good.

Grandpré yelled an obscenity that pulled me out of my daze and raked a hand through his thinning hair. "Nobody move. Don't even breathe without my permission!"

We understood the furrow in his brow: The Paris Ballet was down another soloist. First Sophie Poullain's injury, then Joséphine's death, then Sabine's sudden departure, now Flora.

But not for long.

I licked my lips and took her place, watching as they carted her away and sought a mop for the blood. My heart swelled against my rib cage. This was my chance to show them what it's like to hear the ballet calling, to work for it instead of expecting a place be held for you.

This was what devotion looked like.

"Pay attention," I whispered with a rasp in my throat. All eyes darted to me.

Like Flora, I raised my ankle over my head. There was no music, so I had to keep my own count, but it was fine. I didn't need a pianist to be great.

A full turn on one foot while everyone gaped, forced to concede how smooth I was, every muscle and toe tuned to precision. The gravity in the room changed too—the same way plants tilted toward Andor in the labyrinth, so my disciples tilted toward me.

I'd show them I was more than even an étoile.

Their mouths hung open as I swept up into the piqué manège, fifteen turn-steps en pointe along a broad arc. From the crowd, a hand brushed my arm, trying to stroke me for luck while I conquered the floor. I moved away as fluid as water, as natural as breathing, and met only the determined gaze in my reflection. The muscles in my legs rejoiced, finally being put to good use instead of standing around.

"**Witness a god in the making**," I breathed, holding them close.

The pressure in the room hiked as I whipped around again and again, eyes locked on the seam in the mirror, on myself, on the savage creature staring back. It stretched against skin and slicked me with sweat, and the shard of Acheron that had climbed deep inside me writhed in delight.

We were one in this moment, the river and I, devouring all. How we were meant to be.

Give me all that I deserve, I willed them.

I set sail with a jump and landed in a strong chassé, sweeping my arms to the side in delicate form. A ringlet had come loose from my bun and fallen into my face. My smile gleamed, sharpened. My shoulders rose and fell rapidly.

And around me, the crowd hesitated in their release. Eyes glossed over, unfocused, they blinked and stirred awake. Aiko nodded her approval, and Nina, still in the corner waiting for her entrance, applauded. Her smile didn't reach her eyes, but I didn't care.

Hugo Grandpré clapped a hand on my shoulder, just like he did before *La bayadère*, before Sabine insulted my integrity. It shocked me back into my body. Up close, he looked exhausted and wrinkled with age around the eyes. He asked, "What's your name again?"

Sweat ran down my neck. Over his shoulder, Coralie stared, her mouth pursed, and the force of her disapproval sent a shiver down my spine. She should've been celebrating.

"Mesny," I whispered, breathless, assured that after this, he'd never forget. "Laure Mesny."

"Well, Mesny, I guess you're Dancing Girl number two now," he said in an unceremonious tone. He grimaced as he walked away, mashing the heels of his palms into his eyes. Then he bellowed over his shoulder, "Be careful. You're all dropping like flies."

I didn't move.

If an apprentice danced her way up to a sujet's role, they'd have no choice but to promote me. Now. It was a feat they couldn't deny. And *Études* was a short run, making *Petrushka* less than a couple weeks from the stage; the board would have to do it soon.

I brought my fist to my mouth to bite down a laugh. Teeth cut into my knuckles.

I'd skipped the line. Sure, I might have forced their hand, but that made me a dark horse, not a thief. A clever hero, not a villain. The savior of the ballet, not its ruin. I triumphed while Rose-Marie murdered and still failed.

"Congrats, Laure," said Alain as he passed. The girl gabbing at his side gave a bland smile. Someone squeezed my shoulder.

Wetness gathered at my nose, running down and coating my lip. It tasted metallic. My fingers came away bloody. I took a step back.

"Guess I danced too hard," I mumbled to no one in particular before turning on my heel.

Out of the room, into the hall, and into the restroom, I scurried to tend to the havoc I wreaked on myself. Blood clung to the curve of my lips and chin. Coated my teeth. Dotted the chest of my leotard. My fingers trembled as I washed away evidence of Flora's disaster, as if at any moment, someone might walk in and put the pieces together.

A spark of panic flared bright in me, chanting over and over again that *I did that*. It didn't matter anymore whether the mark had changed me or if I was always this crooked because the horrid deed was already done. Joséphine never wrote in her notes about Acheron corrupting, but since when did blood and domination thrill me?

Then as quickly as it cropped up, another voice, calmer and more grounded, followed. I knew I didn't have to listen to it, but I did. I wanted to. And I let the guilt and panic dissolve. Scatter. Chased away like Keturah bargained away her pain.

My fingers went steady with godly calm as I dried my face. The girl in the mirror with fully red irises had no time for either guilt or grief; she was busy thriving.

Stifling a yawn, I rounded the corner in search of a quiet hall to hide in. Sound traveled far, even in the depths of the opera house, and ghoulish paintings of opera starlettes followed me through every remote corridor. I'd taken to napping before my shows, and after Ciro's discovery and this morning's events, I verged on delirious with sleep deprivation. Every step felt like weights on my ankles, my heartbeat irregular, my breathing labored. I was a zombie walking, but the figure I found standing beside a Firebird costume shocked me awake.

"Keturah?" I rubbed my eyes, scratching my face in the process with the nails I'd just trimmed haphazardly in the bathroom.

Wearing her usual spiky leather coat and bulky boots, she looked so out of place amid the marble floors and gilded walls. She turned and sagged in relief. "This is even worse than the tunnels."

"What are you doing here?" I glanced around for *him*.

There was no one but us, however, and briefly, it was the worst thing in the world. My heart stopped, and my eyes widened, questioning why she'd come. To deliver more bad news—

"He's fine!" insisted Keturah, putting a hand on my shoulder. Because she knew what I was thinking, who I was looking for. "I'm here to get Ciro's things, but this place is a maze. One that reeks of stolen wealth."

She wrinkled her nose and curled her lip. She'd swept her hair up into a pineapple 'do wrapped in a red bandana, and despite the heavy eyeliner and dark red lipstick, there was no hiding the bags under her eyes. She and Ciro were friends, just like she and Joséphine were friends.

"Can you point me toward the office?"

I nodded thickly, feeling terribly transparent. We started back where I'd come from, moving at a slow pace because it was all I was capable of.

"I didn't know if you'd be working today," Keturah said to fill the silence, the body that lay between us.

It took a couple tries to find my voice. "They don't really give days off here. Plus, the work keeps you busy. It's good to stay busy." And I tried to smile, to be convincing.

"I bet. But you look exhausted. Did you sleep at all?"

Considering I still hadn't told anyone about the phone, I only shrugged. There was no easy way to explain foregoing sleep because I needed to dig through it. How, without knowing why Ciro and Joséphine died, their deaths weren't just cruel but senseless—all the signs pointed to me being next. There were no other Acheron marks walking these halls. And because I was selfish, I sat on potential clues and wore that guilt like a crown of thorns.

Sleep could wait.

Down another hall, the administration office sat with its glass doors propped open and a sign that was easy to miss. We paused at the junction, the latest recruits of a dying clan. Opening night of *La bayadère*, when she'd thrown her arm around me, felt so far away.

Keturah tapped the barbell of her tongue piercing against her teeth, contemplating what she said next. "I know it's hard right now, but if you don't rest, your body will rest for you. And then how do you expect to keep going?"

"Thanks, but I'm fine—"

"Your eyes, have they always been red?" She stepped closer, peering down into my eyes, marveling at the color. The proof of what I'd done, who I'd become. "Sorry, I'm the oldest of four—I can't turn it off."

I turned my head away. "I have to get going. We have a show tonight."

She nodded, throwing me a wicked grin. "Break a leg."

My eye twitched, but Keturah didn't notice. We parted, with her heading down the hall toward the office and me remaining still, considering where I might sneak off to or if it was quiet enough to just drop where I stood. If I even *could* close my eyes.

"Keturah?" I asked before she got too far.

She stopped.

"Do you *really* feel no pain? Did it really take everything?"

I considered her brightness in the tunnels, lauding *La bayadère*, her solemnness at finding Ciro. And now, here, she seemed like someone in mourning. Or at least, trying to. Without pain or fear, she'd make a perfect soldier if that was what Acheron was after.

"Yes," she admitted quietly, cocking her head and gazing down the hall. "I have memories of emotions, the *reflex* of them, but before, it was almost too much. I couldn't get out from under the weight of the world. And now…I feel lighter. More in control, confident. I don't feel like

I'm drowning anymore. It's tiring, carrying around so much shame, you know?"

I chewed my lip. "Do you regret it? Or ever feel like you're someone else?"

"Not one bit. Are *you* okay?" She had a look on her face like she'd listen if I told her, like she'd try really hard to understand.

If only I had the words.

I gave her the thumbs-up, waiting for her to walk the length of the hall and vanish inside. Open doors sent a gust of winter wind through the corridor, and I shivered as they clattered shut. Goose bumps covered my arms. And when I glanced back, I found Coralie watching me.

CHAPTER 22

The apartment smelled of Greek food when I got home the next evening. Moussaka-flavored air greeted me as I kicked off my shoes, vapors from spiced eggplant exciting my tongue. I pulled off my coat, ogling the trays of takeout from the traiteur nearby, untouched, hot and ready to celebrate my incoming promotion.

But my stomach turned sour at how Coralie sat waiting.

It was a trap, and I was the mouse.

"I got dinner," she stated, her smile disconnected from the rest of her face. She sat stiff as a doll in her chair. Her once-shiny, golden hair lacked its usual luster in this light, the curls limpid and dripping around her shoulders.

I inclined my head. "Feeling better?"

Coralie patted the seat beside her and offered a container of feta wrapped in phyllo and drizzled with honey—my favorite. My mouth watered in spite of my unease.

"Things have become so tense between us," she admitted, ignoring my question, watching as I neared slowly, her eyes too wide and too shiny. "I wanted to make it up to you—to treat you."

"You know *I'm* the only one with a job, right?"

The corner of her mouth ticked.

The spread was even more decadent up close, juices pooling in the plastic and steam heating my face. My stomach rumbled as I examined it, and, content to see there were no hidden knives with which to kill me while I gorged myself, I sat opposite her. Just to be sure.

"It looks amazing," I conceded, my gaze darting between her and the feta that my hands were already cutting into. After eight hours of dancing, I was starving and sure that Coralie, my best friend in the whole world, wouldn't have the heart to poison me. "You shouldn't have..."

She poured a glass of water, her smile still painted on, too rigid to be natural. It occurred to me with fork poised before my mouth that, while Coralie wouldn't poison me, *her mother* wouldn't have those same qualms. Or better, pins and razor blades hidden inside like they did with pointe shoes.

"Not having any?" I asked cautiously.

"Not hungry."

So I put down my knife and fork, slid my hands under the table, and pinched the skin of the mark on my wrist. She couldn't kill me while I had it, I'd recover—that was what Andor had said, right?

Not exactly. He said it was *harder*, but still possible. And Ciro and Joséphine had lost their marks.

"You should try the courgettes," said Coralie, pulling me from my thoughts. She slid a tray of crispy zucchini closer.

The dinner was a precursor for something. While she stared at me, silent, unmoving, and showing way too many teeth, I ran through the list of what it might mean. Perhaps the food was an apology for asking me to give up my dream, for expecting me to surrender to her the way everyone else did. Only she'd never apologized for anything in her entire life.

Perhaps her mother had told her everything.

I eyed the gyro wrapped in foil and clenched my jaw. I wouldn't be bought with food. "Okay, what is this about?"

Coralie blinked, a long moment passing between us as her mouth weighed her next words. The room temperature fell several degrees. Then the pretense dropped: Her smile vanished, her shoulders slouched, and her shiny eyes narrowed to near slits.

"Your deal."

My knee stopped bouncing under the table. "Wh-what?"

"Give me the terms of your deal with Acheron and what happens if you break them."

Dread tore through me like a serrated blade, exposing every nerve from my scalp to my weary feet. It was a moment I had both hoped for and feared, telling Coralie what I bargained and what I took, which was exactly what she believed she'd lost. But not like this. Her finding out from someone else was worse. If she knew about Acheron, how much did her mother tell her? And why hadn't she turned me in to Auger, her golden ticket to admission?

Coralie fetched something from behind her back and sat it on her empty plate with a *thud*. A phone in a gold glitter case.

The one I'd left on the table this morning, tired and not thinking.

"I'm listening."

I folded the napkin in my lap. "A few months of ..." I considered my words carefully, not seeing the point in lying or further incriminating myself with two assaults on fellow ballerinas. "Power in exchange for blood. If I cut it short, I lose my ability to dance. Forever."

It sounded so simple, but a weight still lifted from my shoulders when I said it aloud. It was a secret not even Acheron's others knew because if they did, that meant showing them everything—every desperate, pitiful part of which Coralie had already caught glimpses.

"What kind of power?"

Suddenly I was grateful for the water she poured and finished my glass. My thumb stroked idle circles around my mark. If I played this carefully, I could keep things from unraveling. My solo was secured, a promotion soon to follow, and Coralie would step right into an apprenticeship like nothing happened. Rose-Marie would see to it. "Let's just say I can be *persuasive*."

"Have you ever 'persuaded' me?"

"No."

"Did you want to?"

I hesitated and pursed my lips instead of answering. Coralie's brows rose as if she didn't expect it. She was taking it better than I imagined, but that only made me more tense instead of relieved.

"What do you do in the evenings? And don't say dancing."

Again I clamped my mouth shut. I couldn't tell her about the others, share any more with her than she already knew. The mess I'd made was my own, not theirs, not while they were grieving.

Her nails drummed on the tabletop. They were ragged, long and uneven, cracked in places and yellow. "Don't want to tell me, huh?"

I stared at the cooling meatballs in their sauce.

"See, I've been observing you, Laure. You're my best friend, so I knew something was up." She rose from her seat and began pacing the length of our living room, her hands clasped behind her. "I gave you every opportunity to come clean, and you failed."

Even with her back turned, I didn't dare release my grip on the table or breathe too deeply in case it came out with a shudder. This was her plan all along, and I backed myself into a corner. My mark squirmed. The monstrous thing in me begged to sink its teeth in her.

"I had my suspicions, so I followed you and Joséphine. I watched you enter the Catacombs, and you came out different. You seemed happier. Less...abrasive."

With Joséphine? That meant she knew from the beginning, had been asking and watching me lie from the beginning. Before she'd even glimpsed my mark, before Joséphine even died.

As if she followed my realization, she beamed and began enumerating on her fingers.

"And then my mother *apologized* to me. You danced the best you ever have at auditions—my god, I was so proud." Her eyes were dreamy and faraway. "At the gala, people who caught your eye seemed clumsy, forgetful. Olivia said class ended early. Then you got a feature and money, somehow. And you started staying out late, coming home tired every night." She nodded sympathetically, like a priest during confession. "Then Sabine packed up and left the city out of the blue. Then, yesterday, Flora."

Every ugly deed laid out before me where I wouldn't escape. But I didn't regret any of it. None of it horrified me, no matter how much the river guided my hand. It gave me the knife, but I drove it in.

"You forgot Olivia's fall," I added with a glower.

Coralie stopped pacing. "You're the first apprentice probably in company history to land a solo, you know."

Oh, I knew.

She leaned forward, her wet hair dripping in the moussaka. "What did it feel like ruining their lives? Do you feel big and tall? Powerful? Important?"

And then she gave the biggest shit-eating grin I'd ever seen.

I said nothing. She wouldn't make me feel ashamed. Not when I never punished her for being rich and blond, with that mousy face and rosy cheeks, bending everyone to *her* will. We were equals now whether she liked it or not—I was just better at getting what I wanted.

Coralie caught her cracked and bleeding lip between her teeth, bemused, and settled back in her chair. "I want you to quit."

My thumbnail broke skin over my wrist.

"Tomorrow, you'll go to the president and tell her you're overwhelmed. You'll resign immediately and request that I take your place so it won't go to waste. Thanks to you, the ballet can't afford to lose any more dancers."

My mouth went dry.

"And then you'll end your pact, get rid of the power. No more cheating your way into a promotion," announced Coralie, hands folded on the table, the kind of pose for negotiating household chores, not my fate. "You're better than that."

I measured my words. "And if I'm not?"

"Then I'll tell my mom and get you fired," she answered coolly.

But Rose-Marie already knew. Auger probably told her about the blackmail, and she killed Joséphine just like she admitted she wanted to do at dinner. *Wring her pretty little neck*, she'd said, and then she killed Ciro too for good measure.

"No ballet in the world will take you after getting fired for sabotage, but resigning?" Coralie continued. "No shame in prioritizing your health, acknowledging that you just weren't cut out for it."

"No one would believe you."

She scoffed. "Be realistic, the picture paints itself—the street thug intimidating all their dancers."

She'd rehearsed this speech, every word practiced like a lawyer in a courtroom, confidence brimming with the set of her jaw. She thought she'd win. And maybe she was right; Joséphine and Sabine were enough to get the imagination going. They didn't need proof to confirm what they already suspected about people like me.

"Please understand—my dream was unfairly taken from me—"

"Yours or your mother's?"

She flushed.

Now was my turn to show her I wouldn't be threatened. I leaned on the table. "What makes you think I won't just make you forget right now?"

Her shiny eyes widened. "But you *haven't*, have you?"

My nails dug into the wood, fighting against the roar in my blood. I couldn't hurt her, not like the guy at the bar, not like Flora. Even if she was foolish enough to bask in my ruin, not knowing it was hers too. "I have a plan for you, if you'd just listen to me—"

"No. Quit now, say you're not ready, and next year, you'll have your fresh start. No deal, no persuasion, no Joséphine or that girl I saw you with—just you and me like old times."

I stared at the open palm she wanted me to take. My appetite was gone, and it took all my strength to keep down what little I'd managed. Without a word, I pushed back my chair, let it scrape against the floor, and stood. Her eyes followed me to the door. The apartment had grown too small; the walls were closing in, and I had to get out.

As I pulled my coat from the hook, she said, "And I'll have my best friend back."

I shoved on my boots and slammed the door behind me.

Coralie had lost it. She was out of her mind to think this would work, to destroy me when she could have just taken the place I was already vacating. To threaten feeding me to her shark of a mother.

My hands raked through my hair, snatching out pins until it was loose and crimped at my shoulders, ends billowing as I stormed down the street. Walking toward anything that might bring this to an end.

No way I'd sleep tonight. Not when I could hardly breathe.

My phone buzzed in my pocket, and for some reason, despite my running and gasping, I answered. I put it to my ear and slipped on my mask of calm. "Hello?"

"Laurence?"

My legs stopped in the middle of the sidewalk, my spine pin-straight. *Julien.* My father's name had blared across the screen, proving once again that the man and his ex-wife always chose the worst times to pretend they cared.

"Papa, hello." That name spilled out of me, a reflex.

And judging by the long silence on his end of the line, he wasn't used to it either.

He cleared his throat. "Your birthday's coming up. Eighteen. I-I wanted to, I thought we should meet. Let me take you to dinner, hear how it's . . . coming along."

The ballet. He still wouldn't call it "the ballet." Always "it," my "little thing," a hobby. He was warring with my career before I understood the rules of battle, all because it reminded him of her.

The backs of my eyes stung, my throat thickened. His timing—when "it" was all going horribly awry, and by the next night, everything I'd worked for, everything I had, would be ruined. It took all my control, nails cutting into my palm, teeth breaking skin on my lip, to stop from throwing the damned phone across the street. To stop from screaming and tearing the whole city apart.

"Sure," I squeezed out, just to get him off the line.

I didn't want to be disappointed again, but I had no more energy to fight back.

Julien gave a nervous laugh but chose a restaurant downtown, a date, a time. He thanked me twice. The single tear rolling down my cheek seared. I seethed harder. The emerald ring on my finger was heavy as an anchor dragging me to the seafloor, but I picked up my pace, running again until there was a face in mind. And then, a place to go.

Twenty minutes later, I met Andor beneath a bank of elm trees outside of Parc des Buttes-Chaumont. He was reaching up to touch some branches while the branches stretched down to him, silence on the other side of the concrete wall. Its winding pathways were thrown into shadow, and the cold wind whipping at my ears ensured the street was vacant, leaving us alone.

And he was waiting for me.

He'd answered the moment I rang, the baritone of his voice calm while I was shy of imploding. I'd wanted to see how he was holding up, and he wanted to get away, and the park spilled out of me before I'd even realized what I was asking.

It was instinct that drove me toward him. When he turned around, brightening at the sight of me, my heart seized. The pure blacks of his eyes still shone despite the dark circles underneath. Streetlight illuminated little flower blossoms woven through his braided hair. The small smile that curved on his lips was dim and laced with hurt, but he was trying. And still it disarmed me, and the sting in my wrist from my digging nail, the inside of my cheeks bloody from biting—all of it turned bright and new. As if my pain demanded he come take a look.

I stopped walking before we drew any closer and I made things worse. "Thanks for meeting me. I know it's late . . . How are you?"

Andor tucked his slender hands into his pockets and glanced back at the trees, the ease on his face soothing my breath some. "I needed a break."

"Have you been to this park before?" I asked, pivoting toward the entrance. It was my turn to lead, and he followed with soft steps. "I thought you might like it. It's kind of like a labyrinth of its own. Sometimes you can't even hear the city."

And at night, it was only starker, stripped of its dog walkers and running children and picnics with speakers turned low. I kept a moderate pace, hoping I might shed the cold sweat from Coralie behind me, but everything she said had permeated through skin and into bone. She not only knew about my arrangement but was planning to have me fired. It didn't matter that my victory helped her too; she wanted my total surrender.

"Do you often go on walks so late at night, when it's so cold?" Andor asked with a sideways glance. Though he rubbed his arms against the chill, the shape of the willow trees as they dangled over the lake caught his rapt attention. "Is this some prima ballerina routine?" When I kept walking and said nothing, he added more seriously, "Laure? What's wrong?"

A pang of guilt sliced through me. Without thinking, I'd dragged him here, grieving, to the cold, dark, and quiet, and he dropped everything without hesitating while I chewed my lip bloody. But if I didn't say something, I'd explode.

"She knows."

He slowed near a copse of oak trees. "Who knows what?"

"My best friend. Coralie. Rose-Marie's *daughter*. She knows about Acheron, me," I said, my heart climbing into my throat. "She'll get me dismissed if I don't quit and revoke the favor on top of everything else going on."

His warm hand closed around my arm, burning through my sleeve, reminding me of the heat from his lingering touch in the labyrinth. My mind cataloged every sneaked glance, putting meaning to things that should have been meaningless, and it cast doubt on why I called him in the first place. And why he'd come running, especially now.

My mark twitched with the impulse to draw him closer, fingers craving to fist the front of his coat, but I stayed still. And pulling away was out of the question even if I wanted to.

Andor regarded me softly and said, "I'm sorry to hear that."

"She's handed everything, and the one time I get something she wants—" My breath caught. The cold air stung my eyes, and a sob threatened to sweep me away, even as I gritted my teeth to fight it. "If I walk away from Acheron, I lose my ability to dance. And then what's the point? All this death for what?"

Strong arms wrapped around me, reeling me in until I was folded into his chest, his face pressed into my hair. The sob that I pushed down rose again, and I saw Coralie's smug grin when I squeezed my eyes shut. This was what she'd wanted: to see me weak and in need so she could be my savior. But I wouldn't give her that, and I wouldn't surrender the ballet so easily.

"It's not fair to ask that of you. None of this is fair," Andor whispered into my hair. Breathing me in.

And I knew he was talking about Ciro too. I stiffened.

So close, his heart thrumming strong and clear, wafting waves of moss and earth from his shoulders that drained the frustration right out of me. I timed my breaths with his, the steadiness of his frame holding up mine in the dark. Within the park's boundaries, the world stopped fighting us for just a minute. I'd claimed a momentary respite away from the predators on my heels, but the instant we budged, time would demand I don my armor again.

"I'm sorry," I said. "You're grieving—"

Andor hovered close when I raised my head to look at him, the flash in his eyes dangerous. Both sorrowful and starving, stilling the air in my lungs. Inviting me to move closer, comfort him. Him or the Acheron under his skin, I still couldn't tell. It still didn't matter. Just like the steps in our dance together didn't matter, not when it was only us two.

As his gaze brushed my lips, I pictured him consecrating my blood to hungry roots in his garden. The moss in Elysium could make a home of my bones and I'd welcome it wholly just to feel permanent and part of something. The darkest part in me hungered for that brand of ruin.

His eyes implored me with a message I dared not translate. His pulse radiated from his skin into the surrounding air, my monstrousness attuned to it and yearning for contact.

I pushed his arms away. "Andor, you're *grieving*—"

His gaze darted past me.

A chill ran its fingers slowly down my spine. The air turned still as a tomb. The flesh under my mark shifted. It was here.

Grass stirred behind me, and Andor jerked me out of the way. Then came a flash of light. Cold and sharp, there and then gone, as everything fell silent. It sliced past me, singeing a lock of hair.

A blow to my shoulder blade sent me sprawling face-first in the dirt. Chin stinging, pain flaring through both wrists. At my back came Andor's shout, and too soon he collapsed in a heap beside me, his head striking a gnarling root. He went still. Blood flowed quickly down his face.

Reeling, I rocked back on my heels just as another strip of light sailed toward us. It nicked my cheek, burning like ice.

Then the bloodlust in my bones rose to a scream and seized control.

I bared my teeth and wrenched the heartbeat behind the blinding white light with all my might, forcing the faint, slippery pulse to a standstill. My knuckles cracked with the effort, so forceful and certain and sated that it should have scared me. But the mark saved us. *Acheron* saved us.

The light petered out, my retinas still burning as the culprit who marred my face and laid a hand on *my* monster dropped to the ground. On my feet, I managed one prowling step to finish them off before Andor let out a pained groan at my back.

The wrath bled out of me instantly, replaced by relief. And then fear. Andor hadn't moved. Blood ran heavily down his face. And across the path, that featherlight heartbeat started up again. There was a choice to be made: retribution or *him*. I might never get another chance to strike, and Andor was a distraction yet again. Between who I pictured "Laure" to be and the beast lurking beneath the surface, I didn't know who preferred what.

"We have to go," I whispered, kneeling down to shake his arm. In the shadows, there was no telling where the blood came from, but it was all over. So hot and fresh, my own mark sang in its proximity. "I can't carry you, but we have to go before they—"

Andor groaned again, and his warm, blood-soaked hands closed around mine. Wind lashed through the trees. Skeletal branches shook loose. And before the assailant stood and tried again, my stomach lurched, and we flopped hard onto the cottage floor.

CHAPTER 23

We weren't in the park anymore. We weren't in Paris anymore. Beside me, Andor released a pained breath, and I rolled up and away from him, gaping at his bloodied form. His pinched eyes. The red ink peeking from beneath his sleeve.

Four deals.

And one of them just brought us to Elysium in the blink of an eye.

"You…" I started, groping for words, but there were none.

Footsteps thundered down the stairs, and soon, Keturah was shouting questions and commands. The room was still spinning as she clutched my face in her small hands, demanding to know what happened. All I could do was stare at Andor, whose blood was pooling in the floor cracks. It looked worse in the firelight. But I couldn't answer. I didn't understand what had happened and how we got here, why it was so hard to focus and make sense of it.

"We were just talking and then the light…"

I was in shock. Even as we hauled Andor into the bathroom, as Keturah assessed the damage and he said he was fine, I couldn't stop shaking. He'd been hurt taking a blow meant for me.

It took a long time to scrub Andor's blood from my skin, but the buzzing numbness of poison lingered. Rust and dirt had settled deep in my nail beds, and every so often, I had to keep pausing to check my reflection. In case someone was there. The discomfort hadn't left my bones, and it reminded me of every time I'd encountered it: around the ballet, outside my apartment, in the Catacombs. Now there was another attack, and if Andor hadn't been there, I'd be the next dead body to discover.

If it weren't for me, he wouldn't have been anywhere *near* the park. And if it weren't for the beast in me, we would have died. I gave into it, so it protected us.

All cleaned up, Andor relocated to sit by the fire, his long legs stretched out in front of him, dark hair covering half his face while Keturah stood with needle and thread at his scalp. She was smart to wear gloves—blood clotted sticky around his hairline and down the side of his shirt. I didn't know if my own dizziness was from exhaustion or exposure. But he was upright at least.

All the horrors of my spoiled dinner paled by comparison.

Keturah nodded toward the tea set on top of a velvet ottoman. "Sit down, Laure. Warm yourself up."

Nodding, I poured a cup of English breakfast and sank into the couch. The adrenaline had faded, and I was too tired to do anything else but watch Andor wince beneath Keturah's stitching.

"I still don't understand what happened," I mumbled with a sigh. "And you're sure you're all right?"

"I'm fine," he said, waving a hand. An oleander blossom appeared at his fingertips, and he tucked it in the front pocket of his ruined shirt.

Keturah snorted bitterly. "Don't forget to show her the best part."

I glanced between them.

Then Andor swept the hair from his face to reveal a thin, violent scar. It crossed from the top of his brow to the edge of his cheek, turning the whole of his left eye milky white. The corners of his mouth were too tense for the valiant smile he tried to give. He was rigid with anger. And loss.

"Will it . . . ?" I asked, and then swallowed the rest.

"No. I don't think it will."

I dropped my gaze, but not before glimpsing the clench of his jaw. The crackle of the fire was too loud for the room and how badly we were faring. If this was the same thing that killed Ciro and Joséphine and burned their tattoos, then he was lucky to be alive. To walk away losing *just* an eye.

"We're not supposed to scar," Keturah spoke up, hands stitching slowly, "don't know if you noticed. Ciro told me, bruises and cuts, those things heal without a trace. Whatever attacked you was something special."

"Special like us?" *Something primeval, something fueled by primordial power.*

She frowned. "Or worse. Look around—Elysium's a lot bigger than our little gang, and there aren't exactly rules or a welcome committee."

"It was the same thing from the ballet," Andor started, hidden once again behind his curtain of dark hair. "Like spiders under your clothes, and cold..."

My fingers went to the cut on my cheek, and I shuddered remembering how my mark had itched right before the attack. The scorch marks on Ciro and Joséphine, her experiment with the jars, the exploding glass, all the unease around the halls of the ballet, outside my apartment, how my blood recoiled—

"Cold like Lethe," I finished for him.

From above, Keturah froze in the middle of snipping thread and stared blankly at me. Cornering me so I could no longer avoid sharing what I knew. "You're kidding."

I turned my head to the window as if that twin river was visible through the trees. It was always there on the horizon when I walked through the meadow, the silvery-white echo to my monstrous benefactor. If Joséphine was right, then there had to be something within the

Catacombs. Maybe Lethe found its own crack between worlds and was recruiting just like Acheron.

"Did Joséphine ever find Lethe's altar?"

Andor's visible eye widened. "I didn't know she was looking, but she would have told us if she did."

"Unless she didn't get a chance to," I mumbled, to their horrified expressions. "Unless she got caught."

Coralie's mother leaving our apartment, the sinister air that followed her to her car, the only other person with a key. Rose-Marie was beautiful, powerful, undeniable—she could have a deal of her own.

"How do you know? Did she tell you?" Keturah pressed, distractedly shoving first aid supplies back in the bag and unwilling to look away from me.

I tucked my bottom lip between my teeth and averted my gaze. "I . . . took her phone when I found her. I've been going through it—"

"You've had it all this time?" She cursed.

I drank my tea in a single, scalding gulp and wished for something stronger to knock me out. My limbs were tired and my mind still reeling, and my heart was racing just to keep me awake. The night had dragged on far too long, and the yawn that escaped insisted as much. It was bad enough that Andor lost an eye because of me, but now, with my guilty admission, it was only a matter of time before they cast me out and I had nowhere left to go. I let my monstrousness turn me into a liability.

Finally, and with an exasperated sigh, Keturah spoke. "Well, it's a good thing you were together. They weren't prepared for both of you."

I flushed, not bothering to look up from my teacup. Heat rose in my neck, spanning my cheeks, and the meager cut on my cheek throbbed. Pulling my knees to my chest, I just nodded, because I didn't know what else to do. About Andor, Rose-Marie, Coralie, the ballet, all a tangled mess with me at the center.

It was different when I'd hoped the killer didn't know or care about me; now I might die before I had my few minutes of glory and take these two with me. The world might never learn my name.

I didn't remember falling asleep, but I woke up curled on the couch, a patchwork blanket thrown over me, inhaling an aroma of moss, nettle, rain, and blood. Andor's head was a pleasant weight and warmth on my arm, soft black hair pooling over. His eyes were closed, his shoulders moving with deep, slumbering breaths, and in front of him, the fire was nothing but cinder. Keturah curled like a cat in a nearby armchair. Reddish dawn broke through the windows.

I hoped Coralie stayed up frantic, worrying where I'd slept on such a chilly night. I hoped she suffered my absence.

Andor's expression was peaceful beneath his new scar. It notched through all of his thick brow, indented and still red as if a whip had stripped the flesh away. My fingers itched to trace the curve of his cheek, the pout of his lips, the curl of his tresses, but I pulled my bloodstained sleeves over my hands to smother the urge. It was exactly this kind of thought that got him hurt. And still he dozed sitting within my reach. His brother, his eye—how much more would he lose when I was through with him?

He stirred.

I shifted away and pretended to stretch, though I'd slept in worse places—hallways, carpeted auditorium steps, anywhere flat enough between classes and shows. Keturah lurched on the other side of the room, neon-yellow coils sticking out from her wrap. She rubbed her face.

"So, what's next?" I asked, massaging my calf, awaiting my sentence. Putting Andor in harm's way, stealing Joséphine's phone, letting it get this far—did I confirm their worst fears about selfish, obsessive ballerinas? "You'll go looking for Lethe in the Catacombs?"

Keturah arched a brow. "*We*'ll go tonight. Because you should get to the ballet, don't you have class?"

I scoffed and rolled my eyes. "Who cares about the bal—"

My voice stopped in my throat as I heard myself. *I* cared. Or was supposed to. It was my everything, my only constant, woven into the fabric of my DNA. Everything I was and would be was entwined with ballet, and had been for as long as I could remember. It was why I walked through fire and bled in the first place.

Which meant I wouldn't roll over and play dead. I wouldn't let Rose-Marie win.

Rehearsal for *Petrushka* was already underway when I arrived. Late.

It took time to trek to the apartment, shower, dress, overturn all the cushions and drawers in search of Joséphine's phone with no luck, and venture back south to the gilded halls of Palais Garnier, Keturah's nervous smile by my side. All the while I replayed the horrid highlights of the night over and over again: Coralie's ultimatum and that look in Andor's eye, his new scar and the killer walking the streets. I didn't know what I'd say to President Auger if Coralie ratted me out, or what I'd do if Rose-Marie caught me all alone. And though Keturah could tell I was preoccupied our whole trip, she didn't ask. For that, I was grateful.

With only a couple hours of sleep in me by the time I arrived at Palais Garnier, I was tired before the day even began.

Music spilled through the seams of the studio doors, flooding me with shame. It was from the third tableau, which meant not only had I missed morning class, but I'd also missed my new solo. And Laure Mesny was never late.

When I pushed on the metal door, it rattled loudly, announcing my presence. Dozens of eyes turned to gawk.

"Sorry," I mouthed, cheeks burning as I flitted to a corner and dropped my bag.

Alain and Nina were in the middle of a duet, swirling across the floor as "the Moor" puppet and his delicate Ballerina. When the casting was announced, my classmates had lauded it a thoughtful touch that Alain was chosen instead of another dancer caked in dark makeup like other city ballets had done. I'd rolled my eyes.

The soloists danced beautifully, moving as if they shared a single breath that they passed between them, the combination of talent and years together. Alain's parents had produced a film with Nina as their star, and Nina's review of his partnership would no doubt elevate him to premier in the coming year. Maybe she'd invite him next summer to London too in the perpetual duet of powerful people doing each other favors. An ouroboros of privilege while Coralie was busy punching down when we could've been working together.

I shook out my pointe shoes, biting my lip as two small thumbtacks meant for the pads of my feet tumbled free. On the other side of the room, the pianist brought the waltz to an end.

"Well done, Nina," the junior director Yelena shouted, hopping to her feet. "Let's break for five and then move to Petrushka's entrance. Laurence?"

My name jolted me around. She glared at me through blunt bangs, her rose-pink lips pursed in disapproval. And she didn't wait for me to approach before she continued, loud enough for everyone to hear.

"I expected more professionalism from you, as an apprentice with so much ambition and a member of this production. You cannot show up whenever you want, toss a little effort our way, and expect to be showered in praise and a contract."

"That's not what I expect at all, actually," I retorted, leveling my gaze to hers in challenge. It slipped out of my mouth before I had time to reconsider how it'd look, but I wanted a fight. With anyone. It was better than always sitting politely, stoic, taking kicks as they came.

My gaze drifted to Coralie, parked at Yelena's side with a clipboard in hand. Watching, not even trying to hide her smile.

Yelena squared her shoulders. "This isn't your world, where you're some hotshot breaking all the rules because you can. This is a job, and you're just an intern. We expect you to show up and do the work—"

"Are you finished?" I interrupted, doing my best to look bored because I knew all this. I understood more than anyone how important this was, how far I had to go, what it meant to show *respect*, and I was sick and tired of simultaneously being apart from the rest, the standard to beat, and the object to point their frustrations and failures at.

I just wanted to dance.

She crossed her arms. "You may have Grandpré fooled, but this is a company full of everyone's life's work. If you want to survive long enough, act like you give a damn because the ballet will be here with or without you. And if you pull something like this again, I'll replace you with Coralie."

At that, I might as well have turned to stone. I clenched my jaw so hard it hurt, and my face stung as if someone had slapped me. "B-but she's not even a member—"

"Maybe I'll make an exception." Yelena shrugged. "Or are *you* the only one who gets special treatment?"

All eyes narrowed on me. All of them hungering for spectacle if I exploded. Everything I strove for was so close to being snatched right out from under me, and they circled overhead like vultures, waiting for me to fall.

Maybe I didn't want to play this game anymore.

Worse, Yelena was right: If my career ended tonight, they'd all be back here bright and early as if nothing had changed. And all of this—the deal, the mark, Joséphine, the past twelve years of my life, and the relationships ruined for the sake of this dream—would be for nothing. And I would be no one, while the girl who couldn't even pass her audition failed upward into my place.

Yelena arched her brow, waiting for a reply that I wouldn't give, an excuse to send me packing.

My jaw quivered at the threat of crying, and I turned away. Back to my shoes, and then tendus, pulling from the hip and the core, taking deep breaths, biting my tongue until it bled, until pain was all I felt. Until it subsumed everything else because I wouldn't cry in front of them. I wasn't their entertainment or their supper.

"Ready?" Yelena asked in a softer voice.

The piano rumbled to life moments later. My breaths remained shallow, even as I took my place with the rest of the chorus. Aiko shrank away when I lined up, and like an electric charge, my frame repulsed everyone for the rest of the rehearsal.

Anger nestled in my ribs, rendering my every movement in the final tableau forced, stilted. It was all twisted—Yelena's assessment of me, Coralie, her mother, the scathing looks everyone gave. I always showed up on time and did the work. I *tried*, dedicating hours to smoothing out my hair and slipping on expensive new leotards I had to steal to afford, practicing until my bones ached and my feet bled and my toenails fell off. Not even prostrating myself before an eldritch god could change them.

Every jump was a knife through my shins. Every turn was a sob about to tear free. And I hated every moment of it—for the first time, dancing wasn't worth all it took to be here.

As I packed my bag, a shadow loomed over me and turned my

stomach sour with dread. Coralie clutched the clipboard to her chest, the hollows of her eyes deeper than they were the previous night, but her grin bright. "Bold of you to show your face here."

I slung the bag over my shoulder and released a full-body sigh I had no strength to hold back. On the metro ride over here, there were a hundred things I'd thought to tell her, brave, cowardly, and perhaps too honest. I even fantasized about breaking in her front teeth. But instead, because I was *always* the bigger person, now I just quipped, "You get your mother to fight your battles for you—what do *you* know about bold?"

And with a shove, I pushed past her and headed into the hall.

Coralie followed. "Will you go to the president now, or should I?"

She was baiting me. It was in her posture, head high, smile unshaken and triumphant, as if I'd already signed the apprenticeship over to her and all she needed now was to be crowned. Well, I wouldn't do it. She'd have to take it from my cold, dead hands.

"I'm not afraid of you," I answered blankly. And for a moment, when I turned into the great atrium, her footsteps didn't follow.

"You don't mean that," Coralie countered after a beat. "I know you better than you know yourself. You don't want to go to war—"

"Oh?" I snarled, whirling around to grab her arm. My nails elongated to points in the span of a breath, piercing skin and scraping bone, my canines sharpening to wolfish points in my sneer. A thrill ran through me at how her eyes rounded, the flash of fear in them as she finally, *finally* noticed the red in mine. The beast that was tired of feigning deference, waiting patiently for scraps.

I squeezed a soft yip out of her and growled, low and full of malice, "Do. Not. Test. Me."

The warning was as raw as I felt, monstrous and rolling through my chest like thunder, and this time, there was no flicker of guilt to follow.

It was too late to care just how wretched I'd become—the varnish had worn off, and the night before, whatever I was now had saved me. And I had bigger problems than this vindictive little girl.

Heeled footsteps echoed along the balcony, and I dropped my grip just in time for President Auger to cross into view.

"Laurence? A moment?"

My blood chilled.

Her expression had the same severity as always, neutral, and beside her, Coralie continued to gape at me, giving nothing away. She might have already told the old woman before I arrived.

Still, I followed the president down the marble stairs, across the mosaic floors, toward the office. We walked in silence, her jasmine perfume singeing my nostrils and the *click* of her shoes piercing my ears. Every step was torture, wondering if I would get to finish the season or pack my locker before the day was up. Where would I go?

She closed the door to her office behind me.

"Please sit," urged President Auger as she walked around her dark wood desk. "I expect your rehearsals are going well? And you're adjusting well?"

Ha.

I smoothed a thumb over my mark. "Yes, it's good. Everything is great."

Unlike her desk, the walls were covered in framed photos of famous dancers, most of them signed and addressed to "Fiona." I tried to look everywhere but the woman's face, lest she see the red and recoil. She wasn't the one who should be afraid.

"Good. That's why I wanted to talk. The board and I have been discussing feedback from the directors..."

A line of cold sweat ran down my spine.

"With Flora's injury and Sabine's sudden departure, we are in a tough place when it comes to dancers," she added, her voice tapering into silence. A bus roared outside her window.

"**Spit it out**," I snapped accidentally, power rolling from my tongue to ease my bouncing knee and racing heart.

Her eyes glistened instantly, and in monotone, she announced, "The ballet would like to make you an offer."

I sat back in my chair, blinking. Stunned.

The woman squinted at her paper as if to confirm what it said and then nodded. Her soft blue eyes locked on me. "It would be a temporary contract for the rest of this season and the next, for the rank of coryphée."

Leading the corps.

"Not quadrille?" I blurted, struggling to keep up.

Everyone hired after apprenticeships entered as quadrille first because it was the lowest rung on a tall ladder. Promotion to a higher rank wasn't *impossible*, but it was as rare as étoiles. As rare as Joséphine. And now me.

"Well, the contract is temporary," Auger explained. "You wouldn't be a regular member. But once it's over, you'd be free to go anywhere in the world, and they'd be lucky to have you."

Which meant I wasn't free to stay. When it was done, so was my time on this stage.

The ballet reserved temporary contracts for special guests, soloists with home ballets elsewhere who didn't need steady employment. It wasn't the same as belonging. By the summer, I'd be turned loose, no job, no ballet, and nowhere to go. But I'd also be free to try someplace new with proper productions at a proper company on my résumé, adorned with the highest rank any brown-skinned girl had reached in years. It was the kind of promotion that made legends, temporary or not.

"After all, your mother is American, right?" continued Auger with a wink as I rose from my chair.

I stiffened. My heart deflated. The ring on my finger tightened to a vise.

"You can go to New York after. You're an extraordinary dancer—I'm sure you'll adapt to the American style of ballet in no time. Plus, you'll feel more at home. Sabine's there!"

CHAPTER 24

I stumbled out of the Opéra in a daze, letting my feet carry me across the Seine and its black, hungry waters, far away to someplace quiet. Taking me *there*.

Tomorrow, I'd become coryphée, and by summer, I'd escape it all: the stares, Coralie's ultimatum, death lurking in the halls. It'd take me far from the Catacombs, Elysium, Acheron, its monsters—I could be free from the wickedness I'd been nurturing just to survive this place.

My heart stumbled in my chest, and then I was running.

It was doable: Accept the ballet's offer, grin and bear the isolation awhile longer, rise victorious in another city. I'd never been to New York; there, I could become someone new, normal, respected. It wasn't Paris, my *home*, but home was beginning to chafe. I could climb again without Acheron's help, though I'd feel the void it left behind.

Soon the balmy heat of Elysium was billowing in my face.

In ballet, what mattered most was transformation, and transformation demanded sacrifice. We whittled down our bones to take the shapes we needed, dancing on splints and sprains, stretching tendons until they strained, all to reach new heights. Perhaps my life now was what I had to sacrifice to become the dancer I needed. Set aside my attachment to Coralie, who was hell-bent on sabotage. Shed my reliance on Acheron like dead skin. Walk away from Andor and Keturah, distractions. I was first and foremost a ballerina, and if I broke all these chains, I'd be better: the Laure I always wanted to be instead of the Laure I was forced to become.

At the end of the day, I had to put myself first, because no one else ever did. And they never would.

"Get ready for me at my worst!" I screamed into the forest canopy, craning my head back, sending birds flying. My legs tangled over a fallen log, and I choked down a laugh that bordered on a sob.

And by the time I caught my breath and stopped feeling like I was going to burst, I'd arrived outside the labyrinth. I'd only wanted a quiet place to think, but that meant Elysium, and then Elysium came to mean *here*. Still, I ambled closer.

Tall hedges rose among the trees, beckoning. It evoked the park all over again, my instincts warring with rational thought, strolling toward a poison garden when I should have been considering my escape.

Unclear if it was me or the beast deciding, I ventured inside. There was no way to remember which paths led to the center, but I was content to idle among the Christmas roses that glowed in dusk. Getting lost was almost preferable—the longer I stayed, the longer I could put off choosing. Maybe the stink of night-blooming corpse flowers would clear my head. Maybe while I was here, I'd say my goodbyes.

But if I took the ballet's offer, eventually all this would be gone, and why should I have to leave? What kind of victory meant giving up more than I started with?

"Laure, is that you or did the flowers finally get to me?" Andor's soft voice drifted out from a shadowy passage as I breezed by. The rustle of his footsteps followed along with the thrum of his pulse, so vibrant my mark latched on it. It itched against the roof of my mouth. He was in his most primal state, towering antlers decorated with a circlet of daffodils and baby's breath, half of his shiny, iridescent face obscured by wild, dark hair, ink overflowing in his four eyes. He was still a thing of nightmares, of terrible dreams I knew I'd miss, whether I won or Coralie did.

Despite everything, I found my traitorous mouth mirroring his smile. The storm retreated. I forgot all the reasons I was supposed to be cautious.

"Just going for a walk—I hope you don't mind," I said, pretending to study the hedges rife with belladonna sprouts that stretched from their shoots toward him. That they were so carefree in yearning made me envious. "It seems I keep stumbling on this place."

"You're welcome anywhere. Want my help getting to the center? Whoever designed this place loved complexity a little too much." The groove of dimples in that macabre mask brought heat to my face. And when he stepped around me, engulfing me in the musk of blood meal and oleander blossoms, I couldn't help but drink him in. And join him in the dark.

Andor's knuckles brushed mine as we walked, each point of contact humming. Every thought that didn't revolve around that sensation fell away like autumn leaves until he asked, "Still deciding what to do about Coralie?"

I could have told him the truth, been honest about my dream being served as a shiny apple with a rotten core. But I didn't. The last thing I wanted was for Andor to feel pressured to care, because he had his own losses to withstand. And if he encouraged me to leave? That scared me more.

"It's fine now," I lied, slipping my hands into my pockets. A cool mask of calm. "We worked it out. How are you feeling?"

We were dancing again around what we wanted.

He turned a corner slowly and hung his head, careful not to displace the hair hiding his scar or to show how affected his vision was. Even in this form. It must feel terrible to wear the price of power on a cursed face when all you wanted was to be marvelous. A god reminded that he was at once proud and fragile.

"It hasn't healed, if that's what you're asking. Can't see out of it, but I'm not dead, thanks to you."

When he looked at me, I looked away, pursing my lips to avoid pointing out that the only reason he got hurt was *because* of me.

And as if he read my thoughts, he mumbled, "It's not your fault, you know."

No, I didn't. And worse, that still didn't stop me from coming here.

It was foolish of Coralie to think she knew anything about me. She didn't. Maybe no one did. Single-minded, heartless, once-a-ruffian-now-a-ballerina Laure didn't do what I was doing. Through river or circumstances, I wasn't the same. Coralie couldn't have her friend back because *she didn't exist.* And maybe never did.

The world didn't know a Laure that was allowed to want and take.

I'd give in just once and get him out of my system. Once, and I'd be back on track. There had to be some solution to all my problems, one I couldn't see because I was distracted, imagining what his lips felt like, the heat of his skin. It had to come from the same dark place as my desire to break things. I'd give in and this brand of hunger would fade. Because the alternative, if it came from *me*, well... It just couldn't.

Once, and my fascination with this place would die. A clean getaway.

"It's a little messy," Andor warned as the passageway opened to the center of the labyrinth, worrying his lip. "We just finished our semester showcase, and I haven't found anywhere to put it all yet."

It was cluttered. A hammock made of vines and flower petals now swung between the oleanders, framed by the wicker benches half consumed by lichen. And the canvas on the easel was no longer blank, the painted face staring back at me immediately familiar. My own.

Sharp eyes and a dimpled chin, the severe widow's peak somehow softened. In the middle of blowing a kiss, in a field of poison hemlock. The same kiss, in fact, from my audition for *Giselle*, when I danced Kitri in that room full of vipers. The first day I saw Andor, tucked in a corner, scribbling away. There were others and drawings scattered on the benches—me en pointe, in arabesque, wearing the veil from "Kingdom of the Shades." Asleep in tall grass. Glaring.

Carefully rendered vignettes of a girl I didn't recognize.

He'd even painted the portrait of Joséphine from the vigil. I sank onto a bench, hands full of scraps of others: Ciro posing and looking bored, Keturah sitting eagerly behind the drum set now wedged in a corner of the cottage, Joséphine with her nose in a book, and more of my resolve chiseled away.

Andor settled beside me as if to destroy the remains of it, close but not touching. "What do you think? You can tell me if it sucks. I don't bite, no matter how I look," he prompted, his fists clenching and releasing on his knees.

He's sitting out of reach because he's poisonous, some tempered part of me insisted, though it did my racing heart no good. That voice was too quiet, too practical.

I laughed in spite of myself, aware that it would only get harder from here. That I had to ask before I chickened out and had to leave. "Did it make you poisonous when it gave you beauty or after?"

This threw him off.

Andor's brows knit, and he cocked his head, thinking over his answer. "Well, I was obsessed with beauty. I painted it, I sketched it, I photographed it—then I wanted to become a work of art. And then I wanted to create it myself."

"And then it changed you," I supplied the ending.

"And then I craved it so much, I let it change me," he echoed.

I swallowed, locking my eyes on the loose thread at the bottom of my coat. I started picking at it. "What would happen if ... I lost my favor tomorrow? If I moved far away and couldn't reach Elysium anymore."

Will it hurt when I'm gone? Will I be missed?

He took a long time to respond, mulling it over on his tongue before he said slowly, "What do you want to happen?"

"I don't know." My shoulders deflated as the dangling thread came loose. Since when did anyone in the world care what I wanted? "I spent my entire life on this one long performance: being so good and perfect that everyone would *have* to see me. I never had time to stop and think if I really wanted it. It never mattered."

The cracks in my mask had deepened until there was nothing left to stop this from spilling out. Ballerina Laure wasn't allowed to admit such things, but what did appearances and armor matter if I was leaving? I couldn't have this and the ballet too.

I kept pulling thread, more and more, wrapping it around my finger and watching the end of my coat unravel to a mess. "And maybe I don't want to be good. Maybe I'm tired of being perfect and polished and *pretty* all the time." I wanted to be messy, to make a mess of everything. I was so sick and tired of *order*.

"Maybe I just want to be enough," I said, my voice definitive and so sure for the first time in a long while.

"You are."

When I raised my head and met his gaze, darkness flickered behind Andor's eyes. Like the primordial thing beneath his skin was waking up. Or pacing and impatient, perhaps. Warring internally, the same battle between instinct and rational thought. Because he was poisonous, and I wrought destruction.

Still, I reached toward him, and he didn't flinch. He didn't shrink away or change form. He only flushed and went rigid, as if any sudden movement might scare *me* away. I, however, was undeterred.

Just once, I'd give in to the monster, and then I'd know peace.

"Can I?"

He nodded. Barely. "You're not afraid?"

"I am," I whispered, "of myself, mostly."

A shiver rolled through Andor when my fingers brushed his forehead and swept the hair from his face. His long scar clipped both left eyes, leaving a trail of silver bleeding into the whorls of black. His jaw flexed as I traced the length of it, and by the time I reached his cheekbone, he'd shifted back to his mortal shape.

An offering, for the want in his eyes.

And, like any flower here waiting to be pruned and crushed by godly hands, I leaned in. Andor held his breath.

The first kiss was soft. A question. The labyrinth crescendoed to deafening silence when we met. Warmth on warmth, captured in a heartbeat and a prick of static.

It was a peck, really. But the sensation echoed through my feet.

The second kiss—it was hunger. His answer. Tasting, a collision of lips and sharp teeth, herbal like thyme and sweet like rose water. Feverish with want, I pressed closer, wood biting into my palm. His hand cradled my jaw.

"What if I—" he mumbled, but I cut him off.

Because the third kiss was all-consuming. There was no space left for thinking. It was base, a creature given over to only feeling. Flower-petal-soft lips, his impatient fist through hair, the brush of claws along my spine and shoving my coat down from my shoulders. My skin buzzed, the fire in my blood spreading.

I dived in.

Somewhere amid breathless breaks and restless hands, Andor shifted again. Mortal and immortal, he flickered like lightning, antlers sharp and then gone, primeval and powerful, both predator and prey but unable to focus on one shape long enough, and I forgot myself too. I forgot about the choices to be made, the ballet's offer, the ticking clock. There was no more death, no stares, no rumors, no Coralie to tell me who I was supposed to be, no *Laure*.

There was only the kisses pressed to the column of my throat, stinging like poison where no one would find me, and the monster I unleashed just because I wanted to.

When my hand brushed over Andor's heart, the tattoo on my wrist twitched. His eyes fluttered open.

"Do it."

Seizing that spark of power, knowing I could affect him, I pinched. Lightly. Just enough to make his pulse stumble, gentler than the last time we were here. Blood trickled from his nose, but he only shivered, flashing half human and half monster, setting off a quake in my own chest.

Drawn to him, I grinned back, bringing his face to mine, and licked the red gathering on his lips. His blood, and Acheron's blood, the coppery tang delightful and rich, and the kiss that followed even better. His laugh throaty as he held tight, squeezing, soothing the ache that drove me to the labyrinth in the first place—

"Andor, you in here?"

Keturah's voice was ice water splashing over me. Her soles rustling against grass propelled me back like a shock, legs shaky as I dropped ungracefully back onto the bench. My face hummed. Andor pressed a hand to his garnet-carved mouth, as if to keep the last kiss from escaping.

It took me longer than it should have to focus on the yellow puff rounding the corner. Immediately Keturah froze, wide eyes flicking between Andor and me, disheveled, breathing heavy, gaping, sitting unusually close. I still tasted blood. My head throbbed.

She cleared her throat and averted her face to the sky. "We still going to look for Lethe's altar in the Catacombs, Laure?"

Right.

I unhooked myself from Andor's burning grip on my side. The absence left my skin clammy, and the instant I was free from the bench and his gravity, I tottered to the side. The hedges spun. The air thinned.

"Are you okay—?"

I spilled to the ground, my hands splayed to catch myself. Darkness swam in my vision. A hot hand touched my forehead, and another squeezed my wrist. Keturah cursed.

"I just need to breathe..."

She threw Andor a scathing glare. "No, you *need* a doctor. It looks like you've been poisoned. Let's get—"

"I'm fine," I snapped, pushing up to my feet, ignoring their worried glances. It hardly mattered when Acheron would heal me. In a few moments, the maze would right itself, and sure enough, I began to take uneasy steps.

Andor vaulted forward to take my arm. Even in the shadows, the guilt and mortification on his face were unmistakable. Unbearable. "I'm sor—"

"Let me just walk it off." I backed away.

"Please—"

But I couldn't hear more because I was already slipping back into the maze and running. Instead of getting him out of my system, I tangled deeper. There'd be no easy goodbye, not after this. And the farther I ran, the more the heady fog receded until I was left with my own carelessness. More proof that I should leave, for everyone's sake.

The sticky breeze smothered me on my retreat out of the labyrinth, through the meadow, and into the tunnels. In the dark, I arranged my clothes and smoothed my hair, still waiting for my feeble pulse to recover, but I couldn't, for the life of me, erase the *feel* of him. He was insidious.

"Goodbye," I practiced through gritted teeth, to him, to the monster that I let crawl out, to Elysium, before turning away.

Only my march through the Catacombs was not so alone as I thought. I sensed it all in rapid succession: rock sliding underfoot, a chill in the dead air, my mark shuddering meekly, skin crawling, and the slippery muffle of a heartbeat, brushing against my consciousness.

Someone was here.

But then the poison took hold, and the ground went out from under me, and I crumpled.

CHAPTER 25

I lurched awake on the cold ground, sucking in shuddering breaths that tasted metallic and dirty. The back of my head throbbed, pulsing in tender waves through my eyes and teeth. My fingers came away sticky with blood.

Every thought was as thin and hard to grasp as smoke, all of me sluggish as I remembered: I'd fainted. It took a moment for the room to blink into focus, but judging by the darkness, cavernous walls, oppressive silence, and stale air mixed with mold, I was still in the Catacombs.

Just not where I fell.

A disembodied groan hung in the air, sounding both mine and foreign, as I tried to prop myself up on one trembling elbow. It collapsed under me, taking most of my strength to stay awake with it. My eyelids drooped despite the voice screaming that something was wrong.

There came the whistling from somewhere in the alcove. It bounced around the walls, a haunting melody I recognized, had heard before. The same tune from Joséphine's apartment. "Danse macabre." Saint-Saëns.

On the other side of the room sat a low table, cracked down the middle, the wood worn and rotted with time. A rusted pair of pliers, a dull knife, and small, yellowed animal bones scattered across the ground. Another altar like Acheron's grotto but abandoned. Forgotten. Soft, cool light gathered overhead, the ceiling covered in molten white so bright I threw a floppy arm over my face.

"Where am I?"

From the corner, someone answered, "You're safe now. I saved you. You're welcome."

Then I woke up.

At that voice, the heavy sleep drained from my face. At that voice, I pushed up against the fatigue and whirled around to face her.

Coralie curled against the wall, picking nonchalantly at the split ends of her hair. Under the harsh light, her skin looked as pale as death. The smile on her cracked lips was cold, detached. I shivered.

The mouth of the cave stood behind me, and without another word, I leapt into motion, skittering back on my hands and feet, tripping over myself, fleeing. I didn't know what had happened, but the loudest voice in my head, in my *blood*, was telling me to go. Now.

"Stop!" she shouted, but I was on my feet and bolting, legs stretching far, dizzy and blood racing—

Something sharp as razor wire wrapped around my ankle and pulled. It seared into flesh, sending me crashing onto the cold earth with a scream. Then it seized the other foot. Both legs dragging me back, away from freedom, nails clawing bloody through sand and rock until a tendril made of light slithered close. Like a snake, it darted out and took my wrist, then the other. My cry came out hoarse.

The light was so cold it burned. It cut through skin and suffused muscle with the pain of frostbite. The tears welling and spilling over crystallized and pricked skin. Every part of me was screaming.

"I'm so sorry, Laure," said Coralie as she climbed to her feet.

With the flick of her wrist, the thing gave a sharp tug and jerked me off the ground, carving away more flesh where it held me. I hung suspended in the middle of the cave, limbs outstretched painfully and ready for quartering. Blood rushed down to my head as I stared at her, at the monster wearing my best friend's face. The light breathed a sinister chill down the back of my neck. The mark on my wrist rioted.

"Let me go—"

"You didn't do as you were told," Coralie retorted, "so I'm clipping your wings."

I kicked out and struggled, but the cables of light only hurt worse. They cinched tighter, and Coralie shook her head, crossed her arms in disappointment.

"No use in trying to fight *oblivion*, Laure." She lifted her sleeve, flashing the pale mark on her wrist that looked more like an old scar than a tattoo. It glowed white like the ceiling, like the chains that bound me, like the thing that took Andor's eye. She grinned conspiratorially, as if we shared a secret, and I recoiled. Whatever this was, it wasn't like me at all.

"What have you done with Coralie?" I demanded, because *my* Coralie would never. This thing wasn't my friend, just like the beast wasn't really me—

"I told you I followed you that night, with Joséphine. I watched you offer yourself like a common beggar and vanish right before my eyes." She wrinkled her nose in disgust. "And when Joséphine ran, I tried to offer myself. You know what it did? It said no."

When I flinched, the chains grew tighter still.

"It laughed at me! Why would anything choose you and not me, if it's so good and noble? So imagine my disappointment when you went back a second time and let it take more." Her voice climbed to a feverish shout that ricocheted off the walls and made my head spin. "But it's all right—I found something better. *Real* power."

And she raised her arms in veneration to the ceiling, the glowing white mass to my pool of blood. Only, where Acheron played music, Lethe was dead silent.

This wasn't Coralie. Whatever crawled inside had changed her, corrupted her into something I didn't recognize. And this thing had been at it for *months*, biding its time, giving me a chance to do what she wanted, all while it carved away at her. All while my best friend was wasting away.

I fought against the light with renewed effort, hoping to find some weakness if I pulled hard enough, twisted at just the right angle. Instead, it only stripped away more flesh. And if Coralie was possessed by Lethe, then I'd seen it was capable of worse.

"It asks for bones, you know. I ripped out some of my *teeth* to keep you safe." She tapped her cheek, where her molars once lay. And certainly I'd noticed a new roundness to her face that I was too busy to fret over. "To clean up your mess—"

"You wanted to one-up me," I snapped, frustration rising.

Joséphine, Ciro, Andor—none of this was for me. The Coralie I knew didn't lift a finger for anybody or anything, never got off her ass to help me, much less pry out her teeth and kill. It had to be Rose-Marie's idea. Coralie was always so desperate to please and too spineless to refuse her.

Coralie angled her face up to the light like a phantasmal sunflower, cheeks hollow, making my stomach churn. Two were dead and another maimed, and now I was strung up like a hog for feasting. My Coralie was spiteful, but the vengeance in the withering shell beneath me was unrecognizable. *Months* of misery and death, all because I earned something she wanted. But that didn't make it hers.

I had to force her to see reason.

"Is your mother making you do this?" I whispered, gritting my teeth at how my voice trembled. Due to the bitter cold, there were no tears to cry, but they swelled in my throat nonetheless. "We can help you, but please, Cor, people are dead!"

Her smile didn't falter. "No one's making me do anything. And they weren't *people* anymore. They were corruptions, too far gone, and they were going to ruin you. Though, I admit Andor surprised me."

The way she spat his name made me lunge. I strained to squeeze a fist, to grip her heart and stop it—stop *this*—and failed. My restraints seared down to bone, leaving me panting.

"He thought I was aiming for you and tried to protect you," replied Coralie in a low voice, her lips pinching into a hard line. "Anyway, it appears I can't reason with you just yet. You'll understand how I'm doing this for us. So we can go back to the way things were."

With the same lack of grace, she hobbled closer and drew a lighter from her pocket.

"Tell me where to find the others."

What was left of my heart split open. If I answered, she'd kill them. And it didn't matter what control she thought she had right now—the void wouldn't let her release me or release her when I gave in. I was going to die here. So it was either laugh or sob because I wouldn't grovel.

"I'm doing this for you," she added. "Please don't make me apply extra motivation."

Pain tore through my flesh as the chains of light pulled my arm taut. The red of Acheron's mark exposed, the skin writhing, for her to see. And reach. Unease spread through me. This far underground, no one would hear me scream. No one would know to miss me. My parents had long since mourned me—I'd just be another pile of forgotten bones for the ossuary.

My teeth were chattering too much to spit out a curse, to do more than swallow the whimper rising in me.

"They aren't looking for you," Coralie pronounced as I fought to catch my breath. "When the mark is gone, you'll be worthless to them. You'll be nothing—they'll forget all about you, just like everyone always forgets. But not me."

Except this wasn't my best friend, not anymore. Acheron and I had learned to coexist, to share and cede control, but her? Lethe must have subsumed her. Not that I could point out as much.

"You know what…" I couldn't stop shaking. "What'll happen if you burn it."

I'd never dance again. My life would be over, everything I sacrificed for the ballet wasted. My will to dance reduced to ash. To protect Andor and Keturah, distractions, people I hardly knew, but not the monsters I should have been wary of.

Coralie was unfazed. "Tell me."

Would they do the same for me? It didn't matter.

"No." I squeezed my eyes shut.

The flame set all my nerves alight. A bloodcurdling scream from a voice I didn't recognize as my own filled the room. The chains held me tight, stripping away flesh even as I twisted, wrenching to get away. So fast but so bright, it took air from my lungs. Charred skin mixed with melted fat and blood dripped to the ground, the stench tilling my stomach.

Still she couldn't have them. The only people standing in that crowded hall with flowers for me—I wouldn't. I'd earn my vigil, deserve my mourning.

"Go f—"

Lightning crackled through my arm, into my shoulder, and down to my feet. I folded onto myself again and again, leaving my body only to get welded back inside. The scream that followed gave way to a wretched sob I didn't think myself capable of, frost stinging my cheeks from sweat and tears that couldn't fall.

"I promise I'll make it quick," Coralie offered, like I was a child. "In/out, the devils are dead, you're all mine again, and order is restored. I'll get rid of this, and we'll—"

"You really think you'll just give it up when this is over? You think it'll let you?" I rasped, right before another bout of flame licked at muscle, carved me away. A tooth cracked, and long after she stopped, the spasming continued. Then at last, I felt the vibrancy, the warmth and buzzing, the primordial presence deep inside, all bleed away. "If you're still in there, Coralie, if you let it win, I'll never forgive you."

"'Forgive' me?" she shouted before barking with sharp laughter. "I don't need you to forgive me! I need our lives back. Ever since your little trip with Joséphine, *my* life has paid the price. You got greedy, and somehow, I lost everything."

She took a step closer. A rope of pure light slithered around my throat at her command.

"Cor—"

"You don't understand what it's like when people expect things from you. To want something so badly. They told me I was a shoo-in, and then you reached for what wasn't yours."

My plea was lost to gagging. The light tightened until she was choking me, and limbs restrained, mark dissolved, I was powerless to resist. This was it—I was going to die.

"I'm doing what I have to, to save you and myself, because that's what a best friend does."

Like a blade, the light dug through skin and muscle, constricting against my windpipe. My lungs burned, and my head ached, my thoughts dissolving to nothing. Coralie was taking and taking until I was reduced to nothing. Any attempts to pry the restraints away only meant more digging, more agony until light cut through bone. If I didn't die of asphyxiation, soon I'd be in pieces.

We stared at each other for what felt like eternity, her bright eyes glossed over with sparkling white film, zealous and unfocused, while my brain cells fizzed out one by one. Dark spots danced around my vision, making her look like famine and death, pale and thin-skinned and gaunt, witnessing my final descent.

From far away came an echo. One phantom voice calling, indiscernible, waiting for a response. And then another.

The cave's light dimmed. Either that or more of my brain was dying. The edges of Coralie's face blurred, and in a blackout moment, my stomach flipped into free fall. I dropped to the floor.

"Seems I was wrong about one thing," she said, standing over me.

The ghostly voices were growing louder, formless over the blood racing in my ears and my own screams still reverberating in my skull. The stink of smoked meat. Gasping coughs racked my body, every jerk and twitch a fresh round of excruciating pain from my scalp down to my toenails. Footsteps through the gravel grew closer, shouts in the shape of my name. Because the beast was gone, leaving just Laure. Weak, powerless, fragile mortal Laure.

Kneeling close to my ear, Coralie warned, "I won't abandon you. You're mine. So if one of us burns, we both will." And then she left, the light retreating with her while I pressed my forehead to the dirt, waiting for the dark to claim me.

Acheron was gone, Coralie was gone, and I was all alone. Brutally, painfully, unbearably alone.

CHAPTER 26

When I resurfaced, it was to the tune of machines. There was the low hum of air, distant beeping, muffled pages on a loudspeaker. Hurried footsteps squeaked on linoleum. Gentle hands combed through my damp coils, smoothing down baby hairs with something coconut-scented. And underneath that, it smelled of antiseptic.

A hospital room.

"What—"

Keturah foiled my weak attempt to stir by turning my head. To finish braiding my hair. "Don't move, I'm almost finished."

I scowled and took in the rest: Everything was swathed in shades of mint down to the paper-thin gown I wore. Thick bandages covered my ankles and wrists, bunching at my throat. My lips cracked and bled. My mouth was dry, jaw tender.

"You have such beautiful curls. I don't know why you won't let them be," she remarked as she swept a lock from my face into her fold. "And you should take it easy, by the way. They said you had severe hypothermia."

I rubbed my eyes and asked drowsily, "How did I get here? What day is it?"

"Sunday. You've been out for two days," she answered, matter-of-fact. "Andor and I found you bleeding and unconscious in the middle of a cave."

My skull felt like it was splitting in two. I didn't remember being found—only retreating into the dark and finding that nothing was waiting for me inside. But I remembered all that happened before, in the light. "Oh."

"I don't know what you were thinking, running off like that," Keturah continued, fingers catching on a tangle. "You could have died. You *would* have died if we didn't go after you. So what happened?"

We stared at each other, even as my eyes stung as I was forced to relive all of it. My screams. Coralie's twisted smile. Dying a hundred deaths as she burned the mark from my arm. And then I finally looked away, because I didn't have an excuse. Coralie had been rotting away right in front of me, and I kept brushing her off.

Besides, I was no longer Keturah's problem now that my mark was gone. I was back to being no one.

"My roommate," I mumbled, fingering the crisp white gauze where Acheron's tattoo should be. Once was. I felt her braiding freeze for a beat, just long enough for me to notice before quickly recovering. Then I shot up. "You're both in danger—where's Andor?"

A hand closed on my shoulder and pushed me back down onto the sad excuse for a mattress. "Relax. He's been glued to your bedside since we brought you in, so I sent him to get some rest. Now, you were saying?"

Pinned, worn down, and stripped bare, I told her everything: Coralie's plan, her jealousy, her confession. All the while, Keturah said nothing, working my hair between her fingers, a deep frown settling over her beautiful features. Ciro and Joséphine were dead because of me, because I got greedy. Because I reached for too much. And when the lights went out, Lethe wearing my friend's skin would come back to finish the job. So Keturah and Andor had to stay far away from me, I insisted, in Elysium, where they wouldn't be found.

She merely nodded, weaving until my face was framed by two immaculate, shiny, soft plaits. It said more than words, her carefully tending to me when I was a walking death sentence. After, she turned her head and pretended not to see my lip trembling.

"Two friends dead, one mutilated, and a girl in the hospital, all over *ballet*. Brilliant time to start all over, Keturah," she muttered to herself as she crossed the room, sinking into the lone chair and stretching her legs in front of her. Then her gaze met mine. "Still, I suppose I don't have anywhere better to be."

"But you're—"

"Your martyr act is getting boring."

Stunned, I clamped my mouth shut and stared at her, how she lapped her tongue piercing against her front teeth in thought. It was like she refused to comprehend that I was a nobody again, determined to find me worth knowing where even my parents had failed.

Keturah shrugged. "It's nice to not be alone sometimes. To have *friends* and all that."

Coralie was my friend too, and look how that went, I wanted to counter. But it was childish, and I didn't want to risk sending her away.

"Also, you're so reckless, you know that?" she added. "For going out there by yourself, taking Joséphine's phone and lying about it, having a world full of normal people at your disposal and instead choosing to get involved with a literal toxin."

I blushed when her eyes narrowed on me, heat rising from my chest and into my cheeks. "I—"

"But I suppose you're my walking disaster now."

My fingers stilled on the wrist bandage, my brain trying to process what she'd said. What she'd meant. Filtering through the long list of reasons why a vulture like me didn't deserve it.

When I took too long to answer, Keturah griped from her chair, suppressing a smile, "I'm trying to keep you in one piece. I think a thank-you's in order."

"Thanks," I replied quickly. Eagerly. Before she had time to reconsider. "And you don't have to worry about... the *labyrinth* happening anymore. My deal's gone, so I won't be doing that again."

There wasn't any point in justifying it, how I thought Acheron's mark would save me, how it was gone now and all its monstrous desires along with it. But she only cocked her head as if I'd spoken gibberish. As if I didn't understand. And in the ensuing quiet, still racked with exhaustion, I lay my head back and stifled a yawn. It'd been months since I last had a moment of rest—no, *years* of outrunning myself to become something better. Now it had all caught up, and I had nothing to hide behind.

"It was really foolish, you not saving yourself and telling her about Elysium."

I laughed. My eyelids drooped, heavy. "Yeah, well, I make a lot of bad decisions, don't I? I was gonna die anyway, was I supposed to take you both with me?"

"Your oldest friend betrayed and tortured you. I'm just saying, no one would have blamed you for wavering. For hurting. God knows I understand." Keturah's voice had grown quieter, or perhaps the call of sleep was pulling me further under.

I knew she of all people understood, because who else could make such a deal? *It's tiring, carrying around so much shame, you know?* And in the hall, she'd had such a sad smile, like she had a well of it so deep I couldn't fathom.

Yeah, I wished to go back in time and tell her, *I do know.*

The burn on my arm, the emptiness in my spine, they were now a persistent nudity, a cosmic loneliness I didn't realize I carried until now: having to do this all on my own. Again. And I was so damn tired and ready to rest.

"We could never have stuff like this," I remarked, wriggling my freshly polished fingers under the drab, fluorescent hospital lighting. And though I tried to make my tone light, though I tried to smile, there was no hiding the sadness in it.

Keturah had painted my nails blue green. It was a beautiful shade, the color of the ocean, but it wasn't the nude tones the ballet academy required. There was no such thing as a swan queen with purple polish—visually, it'd disrupt the smoothness of your lines. Classically, it was uncouth.

Personally, I kind of liked it.

She snorted as she rifled through the bounty of bottles dumped into my lap. It was my turn to do hers. "How anyone puts up with that tyranny is a mystery. No wonder you're all so neurotic."

I rolled my eyes.

Coralie didn't come to kill me in the night. In fact, when breakfast arrived, my eyes stung seeing Keturah sound asleep, shoulders moving softly as she leaned at the foot of my bed from her relocated chair. She'd *stayed*.

Once again, I was no one with nothing, but she was still here. And Andor had done the same.

"It's just a job like any other," I mumbled, holding up a few colors to the light. She cast a sideways glance that said she didn't believe me; I didn't believe me either. It was an upbringing, a culture, a lifestyle, an escape, a religion. It was whatever I needed it to be.

Finally I settled on a bottle of neon yellow that matched her hair and might brighten her persistently dark wardrobe. Applying coat after coat would stave off thoughts of what was coming, what waited for me on the outside. And what *didn't* wait at all.

"So, ready to talk?" Keturah asked as soon as I started.

I didn't look up. "About what?"

Next finger.

When she painted mine, she'd talked about her life—touring small clubs across Europe, street brawls in Birmingham, moving to Paris with her tattooer fiancée, the death of her brother. Her thinking was, if we experienced something so horrible together, maybe we should get to *know* each other too. She delivered everything blankly, though her eyes creased at memories that rose to the surface, and I offered up little things—how ballet was my mother's idea, the divorce, my on-again, off-again father, stealing.

"It's okay to be honest. You can stop hiding."

A lump formed in my throat, more horrible than the pain in my arm or my cracked tooth. We both knew I was full to the brim with something that was threatening to get out, and no amount of swallowing would keep it down for long. I feared what would happen when I reached my limit and started to overflow. Nothing pretty or soft like ballerina-pink satin would come out.

Like how I missed my best friend and roommate turning into *that*? She'd needed me, and I failed her. So I kept painting, finishing the first coat on one hand and moving on to the next, and shook my head. "I just can't believe I didn't see it coming, that's all."

"Well, of course you didn't. You love Coralie, that's clear—"

I balked.

"You seem like you've known each other for a long time, so how could you not love her? How could you have known she'd do what she did? And hurt you of all people?"

For twelve years, we'd been inseparable. Before the academy, before they taught us to hate each other. We started in the same class, learning how to prance and jump, color-coordinating our leotards and the scrunchies on our buns. For as long as I knew ballet, I knew Coralie.

"No one would blame you for complicated feelings about her *or* the ballet."

Keturah squeezed my hand.

The moment I stepped out of her shadow, Coralie sought to drag me back. But *torturing* me? The thing in the cave couldn't be her. Just like I wasn't the same with Acheron.

Keturah cleared her throat and wriggled her fingers. "Now, what will you do about the ballet?"

I glanced at my phone on the table.

There was nothing from anyone at the ballet. No calls or texts, no emails of well-wishes or flowers for recovery. Keturah had reported my absence as severe flu, and the place where I spent most of my waking moments didn't care. The world I consecrated my life and body to never noticed when I was gone. And maybe, no matter what, nothing would change that.

The pressure in my chest grew. Just the thought of the ballet was enough to start a rupture, and I had to believe that she wouldn't run away now.

"I'm not going back. To the ballet."

The words dropped like stones. There was no taking it back now.

Keturah looked up.

I waved my bandaged wrist. "If I forfeited the bargain, I lost my ability to dance, and she, um, burned the mark off. So."

The laugh that came out of me was shaky, but I couldn't stop myself.

"And anyway, they gave me this garbage offer that would leave me without a job in six months, dressed up in pretty language to hide the fact that they only want to use me and then kick me out! They wouldn't dare insult her like that."

By the end, I was shouting, rage and hurt spilling out in waves. Because it was devastating. Every day was brutal. I'd given my body to them, dedicated my life to them, and pledged myself to a proto-god in the dark, all for them, and after all of this, everything I had was still taken from me.

I settled her hand back on my knee and continued painting, little angry strokes thinking of all Yelena had said. Then, because she was still listening, I muttered, "I have to quit. Basically."

In the end, I was tired of fighting and didn't want to do this anymore. They wore me down, and I wanted more. Coralie could have it.

For a long time, there was only silence. Then, with all the bravado one would expect from a woman with the sleeves ripped off all her shirts, Keturah exclaimed, "Who cares about the stuffy old ballet, anyway?"

And it might have been the stress or exhaustion, but I laughed, consoled by the blink of her long lashes and the scent of shea butter from her skin. Every throb and ache lessened a little. It felt so good to give in for once, to stop moving and rest.

CHAPTER 27

I found Andor sitting comfortably at the base of a tree, gazing out on Acheron's gory torrents, a sketchpad in his lap. He was in his monstrous form, antlers decorated with flowers, a fitting fixture for the reddish haze of the banks. And though there was no mark, no primordial magic in my bones to inspire it, my pulse still quickened at the sight of him.

Longing bubbling up inside of me, *from* me.

The realization turned my stomach sour, and I halted, dismayed.

It wasn't our two slivers of blood river calling to each other. The reason I was so drawn to him couldn't be chalked up to preternatural human beauty when I preferred his most monstrous form. Acheron hadn't driven me to Andor at all. Those impulses were all mine.

High grass and wildflowers rustled around my stilted steps, capturing his attention.

As I froze, stunned, Andor turned and stared at me, four dark eyes brushing over the gauze sticking out at the neck of Keturah's borrowed shirt, the wad of bandages bunching at the wrists, covering one forearm. Proof of how ordinary I'd become.

So different from how I'd left him.

Everything I'd planned to say died on my tongue. Did I start by apologizing for my best friend who attacked him and killed *his* best friend? Or for kissing him and running away when the poison struck? The labyrinth wasn't so far from here, and I flashed hot at memories of tracing the scar, how soft his lips were, how he held tight as if I'd vanish. It was too late to admit that getting him out of my system hadn't worked. That even now, even without Acheron, my blood rushed just standing here.

"I'm alive," I announced instead, rocking back on my heels, my voice ringing hollow. He didn't laugh with me.

Smooth.

Keturah's voice cropped up as I studied my boots, loud and clear: *You can stop hiding.* Which was exactly what I came to do: to stop carrying everything inside, to stop *running*.

So I forced a deep inhale, steadied my limbs before I lost my nerve, and started again. "I'm sorry I ran away from you. I was embarrassed and thought if I stayed away, no one would get hurt. Again."

The words came out in a rush, a mess of new feelings not yet cleaned and ready to be rearticulated into shape.

"But I'm tired of running," I tacked on at the end over the roaring of my heart. Sweat ran down my sides. The bandage tape on my wrist was starting to fray from picking at it. "And being alone."

The agitation of the river was all the noise that followed for a long time, until Andor asked in a tight voice, "Are you finished?"

"Not yet."

The memory of his mortified expression flashed in my mind, urging me forward.

"And I don't care if you're poisonous, by the way. Or that you look like that. I kinda like it, actually." My jaw trembled with the effort. This was all so much harder without Acheron reinforcing my every word, even if I needed to see that I could do it on my own. "I dunno—I like you, even."

With the truth finally wrenched free, I squeezed my eyes shut and turned on my heel. Retreating to what I originally meant to do. "Okay, bye!"

Behind me, Andor called out, "Where are you going?"

"To get my favor back." My favor, my claws, my armor, my *nerve*. To figure out why the river chose me and not Coralie. And the faster I got away from here, the better.

"Well, can I walk with you?"

I stilled. Not breathing, uncertain if I'd heard correctly, unsure if he'd ask again. It sounded like an olive branch. Like... acceptance. Like he forgave me for leading a wolf to their gates. And though I didn't know if I deserved it, I was trying.

Nevertheless, I nodded stiffly, back ramrod straight as he climbed to his feet and sauntered over. His hair was decorated with little hemlock flowers again, gold jewelry hanging from his ears and twinkling in the sky's red glow. And when he noticed me noticing him, his mouth twitched in a smile.

"Thanks," I mumbled, hanging my head, neck and face flushed.

We took the winding path through the trees in silence, the smell of pine needles and rainy days filling my nostrils as his shoulder brushed mine. He twisted an aconite blossom between his fingers, and it was hard to focus on anything but his warmth, picturing how beautiful the flower's rich, dark petals would look in a crown. How I wanted just this moment to last forever.

But there was something else, one more thing that had to be said aloud again to make it real. I traced the edge of the bandage where my mark once was, the blue-green nail polish looking so odd it could only be right. "I'm leaving the ballet."

The blossom stopped turning.

"Why?"

Because I couldn't dance anymore.

Because my best friend tortured me over it.

Because they wouldn't allow me this, even if I could.

I shrugged. "It's exhausting. And I'll never win, trying to be liked by people who hate me, stuck in a place that doesn't want me. It'll give Coralie some space from me, and I just...I can't go back to that place. That may sound weak, but—"

"I don't think it's weak," he countered softly. "In fact, there's strength in knowing when to walk away."

The Paris Ballet existed long before and would dare to survive long after me. We were all ephemeral, both on- and offstage. Blink, and Joséphine was gone. Blink, and another filled her place. Blink, and I stopped existing completely. The fresh blood would keep flowing, the ballet would keep swallowing people, keep cleaving dancers in two like a knife. There wouldn't ever be glory in a place determined to forget me, a place that only begrudgingly looked at me because I'd forced them. Holding on to pieces of her, hoping it'd fill the gap she left behind, was killing me. The emerald ring that started all this tightened on my finger like a noose.

"I just...thought you should know."

"Well, it's not as glorious as Opéra Garnier, but you can stay here if you want," he offered, holding out the aconite blossom and turning to face me. Framed by dark plum trees and their deep violet leaves, he looked divine.

Though I distrusted the want back then, thought it only because of his beauty, it was by choice that I leaned toward Andor now, like the day in his labyrinth, another blossom waiting to be inhaled or caressed. Just to be around him, to nourish what was growing in me. I wasn't sure I had strength for anything else.

Dark eyes locked on my mouth.

"You can stay here, with us," Andor repeated, taking my hands in his, stopping me from fiddling with my ring. "We see you, and we aren't going anywhere."

Andor brought my palm to his lips and kissed it softly. Warm, painfully slow, deliberate kisses, black gaze beseeching, burning through skin and sinew, engraving directly onto bone. He remained in his primeval form, no flickering, antlers imposing, claws careful. Still the monstrous thing from so long ago in the same place I'd found him.

And it was everything I wanted: At his most fearsome, he was asking me to stay. An invitation to a space where I belonged.

"I'll beg if you want me to," he murmured, brow arched in offering.

With every kiss, working from fingertip to the pulse point of my wrist over my bandages, doubt and worry and fear were burned off. They were faint enough to leave only a light tingle where skin met, until it left me craving another dose and another. Without Acheron, was I brave enough to say yes?

"What if I told you I wanted to be my most monstrous self all the time? What if I wanted to be a god? Would you pray to me?" I bit my lip at the thrill running through me, at the flicker behind his eyes when I ducked out of his reach and retreated. Baiting him to follow. To chase me.

Andor didn't hesitate. He stalked closer until he was a shadow looming, until I pressed against the trunk of a tree, moss soft along my spine. The hunger, even without Acheron's encouragement, reared its ugly head, but I wouldn't run. Not when I'd lured my prey into *my* trap.

"Of course I would pray to you." He frowned, eyeing lips he couldn't have. Because the last time we kissed, I lost it. "I'd worship you any way you please. I'd melt Palais Garnier down and build an altar in your name, if you so wished." It was a reverent whisper, the kind uttered in the wings of a stage, before an audition, with desperation.

Soft lips pressed to my forehead. And then my temple. My ear. My jaw. My throat. My heart sped up with each kiss, fire trailing along my skin.

When I tried to bring his mouth to mine, to bask in that warmth and taste the herbs and wilderness in it, he lurched away. The better of us two. A grin quirked on his lips as he shook his head and said, "I don't think so."

"Come on." I pitched off the tree and took his hand. This would have to wait—I had a monster to tend to.

"And you're sure about this?" Andor asked as we climbed the hill, its freestanding iron door stark against the meadow of white asphodels. My fingers closed over the cold metal handle, and his scorching hand closed over mine. All levity from the woods left his face, lending his features a wash of disappointment. Or sadness. *Worry*, perhaps, at what I was about to do.

But all I thought about was what I'd gain, what I'd already lost, had taken for granted and wanted back.

"Because you don't have to," he continued. "You can still be normal, free from…"

Free from *it*. The moldy tunnels, Coralie's rampage, and the wicked darkness always rearing its head. What I might lose next in a bargain. But it wasn't that I needed Acheron's favor anymore. Just because I could do this on my own didn't mean I had to.

Besides, power looked good on me, and I simply wanted mine back.

A warm, blood-scented breeze tickled my skin. Over his shoulder, Acheron and Lethe sliced through the land, bloodred and bone-white twins, beckoning. Singing their immortal song. Telling me to stay. And now I was going to demand it tell me why.

"Do you trust Acheron?"

He flinched.

I looked up at Andor, who protested after pulling me from the river.

Who cornered Ciro after he brought a bloodied Keturah to the cottage. Who warned me to be careful and taught me control. Andor, with four deals of his own, so entwined with Elysium that he was equal parts uncanny and human, caring for a fortress of poisonous flowers.

He dropped his hand from the door. And then with a wistful smile, like a private joke, he answered quietly, "With my life."

"Then why—" I started to say but stopped myself.

Because it's harder to be seen when you're dwelling in the dark. And that was what I wanted once: a theatre full of devotees. For all he knew, I was trading two thousand a night for just two and a set of claws. The river had made him formidable, granting him beauty and then ensuring it didn't matter by turning him poisonous. Until me. It was a bittersweet god, delivering life and turning you into a monster for taking it. What Andor offered me instead was an out, a place without conditions or fine print.

I didn't *have* to be a monster, I didn't have to be exactly like them to belong. But I wanted to. And I wouldn't deny myself anymore.

"Will you tell me about your bargains now?" I leaned against the door, still close enough to breathe lungfuls of petrichor and cedar from his skin.

Andor crossed his arms. "Well, you know most of it. The first was for beauty. I was tired of imitating it—I wanted to be looked at the way people looked at my work. But that wasn't enough, not when I was… alone."

He plucked flowers and their stems from the meadow as he talked, fashioning another crown with deft fingers. At the last part, his shoulders drooped, gaze locked on his weaving to avoid mine.

"So the second was to create beauty, real beauty at the tips of my fingers, so I'd have something." He conjured larkspur with a flick of his wrist. "Then it got easier. I wanted to see the world, to travel anywhere, be anyplace but here. And there was so much to see and paint and create, I asked to live forever."

I gaped.

Finally Andor glanced back to face me so I *really* saw his frame, his staggering height, teeth filed to points, antlers long and lethal, eyes multiplied and filled with night, excluding the left two slashed with silver. Even as he settled the crown on his brow, his gaze was imploring.

"I didn't understand at first, what it meant, what I was signing up for. I'm not ashamed, not anymore, but it can be … isolating. People won't always understand."

He stepped in close, larkspur blossoms kissing the top of his scar, mouth grimaced in a line. Striking enough to make me shiver with both desire and fear.

"Just be sure."

"This is the surest I've ever been," I told him, nodding, opening the door, and pulling him into the dark behind me.

The red glow and warmth of Elysium was instantly replaced by the musky-scented cold of wet rock as we crossed the threshold. The quiet was heavier. Turning corners, we came to the pool, which glittered in greeting when we approached, its garnet light filling the cave. Tinny music tweaked in the distance like an invitation.

My feet slowed at the scent, the promise of what lay beneath the surface. Hunger called louder than everything, even as I wondered what else I had to give. If it bargained my dancing back to me, would I march back to the ballet and change my mind?

It was that hunger I thought would be extinguished.

Even without Andor or Keturah, without Elysium or the ballet, I would have returned to Acheron. I found home in the monster's embrace, in its sinister whispers and unabashed cruelty, in being not just seen but *felt*.

I liked who I became because of it.

By the pool's edge, I stripped down to underwear to spare Keturah's borrowed clothes, folded them, and took up the rusted dagger. Andor stiffened and averted his eyes. Warm blood lapped at the gashes on my ankles as I waded in.

"Will you find me on the other side?" I asked, my gaze searching Andor's, bracing for his refusal.

But he only straightened and inclined his head, clutching the folded clothes to his chest. "Always." Then he left before I made an incision deep enough to merit stitches. Gone in a gust of wind to wait by the shore.

All alone with the altar, my mask fell.

"I gave you everything," I whispered to the river, my arm trembling under the riot of pain. Blood ran in rivulets, fast and dark, pitter-patter of the drops dancing around the room. I wouldn't let it refuse me. "You promised me godhood, and then you let her take it away."

My voice cracked as I tore the ring from my finger. It was dingy after all these years, metal scuffed, emerald dull. It weighed heavy in my palm with all the things I couldn't have, that I'd never hold on to no matter how I bent myself into shape. And I was done with its curse, with being discarded.

I pitched it in.

"You left me. You *abandoned* me!"

Blood churned at my feet, voracious and awake, thinning until the floor vanished, and it swallowed me whole again. Lightning rolled across the dark heat as I plunged and then set like concrete. My pulse fluttered as I waited for the presence.

The sudden shift in gravity.

"I need to know why you choose some of us and not others. Why me and not her?"

Would you not rather become divine? It asked, just like that first night.

My eyes drifted shut. "Not until you answer me."

Silence stretched out long in the dark, and for a moment, I wondered if it wouldn't answer at all and send me back empty-handed.

But then it rumbled: **What is life but hunger and resilience? Persistent thriving no matter the conditions? What better kin to have?**

I shuddered as the temperature flared around me, licking my skin like flames. We were kindred spirits in our drive, where Coralie had neither wanted nor fought for anything.

Maybe even gods get lonely, Andor had said in the labyrinth, and I didn't think he knew how right he was.

Now for your steadfastness . . .

"My life," I muttered, trembling. "Everything."

Every last ugly, monstrous impulse, anything it wanted, just to be made anew. I was done being weak, playing at good and perfect, fearful, *mortal*. I was ready to feed and be fed.

Three years, it said as filaments parted skin, **and forgiveness. For your loyalty and the mark stripped against your will.**

Something brushed against my forehead, doting, like a paternal kiss.

And then it spat me out. Back beneath Elysium's wondrous red skies, my head broke the river's surface. Andor's fearsome face brightened as our eyes met.

And there was only one desire in my blood, one thing I needed most.

I craved annihilation.

PART FOUR

REDEMPTION

CHAPTER 28

Place de l'Opéra was crowded, even on a Thursday afternoon. Cars playing their horned symphony inched slowly down the avenue, filling the December air with exhaust. Christmas shoppers ambled beneath skeletal trees, venturing into bone-white buildings from the belle époque and swerving around tourists snapping photos and shivering in their light coats.

I welcomed the sting of cold in my lungs, taking in Opéra Garnier's green dome and two golden angels crowning the front. Nestled between columns were some of the West's greatest composers, Beethoven and Mozart scowling as we approached as if to chase me away. Or change my mind. Would they have made the same choice in my position?

"We'll be here when you're done," Andor said with an encouraging smile before he and Keturah turned away.

Fingertips numbing in the wind, I flashed my badge to security one last time and went inside.

I'd weighed my decision again and again, day bleeding into evening and then whittling off into night, and fretted about what I'd do next, where I'd go, who I'd become. The ballet would remain with or without me, but when I stripped the ballet away, what would be left of me?

Every step toward the grand atrium was a knife digging deeper and deeper into my heart, just hours before *Petrushka* opened. Passing the hall that led to the locker rooms, the staircase that rose to the studios, the doors leading backstage—they all dampened my anger bit by bit.

Because despite everything, I loved ballet. I loved dancing, I loved making poetry with my body and living music with my movement. I loved spinning, shooting across the floor, burning bright and hot until there was nothing left.

It wasn't the art that was the problem—it was the company. The art I loved and would keep with me, but the place would kill me if I let it. I spent more time worrying about making mistakes and losing their favor than dancing and enjoying it. The dream I'd been fed was a lie, and why should I shoulder that burden?

So I balled my fists and kept going until I got to the office. It smelled of lavender fields, and the hum of guided tours outside vanished when the door shut. All I heard was my own heart.

The receptionist was unchanged, the *o* in ISABEL GORCES marked with a gold star sticker this time. Her softness only made me angrier.

"Is President Auger in her office?" I snapped, more forceful than necessary. I didn't know what I'd do if the answer was no—trash the office, turn away politely, wait with my knee tapping incessantly.

When her attention drifted toward me, she flinched. I could still picture the blood, bright and thick, running from her ears at my voice. We lived in a world of predators and prey, scavengers and the living who would always die. I wouldn't feel guilty. At least I never picked apart children, choked their hopes, and then killed their ambition, leaving them gnarled and broken. I never murdered anyone either.

I cleared my throat and nodded to the office door. "President Auger? Is she inside?"

The receptionist didn't move, even as I started walking. If I was a better monster, I might have smelled her fear.

"Laurence! I've been looking for you," Auger chimed, closing the ledger she'd been scrawling in and capping her fountain pen. "Seeing as the show opens in a little under two hours."

The frost of her demeanor never softened even when it did, even when her voice pitched up an octave in greeting. Now that I was resigning, she was less terrifying; an older woman with graying hair who demanded too much, but that was all. No teeth, no claws, no tendrils of life fidgeting to snuff me like a candle. For once, I was bigger than her.

And it didn't slip my notice that she didn't ask how I was recovering. From my "flu."

Calmly, I settled into the leather seat opposite and inclined my head. I had rehearsed my speech, talking points on my phone in case I lost either my way or my nerve.

This place wasn't meant for me this place doesn't want me this place doesn't deserve me so I'm letting it go—

She asked with a tight smile, "You've decided to take our offer, then?"

"Actually," I began, clasping my hands in my lap to stop from biting my nails, "I'm here to resign. I won't be completing my apprenticeship."

She cocked her head, watery blue eyes dancing with intrigue. Her gaze was catlike, tracking new mice across a field. "Oh? Is there another?" And with the acumen of a businesswoman used to getting her way, she readied a notepad and pen. "What was their offer? I'm sure we have some discretionary funds to match."

That only made my stomach go sour, made the imminent more pressing. If they had more to give, then why didn't they from the beginning? Why wasn't I important enough on my own?

Another deep breath, as elongating nails prickled my palms and heat suffused my skin.

"There isn't another ballet."

She stopped writing, pen stilling in her grip, and raised her attention back to me. Head still cocked, but now the fine arch of silver brows bunched together because nothing was making sense, not in this cultural institution that ballerinas bribed and prayed to dark gods to get into. What I said was unthinkable.

"I wanted to come tell you in person that I won't be accepting the offer, and I also won't be dancing here anymore. Thank you for these past few years and granting me the opportunity to do what I love, but I ... I won't be coming back."

My line, drawn in the sand, calm and detached, diplomatic to avoid doing what I really felt, which was smashing this place to pieces. Burning it down, a scream so loud it shattered every mirror inlaid in marble, wrecked every statue until all of it was sundered. It was for my sake that I didn't, because they weren't worth my energy.

For what felt like eternity, President Auger and I stared at each other, the only noise a hiss from the heater bringing the room to just above a chill. Even the traffic beyond the window was muffled. She studied me, appraising me like those academy days of evaluations, searching for misplaced pounds and lies written across my face. And finding no flaw but defiance.

She straightened up. "I see. And may I ask why? You're our strongest apprentice."

Another bitter ache cut through me, wishing she'd told the whole room this when they doubted me, not now when we were alone, and I was on my way out. I averted my eyes to the window, where fog climbed the glass panes and obscured the gray city sitting just outside.

"I don't think I'm a good fit. I'm not ..." I pursed my lips and tried again. Less of a whisper, stronger, with my chin up. "The ballet has a very clear picture of what it wants, and I'm not destroying myself anymore to meet it. It isn't right to demand so much of me but give so little. And everyone treats me like the enemy, so nothing I do will ever make this place feel like home."

Feel like Elysium, like *them*.

And somehow, some way, I'd find other things that nourished me.

President Auger inclined her head, as much of a nod as I'd ever get, and cleared her throat. "I see. Well, it's disappointing you feel that way." Then she realigned the papers that were already perfectly perpendicular. "Ballet requires an immense level of dedication from its members. It isn't for the weak of heart. Or the faithless."

Her gaze narrowed on me, the jab clear. My heart skipped a beat.

"I never thought you one of those people who expect everything handed to you. You were good..."

But I was more than good—I was perfect.

My fingers drummed the carved arms of my chair. I wanted to bite the tongue from her mouth. It was easy for her to call me weak when she sat in an office, unaware of how much I'd given just to be invited through these doors. If anything, I was foolish for thinking she was on my side, that she'd understand.

And to say I was entitled for asking for *crumbs*?

I rose slowly.

Auger waved a dismissive hand. "And no need to worry about *Petrushka*. We assigned your replacement yesterday. You can just empty your locker, get your things."

I licked my teeth and paused. All the burst blisters and discarded nails, the blooming bruises, our bodies like spring gardens—it meant nothing if we weren't lining their pockets every minute of every day. And screw professionalism, keeping it in.

Before her, I shook my head and laughed. Speechless. And then furious. "For years, I practiced every day until I was bloody and sore and exhausted. For years! I gave up my family. I lost my best friend. My body is mangled and twisted—I was *devoted*. I did everything you asked, and I did it all for a place that never once said 'please.' You think *I'm* entitled? For scraps?"

The woman shrank in her seat as I leaned on the desk, claws biting into the wood, fire roiling in my blood, and sneered.

"Go fuck yourself. **I can't wait to watch this place burn.**"

Auger was lucky all I did next was turn on my heel and slam the door.

Freed and raging, I stalked back into the white-veined marble halls. There was no knowing how much time I had before they took everything I once was and dumped it into a trash bag too. No telling what I'd do if they tried. The locker room was empty, sparing me a confrontation I didn't need. With the way my mark itched to smash everything, it wouldn't be pretty. My spare leotards and tights, brand-new pointe shoes still in their packaging, makeup, hair supplies, tapes, muscle creams—all of them, I shoved in my bag until the seams were near bursting, and then I added a few more pointe shoes because I wanted to. Even if the zipper wouldn't close. It was the least of what they owed me.

From Auger's callous indifference to whoever was on my stage dancing my solo, I had every reason to be fed up. I had every reason to tear this place apart in grief.

"Still glorious!" I shouted at the costume cases in the halls, a finger high in the air.

As I crossed the atrium, I blew kisses to the cherubs on the ceiling and waved my goodbyes to the statues cloaked in gold guarding the amphitheatre. A tourist threw me a scowl, and I hissed in reply—this was between me and the Palais. We had a love affair. It supped its fill on my blood and tears, and I left a heaping pile of shattered mirrors and bulbs in the dressing room as my parting gift.

A security guard lingered near a pillar, his soft focus turned toward the nearly empty lobby, unaware that the ballet had eaten another spirit.

"You're looking the wrong way," I said as I slid on my coat. "The real monsters are already inside—"

Julien Mesny rounded the corner. I recognized his figure, his rounded shoulders and walnut skin, his shaved head and shuffling steps. He turned in circles, scanning the lobby for something.

"Papa?" I asked softly.

It was incremental, but the more I used the word, the more familiar it became. Not that I wanted it to, not now. If the title became familiar, I might start to care what he thought. I might change my mind.

His head snapped up. He wrung a dark skullcap in his hands and gestured to the polished red booth at the entrance. "I saw your name on the cast list and came to buy a ticket..."

A perfectly normal answer for a perfectly normal parent. Only *he* didn't buy tickets. *He* didn't attend ballets. He made that clear from the beginning.

My teeth were grinding, fingers twitching at my sides, and all I brought myself to say was, "Nobody actually buys tickets from there anymore. It's all online."

"I see." His cheeks flushed pink, shiny hazel eyes dipping shyly. There was something so very mundane, so annoyingly human, about the gesture. That reminded me of... *me*. "I wanted to see you. Make sure you were okay. You didn't show for dinner; you're always so busy, I figured—"

I cursed.

Dinner. That thing I'd agreed to, right after Coralie threatened to end my career, right before she attacked Andor in the park. That night was a whirlwind that turned into a week of tense rehearsals, torture, and a hospitalization. Already so long ago.

I rubbed my forehead and sighed. "Yes, sorry. I was in the hospital— flu, nothing serious. I forgot. Rain check?"

"Sure." He nodded, shifting his weight from foot to foot. "I'll call you. Are you heading to rehearsal? Am I keeping you?"

His attention flickered to the bag on my shoulder, and I jostled the strap. Was this where I told him I quit? That he shouldn't have bothered because it was too late? I didn't know the rules of etiquette surrounding reconciliation with an absentee parent. I didn't know what I'd do if he said, "I told you so."

Julien cleared his throat and looked away. "I'm sorry this feels weird. It's been so long, and it's my fault." He took a step closer. "I was feeling insecure and inadequate, especially after your mother left."

"So you let a twelve-year-old and seasoned petty thief run off on her own?"

Because it didn't matter what he'd felt. He and his estranged wife were my earliest lessons in packing up and walking away. Their disengagement taught me the value of selfishness. They shaped the beast that slumbered inside of me.

My bag felt full of stones, and here this man was, waiting for my forgiveness. But I wasn't like Andor; I didn't know how to forgive people who ran away from me, and I didn't want to learn.

I smoothed my hands down my coat and navigated back to easier waters, even as the words scraped on their way out. "I actually quit. I won't be dancing in the show, so it's . . . It's good I caught you."

"You quit?"

"I think I might travel for a little bit," I added, fingers fiddling with my coat buttons. "Just to figure out what comes next. And who knows? Maybe I'll do more contemporary or try a company in another city."

Though I shrugged, just saying it aloud brought stinging to the backs of my eyes. The ballet hadn't turned me away, and my body hadn't failed me—I was the one leaving after all this time.

"You'll call when you get back?"

My throat tightened. The most I was able to do was smile. If he realized something was off, he didn't say. After an awkward hand extended but never reaching my shoulder, we headed in separate directions— him, back home to a housing complex far from downtown, and me, to the amphitheatre to say goodbye to the stage.

And maybe steal a program and see what peon they chose to fill my shoes.

CHAPTER 29

The amphitheatre wasn't empty.

I strolled through the gilded doors propped open, my footsteps muffled by rich, red carpet as the noise of others drew me to a halt.

The cast of *Petrushka* stood onstage in their leotards and sweatpants, faces tired, listening to Grandpré bark his final notes before being sent off to get ready. I should have been one of them. And standing on the edge of the crowd, marking through the opening number, Coralie Baumé held her ankle high over her head. She'd already changed into the costume, the white ruffles of a drab blue skirt dangling around her bony knee. A matching scarf pinned her golden curls away from her face. All ready to play my part.

The blood drained from my body.

"How nice of you to finally join us, Laure," Yelena said without an ounce of warmth, catching my attention. Parked beside her was Rose-Marie looking victorious. Everyone got what they wanted but me.

All of me went numb staring at that girl in my place, all of me except the scars on my wrists, ankles, and throat. They burned like they were still fresh.

Yelena gestured to Coralie's wobbly turn. "In case you weren't aware, we've reassigned your role. Keep that in mind the next time you want to slack off."

"I was—" My fists balled at my sides.

It was the same as Joséphine, replaced as if we had never given our bodies in the first place. They sooner replaced me with someone unqualified than show me an ounce of grace when I needed it most. When I was recovering from what *she* did.

And it wouldn't matter if Coralie broke every bone in her body, or if there were no other dancers in all of Europe available to take this part. A house that would replace me with her, for all their posturing about high standards, wasn't a house that cared about quality at all. They didn't even care about her, or Joséphine, or Sophie Poullain, who was thrown a funeral instead of a retirement party for a busted hip, and definitely not the horde of fresh bodies touring the lobby and praying for chances in this glorified meat grinder.

Ciro was right—we were nothing but pawns.

And though she knew it deep down, Lethe convinced Coralie to sacrifice her only friend anyway.

"**Get out**," I growled, my voice carrying through the domed ceiling, shoulders moving with labored breaths. My walk down the aisle was painfully slow, painfully calm, rage welling at the cracks and ready to seep through.

To make them all tremble.

A fog descended over the room. Sneering, cunning faces turned blank and sleepy as dancers streamed offstage through the wings like zombies. Grandpré, Yelena, and Rose-Marie filtered out through a side door, leaving only Coralie to resist, the Lethe in her bones fighting back against my command. Our two beasts were twins, two sides of the same vicious coin, only she was too weak to take control of hers.

Everything about her was weak. Including her turnout.

She arched a brow. "Just what do you think you're doing?"

I pushed open the little door to the orchestra pit, the only thing standing between me and my stage. My bag slid from my shoulder, spilling pointe shoes and tights all over the floor. Coralie took a cautious step back.

"You got what you wanted," I ground out as I stalked through the sea of black chairs and music stands. "And *this* is what you do with it?"

Twelve years of feeding this dream, cutting down anyone else who stood in my path, only to have the one girl I spared turn around and bite me.

And she had the audacity to be mediocre.

"What do you want me to say? That I'm not worthy?" Coralie scoffed, even as she backed away. When I stepped on a chair, onto the piano. She was putting distance between us. "This is my *birthright*—"

Then I was running, leaping, flying.

We crashed to the floor in a tangle of limbs and snarls. Lethe's power had picked her body clean and left only bones—none of the muscle needed to be a ballerina. Though she was taller, though every command to **stop, stop, stop** was rebuffed, I was stronger, heavier. And I was pissed. I closed hands around the corrupted Coralie's throat, even as she gouged at me, seething into the only tangible place to put my rage.

"Don't you realize what you've done?" I shook her. "I loved you, I would've helped you—"

Coralie brought her knee to my ribs, knocking the air from my lungs. It was enough to soften my grip, for her to break my hold and slither out from under me. The scratches on my face and arms stung as I pushed onto my side.

"Helped me?" She sneered, climbing to her feet. "You left me to fend for myself while you took everything!"

"It wasn't *yours*!"

When I reached for her, she caught me by the wrist. Searing pain, bright and white, tore through my arm under her grip, wrenching out a scream. The darkness under my skin curled to get away from the biting cold.

A slippered foot caught me in the ribs before she let go, but the stinging lingered. A light bulb in the great chandelier shattered.

"I don't even recognize you," she said.

As Coralie glared down at me, another light bulb flared bright and shattered. Then another, and a fourth. Her next kick landed in my shoulder, bowing my back.

"The Laure I knew was focused. Cutthroat. Real competition. But she didn't cheat. She didn't quit. This?" She waved at my wincing form on the floor. "I don't know who this is."

A row of lights crackled and sputtered in the chandelier, across the opera house, oblivion leaching out like mist from the filaments. Dread rolled through me at memories of the cave. All my righteousness retreated.

"And don't tell me—your *new* friends are waiting outside? Should I go see them? Such a brave, selfless little hero for those monsters you hardly know. My Laure wouldn't have spared them a glance, much less her entire career."

She spat the last words, her lips curled in disgust. It was such a familiar expression, one she'd make speaking of Joséphine or in envy of another dancer, one I recognized well. So well, it jarred me. Was a knife in my heart.

I still know this girl.

"What happened? What are they offering that's so good you forgot who you are? Did they make you think you'd be like Joséphine Moreau? Did they promise you money? Immortality? *Love?*"

It was the saccharine quality in her voice that made my fingers twitch and jolted me into action. I groped for a heartbeat in her direction, something soft and mortal that would shut her up. If I rendered her unconscious long enough, I'd find something to strip the mark from her skin. Save her. Purge whatever toxin coursed through her, and show Lethe exactly who it was messing with.

— 313

Only there was nothing. No echo, no warmth, no pulse. She was little better than a shell—that was the weight of her silence.

"What have you done?" I asked, horror rising in my voice as I scooted away. Downstage toward the orchestra pit where my discarded bag lay overturned. The kit for customizing my pointe shoes had a knife, a lighter. Either would work.

I could save her—

"You don't get it, do you?" She doubled over, laughing.

It was even the same bitter laugh as my friend's, though this sent light bulb shards raining down, plunging the hall and stage in darkness.

"I want to be the chosen one. I want you to choose me. To look me in the eye and crown me the victor. It's time everyone finally chooses me, and I'm not asking anymore."

I shook my head adamantly. Because all I ever did was choose her. Her feelings, her friendship, her future. I'd always planned to bring her across the finish line with me. We were supposed to be stars *together*.

When she neared, I lashed out, kicking her square in the stomach. She stumbled back, and I threw a command, **"Don't move,"** over my shoulder as I vaulted off the stage. Down into the pit, legs wobbling, stands and chairs toppling over as I barreled to the gate, the carpet, my bag.

All the while, lights around the theatre shattered in rapid succession, shards like gunfire giving way to more shadows. More cold encroaching. The unease prickled at the back of my neck.

"We had everything!" Coralie's shouts filled the opera house. "Things were perfect until you got greedy! You stole from me and knocked me down a peg just so you could, what, *quit*?!"

The piano creaked as the *thud* of something heavy landed on top. A chair flipped over and crashed behind me. My hands trembled as I ripped polyester fabric and stretchy tights from my bag like ribbons from a magician's sleeve. More and more unraveling, unending, heart racing in my ears.

"All because you have some shiny new friends? Well, where are they?!"

Her voice neared as I reached the bottom, unzipping the little black pouch filled to the brim. Scissors, dental floss, a plastic case of needles, weighted metal that fit in my palm—

I shoved the folding knife into my pocket and whirled around just in time for a black rectangle to swing my way. Sharp, blinding pain struck the side of my head, so loud it rang through my skull, and I collapsed.

Dragged along the soft red carpet, tired, throbbing, and dizzy, my thoughts reeled. My pulse was hummingbird fast and faint. Pains in my skull and wrist dialed up to full volume, and it took everything in me to stay awake, to pry my eyes back open every time I blinked.

Where are we going?

I tasted blood.

We waded out of the dark, quiet amphitheatre into the vestibule full of light and sound. Gatherers in their gala best, in gowns and suits, jewels and shiny metals, waited in the magnificent halls of Palais Garnier, unaware of who was coming.

"This won't end well for you," I rasped, yanking against her bony grip on my wrists, to no avail.

"You can't threaten me, Laure," replied Coralie as she led the way toward the atrium.

I kicked out, twisting and writhing even as nails dug into my scalp. Her hold wouldn't budge. My stomach churned.

The vertigo was in my bones, from where Acheron had probably taken too much. I'd strained hard to compel the cast and crew and her—it was probably through the grace of adrenaline alone that I was still conscious. Trying to compel her now, I couldn't even make her flinch.

"Killing me is killing everything you know about yourself," she continued, so self-righteous. "And who would you be without me?"

I mumbled, "Someone happy, scar-free, probably employed," and she laughed.

This corrupted thing with my friend's face was what I would've become without an anchor, swept into an ocean of resentment without limits, incapable of being sated. There was no one to teach her control or pull her away before she'd hurt somebody, no kiss as salve for her burns, no one waiting if she surrendered. We weren't the same; I'd tamed my beast and walked away from this place. And I didn't know how much of my Coralie was left. If there was any at all.

We crossed into the atrium, the polyrhythmic chorus of beating hearts huddled close together filling the air. Though I couldn't see the attendees, the buzz of their voices sawed in my head.

I became the latest exhibition at the famed opera house.

Cries of shock rose from the crowd as we spilled into the open. They parted around us, faces contorted in horror, while I dragged behind Coralie in a macabre funeral march. My fingers craved to stop them from looking the same way my world had been stopped when they forced me out. The way Joséphine's and Ciro's worlds just stopped. For only a moment, I wanted to shut them up and yell in the ensuing silence.

But all I could do was loll as she pulled me along.

Of all places for Coralie to give her show, it had to be where so many dreams came to die.

She flung me down the stairs for all the ballet's audience to see, each marble step beating at my bones. Blood pooled from my scalp onto the beautiful marble floor, and I watched Coralie step in it as she descended calmly behind me.

"This is where you're meant to be, Laure," said Coralie, wrenching my head back by my hair.

She wanted me to see the heavenly glow of the skylight, the cherubs and gilded angels witnessing my defeat. That she'd finally bested me. Fine cracks blossomed in her skin like aged porcelain, filaments covering her gaunt cheeks and thin arms, threatening to rupture. *How much longer can it last like this?*

"You wanted an adoring audience so bad? Think you can live without me? Let's see it!"

She threw me back to the floor with a flourish and began to pace. This was every bit of the Coralie that I knew: loving a show, basking in the light even if she didn't deserve it, full of disdain. Only now, it was twisted. Worse.

There wasn't a quick, easy, perfect way to end this, end us. Quitting the ballet wasn't enough. Giving in wasn't enough. She'd just find some new way to keep her hold on me, something else to take from me until she was all I had. I didn't know if saving her was possible, how, if there was any point—I only knew I no longer wanted a part in her play.

On the edge of the crowd stood Rose-Marie, back again, and not a hair out of place, in a royal-blue gown and covered in diamonds. She pressed a hand to her mouth and stared at her daughter, her horrible, wicked child, the monster she helped create. I'd never seen that expression on her face before: horror.

"What..." Rose-Marie began, sliding a hesitant foot forward. When she took Coralie's arm, felt the dead cold of her skin, her gaze flashed to me with worry. "What have you done?"

Coralie shoved her mother back. "I'm doing exactly what you asked me to. You want me to be great?" My friend thrust a hand toward me. "This is the cost of greatness! This is what it takes these days."

I tried grabbing at her, commanding her to stop, to leave, grasping for her pulse again and again. But my grip was feeble, and I was so tired of having to be better. All around us people watched, Rose-Marie cried, but no one intervened for me. They didn't do anything. They never did.

"Fight back." Coralie sneered as she stood over me.

I raised my gaze to meet hers. "No."

Every feat I ever accomplished was glorious and in the name of glory, and I didn't need to play her game to prove it. For the mark burning through my arm, I'd been chosen three times over. It wasn't cheating if all I demanded was a chance. And if she wanted an enemy, I wouldn't give it to her. Just like this place, she wasn't worthy of me.

As Coralie glared down at me, tendrils of white seeped from her skin like solar flares. They licked the air, singeing everything they touched. She grabbed my collar, and when a thin, little wisp of light brushed my chin, it burned.

I winced. "I'm done with you."

It was my most honest confession in all the years of our relationship, wrought from the pit of my chest, ribs broken open. Even in her weird and twisted way, Coralie thought she loved me, but I was done putting up with her, deluding myself into loving her. It wasn't enough. And if she couldn't let go, the Lethe inside her would kill me. Unless I put an end to her first.

If Acheron was destroying me, wasn't that what I'd want her to do?

I flexed my knuckles and held my ground.

Tendrils made of oblivion billowed and swelled, and the cracks in Coralie began to rupture. There was too much inside—she was too angry, and it was breaking through. From the seams, blood fell thick and colorless. She seethed, still fisting the front of my sweater, even as a flare shot out from her skin and sundered the skylight.

I flinched.

The shattering glass was deafening. Screams of the crowd fleeing in every direction turned silent while Coralie and I locked eyes. In the end, Rose-Marie didn't reach to save her daughter; she ran to save herself. And despite myself, I pressed in to avoid the falling shards, and Coralie stepped in to shield me.

I didn't know if I had enough in me to stop her. It wasn't a matter of strength or Acheron's primal magic—I didn't know if I was *monstrous* enough to use it, to slay whatever remained of the fractured girl standing over me. But I wouldn't survive her if I crossed her again.

Glass rained from the sky, striking down ballet attendees in their rich, bespoke garments. The shards cut through bodies and cloth, slicing through my sweater sleeves and the arms I'd thrown overhead to cover me. Meanwhile, from Coralie, tangles of light rooted through the marble floor, creating fissures that fragmented the mosaics and wrapped around the fine sculpted columns. Another flare lashed out and severed the face of an angel, sending chunks of stone flying.

A large glass shard pierced Coralie's shoulder. She didn't react.

Not even then would she look away from me, even as my fingers twitched to draw the knife from my pocket. The imprint on my wrist seared, urging me to take the shot, even if I lost. I'd pry the mark from her or die trying.

I begged, *prayed*, that Keturah and Andor weren't inside.

"This is why even your parents left you," she yelled over the cacophony, shoving me with a bloody, glass-pocked fist. Pain spiked in my palms where I'd fallen. "Because there's nothing about you worth loving. We were only friends because I felt sorry—"

I snapped.

A feral growl tore out of me as I lunged at her, knife drawn, teeth bared. Coralie crashed onto the ground, eyes wide with fear. Her spreading roots of oblivion ruptured on impact. I only managed to raise the blade before the earth quaked.

And then the floors of Opéra Garnier crumbled, bringing us down with the house.

CHAPTER 30

Stone, glass, and bodies jostled us apart as the floor caved in. Tendrils of Lethe had rooted down several stories, carving away hungrily, and now we tumbled through one level just to fall down another and another and another. A crack reverberated through my skull. Pain flared through my arm. Everything moved into free fall, slabs of rock battering my ribs until water finally closed over my head.

I plunged into the pools beneath Palais Garnier, the instant cold making my lungs seize. Salt and filth filled my mouth, metallic and mineral, and the roar of the collapse dulled to silence under the surface.

Then my body was paddling of its own volition, still clinging to my knife, kicking up over cement, marble, wood, and corpses crowding my path. I treaded water and scanned the disaster, gasping, twisting to find my prey. It wasn't over yet.

Someone called my name in the distance, lost to the ringing in my ears. And then Coralie sputtered and coughed nearby.

She heaved herself out of the pool and onto a boulder-size block of concrete, dangling a limp arm over the edge. Her face was slicked in silvery-white blood from a split seam over her brow, her eyes closed, chest rising and falling while she lay on her back. The pale tattoo of Lethe glowed in the emergency lights.

My knuckles cracked as fingers tightened around my blade. She would not leave this place, I'd see to it. And for once, I didn't have to wonder if the thought was all mine.

Adrenaline and Acheron in my blood subsumed every ache in my body. Some of my ribs had to be broken and my arm twinged with every stroke, but I slipped under the surface and pushed toward her with more strength than I knew my limbs had to give.

I was a monster succumbing to the hunt, a predator out for a kill. The world had let me starve for too long, and eventually, the hungry stop caring what we eat so long as we're fed.

My heart thudded in my ears as I reached slowly from the water. I hoped she could sense me coming, so I could drink her fear in. Like a serpent, I struck, first in the face, then claws sinking into Coralie's arm. Silvery-white blood gushed from her nose.

The more she squirmed, the deeper my nails pierced, thickened and curved to hold tight. The pitter-patter of her heartbeat tickled against my fingertips. Her whimper transformed to a melody when the brittle bones snapped in my grip.

Then Coralie wrenched back, and I finally lost my grip on the blade. It sank down into the muddy water, and in an instant, she flung herself from her perch to escape, dragging us both below. Water closed over my head.

When she kicked up to the surface, a vicious sneer settled on my features. I fisted the back of Coralie's thin, wet hair and licked the blood and tears from her cheeks. They tasted sour and sweet like rotting, fermented fruit, and I took my fill by sinking my teeth into the flesh of her shoulder before pulling her under with me. Fear shuddered through her as she writhed, trying to wind around and get a final look at who I truly was.

But I only held her to my chest.

Coralie bucked and scratched, thrashing as I wrapped my legs around her hips. I embraced her steadfastly, even as she fought, even as she choked, our hearts pounding in sync. Something sharp pinched my ribs, but I wouldn't let go of the remains of my best friend—for Joséphine, Ciro, Andor, Keturah. For her. Most importantly, for *me*.

If we both drowned, so be it.

And she was right—I was killing her, and I was killing me. I needed this if I was going to walk out alive, start again as something new. This girl in this place to shed the last of my grief. Or the water would be both our graves if I failed.

Don't fight me, I willed through gritted teeth, lungs burning. Her gold necklace full of bite marks broke away. But possessed with Lethe, she kept kicking. I shut my eyes and held tight. **Go to sleep and dream of something beautiful.**

And eventually, she did. Eventually, her fighting slowed, and my embrace won. Coralie softened and eventually stilled, her pulse dimming like a candlewick on its last burn. A quiet, nominal end without the sputter and crackle and hiss and bite. No fanfare, no gun salute.

I fed her to the beast, and the beast was me, and the beast was within me.

As my first love's body sank to the bottom and I raced to the top, to our rightful places for the last time, I glimpsed her face. Angelic, eyes closed, a halo of golden hair, a smile on her cracked lips. Something like a sob broke from my chest.

On weak, shaky hands, I hauled myself out of the water and swayed to my feet. The world was loud on the surface, filled with moans of the hurt and dying, trickling from broken pipes, sirens. People fretted over friends and family, loved ones and strangers lying in the rubble, hazarding me with their worried glances as I propped myself against jagged stone. Shrinking away, shoulders tight, noses turned up, faces ashen.

As if *I* was the one who wrought such destruction.

Adrenaline fading, every breath ached sharply. I was hurting too.

"I s-saved you. Won't you thank me?" I demanded, my words

trembling, more sigh than sound. Someone hurried past. **"Will you not bow to me?"**

Electricity crackled under my skin as I pushed off the rock. The command unfurled from my tongue like darkness, and the standing bodies all went rigid. They gazed upon me with vacant smiles, faces caked in dust and blood, and lowered their heads. Sank to their knees.

I basked in their submission in place of their gratitude, their fear in place of their applause, and the singing in my veins climbed to a hum nonetheless.

Until the pain in me screamed louder. Too much pain, the wrong kind of pain. I doubled over, my hands flying to my chest, grazing something solid. And came away slicked red.

"Laure!"

Rising over the mounds of rubble was Andor, Keturah clinging to his side. They were scraped and bloodied, coated in dust and dirt like the lesser disciples, but they weren't bowing. No, they were running to me with their arms wide. My heart was going to burst, but for the wrong reason.

I looked down and glimpsed the large shard of glass sticking out of my side. Coralie's parting gift to me, and it didn't miss.

"Wow," I whispered, stumbling back. The searing pain with every breath threatened to tear me apart from the inside. I needed it out of me.

So I gripped the glass tight, fought against the voices shouting *no*, and jerked it free. Blood flowed like wine.

My knees gave in, and I fell into Andor. Heat rushed down my front fast as we dropped into the debris.

"I k-killed her," I mumbled, face hot and wet. "I had to—"

"It's okay," Andor whispered. He pulled me into his lap and brushed the hair from my face. Keturah was a shadow that folded over me, poking and prodding, split lip pursed, brow furrowed. "It's okay, Laure."

There was a choking sound. It might have been me.

The silence was never a good sign, and the comforting weight of the blood river in my bones was seeping away too fast—there wasn't enough of me left to hold it in. I was dying faster than it could heal me.

"It's t-too bad we're not on Acheron," I whispered, feeling my eyelids grow heavy. Because the river of life would have saved me, its favorite creature. I would have made the same bargain again and again.

But there was no more breath in me to apologize like I wanted, for driving Coralie into this and not being strong enough to stop her sooner. For Joséphine and Ciro, who paid the price for my ascension. Even if I didn't kill them myself, I loved and made excuses for a monster.

This place made monsters out of both of us.

"Stay awake, Laure. We'll get you there soon..." said Andor in a trembling voice. Like he was running. There was wind on my face.

My heart stuttered in my chest.

I took one last look at the collapsed chandelier and gilded ruins of Palais Garnier, the people bowing around me, the ghost girl floating away, the handsome duke who would cry at my headstone. "What a fitting grave."

Then the music finally stopped, and the lights went out.

CHAPTER 31

The first thing I did when I woke up, once again in a world of light and noise, was retch. I heaved myself from the cocoon of pillows and wool, crashed onto the floor on rickety bones, and hurled. My dying soul tasted like sour milk and filled my nostrils with the cloying stench of overripe bananas, thick and chunked and faded silvery white like oblivion. Like Coralie. It flowed in wave after wave of vomit, while I clenched hard, until there was nothing left but spit flavored sickeningly sweet.

It seeped into the wooden floorboards and bleached them white.

Every breath racked my new body in shudders, but I was alive.

Death had been too quiet, too cold, and too still. So far from Acheron, I had plunged into silence, swallowed by the void. It was everything I imagined it would be, a dancer finally put to rest, beholden to nothing and no one, no burning hunger to force my hand.

But Coralie didn't get to decide that for me, and I wasn't finished dancing.

Oblivion held me for only a flash, one perfectly quiet, perfectly cold, perfectly still moment, before something opened the door and I fled. Then only fragments remained: the bitter stench of blood, a music box warped far out of tune, flashes of lightning in the heat.

At Acheron's altar in the dark, I laid the only thing I had left to give—my soul. And then came that voice, red and primordial, that whispered, **"Forever, for you,"** as we bound ourselves in searing chains. As it saved me from oblivion.

I groaned as I pushed up on wobbly hands. The fever coursing through my veins with every heartbeat writhed down my arms and legs and spine, sweat slicking clothes to my body.

I was really alive.

Then I felt it—Acheron getting comfortable in its new skin. The unease of joints demanding to be popped, fluid to be resettled, making room for both of us. So I'll never be alone again.

Red sky streamed through large windows, painting the cluttered cottage bedroom in shades of crimson. Except for the single steady pulse below, the house was quiet. When I walked to the door and passed by the mirror, my reflection drew me to a stop.

It wasn't the fully red irises or wolfish teeth and claws that caught my eye. It made sense, giving as much as I did, that the monstrousness was something I couldn't just escape. Instead, it was the *other* thing staring back at me that I studied.

Beyond dreadful, chilling, even as I found myself grinning.

It surrounded me, a shadow made of deep crimson that moved like angry static. The edges shifted constantly, drawing over itself again and again, fuzzing in the shape of a body. When I raised a hand to touch it, my fingers found only air. It was a cursed duet revealed only in the mirror. And when I smiled, I knew Acheron smiled back.

"Hello," I whispered, watching my primordial shadow flicker on the floor and follow as I slipped into the hall.

From below came the shuffling of footsteps and a soft, feminine sigh. The steps creaked as I descended, and when I rounded the corner, a dark-skinned face poked out from the kitchen followed by a mass of tight, neon-yellow coils. Her smile was made of glass.

"I didn't hear you wake! We were getting worried," said Keturah, stepping into the hall with a teacup in hand. "Come sit, have something to eat. I'm a nervous baker. You must be hungry—"

Nervously, I glanced over to my shadow, just in case she saw how it moved. How alive it was. She didn't.

"Can…" I cleared my throat, dusty with disuse after so much screaming and death. "Can I go for a walk first? There's a lot to get used to."

She leaned against the frame, gaze suspicious and scouring over me in search of deficits. But Keturah knew what it meant to be broken, to tape yourself together again, so she nodded anyway, and then I was rushing out into the spiced, humid air, cheeks kissed by a coppery breeze.

Breathing deeply.

My fingers pressed into the phantom twinge in my ribs, but before the memories rose to the surface, I took off.

The forests surrounding the cottage weren't any darker or any wilder like I'd hoped they would be in the aftermath. They sat unchanged, the tall grass and wildflowers by the makeshift fence, the dark trees obscuring the red of the river that glistened. It flowed calmly today, not the choppy, sloshing waves that battered rocks but the smooth, welcoming stream that invited woodland creatures to drink.

That was what I sought—for the proto-god to wash away my confusion and tell me where to go next.

"I'm alive," I reminded myself again, feeling a smile grow, running my fingers along the trunk of a tree.

In my head, I ran through the list of people who died, all the things I survived and was supposed to mourn. Not just people but my career, Laurence Mesny, ballerina for the Paris Ballet Company. But grief welling up too fast made my pace quicken.

The meager, hurried heartbeats of tiny animals, birds and rabbits and deer, quivered through my bare soles. They were hiding, lives I couldn't touch before but were available to me now that I was changed. Every footfall hummed with power, stronger, assured in the impressions I left in the dirt. The creatures sensed me coming and shied from my path, hoping to escape my notice.

Fearing my wrath.

On the other side of the shore, a two-headed deer watched me. It stood on the riverbank, one head dipped to drink, the other wound back, jaw working at a loose, bloody strand of velvety pulp from its antlers. Eyes unblinking.

There were no road maps for where I was and whatever I'd become. I was still insatiable, still needing, but what did I reach for if not power and belonging in that world? What would I claim as my next prize? What more did I have to conquer?

As I stared back in silence, the river whispered something. A feeling I couldn't translate, like static directly in my veins. And I nodded in understanding. I was fed on sidewalk weeds, grown on distended knees and broken toes, chosen by the blood river and a pack of monstrous beings. Voraciousness was etched into my bones; I'd hunt again.

Then there came more stirring, rustling from the bramble that carried an eager heartbeat. The deer bounded away before the intruder revealed himself.

Andor started for me, hair wild, antlers crowned with hemlock, and blood-rich, molten skin speckled with dirt and debris. As if he sensed me wandering and knew exactly where I'd go. He stopped an arm's length away, shiny black eyes scanning for signs that I was different, fingers twitching at his sides to make contact.

I was fragile, a mortal body stitched together with divine thread. We weren't supposed to make a habit of swimming in the power of a god.

Sleeplessness made the scar across his eyes more pronounced, fitting for the living picture of wilderness. I liked it. And every plant on the edge of the forest leaned toward him, their sun, as he leaned toward me, eyes fearful and wondrous, relieved and something else beneath.

I licked my lips and told him, "It's really me."

"How are you? When did you ...?" He swallowed and took a step, his long lashes fluttering in surprise. "I thought you'd be comfortable in the house, but if you want to come to the labyrinth, you can."

Again, that invitation to stay. To remain as is, unchanging, already enough as the monster I was and exalted. It was only a breath's length of silence, but in it, his gaze burned like a brand. His fingers twitched again.

"That," I started, inhaling the blood-flavored steam, "that would be nice."

He stood close, heart thundering, skin blazing. I stopped breathing. We had reset to that state of being close but not touching, as if I wasn't remade stronger and less prone to breaking. Forever. Like he was forever.

How I wanted to put it to the test.

Andor leaned down and pressed a burning kiss into my hair, scrambling my thoughts. It had been kept neatly braided, Keturah's doing, no doubt. And then he offered his palm.

Waiting.

But before turning back to the cottage, I made him bow, just to see if he still would. "Would you still pray to me, having seen what you saw, knowing what I've done?"

Who I killed.

His hand dropped readily. His chest quivered for a moment as surprise crossed his face, and his body lowered to its knees. But he didn't resist at all, though we both knew he could have. Ink-filled eyes flickered, unblinking and earnest, while he willingly sank down in rapture. He raised his fist over his heart. And though he looked the part, I was monster enough for both of us.

"Of course, Laure."

What an awful pair we made.

I took his face between my hands and blessed him with a kiss.

To my surprise, all alone and in the quiet of my bath, I didn't think about Joséphine or Ciro. I didn't see Coralie's corpse sinking beneath the opera house when I closed my eyes, though I should have and probably would in the days to come. My focus remained on withstanding the scalding water, on scrubbing away the grit of death clinging to my skin.

And I almost escaped grieving myself too, until I crawled out of the claw-foot tub.

Raw and smelling of bergamot instead of rot, my buzzing reflection in the steamy mirror evoked an image from *Giselle* that stunned me in place. Long-limbed and slow, gracious movements blurred by heavy fog, I envisioned the Wilis and their queen Myrtha, all ghosts of brokenhearted maidens who haunted the deathly woods. What was I if not a ghost inhabiting a forest now? Like Giselle, I walked in a liminal world too.

It was my start and end and my start again.

In early productions, Giselle broke down after her beloved's betrayal and met her end by a self-driven blade through the heart, which was why she was laid to rest on the unhallowed ground of the Wilis. Why they claimed her as one of their own. Like a macabre dream, the ghosts, all draped in long gowns and veils of white lace, sauntered through the forest on a thick mist, numerous and indistinct, vengeful and forlorn. They moved like sighing winds, cursing any man they crossed with death.

So all alone, naked and dripping and scarred, in steam I tried to become one of them, to do what I came back for. I tried to dance again.

Like the phantoms gliding across the stage, like white smoke, I rolled up in arabesque, reaching, heart yearning for Giselle's spirit in the mirror. There was no trace of the destruction I'd endured, no pain in my lungs or aches in my arching back. My arms folded in gentle waves as I meant them to, hiding demurely behind an imaginary veil. Delicate hands swept out in Giselle's mournful tenor. I soared up into perfect, fluttering steps.

It was intoxicating just to be so close again, to sink into a perfect curtsy, turn a perfect pirouette, strike a perfect pose with my head bowed behind the clouds of steam.

"Perfect" had once been the goal. But now it was too easy. Too detached and uncanny, not *quite* human anymore, but learning how to be alive all the same.

In a final flourish, I sank down to one knee, swept my arm back in a drastic curve, and then folded forward until my forehead pressed against cool tile.

It wasn't human, or perfect in all of its imperfections, but it was more than enough. *I* was more than enough.

I held my pose until the violins in my head finished their cries and there was applause in my blood.

EPILOGUE

T hough I was presumed dead in Paris, I spent my eighteenth birthday in Prague. The air was chilly, a thin coat of frost gathering along the Gothic roofs, snow making the old cobblestoned alleys glisten, and Old Town hummed with tourists ahead of the holiday. We found the Unusual Garden nestled between a jeweler and an Irish pub, and when its ornate Baroque doors swung open, rose perfume and heady fog plumed in my face.

"You're gonna love it," Keturah insisted, patting me on the shoulder before she walked inside, immediately vanishing into the dark.

Her eyes had brightened at first mention of the city, home to another of her lost loves and colorful past. She spent more time here refreshing her Czech than talking to us, and she'd stayed out two nights in a row at underground punk shows, showing up at sunrise with her ears ringing.

When she suggested the Garden, we didn't know what to expect.

Andor and I exchanged wary glances in the doorway. He looked good in the neon sign's green lighting, the nice drape of his coat on his broad shoulders, snowflakes catching in his long, dark hair, thick brows bunched in suspicion.

"You look ravishing," he'd whispered before we left the apartment, plucking a violet blossom from thin air and tucking it behind her ear. It matched my blouse, white chiffon with large watercolor violets on it and a cinched waist.

I wanted to kiss him now—pull him after me and go hide away in some quiet alleyway, pressed close against the chill.

But then, as if reading my thoughts, he broke into a grin and followed after Keturah, his tall frame inviting me to be swallowed by the shadows too.

The trip was a gift, Andor insisted, having inherited the bulk of Ciro's vast wealth and with nothing to spend it on. And since, aside from a couple visits to my mother's family in Athens, Georgia, I'd never been outside of France, the occasion along with my potential death and other events surrounding Opéra Garnier's collapse felt like a great excuse.

Then it was just me.

Waiting for my racing heart to slow, I mumbled to security, "Just a second."

I didn't know why I was nervous—Keturah wouldn't hurt me. At worst, I'd be annoyed with the noise, but still I stalled, studying the entrance.

The closed box office was papered in fliers promoting extravagant burlesque shows and drag artists, but the largest and most frequent was a poster for the Unusual Garden. A woman with full body waves of burnished brown hair hid behind large pink flower petals and foliage, a knowing smile on her face.

THE RAREST FLOWERS IN PRAGUE, it read.

I bet.

The building's sign threw my shadow onto the narrow passageway, and it fizzed anxiously. Static constantly changing shape, wanting. Waiting expectantly.

Tonight? Acheron asked.

"Be patient," I snapped at it, at my feet, scurrying inside before the bouncers looked at me funny.

It had taken two tries to explain it to Andor and Keturah, how being revived in a river of life had turned into sharing my body with it. The way it moved and settled, wanted and purred, soothed and agitated. They couldn't see it, and it took them more time to adjust to me *speaking* to it.

The rest of the world just saw a girl talking to her shadow.

The Garden's perfume was thick and sweet enough to produce a haze that coated my skin, and when I rounded the corner of the hall, I stepped onto the main floor of a theatre. A heavenly glow descended from a low, white-painted dome, shining onto green velvet seats and white tables. Greenery decorated the gallery, ivy on the walls, vines from the balconies, potted plants on nearly every surface. Finely dressed people lingered at a bar, speaking low over some enchanting, romantic piano.

It *was* a garden.

"We're going up," Keturah announced, leading the way to a flight of carpeted stairs marked VIP ONLY.

Andor took my hand, weaving fingers through mine, and pulled me along.

On the upper balcony, we followed Keturah to a corner booth. There were others, some with their curtains closed, and I squeezed Andor's hand reflexively as my pulse hiked.

I checked my phone one last time. I'd sent a text to Julien, my father, from a prepaid SIM card when we arrived at the airport, alerting him that I was, in fact, not dead. A week hiding in Elysium was a week without cell service and venturing aboveground meant inviting questions I wasn't prepared to answer.

Questions about being at the very center of a building collapse, about Coralie. While they were still pulling bodies from the rubble.

Since then, however, we were texting. Little messages: *hello, happy birthday, good night, stay safe*. It didn't mean we were close, that he was *forgiven*, but I still found myself checking when he got home from work. Just because. Even if sometimes I got so angry, I didn't respond.

Seeing the new notification, I set the phone aside and cleared my throat. "So, anyone want to tell me what we're doing here?"

Keturah shrugged. "You'll see."

Andor pressed a kiss into my hair.

Lights dimmed throughout the house, and applause rippled through the theatre. A curvy, porcelain-skinned woman in a formfitting, glittering red dress and matching gloves took the stage, holding a microphone in the spotlight. The color on her was an indulgent shade of rose red, and her dark hair was swept over one shoulder in an elegant curl. And in an equally indulgent, husky voice that reverberated in my blood, she said, "Good evening, and welcome to another promenade around the Unusual Garden."

A server crossed the balcony, carrying drinks: a water with lime, a Shirley Temple for me, and a white soda packed heavy with maraschino cherries. Andor plucked a cherry from his glass and bit it from the stem.

The two of them watched the stage, engrossed at what was to come, so I sipped my syrup and soda and did the same.

"Amaryllis" was the opening act, and heavy curtains drew back to reveal large, peach-colored petals held aloft by chorus dancers dressed as buds.

I straightened.

As the piano climbed through its arpeggios, the petals, and their corresponding dancers, peeled back to reveal the woman from the flyer. Wearing a peach-colored bodysuit, she danced across the stage, gripping buds and throwing them aside. It was bewitching. From the way she rolled her feet and moved her hips, I could tell she was a skilled, classically trained dancer. Ballerina, by her turnout.

And beautiful.

The choreography was *made* for her.

I gaped as the chorus clung to the woman, hands gripping her arms and legs desperately, beseeching until finally she shed them all. All that held her back discarded until she struck a pose on the chair, her leaves and petals open, full of pride.

Applause roared through the room.

"What did you think?" Keturah asked, making no effort to hide her grin. And I only laughed, speechless, unable to stop my own.

It was a variety show, an assortment of dancers and singers, jugglers and contortionists, each more amazing than the last. There was the Peony, a rosy-cheeked soprano performing an operatic aria; the seductive Poppies in a sensual, pulsing modern dance number; Hibiscus Maidens twirling in aerial silks; the Lotus on hoops. Between sets, we talked animatedly: which were my favorites, who I suspected of having formal training, wondering at how the skills translated.

Where ballet was beautiful in its structure, the Garden was breathtaking in its liberty. And it wasn't until we left, buzzing, that I understood Keturah's message: I could be one of them. A Christmas rose or an angel's trumpet, casting a spell over the crowd every night in Prague.

My blood hummed in agreement.

"Did Acheron say anything?" Andor asked as we spilled out into the night, onto the narrow street filled with revelers. The pub next door cheered to the broadcast of a sporting event.

I shook my head and fell in step by his side. "Nothing, I thought—"

A small figure reeking of booze darted out from around a corner and crashed into Andor. The two of them stumbled, and a soft voice muttered a slurred apology, nimble fingers righting him as she hobbled away. Almost like...

"Zloděj!"

We turned.

One of the security guards outside of the Unusual Garden snatched up the thief, wrenching a slender arm from her pocket to reveal Andor's wallet.

She jostled in his grip and sneered. "Let *go*! I didn't do anything."

The tattoo on my wrist burned.

The thief's dark hood fell away, exposing a shaggy cut of dark hair, olive skin, and vengeful eyes. Instead of apologizing, instead of fear, she looked indignant, even as Andor collected his wallet as proof. Beneath me, my shadow flickered with new purpose. With excitement.

"Her," I whispered, catching Keturah's attention but unable to look away. "I want her—"

"What?" Andor's head whipped around.

"Are you sure?" Keturah asked before sighing and stepping forward to quell the guard in Czech.

Meanwhile I kept my focus on the thief. She looked about my age, couched in baggy clothes and an air of malice, glancing, cagey, between all of us. Calculating her escape and the risks. I struggled to hide my smile at the familiarity.

"What's your name?"

She only curled her lip in response.

I sighed and turned to the guard, who wouldn't relent no matter what Keturah said. There was only one way to earn her trust, then.

"**Release her**," I commanded, watching his pupils blow wide and his grimace soften. His grip slacked too, because the girl broke free and rounded on me, gaping. And before she dashed back into the shadows, I blocked her path. "I'm trying to help you. You're a shitty thief."

The girl scoffed nervously and studied me. "Girl's gotta eat. And whatever this is, I don't want your help—"

"I just want to talk," I said, raising my hands and backing away. "I think you'll want to hear the offer, and I'll explain what I just did. And if you don't like it, you can go."

Her eyes narrowed. She weighed my words, her jaw clenched as she flicked between Andor, Keturah, and me. Young, well-dressed, a misfit bunch. We stood in the alleyway in silence, the guard rigid and blank-faced the entire time. When she waved a hand over his face, he didn't stir.

Finally she adjusted the front of her coat and nodded faintly. "The name's Niamh. And just so you know, I'm better with a knife."

"Niamh," I replied with a smile, glancing briefly to my dancing, wicked shadow, "let me tell you about my friend Acheron."

— ACKNOWLEDGMENTS —

Publishing a book is like running a marathon in a poison labyrinth: pushing your mind and body long distances, navigating winding turns and dead ends, toxins around every corner, and trying very hard not to break something in the process. I have a mile-long list of people who gave me water, pointed me in the right direction, delivered an antidote, and even helped carry my withering husk across the finish line. Unfortunately this list isn't everyone, but I hope it's close. I give my thanks:

First to my mother for inspiring my love of books and the magic of libraries. Nana for her horror collection and all those sleepovers. Amber for encouraging me to be a weirdo. Honey, light of my life, sun in my sky, for that date to the Catacombs (and the many after), for listening to my plot problems, for naming characters, for keeping me housed and fed and sane, all while I labored over this book for the billionth time. It would probably still be on its second draft without you, mon amour.

To my kickass agent Jennifer March Soloway, for being brave enough to scream about how much you love feral girls and guiding me every step of the way. It's a better book since it touched your hands, and I'm a better author since we met. To my editor, Jess Harold, and the rest of the Holt and Macmillan teams, for championing Laure's right to be a menace and seeing her story as deeply human, even as she became a monster. And my mentor, Kylie Schachte, for gassing me up, setting me on the path to success, and helping refine this story into something that turned heads.

A major shoutout is owed to my Pitch Wars '21 class for struggling through the chaos alongside me, for being my invaluable village, including Valo, Clare, Eve, Tyler, Nathalie, Tiera, Sana, Sian, Victoria, Chandra, and Phoebe. To my Unearthed witches, Andrea Hannah, Michelle, Fran, Alicia, and Naomi. A loud hurrah for my friends in the fediverse like Mordecai, LJ, Viviane, Artist Marcia X, Erik, Shrig, Green, Zoë, Red, Alice, Ben, Tessa, Duncan, and others I cannot think of now but will be super embarrassed I forgot. And also my earliest readers and bookish friends like Sabrina, Dera, Jen Carnelian, Isa Arsén, Louangie, Anna, and Sara Han.

Lastly, the biggest round of kisses to my cat, Luna, for keeping me company at 3 a.m. when deadlines loomed and for being my inspiration for Acheron, as a fellow demonic entity that never shuts up.

And to you, reader, for giving this a chance.

Stay wicked,

Jamison